Into the Twilight

A Between the Worlds Novel

By Morgan Daimler

ISBN-13: 978-1505677621

ISBN-10: 1505677629

Dedicated to my husband Scott, for always supporting my dreams and keeping me entertained. As requested you're fictional counterpart appears and dies horribly in this story. Love you, babe.

And to my beta readers Maya, Cathy, Tricia, Sara and Jennifer for constructive criticism and feedback.

Novels in the Between the Worlds Series:
<u>Murder Between the Worlds</u>
<u>Lost in Mist and Shadow</u>

Non-fiction by Morgan Daimler:
<u>By Land, Sea, and Sky</u>
<u>A Child's Eye View of the Fairy Faith</u>
<u>Where the Hawthorn Grows</u>
<u>Fairy Witchcraft</u>
<u>Pagan Portals: The Morrigan</u>

Table of Contents

Guide to Characters Names and Pronunciations

Aliaine "Allie" McCarthy–Ah-lee-awnya
Bleidd–Blayth
Syndra Lyons -
Elizabeth "Liz" McCarthy–
Jason Takada–
Jim Riordan–
Sam Kensignton –
Ciaran – Keer-awn
Jessilaen–Jes-ih-layn
Brynneth–Bree-nehth
Zarethyn–Zair-eh-theen
Aeyliss–Ay-ee-lihs
Natarien–Nah-tah-ree-ehn
Ferinyth–Feh-rihn-eeth
Morighent–Mor-ih-hent
Mariniessa – Mahr-ihn-ee-ehs-sah
Salarius – Sah-lah-rih-uhs

1

Prologue

Allie was sitting by the edge of the garden at the side of the house, staring listlessly at the ground. She'd come out planning to weed the small plot which was only just beginning to show signs of growth, but found that her heart wasn't in it, so instead she sat in the grass watching the sunlight and shade shift across the lawn as the wind blew. When she heard footsteps she glanced over her shoulder just far enough to see a familiar pair of battered sneakers and sighed. "If you're going to tell me I need to keep your secret, I already figured out I shouldn't tell anyone. If you want people to know or not know that's your business."

Jason sat down next to her, carefully, "No. I mean yeah please don't tell anyone, but that's not why I'm here. I wanted to see if you were okay."

"I'm not sure okay is something I'm ever going to be again. Can I ask you something?" Allie said softly, reaching out to touch the grass around her knees.

"Sure. What's up?"

"I get not telling anyone about your, you know, history. I even get hiding it. I guess I do that too a lot. Pass as human I mean. And, ummm, not talk about my past, where I come from. So I can't criticize you for it. But I was just wondering…is that why you're friends with me?" Allie kept her eyes down as she spoke, not daring to look at him.

"I don't understand what you mean," Jason said.

"I mean are you only my friend because you feel like I'm safe to be friends with because I'm mixed? Or…"

"No," Jason cut her off, sounding upset, "No, Allie. Please don't think that. I like you because I like you, for who you are, not because of something stupid like your ancestry…"

He trailed off, but Allie smiled slightly, nodding. "Okay. I just had to know."

"Why would you even think that?"

"I don't know. Because I feel like I can't trust anything anymore. Nothing's like it should be. We saved Jenny, but she's…it's going to be a long time before she's herself again, if ever. And three other girls are dead. Bleidd almost died because of me, because I'm too stubborn to listen to anyone telling I'm in danger. And I still just can't let the elves totally take over my life, even knowing that it's probably the smart thing to do," Allie sighed again, resting her cheek against her knees.

They were silent for a while, lost in their own thoughts. Allie knew Jason had been visiting Bleidd at the clinic, and she wanted to ask how he was doing but part of her was afraid to find out. She hadn't dared to go see him yet herself. The two days since the shooting had been stressful even though a kind of fragile peace had settled over everything, and Allie feared finding out how much Bleidd remembered. Allie and Liz had gotten into a huge fight about Jess moving in, and she felt like she'd lost all the ground they recently made up. And there was still a subtle tension between her and Jason. Finally Jason cleared his throat, "Is that what you were thinking about before I came out? That you can't trust anything?"

Allie shrugged, "Kind of. I was thinking of an old Robert Frost poem. He's a poet from regular earth, from America."

"Yeah, I've heard of him. Which poem?"

"It's a short one called Nothing Gold Can Stay. It's about how leaves look gold at first but turn green quickly…basically just how everything changes and nothing stays the way it starts out I guess," Allie finally turned and looked at Jason.

"Sounds like fairy gold turning into leaves," he smiled at his own weak joke.

3

"I guess," she agreed. Then, looking up at him, afraid of what he'd say, "Jason? Do you think this is all my fault?"

"Of course not," he said forcefully. "You aren't making those people kill people. You aren't making them hurt people. You're just trying to help."

"Yeah, and Syndra's dead and Bleidd got shot because I was trying to help," she said.

"And you've been hurt too Allie, don't forget that. And if you hadn't done what you did Walters would still be killing people and no one would have any clue it was a big crazy ritual and not just a normal crazy serial killer," he said.

"It seems so unfair that trying to be the good guy has such a big price tag attached," she said.

He laughed, "You know I kind of feel that way about being a firefighter sometimes. Its hard work and there's so much training all the time, and people get hurt, sometimes even killed. But it's still worth doing Allie. Somebody has to do it or the town would burn down."

"Yeah, I guess," she sighed again.

Jason looked over his shoulder towards the house, "Speaking of benefits of being the good guy, I think yours just got home. Looks like you have a hot date tonight. And wow."

"Huh?" Allie said cleverly. She twisted around to see what he was looking at and realized Jess was walking across the lawn towards them. For the first time in the months that she had known him he wasn't wearing his Guard uniform or his armor. Instead he wore tight dark green leggings and a lighter green tunic, belted at the waist. His hair hung loose, falling to the middle of his chest.

He was stunningly beautiful.

Jason scrambled to his feet, "Wow, ummmm. Yeah. I'll be…ummm, somewhere else…"

4

She barely noticed him leaving, her attention fixed on Jess. He nodded slightly at Jason as the two crossed paths, and Jason tripped over his own feet, blushing and stumbling the rest of the way into the house. As Jess got closer she could feel an odd nervous tension that set her on edge. He had seemed so accepting of her actions after the shooting, but his feelings now were so reserved and uneasy that she fully expected bad news. Then she had a truly horrible thought. Was he here to tell her that he had been called back into the Fairy Holding? The Guard worked rotating assignments and the Outpost was only one possible place they could be set to work. Maybe Zarethyn had changed his mind about Jess staying here with her…

He reached her side and hesitated a moment, then extended his hand down to her. She took it and he helped her to her feet. She looked up at him in mute resignation waiting for him to break whatever bad news was waiting.

Instead he launched into small talk. "Good afternoon Allie."

"Hey Jess, you look…amazing," she said, distracted from her worry by the novelty of seeing him so finely dressed.

He relaxed slightly, his emotions shifting to something gentler, "As do you my heart."

She laughed nervously, "Me?" she gestured down at her grass stained jeans and plain t-shirt.

"You always look amazing to me," he replied. She blushed and he stroked her cheek, his lips turning up in the barest hint of a smile. "Has your day gone well?"

"Well, no one's tried to kill me so far, that's an improvement," she joked, but his face tensed and she regretted mentioning it. "I'm sorry, I was just trying to make a joke. My day has been boring. My arm feels much better today – Brynneth is coming out tomorrow to do more healing work. Physical and non-physical."

He nodded, "That is good. He is very fond of you, you know."

"Wasn't he one of the ones urging you to break up with me and start seeing other people?" she quipped, once again seeing her attempted joke fall flat as he looked distressed.

"Don't think badly of him for that Allie. They worry for me, my family and Brynneth who is my friend. That is a rare thing among the elves, to have a true friend and I value him very much."

"Why do they worry?" she asked, deciding to keep her humor to herself from then on.

"Because I love you too much. Because they fear that if I lose you, through death or rejection, that it will…be bad for me," he answered honestly.

"That you'll Decline you mean," she said referring to the term the elves used for a person falling into suicidal despair.

"Yes," he said earnestly. "They do not understand you as I do. They do not understand that your ways are different, more human, and they judge you by an elven standard."

"They must hate my habit of getting into these near-death situations," she said, grimacing.

"They understand that seeking to fight darkness is a dangerous thing to do and they do not judge you for that. My brother and Brynneth both respect you more for your determination, and blame your penchant for injuries on youth and inexperience," he said sincerely. "What they dislike is the appearance that you don't return my feelings."

Her eyebrows arched upwards. "Even now? When I'm calling you like a hysterical child every five minutes and you live with me?"

He pulled her into him, until she rested her cheek against his chest. She decided the tunic must be silk, and fought the urge to run her hands all over it. "You call me for work related things, and they appreciate the importance of that. But from the outside looking in they do not see the intimacy. You are a very guarded person Allie, and they see the caution and misinterpret it, while they see my feelings only too plainly. And the sex means nothing to them."

"Yeah," she said closing her eyes and sighing, "I don't suppose it would."

"Allie…" he started and stopped. She looked up and then stepped back a little as his emotions were overtaken again by anxiety.

"What is it?" she asked.

He opened his mouth again, then closed it again. Finally he reached down and took her hands in his. When he spoke his voice was rushed, the words tumbling out on top of each other, "Aliaine of clan Draighean, will you agree to marry me?"

She looked at him, completely stunned, and the only thing she could think was, *He's flouting custom, I should be the one to ask him, or his mother should arrange it with me and then ask him…*

When she didn't immediately respond, he rushed on, "You can negotiate whatever contract you want, anything you want, and I will see that my mother agrees to it. Only say that you will take me as your husband Allie, under the law."

"What?" she managed to stutter, her brain still stuck in neutral.

"Marry me," he repeated, squeezing her hands, then raising them to his lips and kissing them.

She stared up at him, completely dumbfounded.

He spoke into the silence, his voice uncertain. "My mother has given me an ultimatum, to accept a contract and marry Avaeryn. If I refuse she is going to go to our clan head, my great-aunt, and ask that she compel me to do so, which she may do. But I can accept another offer that I

7

prefer, if there is one. If you make one. And I do not want to marry anyone else Allie, not now nor ever."

"You – wait. So either I have to marry you or you have to marry someone else?" Allie said, thinking *Gods I really hate your mother. Why does she have to push this now?* Even though she remembered the conversation she had overheard where his mother had been pressuring him to marry, and Jess saying afterwards that she had been pushing him like that for years.

"To be blunt, yes. If…if you do not want me then once my mother goes to my great-aunt I will have no choice but to accept the contract," he said, his voice unsure.

"Gods this is so…so Victorian, except role reversed," Allie mumbled, unable to believe she was in this situation. She loved Jess and her own unhappiness at the thought of him being with someone else aside, she hated the idea of him being forced into a marriage he didn't want just because his culture said that he had to do what the women in his family said. Then something occurred to her. "What if I do offer a contract and they turn it down?"

His hands tightened in hers and she felt a surge of hope from him, "My mother will not turn you down Allie. She knows how strongly I feel about you, she only fears that you do not return my feelings. If you were to ask to marry me, it would show that you do care."

Allie took a deep breath. Her mind felt frozen and she knew, with a rising sense of panic, that she needed to think quickly to come up with a response to this. She just wasn't sure she could. She did not want him to marry someone else. But she also wasn't ready to even think about marrying someone she had only known for a few months, no matter how much she loved him.
"Jess…ummm…would it…I mean, if I asked your mother to marry you," she repressed a hysterical giggle at the words, "how long would I have to actually get the contract written up?"

"Generally it takes several months to negotiate and set a contract, although sometimes it may take years," he replied and she felt a sudden surge of relief. She could ask his mother and get the pressure off of him, but still have time to really think about this. *And,* a small part of her heart whispered, *if you change your mind later you can always back out…*

"All right," she capitulated, embarrassed by her own reluctance. "I'll talk with your mother."

His joy surged up and overwhelmed her fragile shields, which collapsed, and then flowed into her, filling her so that her own doubt and worry were erased. He swept her up in his arms, and she let herself reflect his own happiness back at him.

It wasn't until much later, when she was finally able to extricate herself from his emotions and get some space that she felt a twinge of panic. *What did I just agree to?*

****

"Calm down," the group's leader said, holding her hands up towards the other woman, who was throwing things around the room. Clothing, books, and less easily identified items lay haphazardly around the floor and bounced off the walls. The leader raised one blond eyebrow at the wreckage but wisely didn't move to interfere.

"Calm down? Calm down?" the other woman's voice was shrill, caught somewhere between anger and fear. "You shot her."

"I didn't shoot anybody," the leader replied, her voice completely calm.

"Oh don't give me that," the other woman snapped. "You ordered it done. You weren't holding the gun but you caused it."

"It wasn't supposed to happen that way, it was just supposed to be a warning shot," the woman said, her voice still calm, unmoved by the other woman's hysterics.

"Well that's not what happened, is it?"

"She's fine…"

"She could have been killed!" the other woman's voice grew shriller with each word until she was shouting.

That finally broke through the leader's calm expression. She frowned fiercely, her voice hissing out, "Keep your voice down! Do you want someone to come in here and see this mess and ask what's going on?"

The rebuke broke through some of the other woman's anger and she took a deep breath. When she spoke again her voice was lower, although it still shook slightly. "You should have let me handle things. You promised she wouldn't be hurt again, and she was. She could have *died*. And then I couldn't get in touch with anyone – couldn't find you to talk to – for days. I didn't know what was going on."

"I've already apologized for that. How many times do you want me to say it?" the other woman's voice was sharp. "Since she's fine I'd think you'd be more upset that Amy was killed. Or doesn't that bother you?"

For a moment the woman was tempted to be honest and admit she was glad that the shooter was dead, but instead she said, "Of course I'm upset about Amy. I'm the one that brought her into the group, aren't I?" she paused slightly, surveying the mess she'd created. "What are we going to tell everyone?"

The leader sighed, "The truth, that Amy died for the cause and that they identified Jerry but didn't catch him. We'll all have to share the burden of helping him hide for the next few months until this is done."

"You really think the Elven Guard killed her?" the woman said uncertainly. She knew that they were denying involvement in the shooter's death and as much as she hated the elves she had never doubted their honesty.

"Her throat was slashed. The Guard carry swords. It's pretty obvious what happened," the leader said, rolling her eyes.

The other woman bent over, her brown hair swinging in front of her face, and began picking up the things she'd thrown. "We're so close now. We're almost done with this. But I won't risk her being killed."

"Well what's done is done." The leader said tapping her manicured nails impatiently on her leg. "We can't waste effort being upset about things we can't change. We need to focus on moving forward."

"Fine, but from now on you leave her to me," the woman said. When the leader started to open her mouth to protest the woman held up a hand, cutting her off. "I mean it."

The leader sighed. "Alright, but you have to up the ante. She's doing too much to help them. You have got to take her out of the game, or I won't have a choice but to let someone else handle it."

A look of grim determination came over the other woman's face, her lips pressing together and her eyes going cold. "I'll take care of everything."

Chapter 1 - Monday

There was always something unreal about Monday mornings, as the work week started over again and the weekend was left behind. Allie woke up to find Jess lying next to her, awake. He had clearly been watching her sleep and she found herself caught between finding that annoying and finding it creepy. *Meh*, she thought, trying hard to shield her thoughts from him as she yawned and rolled over, *the novelty of having him live with me has definitely worn off. That didn't take long. Gods who'd have guessed I'd be sick of having him around all the time within the first four days?* She winced slightly at the thought. *Don't complain, if it wasn't for him being here I'd probably be shut up in some corner room at the elven Outpost, safely tucked away from all this madness and slowly going crazy from sheer boredom.* Allie couldn't help but keep expecting Zarethyn to change his mind about letting her remain in her own home, but so far he seemed content to let her go her own way as long as Jess stayed with her. She wasn't entirely happy that he was only living with her under orders, but on the other hand with a serial killer who targeted mixed blooded girls still on the loose, and after being shot by a stranger who was later found dead, she couldn't deny that it seemed a reasonable precaution.

He reached out and stroked her side lightly and she shivered, turning back to face him and feeling bad for not appreciating him more. He was certainly thrilled with the situation and even now she could feel his happiness, like the light of the sun through her bedroom window, as a warm glow surrounding them both. With the combination of her innate empathy and the magical bond she had created between them she could both hear his thoughts and feel his emotions all the time, although normally she could ignore them, like the sound of a conversation in an adjoining room. Physical contact, however, made it almost impossible to block, and as he caressed her side she heard his thoughts in her mind, as clearly as if he were speaking out loud, *If only I could remain here forever, always by her side…*

Allie repressed her irritation, realizing that she was overreacting. To herself she thought *Apparently I am not a morning person today.* Then to him she reached out and thought *"Good morning. You know if you stayed here forever you'd lose your place in the Guard, not to mention we'd both get hungry eventually."*

He laughed, leaning forward to rest his chin where his hand had just been, *"Good morning my heart. How do feel today?"*

She rolled onto her back so she could look at him more easily, her eyes tracing the lines of his face, his long light blond hair falling across his face and arms, the delicate points of his ears visible through his hair, finally meeting his eyes. She fell into their vibrant green, her mood softening. He rested his head on her stomach, looking up at her as if he meant what he'd said, that he'd be content to stay there forever. *"I should feel exhausted. The spell I used to heal Bleidd was at the very limits of my ability. I still don't think I'm up to casting anything more complicated than a minor glamour right now but I don't feel terrible."*

He smiled, *"I'd like to think that I helped with that."*

She blushed, but for once didn't deny it, *"You know you did. When my energy is really down I can't seem to help taking yours."*

"You aren't taking it my love, you are taking nothing from me. I have told you many times that if you can use my emotions to strengthen yourself you should do so," he said calmly. *"I do not understand why you feel so conflicted about this. You weaken yourself by resisting your gift, your own abilities. Stop fighting against what you can do, and embrace it instead."*

He smiled again, his expression playful, *"And I am more than willing to give you whatever you need at any time. Especially as you so strongly prefer the pleasant emotions."*

She started to argue and then stopped. Instead she felt his love and contentment surrounding her, filling her. She frowned but had to admit that his emotions did empower her; she absorbed them and used them to replenish herself. After being shot and using a major spell to save her friend's life she *should* have been exhausted – in the past she would have been – and yet besides a feeling that she couldn't muster the magical energy to cast any spells right now she felt fine. And if she was totally honest despite her fears there had never been any indication that absorbing his feelings harmed Jess in any way. *"You may be right,"* she thought reluctantly. *"It doesn't seem to hurt you."*

His smile widened, but he didn't press the point. Instead he focused on a different subject, *"And how is your arm?"*

She raised her left arm, holding it up so that he could see the faint white lines high on her forearm that were the only evidence of her injury. *"You can barely even see the mark, and it doesn't hurt anymore."*

He reached out, his fingers lightly tracing the scar. *"I am amazed that it has healed so well and quickly."*

"Really?" she thought back, genuinely surprised that he thought it had healed well. *"I've never seen wounds healed by elven magic scar at all, usually it heals without a mark. I was surprised when this one didn't."*

"This was a steel bullet my heart," he thought back sadly. *"Any weapon of iron will cause a wound that is much harder to heal. Brynneth is actually very skilled at healing such injuries, or the scarring might be worse."*

When he said that she didn't think about her own injury but about Bleidd's and she began to understand why it was shocking to everyone that he had lived. She clenched her left hand, feeling the muscles in her arm flex. There was no residual pain or stiffness, even though she knew there should be. Jess watched her closely and she could feel his curiosity. "*Well*," she thought back finally, "*I'm grateful it has healed as well as it has. I will have to remember to thank Brynneth.*"

She switched suddenly to speaking out loud, wanting to hear the sound of her own voice in the silent room. "What's on your agenda for the day?"

He gave her a long look, not liking the change to verbal communication instead of the more intimate mind-to-mind speech that was a unique side effect of their bond, and which allowed him to sense her emotions to some degree. "I am to return to the ritual site and see if any new evidence can be found, and then later this morning we are to meet at the police station to discuss the current situation with the detectives and attempt, again, to convince them to reform the joint task force."

"Do you need me there for that? As an, umm, cultural intermediary?" she asked, reaching out to brush some stray hair out of his face. She still wasn't comfortable with her position in the Guard, nominal as it was, but she also didn't want to shirk her duty.

He hesitated. "Well…ideally yes, but I know you have your store to run and I did not want to ask you to close it for this."

"It's all right," she said, thinking of the blood and mess behind the building from the shooting. "I have to meet with the police this morning anyway, so I already planned to keep the store closed today."

"Detective Riordan has asked you to meet with him?"

"No, I asked them to meet with me," she said, cocking her head to one side.

"Interesting," he murmured, with typical elven evasiveness. She knew full well he wanted to ask her why she had arraigned to meet with the police, but was hoping she would volunteer the information on her own without him having to ask a blunt question.

"Interesting?" she repeated playfully, intentionally mimicking his tone.

"I am curious why you want to meet with the human police, but it pleases me that since you are closing your store anyway you will be able to attend our meeting," he said, caressing her face lightly. She sighed and leaned into his hand, making him smile.

"Well, I'd like to get my car back at some point soon," she said. She wasn't sure she'd have any luck with that but calling and asking politely hadn't gotten her anywhere so she'd finally decided to be more direct. She pulled away from his hand reluctantly. "We'd better get moving. It looks like it's going to be a busy day."

Smiling mischievously he shifted his face against her side and kissed his way up her ribs. She giggled and squirmed away, only to find herself held in place, as he pressed her back. He kissed his way up to her breast and she stopped laughing. "Jess, really we've got a lot to do today."

He smiled wider, his lips circling upwards, making her shiver. She felt the energy of his arousal like honey in the air, thick and sweet, and she drank it in despite her own intention to convince him to stop teasing her. As the energy filled her she changed her mind, liking the way it danced beneath her skin. She shoved him back hard, rolling him over onto his back; his disappointment was palpable until she slid upwards, straddling his waist. "Your incorrigible you know that?"

He filled both hands with her breasts, grinning. "From this perspective it's more than worth it."

She shifted herself back, moving along his body until his breath caught and he arched himself up beneath her like a cat stretching, every muscle straining. "Oh is it?"

"Allie," he groaned, his hands shifting down to grip her hips and move her further, until their two bodies were firmly locked together and she was gasping as well. She had very little experience with sex, even after a few months in Jess's bed because he went slowly with her, and this was new but she let instinct control her actions. She moved the way her body told her to move, following what felt good, allowing the emotions to guide her and feedback on themselves until everything else fell away.

When they were both spent, she lay across his chest their bodies still joined and she decided that maybe having him live with her wasn't so terrible after all. This certainly wasn't a bad way to start the day.

****

The knife rose and fell long after the girl had stopped screaming and long after she stopped moving. Not until his arm started to ache did he stop, and even then he felt a burning, all consuming fury. The others would be angry that he had left the safe house they had set up but he didn't care. He was sick of hiding, stuck in a boring room watching tv, waiting around until they needed him to perform the next ritual. He needed to feel blood on his hands, to hear one of those mixed-blooded bitches begging for mercy, knowing he wouldn't give it.

Looking down at the bloody ruin that lay on the ground his rage settled into a dull resentment. He took a deep breath, letting the adrenaline rush clear his head. He'd lost his home and the girl he'd been keeping there, and that was almost more than he could bear to think about. The thrice-damned Elven Guard and that half-blooded bitch had ruined everything. It had all been so perfect for the first time in his life. He'd had everything he'd wanted and all in the name of saving the human world from Fairy contamination. And they'd ruined it all, everything. Almost everything. He could still serve the greater good by killing the mixed blooded Fairy girls. He still had purpose.

And he still had his freedom.

****

Allie walked nervously into the outer lobby of the Ashwood police station, feeling uncomfortably like an intruder. The small square room was painfully plain with only a single bench against one wall. To the left was a door with no knob, only an odd flat metal piece where one should be, and a keycard reader on the wall next to it. Opposite the entrance was a small plexiglass window, with a shelf in front of it and an opening for passing small items back and forth; the other side opened up to the inside of the police station. On the wall next to the window was a small hand written sign with the barely legible words "Push button for help" and a small red button. Allie walked up to the window and hesitated, unsure if she should push the button or if it was only for emergencies. The few times she'd been to the station before she'd come with Syndra and they'd always gone in the back entrance, not the front. After several minutes standing indecisively without anyone coming to the window spontaneously, she finally gave in and risked pushing the button.

A moment later an older man in uniform appeared, looking mildly curious. "Can I help you miss?"

"Umm, yes. I have an appointment? With detective Riordan?" Allie said, hating the uncertainty in her own voice.

The strange officer smiled kindly, perhaps sensing how nervous she was. "I'll let him know you're here as soon as you fill out this visitor's log," he said, sliding a clipboard through the slot.

"Okay. Thanks," she said, taking it and quickly filling in the information before passing it back. The officer disappeared and after another minute of standing, with her bad ankle starting to ache a bit, she limped over and sat down on the worn wooden bench. She hoped that the police would listen to what she had to say, and she worried that they might take advantage of her coming here voluntarily to ask her questions she didn't want to answer about the shooting. She shifted uncomfortably in her seat and hoped she wasn't losing too much business by shutting down the store today. That train of thought only raised another fear as she realized that the shooting must have made at least the local news. *This is going to stir everything back up again*, she thought. *I'll have even more tourists and curiosity seekers coming in bothering me, wanting to know details....* In her mind's eye she saw again the terrible gaping hole in Bleidd's chest where the bullet had torn its way out and she shuddered, trying to banish the memory.

The side door opened with a heavy click, startling Allie into flinching reflexively. She looked up and saw detective Smythe, Riordan's partner, peering out at her around the door. He smiled when he saw her sitting on the bench. "Good morning, Ms. McCarthy. Come on in."

She smiled back, relieved to see a familiar face, "Good morning detective, I'm sorry I'm a little bit early, I had to get a ride in and I guess I was so worried about being late I kind of ended up going too far the other way." *Oh dear Gods you're babbling shut up!* she thought to herself as she stood and crossed the room.

19

His smile widened as he held the door open for her. "Don't worry about it. It's just as easy for us to see you now."

His eyes flicked down to her waist as she moved past him, and he continued, "I'm surprised you aren't wearing your badge."

"What?" she said, flustered at the reminder that she had let herself get tricked into joining the Elven Guard, the Fairy equivalent of police, even though her work for them was along the lines of a specialist. Her hand immediately grabbed her pocket, the reassuring shape of the badge pressing through the denim against her palm. "Should I be? I mean I'm not here on official Guard business or anything."

"I know, but I'd wear it if I were you. I hate to admit it, but you'll get more respect and better treatment around here if you have a badge."

"Oh," she said, frowning slightly. As they walked down a hallway plastered with various training posters and official memos, she pulled the heavy gold badge out and clipped it to her waistband. "I didn't think most people liked the Guard that much."

He actually laughed, an unexpected sound out of someone Allie had come to think of as typically very stoic. "No I guess most people don't. Not sure why that is, really, but around here a cop is still a cop even if they have pointed ears. Ashwood cops may not like the Guard all the time, especially when there's an issue over who's handling what case, or when the elves get pissy about something, but generally we're all happy enough to see the Guard show up when we need them."

Allie's eyes went wide at what was possibly the most honest assessment of the relationship between the two police forces she'd ever heard. "I guess that's fair enough. Not that I'd dare speak for them, but I imagine the Guard would say something very similar about the Ashwood police."

He gave her a lopsided smile, one side of his mouth twitching up, as if he were trying not to laugh again, as he stopped in front of a non-descript door. Allie felt herself tense slightly; she knew full well that the detectives had desks in one main room because she'd visited it with Syndra. This was something different, someplace she'd never been. As he opened the door, she stood her ground in the hallway. "What's this?"

He looked surprised at her resistance, his dark eyebrows going up towards his hairline. "Technically it's the room we have set aside for non-human witnesses to give statements, but basically we're using it today just to have a quiet place to talk."

She tried to keep her face politely blank, but her hackles were up. Although she understood his explanation this felt a lot more like an interrogation now than just the quick talk Riordan had agreed to on the phone. She moved into the room cautiously, but like the entryway lobby it was a bland empty room with no personality. It contained nothing but a wooden desk and several chairs. Smythe gestured towards the chairs and Allie sat down facing the door, perching on the edge of the seat. The detective sat as well, choosing the seat directly opposite Allie. She couldn't help picking up his emotions and somewhat to her relief she didn't feel any tension or concern from him.

"So, if you don't mind me asking," Smythe said, "how long have you lived in Ashwood?"

"I don't mind," Allie said, understanding the detective's desire to make small talk while they waited. "I moved here when I was thirteen. I had been living with my father and he died in a car accident, so I came here to live with my grandmother. That was about twenty-four years ago"

Smythe's expression was sympathetic, "That must have been tough."

Allie shrugged, "It was hard at first, but life goes on, you know?"

Smythe opened his mouth to say something else when the door opened, interrupting him. Allie stood reflexively as detective Riordan walked in accompanied by a stranger. The man looked to be in his late thirties or early forties; his light brown hair was just beginning to grey at the temples, his goatee streaked with silver. He was dressed all in black, from his slacks to his round-collared dress shirt, and carried a cane even though he walked easily and without any apparent limp. The cane was of course actually a magical tool, wooden with a silver handle crafted in the shape of a dragon's head; unless Allie missed her guess the dragon's eyes were real rubies. He wore an aura of magical power like a cloak, totally unabashed at what seemed to Allie an excessive display of strength. She was familiar enough with ceremonial magicians though that she recognized the energy and extravagance immediately. *Interesting* Allie thought *this must be the department's magical specialist.* Suddenly many things about this meeting were making a lot more sense and she had a sinking feeling this wasn't going to be a quick chat about her car.

"Good morning Ms. McCarthy," Riordan said, looking and sounding genuinely happy to see her. "This is Sam Kensington; Sam this is Allie McCarthy. Sam's the department's resident mage. He helps us with any blatantly magical cases."

Allie shook Sam's hand not surprised when he took advantage of the moment to test her shielding and power levels. Typical mage, more concerned with measuring her potential and assuring himself he was stronger than with politeness. Letting a small smile slip Allie pushed back flexing the energetic barriers that protected her from other

22

people's magic – grateful that for the moment at least they were up and at full power – and put just enough energy behind it to make his protections trigger, knowing that he was stronger but wanting him to know she wasn't intimidated. His face split into a wide grin, his blue eyes twinkling in a way that made Allie think he must be a handful to work with, mundanely or magically.

"Well you aren't at all what I expected," Sam said, still grinning as they all sat down.

Allie's eyebrows went up, as Riordan cut in. "Jesus, Kensington, can't you even pretend to have manners for five minutes?"

"Call me Sam, Jim, I keep telling you – that goes for you too Allie – the world would be so much friendlier if we all just used first names," Sam replied cheerfully, unfazed. Riordan looked pained and Allie tried not to giggle.

"So what were you expecting?" she couldn't resist asking. Riordan and Smythe both looked nervously at the mage for his response.

He flexed his hands together, cracking the knuckles loudly, then leaned back in his chair as if he were completely comfortable. "Well since you're the occult ritual expert they called in to replace me when I couldn't make heads or tails of the first murder I thought you'd be seventy at least."

"That isn't exactly how…" Riordan tried to cut in again, obviously embarrassed.

Sam ignored him and kept talking, gesturing expansively. "And you own a book store so you should be stooped over and bespectacled, dressed in homemade sweaters and smelling of a dozen cats…"

Smythe snorted loudly, his hand covering his mouth. Riordan looked appalled. Sam winked at Allie, who had the distinct impression that he was playing to his audience. Trying not to giggle at the image he was creating

23

– it was hard to deny that the man had a way with words – Allie nodded seriously. "Well, I hate to disappoint you."

"Oh hardly my dear!" Sam enthused, propping his feet up on the table. Absently Allie noted his designer shoes, simple black leather whose label meant they probably cost more than her store earned in a month. "You are quite delightful. Far more pleasant to look at than the rest of my co-workers, and I like your spunk. Now pleasantries aside, let's get down to business…"

"Sam," Smythe's voice held a clear warning, which the mage ignored.

"How can you be sure this new killer is continuing the ritual series and not just mimicking them?" Sam finished, still smiling.

Allie blinked. "Well, you certainly get right to the point."

"Only when you don't want him to," Riordan said, sounding resigned. "If you need him to be direct he'll talk circles around the subject until you want to scream."

Allie struggled not to look as amused as she felt. However since she knew the joint task force hadn't been reformed because the two police forces were arguing over just that issue she wasn't unhappy that Sam seemed eager to discuss the topic. "Well, I'll keep that in mind. Getting down to business then, I know that the ritual itself is being done because there is more energy there and I can feel the same person at the ritual site and around the bodies. Surely you can sense the added energy at the site?"

"I sense something…odd. Unusual. But all the energy there is odd and unusual and uncanny in a way that makes one's skin crawl. I find it impossible to read," he said pursing his lips as if it pained him to admit that much. "I do find it fascinating that you seem to sense something different. I wish you could explain how that works."

And by explain Allie thought *you mean tell you how I do it so you can do it too*…Allie sighed, and tried to choose her words carefully, not wanting to reveal that some of her knowledge came from firsthand experience. The last thing she needed was for it to get out that she had used a modified version of the same spell herself, in her case to amplify a psychic bond with Jess. "I am familiar with the energy that the ritual raises, so I suppose that that's why I have some sensitivity to it."

He looked at her thoughtfully, "What magical system do you practice?"

"Mostly witchcraft – low magic – but I also have some very basic knowledge of elven magic," she replied.

"The advantage of having a foot in both worlds. I would dearly love to learn some elven magic, but alas, my ears are the wrong shape…"

"Damn it Kensington!" Riordan barked, frowning. He glanced at Allie, obviously trying to guess whether or not she'd been offended by the comment. He never seemed sure if Allie should be treated with the extreme caution the elves merited or not since finding out about her position in the Guard.

"What?" the mage asked innocently. "Just an observation."

"One of these days your mouth is going to get you killed."

Sam rolled his eyes and waved both hands in the air. "You worry too much Jim. Allie's a good sport. Aren't you?"

"Ahhhh," Allie floundered. "I don't know what to say to that."

"And honest too!" he smiled at Allie. "I like that. So do you think your knowledge of elven magic is what gives you the inside track with this?"

"No," Allie said truthfully, starting to wonder if they were intentionally using the brash mage to ask her blunt questions that common courtesy would otherwise

25

make it difficult or impossible to get to. "The elves themselves also have difficulty with this."

"Okay, so what's so special about you then? Is it because you have a family connection to this, sort of karmic blood on your hands, or is it some freaky half-elven thing?" he asked, his voice never wavering from polite curiosity.

"Jesus Christ Sam, that's enough!" Riordan raised his voice this time, his face red. Allie could feel the waves of anger and embarrassment rolling off of him, which at least reassured her that this wasn't a set up. Smythe was staring at the mage in open mouthed disbelief. Allie fought back another nervous giggle, hating her tendency to laugh in these situations.

She held up her hand towards Riordan in a calming gesture. Her eyes fixed on Sam, trying to decide if he were assuming a persona intentionally to be able to get away with this behavior or if this were his true personality. "It's okay detective. Sam I'm guessing you don't deal with elves or the other Fey very often, do you?"

Sam's eyes glinted, leaving her with no doubt that he could behave perfectly if he wanted to, "Oh a bit here and there. They don't seem to like me very much though."

"Mmmmm," Allie murmured noncommittally. "I'm an empath and my empathy is rather…intense sometimes. The combination of that gift with my other magic sensing abilities seem to let me connect to the ritual site and the person committing the crimes on some level. That's where the insight comes from."

"Gift or a curse…" Sam muttered under his breath, then louder, "Intense, huh? Shielding isn't your forte?"

Allie struggled to keep her face carefully blank, not wanting to give away her shock. Perhaps she was underestimating how perceptive the mage really was. Or how skilled he was at getting people to let information slip with his particular obtuse approach. "I don't think shielding as an empath is the same as shielding for other things."

"Oh indeed it isn't," Sam said archly, looking at her intently. "I'd say it's even more important though. If you aren't sure of the best methods I could help direct you to some solid training."

"I'll certainly keep that in mind," Allie said, her voice even. "Getting back to the ritual though, I can sense – somehow – that there is more energy there, something that the Elven Guard captain has confirmed. I can also sense that the guy, er, suspect who kidnapped Jenny and killed the other three girls was the one who was doing the ritual. He's doing it at the right times and in the exact correct way, which means he knows how to do it and so logically it seems safe to assume he is doing it to continue the series of rituals."

"In the footsteps of the last killer you mean?" Sam asked, his voice slightly more serious.

"Something like that," Allie agreed as the two detectives looked on. "The original ritual plan called for a full year of dark moon sacrifices, thirteen altogether. Walters did eight. This new guy…"

"Jerimiah Standish," Smythe offered.

"Okay. Right, well, Standish has done another two, on the dark moons since Walters died. That only leaves three more and the cycle will be complete," Allie said, realizing with sudden insight that the real reason she was here was to convince the police to re-form the joint task force. They had stalled in their dealings with the Guard when both sides dug in and stopped listening to the other, too caught up in arguing over jurisdiction. Riordan could get nowhere with the Guard directly but if he was willing to listen to Allie, and Allie suspected more importantly if she could convince Sam, then perhaps the two groups could agree to move forward together. She felt a sudden surge of hope at the thought. "But the only way that he – Standish –

could know what to do and when is if he understood the ritual itself."

"But what about the differences in the injuries and methods?" Riordan asked. "And the victim that wasn't killed as part of the ritual?"

Allie bit her lip, wishing she could give him the solid answers he wanted so desperately. "I don't know for sure. I mean the bleach, well that was probably Walters police training helping him destroy evidence that might get him caught. Maybe he never explained that to Standish, or maybe Standish just doesn't care. And the injuries…well, what Walters did was methodical. This new guy is all about emotion. He likes hurting these girls, so maybe that's why he doesn't just do what the ritual calls for."

"So you believe they knew each other?" Riordan asked, his voice subdued as he spoke about his former partner, a man he'd been forced to kill.

"Obviously I don't know, but I can't see how Standish could do what he's doing without the sort of inside information about the ritual itself that Walters had," Allie said, trying not to wince when she said it and remembered she had that same inside information. Then deciding it was time to ask a question of her own. "What have you found out about the person who shot me?"

"You really think that's connected to all of this too?" Smythe asked. "I know the elves are big on this idea of synchronicity, but in my experience sometimes random things are just that – random."

"I can't be sure, but doesn't it seem odd to you that we find Jenny – the missing girl – and identify the suspect then suddenly someone's taking a shot at me?" Allie said.

Riordan grimaced. "You were being stalked, and we had tried to warn you that the situation might get violent."

"I know," Allie said, struggling to put into words the nebulous feeling that made her sure it was all connected. "But I've been thinking about this a lot the past

28

couple days and I think that there's more going on here than any of us realize, and I don't pretend that I know what that is. This all started up again when Jenny got kidnapped. It was right after that that the first dead animal showed up on my doorstep. Isn't that just too much of a coincidence? And then I help find her and the killer is on the run and the next thing that happens is I get shot. If I have a totally separate stalker then why the correlation? But if there's something deeper here, something connecting these things, then maybe there seems to be a connection because there actually is one."

"You mean that someone was trying to throw you off their track by distracting you or scaring you?" Riordan asked slowly.

"There is a beautiful logic to it," Sam said thoughtfully. "If Allie is right and she is the only one – so far anyway, I don't underestimate my own ability to eventually understand this ritual energy – but I digress, if Allie is right and she is the only one now who can see the way the energy connects between these things, then whoever is behind this would be highly motivated to keep her off her game."

"Then why not just kill her?" Smythe said.

"Well we could certainly interpret the bullet that hit her arm and went through her friend as an attempt in that direction," Sam said wryly.

Both detectives looked annoyed at that. Allie nodded, "Yes, there is that. And getting back to that – have you learned anything about the shooter?"

"A little," Riordan said slowly.

"Oh relax Jim," Sam cut in, waving his hand indolently in the air. Riordan gave him a warning look, obviously not wanting him to say anything else but the mage ignored him. "The woman who shot you was named Amy Blackstone. Been a resident here for her entire life. Receptionist at a dentist office out in Berville, spent several years in the military after high school – which is where she learned how to shoot so well. And here's the interesting bit…"

"Sam, don't…" Riordan started.

"…She used to date the late and unlamented detective Walters." Sam finished.

Riordan pinched the bridge of his nose. "That's confidential and could be vital to our case."

"So they knew each other." Allie pressed.

"Yes, but that could also give her a motive to want to hurt you, if she blamed you for his death," Smythe said.

Allie sighed but nodded. "Yeah I guess that's true. But is she connected to Standish in any way?"

Both detectives looked at her wide eyed. She tilted her head in surprise, "You did check that didn't you?"

"We're working on that" Riordan said, sounding tired. "But we're also working on the arson cases and another murder that came in this morning. The department's spread pretty thin with the amount of crime going on right now and tourist season about to start. We haven't finished following all the possible leads yet."

"And if it turns out she knew Standish?" Allie said, trying to stay focused, earning a laugh from Sam.

"Excellent question," he agreed. "Maybe we can let that be the deciding factor? Let's see if our new friend Jerry-the-lady-killer had any connection to Amy-the-shooter. Who we already know is connected to Rick Walters."

Riordan was frowning and nodding; Smythe looked thoughtful. When Riordan finally spoke his voice was as perfectly neutral as any elf's. "Alright. If there isn't then I hope you'll be willing to consider listening to our ideas about Standish just being a copycat killer."

"That's fair, detective. And if there is a connection?" Allie said.

"If there is, then I'll acknowledge you may be right about a wider conspiracy," Riordan said, smiling slightly. "And we'll investigate them as connected crimes and not separate ones."

"Okay," Allie agreed. He hadn't said it out loud but she could see no way the police could refuse to reform the joint task force if their own investigation proved the cases – old and new – were linked. She had complete confidence in the detectives' ability to find any connections that were there, so now it was just a matter of letting them do their jobs. "Is there any chance I'll get my car back any time soon?"

Riordan looked startled and then sheepish. "Yes, I'm sorry it's taken so long. It's in the impound lot now actually. I can get you the paperwork to get it out."

"I'll have to get a truck to take it to the garage to get new tires," Allie said, already thinking of how soon she could get that done.

"Don't worry about it," Smythe said. "It's got brand new tires on it now."

"It does?"

"Yup," Smythe said, not elaborating. After a moment Allie decided not to ask. She was getting her car back and it was drivable; better not to look this particular gift horse in the mouth. She stood up and the three men followed suit. "Thanks. That's great news. I'll wish you luck in your investigation, and I hope you uncover the truth, whatever it may be."

Sam picked up his cane, not even pretending to use it to walk with, and headed towards the door, while the two detectives lingered.

"It was nice meeting you Allie. If you decide you'd like some help training that empathy, let me know. I think you and I should talk again soon, maybe compare notes on the ritual murders and you can help me understand the energy so that I won't get a headache every time I try to sort it out in that blasted cow field. Given how much the department pays me it would be nice not to get upstaged by a woman who looks like she's not old enough to drink legally. Oh and speaking of that, you should really wear tighter clothes, you know, show off that figure. And lower cut," Sam said cheerfully, giving her jeans and t-shirt a disparaging look and making a sort of half cupping motion half line drawing gesture with his hands at mid chest level. Allie was too busy being impressed that he could make such a motion at all with the unwieldy cane in his hand to think to be offended by the implication of what he was saying, either about her youth or her appearance.

Riordan groaned, prompting the mage to add, as he went out the door, "If you've got it flaunt it."

"You won't ever let him around the Elven Guard, will you?" Allie said into the stunned silence, finally processing the mage's parting words. Smythe laughed loudly.

****

A short time later Allie was sitting in the driver's seat of her car, pulling slowly and carefully out of the police impound lot. The joy of finally having her car back was quickly overshadowed by the fear of not making it out of the tightly packed impound area without hitting something. She suspected that the officer on duty at the impound would normally have gotten her car and brought it to her, but she had forgotten to put her badge back into her pocket. He had taken one look at the Elven Guard badge, handed her the keys, and stepped back. She'd been so embarrassed she'd barely been able to force herself to ask him where her car was as she took the badge off and stuffed it back into her pocket. And naturally he'd told her that her car was at the very back of the lot.

The amount of iron from all the various vehicles crammed together and the heavy steel fence surrounding the lot made Allie's head spin and she kept blinking hard trying to clear her vision. It reminded her forcibly of the one time Liz had convinced to go see a play in New York, on Broadway, and she'd spent the entire time in the city feeling claustrophobic and ill and wishing she were back in Ashwood. She wished she dared to drive faster, wanting nothing but to be out of the maze of parked cars. The lot itself was fairly small, and not designed to handle the amount of vehicles it was currently holding, making Allie feel as if everything was pressing in on her.

She inched forward slowly, starting to make the final turn towards the front gate when a small, dark shape darted in front of the car. She hit the brakes so hard the tires locked, even at the low speed she was going. She peered cautiously around, waiting to see if another shape would follow. She hadn't gotten a good look and she couldn't be sure it wasn't an animal, but with a growing sense of annoyance she guessed it was probably one of the lesser Fey creatures that wasn't bothered by iron. A moment later her guess was confirmed as a small, ugly face poked out around the bumper of one of the parked cars just in front of her. The creature was a sort of rust brown color, and resembled a wrinkled old man in miniature. His face was wider and flatter than a human face, and seemed strangely compact, as if someone had taken a normal face and pressed it in from the top and the bottom. His ears were sharply pointed and long, but tight against his bald head. Eyes black and wet as used engine oil squinted out over a small, sharply pointed nose.

She stared at the gremlin and he stared back at her; she watched as the realization slowly dawned in his little eyes that she could see him clearly, and he frowned fiercely, breaking his silence with a long string of swears in German that made her lips twitch as she fought to keep from smiling. There wasn't anything particularly funny about gremlins in this situation, given their propensity for sabotaging or destroying machinery. They were often found in places where they could run amok unnoticed like junk yards, but occasionally they did decide to move in to other spaces where there was a lot of machinery. Allie had heard stories of gremlins infesting factories, usually causing a high number of deaths and maimings before being found and driven out. She supposed someplace like the impound lot wasn't totally out of the norm for them.

The gremlin hissed at her, showing a mouthful of fangs, and began edging forward. She sighed, realizing that it had decided she must be a human witch and was probably intending to attack her to try to protect the secret of its presence here. Well it was partially right. Tempting as it was to drive off and leave the problem to someone else – assuming the wards on her car would hold against it - she put the car in park and unclipped her seat belt, slowly opening the door and stepping out. The gremlin, doubtless used to scaring most people who saw it, had not expected that and froze, crouching down in front of her car. She pulled herself up to her full five and a half feet, towering over the small creature which snarled slightly. As she closed her door and stepped up towards the front of the car another gremlin, and then a third joined the first. She didn't doubt that if there were three willing to show themselves there were probably at least another half dozen surrounding her among the cars. This was a more serious problem than she had realized and she wondered how many accidents and injuries without an explanation had been going on around here.

Emboldened by the sudden reinforcement the original gremlin crouched lower, doubtless getting ready to spring at her face. They were little things, comparatively, but fierce fighters and vicious, with teeth that could rip through steel. Allie raised her right hand slowly and took a deep breath, getting ready to call a little bit of magic that should impress the ugly little Fey monsters. It was something that any elven child, even very young ones, could do easily, and which took almost no effort, but it was also magic that only elves could do. Holding her hand out palm up she called tinesí, the fairy light, and instantly a bright, pale white glow filled the air over her hand, visible even in the sunlit impound lot, so bright it cast its own shadows among the cars. Even the tiny magic made her feel tired, exhausted as she still was after healing Bleidd and surrounded by iron and steel on all sides, but it had the desired effect.

All three gremlins flattened themselves to the ground, and she could hear movement and muttering around her. She spoke loudly enough to be heard by any of the lesser Fey nearby. "If you can hear my voice metal-biters then come out before me and join your brothers."

The sounds of movement grew louder and a moment later another dozen gremlins, hunched over and grimacing, skulked out from every direction until there was a small mass of the creatures huddled in the narrow space in front of her car. They squinted in the bright light from her hand, shifting back and forth uncomfortably. Allie tilted her head to the side, surprised that there were so many and curious about why, but also glad that even gremlins held elves in enough respect to fear her.

One of the little creatures which was slightly larger than the others and less savage looking edged forward. He glared up at her, speaking Low Elvish in a voice like metal grating on metal, "Why do ye gather us High Lady? We did ye no harm."

She replied in Elvish, giving him a question for a question. "Why are so many of you vexing such a small space?"

35

His small face screwed up unhappily, "We do what we're told, don't we then? High Lords say go bend the metal in this place so we goes don't we?"

Allie's eyes narrowed at his words. Elves had sent them here? She felt the skin on her arms raising in goose flesh but pushed the thought away for later. She knew enough about gremlins to realize that she wouldn't get any further details from the little Fey, and it could be dangerous to risk questioning them too much. If they realized she didn't have the power to back up her elven appearance, that she was in effect bluffing them, they'd probably tear her into palm sized pieces and leave her strewn across the alley. Luckily a childhood in the Dark court had taught her some hard lessons about dealing with the more dangerous Fey creatures that gave her a certain expertise in that area. Careful to keep her posture as imposing as possible, and speaking in a voice that was strong and projected she said, "Leave this place and do not return. Go to the scrap yard across the river where you can delight in destroying metal without harming anyone."

Several of the smaller gremlins hissed angrily but the leader did not seem unhappy about their destination. Reaching out with her empathy she could feel an odd kind of relief in him, that made her wonder how difficult it had been for the gremlins to be packed in the small impound lot in such numbers. Nonetheless it would be against his nature to concede easily. "And why should we do what ye say High Lady and risk pissin' off the ones what sent us here? I'm thinking they's more fearsome nor ye is."

Not long ago this would have presented a real problem for Allie, especially when she was too weak to use any magic. She would have had no choice but to try to bargain with them, or call Jess and use him as a threat to force them to do as she said. But she knew that it was more than time she start using her situation in the Guard to her advantage instead of constantly feeling used by it. She

36

reached into her pocket with her free hand, holding the fairy light with the other, and pulled out her badge, thrusting it forward towards the gathered gremlins. The fairy light hit the gold and reflected off. When she spoke again she tried to imitate the way most elves spoke to the lesser Fey, making her voice sound strong and arrogant, "You'll do as I say because I say so."

The gremlins flattened themselves down looking away from the badge in fear. Even the erstwhile leader bowed his head and winced, "O' course High Lady. We goes right now, we does. Don't want no trouble wi' the Elven Guard, no we don't. Sure we didn't know you was an elf, nor one the Guard or we'd not have troubled ye at all."

True to his word as soon as he spoke all the gremlins dispersed. She heard the skittering of claws on metal and had no doubt they were leaving the impound lot and heading over to the scrap yard she'd ordered them to go to. Allie let out a long breath, not entirely sure if she liked inspiring fear and obedience in anything, but also grateful that she'd come away unharmed and succeeded in clearing the area of a dangerous situation. Now that everything was over she felt shaky and started to think of all the ways that could have gone wrong or ended horribly.

She got back in her little car and resumed her slow progress out of the lot. She gave a slight wave to the officer at the gate, deciding not to bother telling him what had happened; she doubted he'd had any idea about the gremlin infestation anyway. Instead she drove a little ways down the road and pulled over, parking in the first spot she could find. She left the car running, taking a moment to relax and let herself feel relief at finally having her car back. The police had even put new tires on to replace the slashed ones they'd taken into evidence.

When she was certain that she had calmed down and no trace of any fear or anxiety might show through she reached out to Jess. Connecting to his mind she had the impression of him sitting, but movement, and a low conversation going on around him. After a moment she concluded that he was in a car, probably heading to the meeting with the police. She was fairly certain he was a passenger and so she spoke to him, "*Jess?*"

She felt a moment of surprise from him and slight annoyance which surprised her. "*Allie now is not a good time. We are preparing for the meeting with the police.*"

His mental voice was abrupt and distracted and she realized she must be interrupting a conversation. She could, of course, have fully projected into his mind before speaking to him and seen exactly what was going on, but that seemed so intrusive she tried never to do it intentionally unless he explicitly invited her to. As it was she debated backing off, but decided that he needed to know what she had learned immediately; his tone however put her off slightly, enough that her own response was rather snarky. "*Should I call your cell phone?*"

She felt another flare of annoyance and then sudden worry. "*Is something wrong? Are you in danger?*"

"*Not at the moment, but the day is young. I need to tell you something important.*"

"*Tell me,*" he thought back impatiently.

Sitting in her car she rolled her eyes, trying to remind herself that he was under a lot of pressure and heading to an important meeting. And probably wondering why she couldn't have just waited until she saw him there to talk to him. "*I picked up my car from the police impound lot, and stumbled across a rather significant infestation of gremlins…*" she started.

He interrupted, his mental voice sharp and worried, "*Gremlins? Define significant. How many were there? A half dozen?*"

"*No, closer to fifteen or sixteen altogether.*" She thought back, trying to remember the gathered mass of creatures and send him an image of them with her words.

"Sixteen," he thought back, horrified. *"Sixteen? Blessed Gods..."*

She had not expected him to be quite so upset, and she hadn't even gotten to the part she actually wanted to tell him about. *"Well, at any rate, I confronted them..."*

"You confronted gremlins by yourself? Sixteen of them?" now he really was upset, his emotions making her wince.

"Of course. They were going to attack my car. Well, one of them was. I didn't know there were more of them until I got out of the car to stop that one," she thought back, puzzled.

"Allie," he thought to her, so upset now, he was momentarily incoherent. *"Why would you take such a risk? Gremlins are the foot soldiers of the Dark court."*

"I know that Jess," she thought back drily wondering if he'd forgotten what she'd told him about her past. *"They are fearsome fighters and vicious little things, but generally speaking they have as much respect for elves as any of the Lesser Fey and they greatly fear the Elven Guard. I made them think I was a full elf and they behaved themselves."*

"And what would you have done if they hadn't?" he thought back, his agitation making her shift uncomfortably in her seat.

"They did, so it's a moot point," she thought back. *"And at any rate, that's not the real point here. They told me that they were in the police impound lot to begin with because elves had sent them there."*

He was completely silent for a full minute and she could feel his shock vibrating through her. Finally, slowly, he repeated what she'd said. *"They told you elves sent them there?"*

"Yes."

"No Bright court elf would deal with gremlins," he thought back, his mental voice suddenly grim.

39

She bit her lip at his words, not having realized that gremlins were so completely Dark court. Usually most Fey beings had counterparts in both courts. Usually, but not always. *"Then it must have been Dark court elves who sent them,"* she thought, her voice calmer than she'd expected as she stated the obvious conclusion.

"Allie, my heart," Jess thought to her, suddenly sounding less like the stressed Guard commander and more like the lover she was used to dealing with, *"Who is with you?"*

Uh-oh Allie thought to herself unsure of the best way to answer his question. She made a futile attempt at prevarication, *"I hope you don't need to question them further. I doubt they would answer much anyway, but as it is I sent them off to a human junkyard where they aren't likely to cause much trouble and can destroy things to their hearts content."*

"You sent them...and why did they listen to you?" he asked, momentarily distracted.

"Because I flashed my badge. I told you they fear the Guard," she replied.

"And who was with you when you did this?" he pressed again, recovering from his earlier surprise.

She flinched, *"I don't need round the clock supervision."*

"You..." his voice managed to combine stunned and appalled in equal measure. *"You confronted more than a dozen gremlins by yourself? When you are too drained to do even simple spells? Do you* want *to die?"*

"Obviously not since I'm fine, and yes I confronted a bunch of gremlins by myself. And I'm fine," she focused her emotions and reached out to him, letting him feel her calm, and after a moment her love for him. His own emotions were a mix of fear and worry. She wished there was a way to get him to understand that she knew how to deal with gremlins well enough not to fear them. Healthy

40

caution maybe, but not fear. *"Everything is alright Jess, truly. I will meet you at the police station for the meeting, but I thought you needed to know immediately about this, about elves sending some of the nastier Lesser Fey into the police lot to cause trouble."*

"Yes, I'm glad you told me. It may answer a lingering question about certain difficulties that we have been dealing with," he thought back, only somewhat soothed. *"And I will see you soon."*

Allie sighed and put her car in gear, getting ready to pull back out into traffic.

****

With an odd feeling of déjà vu Allie walked into the lobby of the police station for the second time that morning. This time however the little room was not empty, although it was also not as full as Allie had expected. Standing at attention in the middle of the room, radiating tension so sharply that it made her wince, were Jessilaen and captain Zarethyn. Both wore the uniform of the Elven Guard: dark green tunics, multi-pocketed black cargo pants, longswords at their hips, badges clipped to their belts. Their hair was pulled back into the long braid that was the signature style of the Guard, Jessilaen's a slightly paler blonde than his brother's. Feeling suddenly self-conscious about her worn jeans, loose t-shirt, and frumpy ponytail, Allie moved to join them, glad that at least her badge was properly displayed.

The elves turned as she entered and she sensed them relaxing slightly. Jess's eyes traced her form and although his face remained impassive she could feel that he was not only relieved to see for himself that she was still in one piece but also pleased to see her. She moved to stand next

41

to him, gravitating to his side without thinking. She wasn't sure of the best greeting under the circumstances so she erred on the side of caution and went with a very formal, "Good morning captain Zarethyn, commander Jessilaen."

Zarethyn nodded tersely, "Greetings Aliaine. I am pleased that you are attending this meeting with us in your capacity with the Elven Guard. We have had no success in convincing the human police to work with us and attempting to run parallel investigations is proving both frustrating and futile."

"Ah, well," Allie mumbled, "yes I can see that. From the beginning it's been essential for us all to work together, but it's so easy to get sidetracked. And the human police understandably are trying to work within their own system."

He gave her an odd look, tilting his head to one side. Nervous under the scrutiny she kept talking, "You should know, I mean I hope it's alright, I came here this morning. I had an appointment with detective Riordan and his partner. Oh and also the police mage. Well I had the appointment with Riordan but the other two also showed up. Anyway. About getting my car back. But they wanted to talk about the ritual murders and why I thought they might be connected so I was trying to convince them that the cases might be linked."

"Were you?" Zarethyn said, sounding impressed. "Were you indeed?"

She blushed, feeling Jess's approval. "Yes, I was. I know it's probably not my place and all, but it's just so important…"

"And did you have any success?"

"I don't know, but they were willing to listen at least," she said feeling tired. What if she was wrong in the approach she'd taken with the police? That could set things back instead of moving them forward.

42

The Guard captain nodded thoughtfully, clearly pleased with her initiative. Jess reached a hand out, clasping her shoulder in a reassuring grip. His voice in her mind was uncertain, *"My love why did you not tell me that you planned to do this? I could have assisted you."*

"I didn't exactly plan to do it, it just happened – I mean the opportunity presented itself," she thought back embarrassed. *"But when they were asking questions about the ritual I wanted to get them to see it the way I do, the way the energy is building. I wanted to help you, to help see the joint task force reformed. Because I'm tired of sitting on the side watching everyone fight while whoever is doing this keeps getting away with it."*

Zarethyn was frowning. His eyes going between the two of them, and she realized it must be obvious that they were communicating in some way and that her face was probably broadcasting her feelings as well as if she were announcing them. She blushed again and then felt even more foolish for being so obvious in her reaction to his expression. Jess ignored both his brother and Allie's distraction, continuing the conversation. *"You are still in great danger. We are doing our best to protect you and track down whoever is behind this, but it is not wise to keep pushing yourself out into the front lines. I appreciate your desire to help Allie, but you risk yourself too much already. Think of the consequences you have already dealt with, the physical damage, the tromluithe, the recent attack."* He shook his head slightly, his expression grim. Zarethyn looked fascinated.

She knew tromluithe was what the elves called panic attacks and she fought back a grimace at the reminder that if not for Brynneth, a medic with the Guard and Jess's close friend, she would still be suffering the crippling anxiety. Her fingers traced the design on her badge and she bit her lip, thinking that she never would have been maneuvered into her current position working with the

Guard if she hadn't needed a way to trade for that healing…She shook her own head slightly. *"No Jess. I have to start fighting back. Maybe all I can do is little things, a push here and a nudge there, but I can't do nothing. Sitting back and doing nothing but wait for other people to act got my best friend killed and Bleidd shot. I don't want any more blood on my hands."*

"At least wait until you have recovered from the strain of the spell you cast and are able to defend yourself," he pressed.

She would have been annoyed but she could sense his genuine fear for her. Without thinking she spoke out loud, "I don't think we have time to waste waiting."

Jess's eyes widened slightly when she spoke and his hand tightened on her shoulder. Zarethyn stepped closer, his voice calm, "Do we not?"

"Forgive me," she said, looking away. "I don't know why I said that."

"You and Jessilaen were conversing, yes? Using the spellbond you have which ties your mind to his?" he asked, his voice politely curious.

"Yes," Allie agreed, glancing up at Jess who was looking steadily at his brother.

"Fascinating. Forgive my negligence in this matter, I have been greatly distracted by other things, but this connection has not weakened?"

"No," Jess answered, his voice clam but his emotions suddenly uneasy. "It has strengthened in the months since Allie cast the spell which amplified the bond we already had."

Allie did not miss the emphasis that Jess put on that last. He was making it clear to his brother that he believed they had been joined in some way before she had cast the spell. She struggled to keep her face impassive as Zarethyn nodded thoughtfully. *"Jess,"* she thought to him, *"what is wrong?"*

44

"*Nothing is wrong*," he thought back, his eyes never leaving Zarethyn. "*There are many who believed what you did would fade on its own and some few who advocated finding a way to undo it. I have endeavored to explain that it is wasted effort to undo what is merely the amplification of something that occurred naturally.*"

"Fascinating," the Elven Guard captain repeated. "But perhaps a discussion for another day. As to the matter at hand, you say you don't know why you said it, but do you believe it to be true?"

Allie leaned into Jess without thinking and he wrapped his arm around her shoulder. She tried to choose her words carefully, "Do we not have much time to waste? No, I don't think we do. I think the killer who is still out there is too dangerous to allow to stay free-"

"That much we agree on," detective Riordan said.

All three turned to find the detective standing in the doorway leading back into the station holding the security door open. Allie wondered how long he'd been standing there, a concern clearly shared by the Guard captain who nodded stiffly at the human police officer. "Detective Riordan. I'm glad to hear you acknowledge that we have some common ground."

Riordan made a face at that and Allie suppressed a wince. Obviously things between the two groups had deteriorated far more than she'd realized. Riordan stepped back slightly, holding the door open so that they could enter, "I'm sorry about the wait Captain, Commander. We were running some information down and got a bit sidetracked. Ms. McCarthy I didn't realize you'd be attending this meeting."

"Aliaine is the cultural intermediary for Crannuiane Outpost's Elven Guard," Zarethyn said, his voice so cold Allie half expected frost to form on the walls around him. "Her presence is essential here."

"Yeah," Riordan said, his own tone less than friendly, "then it's a shame you haven't dragged her along to all the other meetings in the last week."

Allie reeled slightly as the air filled with anger and resentment, thick and heavy. Zarethyn and Jess both stiffened at the detective's words, but it was Jess who spoke, "Detective don't end this meeting before it begins by insulting us. If the meetings thus far had proved at all fruitful perhaps it would not be necessary to have an intermediary involved in this one."

Riordan's lips thinned but Allie could sense that he wasn't going to apologize, and that the elves were peeved enough already to be willing to leave. For an instant she struggled with the urge to just let things play out and then she kicked herself. "Detective I volunteered to come here hoping that I might be able to help."

"And is that part of why you came here earlier?" Riordan said.

Allie smiled, shaking her head, "No, but I understand why it looks suspicious. I had arraigned to meet with you on my own before I had any idea you were meeting with the Guard too."

"And I suppose the Guard had no idea you were coming here?" he said sarcastically, stopping in front of the same room Allie had been taken to earlier.

"No, detective, I did not," Zarethyn said his eyes glittering with suppressed fury. Allie wasn't sure what had happened but she hadn't anticipated that the normally easy-going, polite detective would act so openly confrontational.

Allie took a deep breath, trying not to get overwhelmed by the miasma of negative emotions or allow them to influence her. Despite her best efforts though she felt herself getting angry, and unexpectedly she thought she heard the voice of her friend Syndra whispering *"channel your inner bitch"*. She reached out and took Jess's hand, desperate to ground herself. "Okay listen. Everybody is

46

mad at everybody else. Fine be mad. You don't trust each other. I can see that. I came here earlier to find out about getting my car back not to advance some kind of Elvish-agenda or whatever you're accusing me of. You were the one who wanted to talk to me at that meeting about the murders, which is fine by me, but let's not act like it was my idea. I don't have any idea what's been going on with you all or why everyone is at everyone else's throats all of a sudden. What's the plan here? We all just stand around and insult each other, we waste time fighting with each other, and watch the bodies pile up?"

"Ms. McCarthy…"Riordan started, but she could sense him wavering so she pushed.

"No, really. I just want to be on board with the plan, so the next time I get shot or whatever and you all stand around arguing over whose jurisdiction it is while I bleed to death I'll know not to take it personally," she said, her voice unnaturally high in her own ears. Jess inhaled sharply and she could feel his horror at the very idea, while Zarethyn turned his glare onto her. She refused to wilt under that formidable look. Swallowing hard she forced herself to keep going. "It's essential that we work together. You think I want to be in the middle of this? Because if any of you think that, you couldn't be more wrong. I want my nice normal life back where no one tries to hurt me and I go to work and go home and don't have nightmares about the terrible things I see and sense, but that isn't possible is it? The Elven Guard is committed to finding out what's going on with these rituals before they are completed and both worlds are damaged. Detective you have dealt enough with the Guard to know that it is not wise to insult them, to question their word or their honor, yet you seem to be out to pick a fight. I don't know why, but at this point we don't have time to bicker like kids over who gets to be in charge. You all want to know what I think? Well let me tell you whether you want to hear it or not: I think this has to be solved as quickly as possible and I think we will never succeed unless we work together."

Zarethyn's anger had run out like water midway through her impromptu speech and he was regarding her now with the same intense scrutiny of earlier. "You have said that twice now. Are you so certain?"

Riordan was also watching her intently and she sensed his anger had broken as well, replaced by a mix of fear and worry. The fear concerned her, but she didn't have time to think about it. "Yeah I am. I don't know why. I just…it's this feeling I have. If either group could solve it alone I think it would already have been solved. But whatever's going on here…it's going to take all of us to figure it out. And we don't have time. I don't know why I think that either, and I know I sound crazy right now, but I just know…feel…that time is running out."

There was absolute silence for a minute, so complete that Allie could hear the distant sounds of phones ringing and people talking elsewhere in the station. And then detective Riordan nodded stiffly, "Alright. Chalk it up to too much coffee and stress and not enough sleep in the past few days. I am…sorry…if I offended anyone."

Zarethyn's head went to the side, still looking at Allie, and she could sense that he was impressed for some reason with her. For her part she was embarrassed that she had lost her temper and said some of the things she had, but it was too late to take them back and at least they seemed to have snapped Riordan out of his weird mood. The Guard captain turned to acknowledge the detective, his own tone also stiff, "Apology accepted detective. Aliaine is correct that we would be foolish now to let our own personal quarrels sidetrack us from focusing on what truly matters."

Jess's hand tightened in hers and Allie felt a wave of love and approval from him. It prompted her to reach out and question him as Riordan opened the door and ushered them into the small room. "*I don't understand. Why are you happy with me for getting pissed off and snapping at everyone?"*

She saw his lips twitch into a small smile as they walked over to the table with its cluster of seats. *"That was perfectly done my love. You said exactly the right thing to get both the detective and my brother, two very stubborn people, to back down and actually listen."*

"Oh, I guess I'm lucky it worked out that way then," Allie thought back, sitting in one of the chairs facing the door. Jess took the seat next to her, with Riordan and Zarethyn sitting opposite. As they sat Jess gave her an inscrutable look, sliding his chair closer so that he could more easily continue to hold her hand.

"Will your partner be joining us?" Zarethyn asked, obviously not wanting to start if the other detective would be joining them late.

"Yes, he should be here any minute," Riordan said, watching the door over his shoulder, "He just had to confirm something."

A moment later the door swung open and both detective Smythe and the police mage Sam walked in. Allie tensed seeing Sam and looked at Riordan but his expression remained calm. Everyone stood and greetings were exchanged; Allie barely noticed, too busy hoping Sam behaved around the two elves.

"Sorry for the delay," Smythe said, sounding like he meant it. He walked over to his partner and handed him a folder, which Riordan took with a resigned look. "We got back here as quickly as we could."

The elves nodded politely. Allie sat awkwardly suddenly feeling very out of place and acutely aware that she really had no idea what she was supposed to do here. Her earlier outburst was entirely out of character for her and while it may have helped get the Guard captain and detective working together – or at least listening to each other – she doubted that it would help for her to keep lecturing people. She shifted in her chair, as the elves sat patiently at attention and Riordan shuffled through the paperwork Smythe had handed him. Sam sat against a wall away from the small table, his cane upright in both hands, a brooding expression on his face as he regarded the elves.

Finally Riordan sighed and closed the file. "Okay, so the cases are connected. Where do we go from here?"

Allie felt the shock that rippled through the elves, a feeling she was sure was plain on her face, but both Zarethyn and Jess stayed outwardly impassive. When he spoke the Guard captain's voice was unperturbed. "What has changed detective?"

Riordan pursed his lips, looking unhappy, but again what Allie felt from him was fear. Out of the corner of her eye she saw Sam leaning forward, regarding her intently and she tried belatedly to strengthen her shields and block the other emotions out. After a moment Riordan said, "Ms. McCarthy asked us this morning if there was any connections between the woman who shot her and the new ritual killer, because we had already found out that the shooter had a previous relationship with the first killer."

Jess's eyes narrowed, "You failed to share that information with us."

"At the time it didn't seem to relate to anything except a possible motive for Ms. McCarthy's shooting..." Riordan began, but Jessilaen interrupted.

"Which you knew we were investigating, since she is a member of the Elven Guard and the other victim is an elf." His anger was plain, and Zarethyn gave him a warning look. Elven culture rejected strong expressions of emotion and the elves prided themselves under most circumstances with projecting an aura of stoicism. Clearly Zarethyn, while also angry about being excluded on this, did not feel it merited an obvious show of such anger. Jess caught his captain's eyes and took a deep breath, leaning back in his chair.

50

"Yes, and I am sorry we didn't share what we knew when we first found out," Riordan said with surprising sincerity. "At the time we were pursuing a separate investigation and sharing information wasn't our top priority."

"And that has changed?" Zarethyn asked again.

"Yes it has," Smythe said quietly. "Not only is the shooter a former girlfriend of Walters, but she knew Standish as well. They went to high school together and appear to have remained friends afterwards. That was what we were running down that made us late getting back here."

"Indeed," Sam said suddenly. "It's a bit convoluted, and suffice to say Ms. Blackstones' family is far from cooperative as they are quite thoroughly convinced that the Elven Guard was involved in her death, but it's more than enough evidence to convince us."

"Why should her family believe that the Elven Guard had a part in her death?" Zarethyn said, not trying to hide how much the idea offended him.

The humans exchanged glances, and finally Riordan said, "It's hard for them to believe that some other random person killed her with a bladed weapon, when everyone knows the Guard carries swords."

"We would have been within our own Law to kill her for her crime, had we been in a position to mete out such justice," Jess said. "But we would not deny doing so, had it been our blades that had ended her life."

Riordan held up his hands in a placating gesture, "I don't doubt that. I have never known the Elven Guard to be anything less than utterly honest."

A residual tension left the room with his words, the praise going further with the two elves than the earlier reluctant apologies had. Allie fought the urge to roll her eyes at the ridiculousness of it; the detective had apologized and the Guard had still been in a snit about

51

being treated rudely, but he gave them a rather offhand compliment and all was forgiven. *Elves*, she thought to herself *care more about their honor than anything else. No wonder most people think they're arrogant jerks.*

"Are we certain that she died the way it looks like she died?" Allie ventured a question.

Smythe shrugged. "The autopsy shows a cut on the right side of her neck, fairly shallow, but it bled for a bit, and then her throat was slit, I think the M.E. used the word 'forcefully', from left to right."

"Interesting," Zarethyn murmured. "So someone held a blade to her neck, close enough to cut her and long enough for the wound to bleed in a noticeable amount. And then after some small time they killed her."

"You think she was...what? Being questioned?" Riordan asked, his voice sharp.

"That would fit the evidence," Zarethyn agreed.

"For what purpose?" Jess asked.

"Hmmmm," Sam interjected. "That would imply whoever killed her wanted information from her first. That doesn't make it sound like they were playing on the same team."

Jess turned and exchanged a long look with his brother, who frowned. Riordan shifted, his chair creaking with the movement, "What? What is it?"

"You think this might be tied into whoever sent the gremlins?" Allie asked, and both elves gave her a quelling look. Jess's voice in her mind was harsh *"Allie do not speak of the Dark court to the police."*

"Of course not," she replied, stung that he would assume she'd be so foolish. *"But the police must know – must be told - that there were gremlins in their impound lot. And if the Dark court has agents here, for whatever reason, and that is tied to the shooter's death, that's important information."*

He looked unhappy but nodded slightly. "*Yes, but they must be told with great caution and without any mention of the Dark court. If there are such agents and they are working against not only the Guard here but also the human police then of course the police must be warned*"

Sam was watching them closely, obviously aware of something passing between them. Riordan however was oblivious to it, "What gremlins?"

"When I went and picked up my car at the impound lot today I found that you had a really serious infestation of gremlins," Allie said.

Sam swore colorfully. "Well that'll be a mess to clear out, the vicious bastards are hell to deal with. How many are there, do you know?"

"Oh, ummm, well. There were about, ummm, sixteen I think. But you don't need to worry about it I took care of it." Allie said, flushing as everyone in the room stared at her with looks ranging from shocked to disapproving.

"You…"Sam's mouth moved but for a moment no sound came out; the usually flamboyant mage temporarily at a loss for words. He stood up, stepping towards Allie, which made Jess stand and step protectively in front of her. "You cleared out sixteen gremlins by yourself?"

"Well, not using magic exactly," Allie said, wishing everyone wasn't looking at her like she'd suddenly grown another head. "Gremlins are still Lesser Fey and like any Lesser Fey they respect elves and fear the Guard so I kind of made them think I was an elf, a full elf, and flashed my Elven Guard badge. And told them to leave, to go to a scrapyard where they wouldn't cause any trouble that is. And they did."

"You took an enormous risk," Zarethyn said tightly.

"Not really. I mean I can see that it looks that way, but…" *but I can't explain this* Allie thought miserably *without explaining how I know so much about gremlins,*

"The point is that they weren't there by chance. And if there is someone around trying to stir up trouble and using the, ummm, more dangerous Lesser Fey to do it, maybe they had something to do with Blackstone being killed. I mean that makes more sense than thinking someone in her own group would question her at knife point and then kill her after she shot at me."

Riordan massaged his temples, "So what you are saying is that we don't have one group acting here we may have two?"

"Possibly, but I think the real issue is the group behind the ritual murders. If Walters, Blackstone, and Standish are all connected and we know Standish is still at large and still in Ashwood, isn't it logical to assume there's at least one more person, someone who is helping him?" Jess said slowly. Allie hoped he was being sincere and not just trying to distract the police from the possible Dark court elves.

"Actually I think it's glaringly obvious," Sam said, sitting back down, his eyes still trained on Allie. Jess also sat with obvious reluctance. "The original group worked in a coven structure, with a single leader and more than a dozen followers, yes?"

"Yes," Zarethyn agreed. "So you believe whoever revived the ritual also revived the coven?"

"If you want to put it that way," Sam shrugged. "I think we made a big mistake focusing on the idea of a single killer from the beginning. Of course I wasn't involved in the earlier investigation since I couldn't identify either the magic or the ritual being used, or perhaps I could have offered this insight sooner…"

"Sam," Smythe said, the single word a clear warning to the mage who winced and waved his hands in the air.

"Be that as it may," he went on, obviously struggling to reign himself in. Allie wondered what the police had told him about the Elven Guard that had him trying so hard to behave himself. "My point is that it's clear now that the three known suspects are connected, and where there are three I believe there are more. Certainly at least a rudimentary coven."

"Isn't it possible it was just those three?" Smythe asked.

"Possible, perhaps," Sam said, resting his chin thoughtfully on the dragon-head of his cane. "But then how is Jerry-the-slasher still loose? He can't escape to regular earth and he can't flee into Fairy. He must therefore still be in Ashwood and yet we have not even a whisper of his presence. Nothing. Radio silence. No I think that Jerry has friends, friends of the magical murderous ritual sort, and they are hiding him, undoubtedly so that he can continue to do their bloody work for them when the moon is dark again."

"That doesn't give us much time," Riordan sighed.

Allie shook her head. "Don't assume he'll wait that long."

"What do you mean my dear?" Sam asked, his voice casual, his gaze keen.

"I mean that unlike Walters he isn't just doing this because he has to. He's doing it because he gets off on it. Now that he has nothing to lose I wouldn't be surprised if this becomes the only driving force for him."

"How so?" Jess asked frowning.

Everyone was looking at her again and Allie fought the urge to look down, instead staring at a point on the wall to keep her head up. "I mean that he doesn't have to worry about pretending to be normal, going to work, paying bills. He's got nothing left in his life but completing this ritual and killing girls, and from the feelings he gives off, around the scenes of the kidnappings and bodies..." she shuddered feeling again that slimy emotional mix of lust, rage, and joy," ...if he was driven before I think he'll be, I don't know whatever beyond obsessed is now."

"Then it essential that we find and capture him quickly, and root out any who may be aiding him," Zarethyn said grimly. The others all nodded, unhappy but at least in agreement.

"Alright," Riordan said, nodding slightly. "Well, we'll start pulling all the personal information we can get on all three of them and cross checking everything. It'll be tedious..."

"If it would assist you detective," Zarethyn said, looking thoughtful, "I will send one of the squad members I have assigned to this case, at Jessilaen's discretion, to help you."

"I'd appreciate that," Riordan said, visibly thawing towards both elves. "We're flat out trying to handle everything right now and this...it's a lot of information, lots of details to go over. Another set of eyes would be a big help."

Allie stood up with the others as everyone shook hands and finalized a plan to move forward with the joint investigation. It all left her head spinning. She found herself silently nodding and unable to follow what anyone was saying, acutely aware of how tired she was. She should have been thrilled at this turn of events, that the task force was reformed and that everyone was finally working together, but she wasn't. She felt numb, as if her system had hit some point of critical mass in dealing with everything and couldn't process anymore.

As they walked out of the police station a little while later, her mind was on an obligation she'd been putting off. She reached her car and hesitated, trying to decide if she should just go home or if she should tell Jess she had to do something else first....

"I have not had time to mention to you Allie, but I want to offer my congratulations," Zarethyn said in Elvish, reaching out and grasping her shoulder. She felt his emotions filling the air around her and forced herself to remain still and not step away as he kept speaking. "I am very pleased to hear that you intend to talk with my mother about a marriage contract with Jess. I think it a very wise solution to settling the disruption caused by the uncertainty surrounding your relationship."

"Oh, uh, well thank you," Allie mumbled reflexively. "But that could be premature, nothing's been accepted yet."

The two elves glanced at each other, exchanging a cryptic look. Then Jess reached out and pulled her in close against his side, "She will not refuse you."

His brother nodded in support, "She has been urging him to marry for many years. Although she may be willing to force him to it now to get the heir she wants she does care for him Allie; she knows he prefers you and I cannot imagine her standing in the way of his happiness if you ask for him."

If I ask for him, Allie thought, the words echoing oddly in her mind. *As if he were an object to be requested.*

"I hope you will not be upset with me Allie, but mother is visiting the Outpost tomorrow and since I told her you were planning to ask for the marriage she would like to meet with you," Jess said carefully.

"Oh, I...of course," Allie fumbled out the words, caught totally off guard. They had only just discussed a possible marriage – her mind refused to think of it in concrete terms – and she had assumed she would have weeks at least to decide how to approach dealing with the situation. But since she had agreed to it, it seemed unfair to immediately turn around and try to delay.

Chapter 2 – Monday afternoon

Salarius watched Ferinyth pace back and forth like a caged animal and he wisely stayed out of the other elf's way. The two Dark court elves had spent the first 48 hours after the girl was shot shadowing her every move, with Ferinyth pledging to take her at the first opportunity. That opportunity, however, never presented itself. The girl was perpetually surrounded by others, her Elven Guard lover barely ever leaving her side, and she proved impossible to get near. Finally in the dark hours of the morning of this, the third day, he had admitted defeat, and the two had headed back to the cheap motel they were staying at.

The older elf had accepted the situation with ill grace and was in a truly foul mood. He refused to eat or sleep, instead walking the length of the room endlessly, devising and discarding different plans to get to the half-elven girl they had been tasked to kidnap. Salarius hadn't dared even speak to the other elf, after one brief attempt when they'd first returned to the room. He'd made the mistake of suggesting that after almost three straight days awake and hunting the girl they should try to rest and regroup and Ferinyth had picked him up and thrown him into a wall. After that Sal left him alone, keeping a cautious eye on the other elf and trying to measure his desperation as the hours ticked by.

It was obvious enough to Sal that they would simply have to wait until the girl relaxed her guard and then seize the ideal moment. There was no way to force that timing and hope to have any success. But there was no reasoning with Ferinyth at the moment. Sal rather hoped that he would work himself into exhaustion and pass out.

****

After finishing up the second meeting at the police station Allie had met with Brynneth for a healing session, which left her feeling relaxed but even more tired. The morning had felt as long as an entire week and Allie would have preferred to just go home, but her conscience pricked her, reminding her that she still hadn't gone to see Bleidd. So with more than a little reluctance she drove to the medical clinic that served as a small hospital for the residents of Ashwood, resigned to doing her duty as a friend. She parked as close as she could get to the building, remembering Jess's anger that she was wandering around alone, and trying to be as safety conscious as possible. She also put as much effort as she could spare into blocking Jess from her mind and awareness, wanting a layer of mental privacy for at least the next little while.

To her surprise she ran into Jason at the entrance. He was still wearing his fire department uniform, but a quick glance at the bulky hand held radio at his waist showed it was turned off. Allie decided he'd just gotten out of work; it must be a lot later then she'd realized.

"Hey Jase," she greeted her roommate distractedly, licking her lips and glancing past him towards the receptionist's desk. "Are you here to visit, to ummmm, see him?"

Jason nodded, "I'm glad you're here Allie. He's been pretty down about being stuck here, and being hurt. It'll mean a lot to him to see you."

Allie looked away, feeling a surge of shame and fear. She did not want to be here, did not want to see Bleidd. They had been friends for ten years but did he hate her now for what she'd done to save him? She was terrified of finding out, and she could feel her stomach churning as she thought about it. He had almost died because of her, and he might hate for that as well. She swallowed hard; in her mind she ran over all the worst case scenarios, from icy silence to him screaming at her until she fled the room. "Right well, can you show me where his room is?"

Jason gave her a strange look, but gestured for her to follow him and headed off into the building. With her feet dragging Allie followed, full of a growing sense of dread. She went back and forth in her head as they walked, first berating herself for not having come sooner, then for coming at all. Finally after a short ride in an elevator to one of the upper floors and a walk down an antiseptic smelling hallway he stopped in front of a door. They stood there for a few seconds and then with an impatient look Jason gestured her forward.

Allie stepped up and tapped lightly on the closed door of the hospital room, more than half hoping there would be no answer. To her disappointment after just enough time to make her think maybe he was asleep or didn't want visitors Bleidd's voice drifted through the heavy door, "Enter."

She hesitated and Jason leaned past her, turning the handle and pushing the door open before shoving Allie in. She stumbled, throwing her arms up to catch the door on the backswing before it could hit her in the face. Taking a deep breath and bracing herself she stepped fully into the small room, while Jason stepped back, obviously planning to wait in the hall. The door closed under its own weight behind her with a thud. Almost reflexively her eyes went to Bleidd where he lay in the wooden hospital bed. The white blanket was pulled up to his chest and his black hair was loose, falling down over his chest and arms. But she could still see the bandages wrapped up and over his right shoulder, glaringly white against his fair skin. Thinking of the terrible injury caused by the bullet made her swallow hard, the polite greeting she'd been ready to say dying on her lips.

He was staring out the window when she walked in, but as the silence drew out he finally turned towards her, his green eyes chill and his expression hostile. Her heart dropped in that first moment but then he clearly registered who she was and his entire demeanor changed, his eyes lighting up like the sun shining through the leaves of a tree, his lips curving in a wide smile. His voice was low and slightly hoarse, but eager, "Allie! Come in."

She saw him struggling to sit up and she rushed over, her instinct to help overcoming her discomfort. "Wait, let me…"

He gave her a wry grin, but settled back down, watching her walk across the room towards him eagerly. She could feel his emotions as she approached, like a cloud surrounding him: frustration, embarrassment, happiness, love. She ignored that last, not wanting to think about his feelings towards her right now. She had enough insurmountable problems in her life without worrying about that one. Part of her was nearly deliriously relieved that he didn't seem to be angry at her; she had almost convinced herself that he wouldn't even want to see her, considering that she was the reason he was here.

She reached the bed and fumbled to get it into a sitting position; after nearly a minute of futile effort she gave up. Looking around she spotted a cabinet labeled 'linens' and limped over to it, relieved to find several extra pillows. Turning back towards the bed with her find she blushed at the amused look on Bleidd's face. It suddenly occurred to her that she probably should have just asked him if he knew how to reposition the bed, but at that point she decided it was better to act like she'd wanted to get the pillows the whole time. His grin widened as she reached his side and she realized she'd have to help him sit up to get the pillows behind him. *Could I possibly have made this any more awkward?* Allie thought trying not to look as flustered as she felt. Then out loud she said, "Ummmm. If I help you can you sit up?"

His expression didn't change and she could feel his enjoyment at her discomfort. When he spoke though his voice was calm, "I can manage to sit up but it would be easier if you helped. If you lean down I can hold onto you."

Feeling foolish she held the pillows in one hand, straining not to drop them, and leaned over the bed until her face was almost next to his. He wrapped his left arm around her neck and she slid her free hand behind his back. His breath was light against her cheek, and before she could think to stop herself she moved slightly until their cheeks were touching and breathed deeply, inhaling the reassuringly familiar scent that always clung to him, something like wood smoke. She straightened up slowly, pulling him into a sitting position. This close, touching skin to skin his emotions filled her as solidly as her own and she was embarrassed both to be reading him and at his overwhelming relief. *He didn't think I was coming to see him*, she thought, ashamed of her own cowardice. *I should have come sooner, not waited because I was afraid he blamed me. Of course he gave up on seeing me. Gods I am such a crappy friend. He takes a freaking bullet for me and I wait three days to visit him in the clinic...*

She pulled back slightly when he was upright, trying to position the pillows behind him, but he clung to her, refusing to let her move away. Despite the difficulty she finally managed to get the pillows set up, more or less where she wanted them. She leaned forward, pressing against him to try to gently lower him back onto the pillows but still he held tightly to her. She braced both her arms on the bed, but he didn't relent. Finally, exasperated, she said, "Bleidd, you need to let go now so I can stand back up."

"No," he said simply.

"No? What do you mean no?" she asked, smiling despite her annoyance. "This isn't the most comfortable position."

"Feel free to climb onto the bed with me," he said archly, some of his usual spirit in the words.

"Bleidd!" she snorted, trying not to laugh and encourage him.

"There's plenty of room," he said, his arm tightening slightly so that she could not pull away without risking hurting his bad shoulder.

"This is ridiculous," Allie quipped, "I'm negotiating a hostage situation where I'm the hostage."

He laughed lightly, the sound a ghost of its usual self, but still a laugh and Allie felt her own spirits lift. "Well then shouldn't I tell you my demands?"

"Oh now I'm afraid," she couldn't control the nervous giggle that snuck out, suddenly genuinely worried. She could think of many things that Bleidd might say next and all of them would create a conflict of interest for her, especially since she felt a huge obligation to him after what had happened.

"Then I shall keep this simple. I will let you go if you will lay next to me in the bed."

"Bleidd!" she said his name again, not entirely surprised by his request but unsure if it was a good idea. Not only because it would let him make jokes later about getting her into bed – which he would – but because she didn't want to hurt him. He had come close to dying, closer than she liked to think about, and even with magical healing and his own innate elven ability to heal more quickly than a human would he was still physically fragile.

"Allie!" he mimicked her tone exactly. "Why not? I'm not asking you to do anything untowards. We are both fully clothed and in what passes for a hospital in this town. I just want to have you next to me, not perched on a chair across the room."

63

She wanted to point out that she could pull the chair up next to the bed, but he had a point that there really wasn't any reason to say no, except that she was uncomfortable about the mere idea of being in any sort of bed with him. *But what's he going to do?* Allie thought *He's recovering from a serious injury, even if he wanted to try to take advantage of the situation he's not in a position to do anything. And it's such a small thing to ask. It must be hard for him, with the way elves are so used to casual physical contact to be trapped alone in this bed in this human run place.* That last thought made up her mind for her and sighing she relented. "Okay."

"Okay?" he sounded cautious, and she rolled her eyes.

"Yeah, okay. Let me go and I'll climb up next to you."

Slowly, his emotions echoing his disbelief, he relaxed back against the pillows, releasing her. She straightened up, stretching to ease her back after staying in that awkward position. And then true to her word she sat on edge of the bed next to him, and scooting back a bit swung her legs up. He reached up, wrapping his good arm around her shoulders and pulling her back against his shoulder until she was lying down next to him, her head on his chest. It was not the most comfortable position either, especially since she was trying not to rest her full weight on him, worried about his injury, but she could feel him relaxing and that made her feel a little bit better.

"Thank you Allie," he said softly in Elvish.

She sighed, not in the mood to deal with the convoluted language, but replied in kind. "For what?"

"For coming to visit me, and for…this," he said.

"Don't thank me for visiting, I should have come sooner," then after a slight pause, afraid to ask but needing to know, "How are you feeling?"

"I can hardly complain since I should by all rights be dead and feeling nothing," he said.

She started to sit up, trying to pull away from him. "Don't say that."

His hand tightened around her shoulder, holding her down, "I won't talk about if it upsets you Allie. Please, stay."

She was surprised by the genuine distress she felt from him. Overwhelmed by his need for her company, she settled back down, feeling his relief with him. "No I want to know. Are you okay?"

"I will mend. The pain is less today than it was yesterday, and that was less than the day before. I believe, as do the doctors, that I will be fully recovered within the week."

"Be glad you're an elf," she said shaking her head slightly. "If you were human it would be a different story."

They were both silent for several minutes, and when he spoke again his voice was serious, "I owe you my life."

"No," she said, shaking her head.

"Yes, Allie, I do. I would have died if not for you. You healed me," his voice was soft again, almost puzzled. "I don't pretend to know how you did it, but I am certain that you did. I remember the pain and falling…and the certainty that I was dying. And then suddenly warmth and light and life returned, and I knew, despite the pain, that I would live. And somehow you did that."

She lay against his shoulder, trembling as she remembered the events of that day. The blood everywhere, the terrible wound, the gurgling sound as he tried to breath and couldn't. And most of all the terrible thing she had done to save him. "I could not let you die Bleidd."

His arm tightened around her, this time not confining but comforting. She accepted the reassurance, still torn by the guilt of what she'd done. "Yes, and that means more to me than I can say," he said. "I know whatever you did was something exceptional…"

"Not exceptional," she broke in bitterly. "Evil maybe, but not…you just, you have to understand that I didn't have a choice. There was no other way, nothing else that I knew to do. And I could not sit there and watch you die."

"What did you do?" he asked, his voice gentle.

She took a long breath to brace herself and then decided to tell him the truth, even if he hated her for it. "I used a spell from my grandmother's grimoire. It…I took the life force from all the birds in the area and used that energy to heal you. I wasn't sure it would work because I was substituting birds for…for what the spell originally called for and I didn't know if the healing would be enough…but I had to do something. Anything. I had to do it."

He was silent for a long time, his arm relaxing, his hand gently stroking her arm. When he did speak his voice was low. "Who knows about this?"

She inclined her head slightly in an elven shrug. "That I did something to save you? That was pretty obvious to everyone I think. What exactly I did, only Jess."

"And he has not told anyone?" his words were sharper now, and she could taste his worry in the air.

"No," she said. "No one."

"Allie, you must not tell anyone else what you did, not the details of it," he said. The urgency in his voice grabbed her attention. "Not even Jason, but especially not anyone else in the Elven Guard. Using death magic is forbidden, and the punishment is…exceptionally harsh."

She closed her eyes, nodding in agreement. "I assumed it wasn't allowed, and the way the Guard is the punishment would be harsh."

"I'm serious Allie," he said.

"I know you are," she replied, puzzled.

"Death magic is one of the only forms of magic that is entirely banned, without exception," he said grimly. "Even during the Great Wars after the Sundering it was not used. The only thing that has kept suspicion off of you so far, I'd wager, is that it is so ingrained in the Bright court not to use that as an energy source that it's almost unthinkable." His hand tightened protectively on her shoulder, pulling her in closer against his chest, and she could feel his worry growing.

"I didn't know that," she said softly.

"Allie…" he hesitated, but she could guess what he wanted to ask. They had never talked about her past, before she came to Ashwood, except in the most general terms. Her last comment though, admitting ignorance of something that should have been well known to anyone raised in the Bright court, had given away too much. She was surprised at how relieved she felt to suddenly have that aspect of her past out in the open with him.

"I was born into the Dark court," she told him simply, intentionally extending her empathy to read his reaction. His emotions barely changed. She sent up a silent prayer in thanks that he hadn't shoved her away or been filled with disgust. She had expected more of a reaction though. "You already suspected?"

"After you were hurt in your store… you spoke of the Dark court then as someone who was familiar with it. I wondered if you had spent time there, but it seemed rude to ask, especially under the circumstances," he said.

"It makes no difference to you? That I was born into the Dark?" she asked, her voice soft but the question sharp.

"I spent 60 years as an Outcast losing myself in drink and pleasure," he whispered back just as softly, his hand stroking her hair. "Our past does not define who we are as people now."

It was a very un-elven thing to say. The elves put a lot of stock in a person's clan, parentage, and personal accomplishments; to say those things didn't matter as much as who the person was now was quite scandalous. "I'm glad you think so, since there isn't anything I can do about who my mother is."

She could feel him nodding slightly. He was silent again for a moment, and when he did speak again his voice was very serious. "Allie, you need to understand that the punishment for using such magic is to have your magical ability, your daan, stripped from you."

She struggled to hide her shock. "How…is that even possible?"

"It is a very high level magic, but every Guard captain can do it. It's considered a punishment worse than death, because it strips away an essential part of the person and they must live the rest of their lives without it. Without any magic," he said, his own horror at the thought evident.

She bit her lip, suddenly realizing how close she had come to total disaster. If Jess had felt compelled to tell the others what she had told him…she felt herself going cold. *Why didn't he?* she wondered. She had always assumed his duty to the Guard would trump his affection for her, yet he had kept silent and protected her, even when she violated one of the Bright court's most vital laws. It should have been comforting, but it wasn't. It disturbed her on a very deep level that he was so enamored with her that he would violate his own closely held principles to protect her when she did something that even she could not deny was a terrible thing, no matter what her reason was for doing it. Bleidd shifted slightly, snapping her back to reality. She spoke to reassure herself as much as him, "I won't tell anyone else. I thought you had a right to know though."

"Thank you," he said, sighing. His hand tightened slightly, pulling her closer and he leaned his head down so that her head was tucked under his chin. "We never need speak of it again. It explains some of the strangeness about the healing itself and it is good to know what was done."

She nodded slightly, content to never mention it again. They lay together for a while, not speaking, and she slowly relaxed. There were still unspoken things between them, and she hadn't forgotten that they had been fighting about his feelings for her, and her inability to deny how she felt about him, right before he was shot. That was the real elephant in the room, making the means of his healing and its possible consequences look irrelevant. She spoke again to fill the silence. "I found some gremlins today."

"Gremlins?" he asked. She couldn't see his face with her head tucked down against his chest but she imagined the curious look based on his emotions.

"Mmmmhmmm," she murmured. "In the police impound lot. They said that they had been set there by elves."

He tensed and she sat up slightly, twisting around so that she could look him in the face. "I think," she continued, "that it's safe to assume they meant Dark court elves."

He met her eyes and held them, his expression giving nothing away, but his emotions sharp and concerned. "Have you told this to Jessilaen?"

She nodded without breaking eye contact. "Yes."

He waited for her to elaborate and when she didn't he finally spoke again, "They would not be moved to do such a thing unless they were moving or planning to move against Ashwood in some way."

"Or Queen Naesseryia's Holding," Allie said softly. "If they can stir up enough trouble in Ashwood by setting some of the Lesser Fey on humans they could weaken her or at least make her look weak. That would make it easier for them to influence her realm directly."

69

His expression turned grim. "There's another possibility Allie. They could still be trying to get to you, to see what you know from your grandmother's book."

She blanched, pulling back further and shaking her head, "No. No I can't believe that. That was months ago. And why would they…no."

"Allie…"

"No," she said more forcefully. In her mind she saw flashes of her captivity and felt a shadow of remembered pain shoot through her bad ankle. Shuddering she fought to push the memories away, gratefully that she had enough healing herself now to be able to. Even a week ago what he was saying would have sent her into an uncontrollable panic attack; as it was she felt her anxiety spiraling up until she could feel Jess's attention being drawn to her. She shook her head again, trying to banish the images. "No Bleidd. I can't believe that."

Something in her face must have told him more than her words were saying because he nodded slightly, still looking concerned, "Alright, we don't have to talk about it. In any case I will be home soon, and well enough to protect you should any need arise."

Allie closed her eyes, groaning inwardly at the realization that he didn't know Jess had moved in. As tempting as it was to not tell him, she felt like she owed it to him to let him know that someone he did not especially like was living in the same house now. "Ummmm. About that. The house I mean. And coming home.…"

She trailed off and he reached up, his fingers brushing the hair out of her face. In her mind she heard Jess's voice suddenly, calling her. She swore to herself, feeling overwhelmed, then thought back quickly "*It's okay Jess. I'm visiting Bleidd at the clinic.*"

"What is it?" Bleidd asked, his voice gentle.

"Jess is staying at the house," she told him, afraid to meet his eyes but unable to avoid his emotions. "After the shooting, with you almost dying and no one being sure who was supposed to be the target, the Guard had wanted me to go stay at the Outpost and I refused, so he is staying at the house instead."

She had expected many different reactions, but he was calm. "Yes I can see why they would want to be assured of your safety. What are their current theories on the shooting?"

"Well, the shooter knew detective Walters, and she also knew the new killer, Standish, so the joint task force has been reformed. They aren't sure who killed her yet, but they've had to admit that everything seems to be tied together somehow," Allie said, trying to summarize everything. In her mind she felt Jess reaching out to her, his words colored by something she couldn't quite define – not jealousy exactly, something more like distress – nothing she had expected to feel from Jess when the topic was Bleidd, "*Is he recovering? Does it upset you to see him injured so badly?*"

"*I think he is very lonely here in this human place,*" she thought back, knowing she sounded defensive. "*And he is in pain and worried. I am not sorry that I came to visit him.*"

Jess sounded less upset and more thoughtful then, "*Yes, it must be hard for him to be there with only humans around him. I had not thought of that.*"

Bleidd blinked slowly, trying to process all the implications. "Why would this person want to kill me? Because I was protecting you? Or as a warning to scare you off?"

"Well, personally I think maybe the second one," Allie said. "But the police and some of the Guard aren't totally convinced that I wasn't the one who was supposed to be killed."

His look sharpened again, his eyes narrowing, "Why? What am I not being told? Did something else happen?"

"No," she said shaking her head. "Well, I don't know what they told you actually."

He sighed, his chest rising and falling beneath her. "That I was shot in the back, which I remembered well enough myself, and that when the Elven Guard arrived my injury had been partially healed and stabilized, which I knew you had done. I am just as pleased by that anyway, I'd much rather be primarily in your debt rather than Brynneth's."

"You aren't in my debt Bleidd," she said, her voice flat.

"Don't be ridiculous," he shot back. "Of course I am. I would have died if not for you Allie. There is no greater debt I could owe anyone."

"And perhaps I would be dead without you," she said stubbornly. "For all we know the bullet was supposed to hit my back and only hit you by chance."

"You are guessing, but supposition does not matter. What matters is that you were not harmed and I was and I would be dead now if not for you, and to a lesser degree Brynneth. But my debt to him is a pale shadow of what I owe you."

"You owe Brynneth…"Allie started, caught off guard by the statement, and then his words really sunk in and she winced looking away. "Bleidd, I thought you knew."

"Knew what?" he asked, his voice that flat emotionless tone that elves used when they were trying to conceal a very strong feeling. Because she was touching him she could not block out the surge of anger and suspicion that filled him even before she clarified.

"Okay, don't freak out about this," she started to say, which only made him tense even more. "But you see…its just…the bullet that hit you, that went through your back, it, umm, kind of hit me too."

"It…kind of hit you too?" he repeated, his voice dangerous.

"Well, yes. In the arm, but nothing serious. Really just a very minor, little…"

"Stop talking," he cut her off, his words so abrupt that she immediately stopped. "Show me."

She pushed herself up, propping herself on her right arm and held up her left arm for him to inspect. His eyes traced the pale flesh until they found the spot just below the elbow where the spider web of fine lines marked the healed injury. His breath went out in a hiss. Then, his expression pained he sat up, pushing himself up off the bed with obvious effort, and kissed the scar. She leaned forward to push him back before he hurt himself and he tilted his head up away from her arm. Their faces hung inches apart, the air tense. Jess's voice was in her mind again, drawn by her emotional distress, *"Are you well, my love?"*

"Yes, Bleidd hadn't known I'd been shot too and he's really upset," she thought back, feeling the inches of air between herself and Bleidd like a physical barrier. "Bleidd there's something else I need to tell you."

"Should I brace myself?" he asked, his voice soft.

"Probably," she sighed. "Jess asked me if I would marry him."

Bleidd's eyes went wide. "He asked you? *He* asked *you*? Is he mad or truly that desperate?"

She made a face at him, "Probably desperate."

His eyes narrowed at that, "And what did you say to his desperate proposal?"

"Bleidd…"

"You agreed to this?" his voice was calm but Allie could feel the waves of hurt rolling off of him.

"His family is going to accept a contract from someone he does not want to marry. If I offer one, that is he hopes that if I offer one his family will accept that instead," she said refusing to look away.

He was silent his eyes searching her face. Finally his shoulders slumped. "Yes, I can see how that situation would engender desperation in him. Or most people for that matter. I could almost pity him, loving you so completely and being told he has to marry someone else. You realize of course that his family may well turn you down, if they prefer the contract already offered?"

"I know."

He was silent again and then, "Allie you said that you owed me your life."

She tensed, sensing trouble. "Yes."

"I would ask a forfeit from you," he said calmly.

She looked at him cautiously. He was fully within his rights by Elven Law to demand it since she had insisted on acknowledging that she owed him a debt, but she felt her stomach drop trying to imagine what he might ask for. Still, she could not refuse him. "What do you want from me?"

"Just a kiss," he said, his voice still soft.

"Just a kiss?" she repeated skeptically.

"Yes," he said, so innocently that she immediately suspected something, but there really wasn't any reason to refuse him either. If she tried to negotiate he could demand something more intimate, and maybe that was his plan...

"*Jess?*"

"*Yes?*"

"*I told Bleidd that I owed him my life, and he wants a forfeit to pay the debt. He wants me to kiss him.*" she thought to him, knowing that if he could pick up on her feelings he would understand how confused she felt in that moment.

"*I do not like the thought of you with any other, but it is just a kiss my heart,*" he thought back. "*He could have*

74

demanded many other things of you once you
acknowledged a debt between you."

"*I know*," she thought back. "*I told him you are*
living at the house and that I am going to offer a marriage
contract."

"*Did you? And he asked for a kiss? It seems a small*
thing."

"*I know. That's what worries me,*" she thought
back.

Allie was annoyed with herself that she had actually
just asked permission to do something that within his
culture was barely more intimate than shaking hands, but
she also felt an odd relief that he seemed unconcerned.
Elven culture was polyamorous, but Allie, who had spent
much of her life in the human dominated Bordertown of
Ashwood, was not and she had struggled for the last few
months to reconcile her monogamous ethics with her
attraction to two people. She could not help but feel a
loyalty to Jess as the person she was committed to, but
nonetheless she felt that she needed to do this little thing.
Not because he was asking her too but because Bleidd had
saved her, because he was so badly hurt, because he was so
upset that she was hurt too. Because she loved him and she
hadn't realized until that moment exactly how upset *she*
was that he had almost died.

She leaned forward slowly, pushing through those
few inches as if they were solid. Bleidd tensed, his distress
being replaced by shock as her lips brushed his. She had
kissed him twice before, or more accurately he had kissed
her, and both times she had fought against the experience
and pushed him away. This time she was the one initiating
things.

She had never kissed anyone except Jess in an
intimate way and the experience was an odd one. His lips
were softer than she'd expected, and after a moment's
hesitation he leaned forward, pressing his mouth harder

against hers. His hand came up and tangled in her hair, holding her head close to his, and she could feel his emotions surging wildly, swinging from shock to joy and lust. His mouth moved against hers eagerly now, exploring, and she relaxed and let herself enjoy the sensations in that moment. She was too nervous for her feelings to match his, but she let his emotions fill her.

The door swung open and hit the wall with a light bang. Allie jerked back immediately, Bleidd growling in frustration as his hand slid free of her hair. The nurse, a no-nonsense looking woman in her sixties, looked up from the clipboard she was carrying as she walked in and her grey eyes went wide. She checked her brisk stride midway across the room, stopping to take in the scene before her. Her expression transformed instantly from business-like to scandalized. "What is going on in here?"

Allie blushed furiously, struggling to sit up and sliding off the edge of the hospital bed instead, mortified to realize how obvious Bleidd's arousal was. For his part he grabbed her arm, his hand like iron on her wrist dragging her back partially onto the bed. He growled at the nurse his tone openly hostile, "I'm certain, Nurse Haynes, that you've seen two people kissing before."

"Not like that, not when one of those people is critically injured," the nurse snapped back, not the least bit intimidated. Allie wondered if they assigned her to all the elven patients, because usually humans were easily cowed by elves. Clearly not this one though. "You are supposed to be resting."

"I am resting," Bleidd said coldly, refusing to let go of Allie's arm even as she tried to extricate herself.

The nurse turned to Allie, "Miss you're going to have to leave."

Allie nodded, mumbling an apology, but Bleidd refused to relent, the grip on her arm tightening further

76

until it began to hurt. He pushed himself up into a sitting position with obvious effort. "She stays."

"No, sir, she doesn't stay. I need to check your vitals, and she needs to go so you can rest," the nurse's voice was firm. Her eyes on Allie were reproachful, and Allie could feel the judgment rolling off of her, acrid and heavy as sweat.

"She stays," he said again, and to her surprise she felt a sudden surge of fear from him. Ignoring the nurse for the moment she turned as much as she could given her precarious position on the edge of the bed and gently pushed him back down into the pillows. He looked up at her, his expression unreadable.

"It's okay Bleidd. I'll go get Jason, he's here to visit you too, and we'll both come back in when the nurse leaves and hang out with you until visiting hours are over, okay?"

The nurse made a disparaging noise but Allie could see some of the tension leaving Bleidd's face and he finally let go of her arm. She nodded slightly and stood up. "I'll be right back in, with Jason, as soon as the nurse leaves."

"Just remember that the patient is recovering from a serious injury," the nurse said waspishly as Allie walked past her, giving the half-elf a scathing look. "He needs bed rest, and any strenuous activity, even if he's being passive during the activity, could be dangerous."

Allie could feel herself blushing at the obvious implications of what the nurse was saying, and she fought back nervous laughter. She had no doubt that Bleidd would be more than willing to passively enjoy any activity he could get her to agree to, but little did the nurse know that the kiss she'd walked in on was by far the most intimacy he'd ever gotten from her. Given the well-earned reputation elves had for lasciviousness and hedonism the nurse's imagination was probably running wild and painting pictures of Bacchanalian orgies in the hospital room that only nurse Haynes could save her patient from killing himself with….

"Right," Bleidd said sarcastically, as Allie was slipping out the door, "So I guess a blowjob is out of the question even if I'm passive during the activity?"

The door closed before she could hear the nurse's response to that. She lost control of her nervous giggling, laughing so hard she had to lean against the wall for support, until tears were streaming down her face and she was gasping.

It took several minutes before she could calm down enough to explain what had happened to Jason.

✶✶✶✶✶✶✶✶✶✶✶✶✶✶✶✶✶✶✶✶✶✶✶✶✶

When Allie pulled up and parked in front of the house, feeling an odd relief to finally be home, she found Ciaran waiting for her in the yard again. The Kelpie was in his dog form, a huge black hound, shaggy and fierce looking, lying across the concrete path to the front steps of the house. She crossed the yard towards him feeling a slight twinge of worry that he was waiting with bad news, but as soon as she was close he rose and stretched, in a leisurely way, and trotted forward to meet her.

His voice coming out of the dog's mouth was a bit disturbing but she was used to it, "Good evening Allie. Are you well?"

"Well enough. And yourself?" she replied smiling at her friend.

"As well as ever," he said, bobbing his head slightly in what she guessed was the canine equivalent of a shrug. "I was hoping you might have time tonight for a game or two of chess?"

Her smile widened. Despite how tired she felt it lifted her mood to think of spending some time relaxing with Ciaran. And it would let her avoid, for a little while, thinking about either the impending meeting with Jess's mother or the situation with Bleidd. The rest of her visit with him had been nice, as she and Jason had kept him entertained and generally distracted, but she could not stop thinking about the feel of his mouth on hers. In retrospect she thought that perhaps his request for a kiss had been brilliant. If he'd argued against her choice to try to help Jess get out of a forced marriage it would probably have just hardened her resolve. She had a sneaking suspicion that he had intentionally forced her to confront some of her own feelings about him instead and she couldn't help but admire his deviousness, even as she squirmed at the feelings it dredged up. She hadn't even begun to sort out how she really felt about him and she was refusing to let herself deal with his near death, but now her mind kept turning back to thoughts of him lying in that hospital bed. With Jess working late at the Outpost to sift through the information the human police had finally released about the cases she had been looking at a long evening with only Jason to distract her. The novelty of Ciaran visiting the house would do a much better job of that.

"Sure, come on in," Allie said, gesturing at the front porch. "Jason's cooking dinner but there's plenty if you'd like to eat too."

Ciaran's form rippled and shifted, the dog blurring and then being replaced by a slim, pale young man with dark hair and eyes. The kelpie looked up at the house eagerly, "Yes," he said, smiling, "I would like that very much."

They walked up to the house together and Allie opened the front door and politely gestured for Ciaran to go in first. The kelpie walked across the threshold with his head up, sniffing the air appreciatively. The smell of dinner

– tacos Allie guessed, her mouth watering in anticipation – wafted down the hall and she could hear Jason moving around the kitchen. While she had run some errands after leaving the hospital, Jason had come straight home to fix dinner. Liz was out on a date with her boyfriend, Fred, and their new roommate Shawn was out visiting family on mortal earth for a couple days so Jason and Allie had decided to make a night of it themselves. As she led Ciaran down the hall Allie felt herself relaxing; for the first time since the shooting things felt somewhat normal. Allie clung to the illusion desperately. She called down to the kitchen to warn Jason that they had company. "Hey Jase, I'm home, and I brought a dinner guest."

"Oh, okay," Jason said over his shoulder. "I may have gone a bit overboard cooking so we can use another mouth to help eat it all."

He was standing at the counter chopping lettuce; bowls of chopped tomatoes, shredded cheese, salsa, and sour cream already sat on the table. Allie was debating the best way to politely warn him about Ciaran's lack of clothing when Jason turned around. His eyes went very, very wide as he took in the kelpie's pale form – all of it, and it was an impressive sight – but otherwise he didn't react. His voice was a bit stunned when he spoke, "Any friend of Allie's is welcome here of course."

"Thank you for that, it is kind of you to be so welcoming," Ciaran said, his eyes roaming around the kitchen as if he were trying to remember each detail.

"Ciaran this is Jason – Jason, my friend Ciaran, He's the kelpie I've mentioned, that lives out in the woods," Allie offered a quick introduction, hoping it was enough to satisfy Jason's curiosity without offending Ciaran. The two men nodded at each other, somewhere between polite and speculative. "Grab a seat Ciar and I'll get you a drink, what would you like?"

"Milk, if you have it, would be good," Ciaran said, sitting down tentatively in the closest chair. "Is no one else home this evening?"

"Nope," Jason said, turning back to the counter to get the freshly chopped lettuce. He carried the bowl over in one hand and a bowl of taco meat in another, setting them both down on the table. "Just us."

Allie was confused at Ciaran's obvious relief, but then thought that perhaps he didn't like the thought of hanging out with Jessilaen. Many of the Lesser Fey – most if she was being honest with herself – did not like the Elven Guard, and certainly few if any would choose to socialize with them.

She shrugged it off as she handed him his drink. "Hey Jason, do you like playing chess?"

Chapter 3 – Tuesday

There was nothing more awkward, Allie thought, than walking into a room when you knew the person waiting there didn't like you. She stood in a back hallway in the Outpost listening to Jess's footsteps retreat into the distance, facing a closed door. Behind the door he had told her was a small sitting room designed for the purpose of accommodating family visits like this one or acting as quiet rooms for visitors to rest in if needed. Allie stood outside the door trying to work up the nerve to enter.

Despite Jess's reassurance that his mother was only worried for him, Allie was convinced that the elven woman did not like her personally after accidently overhearing the woman repeatedly urging Jess to leave her. She had unintentionally projected herself into his mind while sleeping while the two were talking and was now faced with meeting the woman in reality. It was a silly thing to think but she wished desperately that Jess could have gone with her. As it was she ran her hands nervously over the front of her dress, another detail that made her feel off balance and uncomfortable, then stepped up to the heavy wooden door and knocked.

A female voice drifted through the door, reminding her oddly of her visit to the clinic. "Enter."

Allie braced herself and then opened the door, walking into the small sitting room to find not only Jess's mother but two other women as well. Jess's mother looked much as Allie remembered her from the time she had projected into Jess's mind while he and his mother argued: she was tall and willowy, with light blonde hair that curled slightly. The second woman looked very similar to her, being of the same height and with identical hair, but she was thin in a way that gave an impression of ill health. The third woman was closer to Allie's height, slim, and with hair so fair it almost looked white. She radiated power in a way that frightened Allie and told her that this woman was very old indeed. If Allie had to guess she would have said that the third woman was probably Jess's great-aunt, which meant she was the head of his clan – the ruling clan here. Which meant she was closely and directly related to the queen. Allie swallowed hard, inclining her head in the proper polite gesture of greeting. "Good Afternoon. I am Aliaine."

Jess's mother stepped forward slightly mirroring the slight nod, "Greetings Aliaine. I am Jessilaen's mother, Jennaessiya."

She gestured at the other younger-looking elf, "My elder sister, Karealiss."

Allie nodded politely at the other woman who regarded her coolly. Jennaessiya gestured at the elder woman, "The head of clan Firinne within Queen Naesseryia's Holding, our great-aunt, the esteemed Ariessa."

Allie gave a deeper nod and a small curtsey in return for the acknowledging head dip from the clan leader. She fought to keep from feeling intimidated; this entire meeting was clearly far more serious than she had been led to believe. She made a mental note to smack Jess when she saw him again.

"Jessilaen has told me that you wish to offer a marriage contract for him. I am sure you are aware that another contract has already been offered, one which we have been considering for some time." Jennaessiya said smoothly.

"Yes, I am aware of that," Allie said. "I'm sure you are aware that Jessilaen does not wish to take that contract but does wish to take the one I am willing to offer."

"It is not a male's place to decide which contract to accept." Karealiss said dismissively.

"I am willing to hear her offer," Ariessa said placidly. "Jessilaen has earned some favor with us and I will consider his preference as a factor. Aliaine is also known among many in the Outpost for her unique gifts."

"Half-elves are so difficult to measure, each different than the others," Karealiss said, sniffing slightly. "And nothing known for certain. I have heard some are barren, and that would make any contract with her useless for our purposes."

Allie felt herself stiffening at the insult, made all the worse by the knowledge through her empathy that she genuinely was a non-entity to this woman. When she spoke she was relieved that her voice was steady, "That may be so, but much the same can be said of anyone. Each person is different and fertility is hard to measure until proven. Some may be infertile but I have known those of mixed blood who took after their human parent and displayed human fertility."

"Even if we assume that she isn't barren," his aunt, Karealiss pressed, refusing to acknowledge Allie directly, "she doesn't even have a clan. It would be a loss for our family when we could make a much better contract elsewhere."

Allie felt herself tense even more, but she tried to keep her voice calm and polite, "Your pardon, but as my mother's daughter I do have a clan."

"What clan is yours?" Ariessa asked.

"Draighean." It was a risk publicly naming her clan when she could hardly admit which court she was born into, but Draighean was one of the clans that belonged to both courts, making it a calculated risk. As long as they didn't press her to name the Holding she'd been born into, or ask her anything more than superficial questions about her family she should be safe enough.

"Draighean isn't a significant clan here," Karealiss said, refusing to back down.

"No not here, that's true, but they rule in other Holdings," his great aunt said her voice thoughtful now.

"And they are on the Council," his mother, Jennaessiya said demurely. Allie hadn't expected assistance from her, but then she remembered Jess and Zarethyn insisting that she would approve of Allie if she believed Allie really wanted to be with Jess.

"That is so," Ariessa agreed. Her eyes pierced Allie, who was struggling not to fidget over being talked about like a prime heifer at a market. "I find your clan ties acceptable Aliaine, and more than equal to Avaeryn's. She has offered a very generous contract. What do you offer?"

Allie's mind went blank as all three elven women turned and looked at her. Jess had told her it could take months to negotiate a contract and she had foolishly assumed that coming here today would not involve any actual negotiations, just the formality of her putting in her own offer. He had obviously not been aware of how close his family was to agreeing to the contract with Avaeryn. *Oh crap*, she thought panicking *I'm not good at this sort of thing. How am I supposed to make some kind of opening bid or whatever when I don't even know what's already been offered?* More than anything Allie wished she could reach out to Jess in her mind and get his help, but that would be wrong, after it had been made clear he wasn't to attend this with her. She had to do this by herself, no matter how hard it was. It was agonizing though, knowing that if she made a mistake or if they turned her down it was his freedom that was at stake. Luckily for Allie elves thought nothing of long drawn out silences in such situations; the three women stood patiently waiting to hear what she had to say as all of this went through her mind. Finally, not sure if it was the right direction to go in or would be unforgivably rude Allie said, "What has Avaeryn offered?"

Ariessa nodded slightly, the barest movement of her head, but it reassured Allie that she had said the right thing.

Karealiss frowned slightly; Jess's mother's expression stayed neutral. Ariessa said, "After lengthy negotiation Avaeryn has offered a hundred years or two children, whichever condition is met first. She is willing to let a child apprentice with the Guard, if the child chooses to. And should both children be girls she will allow the second to belong to clan Firinne as Jennaessiya's heir."

Allie stared at the closest wall, considering this. She didn't know a lot about marriages beyond the basics, but she did know that a hundred years was pretty generous. Usually a marriage contract would run half that or less, with the belief that if no child was produced after a couple decades of monogamous effort then there wasn't going to ever be one. She nodded slowly, thinking hard. She didn't like these women, Karealiss in particular, and she wasn't going to stand there and let them force Jess into a marriage he didn't want. But she'd have to give them something they couldn't say no to. What would they want that she was willing to commit to? "Alright, then I will offer…as much time as it takes to bear him a female child, which will belong to clan Firinne and be Jennaessiya's heir when the child reaches maturity. And may apprentice wherever Jessilaen approves of."

The stunned looks on all three women were so comical that Allie had to fight hard not to laugh or otherwise show any reaction. Jess's aunt especially was incoherent at hearing this, her mouth opening wordlessly. Allie kept a look of polite interest on her face, but she felt a surge of triumph behind her amusement. It was an offer so insanely generous that there was no way they could turn her down. Little did they know that she didn't personally care about having a legal heir within elven culture, not when she had no association with her own clan or past.

Ariessa recovered first. "Of course it must be added as a term within the contract that should no child be

86

produced within a reasonable timeframe the contract will be nullified."

"Of course," Allie agreed demurely.

Ariessa nodded slowly. "What you are offering is clearly superior to Avaeryn's contract, your clan is acceptable, and Jessilaen prefers you. I see no reason not to accept the contract you are offering Aliaine. I will have the document drawn up and sent to you for review."

Allie nodded, but as soon as she knew she'd won she felt a chill go through her.

What the Hel had she just done?

****

Jess pulled the car up in front of the house, and put it in park, letting it idle. Reaching across he grabbed her hand and squeezed, his joy filling her and almost erasing her misgivings. She turned towards him forcing a smile. He was blissfully unaware of how she was really feeling about his family accepting the marriage contract, and his own happiness at the situation had made her feel worse on the ride back to the house. She wished that she had driven herself, instead of letting him give her a ride, so that she could have the time driving home to think about what she was doing with her life. But when he had suggested picking her up to bring her to the Outpost for the meeting with his mother so that they could discuss how she should behave and what would be expected it had seemed perfectly logical.

"I have to return to work," he said, "but I shall return here within an hour – two at the most."

"I'll be here," she said unable to think of anything else to say.

He leaned forward and kissed her gently, and she slid out of the Guard car and out of his emotional influence.

It was a relief to just have her own feelings to deal with, and she took a deep breath, standing on the edge of the yard and waving as he pulled away.

Inside the house she jogged up to her room and pulled the dress off as quickly as she could, sick of it and what it represented. The stiff formality was quickly replaced with her usual jeans and t-shirt and that made her feel a bit better. She trotted back downstairs, looking into the living room to see if Liz was there reading. When that turned up empty she went to the kitchen and then the den, the realization slowly dawning on her that the house was empty. She felt a tingle of worry at that, knowing that the police and Elven Guard did not want her left alone in the aftermath of the shooting. Jason had stayed with her at the store all day until she'd closed to get ready for the meeting with Jess's mother and then he'd left for work. She had just assumed at least one or the other of her remaining room mates would be home when Jess dropped her off. *Shawn must still be visiting his mom out on mortal earth but Liz's car was there, I know I saw it* Allie thought frowning. She extended her empathy carefully out to check the house but it was definitely empty, except for Liz's cat, Riona, who was sleeping in the den. *Maybe Fred picked Liz up for another date* Allie thought suddenly nervous. It was embarrassing to be afraid of being alone, but she couldn't help glancing around the familiar house with trepidation, half expecting something terrible to jump out of the shadows.

She walked out the backdoor into the yard just to be sure that Liz wasn't out there for some reason. It was just starting to get dark, clouds gathering, and the temperature was beginning to drop. Again Allie extended her empathy carefully, uncertainly, hoping that Ciaran at least might be nearby. Instead she felt two people moving along the tree line on the west side of the house; one she didn't immediately recognize, but the other sent a shock of terror through her whole body. The memory was so intense it was almost physical: the same emotional mix of lust and satisfaction as he knelt over her, his hands gripping her torn dress, the bare bulb of the gardening shed casting a rough light over him and the other Dark court elf with him...

Her instincts screamed at her to run and she did so without thinking, running faster than she would have ever thought she could have. She knew they would not be far behind her, and worse that they could run faster than she could. The thought pushed her on and she crossed the backyard and leapt over the stone wall that divided lawn from forest without a pause. She came down hard on her bad ankle and fell, rolling in the tall grass and bushes. She was back on her feet in a breath, ignoring the blinding pain of her left leg.

She hit the tree line just as something metallic clicked off a trunk next to her. She did not turn to see if it was a dagger or arrow or something worse. She ran towards the deeper woods hoping only to find some way to lose them in the cover of the trees, too terrified to form a coherent thought or call Jess for help.

The dark shape of a large dog hurtled towards her, black in the shadows of the forest. A dozen yards away Ciaran's form shifted from hound to horse and he let out a terrible cry that belonged properly to neither. At the familiar sight Allie changed direction, flinging herself desperately at the fairy-horse. Hitting him was like hitting a wall and he nearly trampled her in his frenzy to get to the Dark court elves chasing her. She ricocheted off of his side and rolled to the ground, still blinded by panic, and he hesitated, torn between protecting her and attacking them. A second dagger cut the air, slicing along his flank; the wound closed almost as quickly as it opened, but the flying blade made Ciaran's decision. Turning with an unearthly agility his head snaked down and he grabbed Allie with his mouth lifting her up and swinging her back. She landed on his shoulders and instinctively grabbed his mane to keep from sliding off. In the next instant he was flying through the dark trees towards his pond.

Allie realized he wasn't going to stop in the same moment he leaped at the water and she held her breath reflexively as the surface of the pond rushed at her face. There was a disorienting moment where she could see the water all around her but could feel nothing except the rush of cold air and the tingle of magic and then they were landing in a small, dry room. With a twisting kick Ciaran threw her off and she landed with a woosh as the breath was knocked out of her. Then he was gone.

Allie sat up slowly, her whole body aching. Her ankle hurt in a sharp way that worried her. She wanted to call Jess, but she hesitated, taking stock of her surroundings instead as her pulse began to slow and the blind terror faded.

Ciaran's home was a little slice of Fairy anchored in Ashville. She could feel the almost intoxicating level of magic that she associated with being fully in Fairy suffusing the air. Looking around, if she hadn't known better she'd have sworn she was in a tastefully decorated sitting room. A fireplace, complete with crackling fire, took up almost half of one wall with two high backed leather chairs positioned to either side of it. The other walls were covered in floor to ceiling book shelves, which were filled with books, everything from leather bound classics to cheap paperbacks. Across from the fireplace was a long leather couch, with dark wooden end tables at each side and a long matching coffee table in front. The horse statue she had given Ciaran as a gift sat in solitary splendor on the coffee table. The floor appeared to be hardwood, polished until it shone with a heavy dark red rug under the cluster of chairs and couch.

Allie crawled over to the nearest chair on her hands and knees, not trusting her ankle to bear any weight. She

90

managed to pull herself up into the chair, her hands sliding across the slick leather. The cushions were softer than they looked and she sank down into them, her eyes unfocusing as she stared ahead at the fire dancing in the fireplace. The entire setting was so cheerful and welcoming and overwhelmingly safe that Allie started to shake, the stress of what had just happened hitting her. "*Jess?*" she reached out tentatively to his mind, aware that he was talking to someone – no she recognized the person, it was Mariniessa the mage assigned to their squad.

He stopped talking, looking down at the papers spread out on the table in front of him. She had linked closely to his mind, almost fully projected into it in her need for reassurance and she heard him telling Mariniessa to wait a moment, then "*Allie what is wrong?*"

"*Don't panic, please, I'm safe now, I swear I am,*" she thought to him. "*But I was just chased by two Dark court elves...*"

"*What?*" his thought cut her off, his fear vibrating through her. "*Where? At the house?*"

"*Yes,*" she thought back, his fear oddly helping her to calm down. "*I was out in the yard and I sensed them in the woods and ran...*"

"*Where are you now? Where are they?*" his agitation hadn't lessened, and she was aware of him calling the rest of the Squad together to go to her home. The idea of impending reinforcements calmed her even more.

"*I don't know where they are. I am in Ciaran's home. He was pursuing them,*" she thought back.

All the tension went of Jess. "*The kelpie was after them? Then I pray they don't escape him. He will do our work for us.*"

Allie thought of that, of her friend tearing the Dark court elves apart and likely eating them. It was a nauseating thought, but also somehow satisfying. After everything she'd suffered at that particular elf's hands she couldn't be too upset imagining him dying horribly, even though it made her feel like a bad person.

"Stay there Allie, we are on our way."

She responded without words, sending him a wave of love and gratitude.

A moment later the magic in the room flexed and then Ciaran appeared, jumping through the wall and landing lightly. Allie tried to hide her disappointment – he was back too quickly to have caught them. The horse's form rippled and shifted and then Ciaran was crossing the room in his human form, his bare feet silent on the carpeting. He knelt down by Allie, reaching out to take her hand, "Are you alright Allie?"

"Yeah," she said. "Yeah I'm fine. Just a little shaken up."

"I am sorry that I threw you down, did I hurt you?" he pressed anxiously.

"What?" for a second she couldn't even remember what he was talking about, thinking only of the elves chasing her. Then the memory came in a flash of sensory input: the horse's mane rough in her hands, his back shifting beneath her, the air as her body flew through it. The hardwood floor when she landed. She flushed, "I'm okay."

He nodded slightly, relaxing. "I am sorry that I could not catch the ones pursuing you. By the time I returned to the world-above they had already fled. But I pledge to you Allie, if they return here they will not escape me again."

"I know they won't Ciar, and if you catch them feel free to eat them," she said, swallowing hard, but not looking away from his eyes.

His dark brows rose at her words. "Indeed. I wouldn't expect such ruthlessness from you."

She sensed disappointment from him and then she did look away. "One of them is the one…the one who broke my ankle."

Ciaran's eyes narrowed, his rage making her flinch away. "Is that so? The one who tortured you came back here seeking you again?"

She closed her eyes at the word "tortured" wanting to deny it, but unable to. "Yes."

His nostrils flared, an oddly equine gesture on his human face. "If he does come back would you like to watch me tear him apart one piece at a time?"

A nervous laugh bubbled up and she covered her mouth with her hand trying to hold it in. It spilled out anyway, which was just as well; hearing her laughing Ciaran relaxed and his own rage ebbed. "That's a really tempting offer but I don't think I actually have the stomach for it."

He nodded, his expression telling her without words that he understood. She took a deep breath to steady herself, suddenly remembering her manners. "I like your home. It's very nice here."

He looked around the room, pleased at the compliment, "Thank you. I'm not surprised you appreciate a room furnished mostly with books."

Allie smiled, "Well it is my kind of decorating scheme."

He smiled back, briefly, and then sobered. "Allie I should return you to your home. In truth you are safer here, for no elf nor any other being can enter my home by force without great effort, but I think the others will be worrying about you already."

Allie winced reaching down to rub her left ankle which she was certain was sprained from when she had fallen after jumping the stonewall. "You're probably right but I'm not sure I can walk."

He looked alarmed. "You said you were not injured."

"I said I was fine," she repeated, trying to calm him. "And I am fine. But I twisted my ankle when I was running. It's nothing major…"

Her words were cut off as he knelt down in front of her again and ran his hands over her bad ankle. He frowned, "No you should not walk on this. Well that is a simple enough solution. I will have to carry you."

"Ciaran, I don't want to burden you and it's a long walk."

He smiled broadly, keeping his lips closed politely over his teeth. "Allie surely you know how to ride a horse?"

****

Jessilaen moved quietly around the east side of the house, his sword in his right hand, a small dagger in his left. Even in his battle armor he moved silently, the young grass making no noise under his boots. There was no sign of any disturbance, indeed the birds sang in the woods and he could hear small animals shuffling in the underbrush. It was likely that whatever had occurred was finished and the danger had passed, but he remained cautious. It was unwise to ever underestimate the Dark court.

He reached the back corner of the building and edged slowly and carefully around to the back. The yard seemed to be devoid of activity as well. A moment later his brother appeared around the other side of the building, sword in one hand, the other held ready to cast a spell. Zarethyn's gaze swept the yard as Jess's had and then he briefly met his brother's eyes, nodding slightly towards the center of the back wall. Both elves began moving towards each other, still on guard against any possible attacks.

When they met they stood with their backs against the wall of the house, standing facing out so that they could ward against anything. Zarethyn's voice was low, "Where is Allie?"

"I shall ask," Jess said and then paused, gathering the focus he needed to reach out to his beloved's mind. It was like closing his eyes and trying to touch something he knew was there but could not see…"*Allie?*"

"*Jess? Are you okay?*" her voice in his mind was calm, and he relaxed subconsciously at the reassurance it held.

"*I am well. We are here and see no sign of anyone. Where are you?*" he thought back.

"*With Ciaran. He chased the Dark elves but they escaped. He is bringing me back to the house now. I twisted my ankle, my bad ankle, running. But I'm fine really,*" she thought back. He repressed a wince, having learned that her idea of what constituted 'fine' and his own were not similar concepts. Allie bore the stubborn conviction that to admit any weakness was to make herself less in the eyes of others and he thought as well that because of her childhood in the Dark court she feared that weakness would make him repudiate her. *How difficult it must have been for her* he thought to himself *to grow up in such a place and live always feeling that her value to others is measured only in her strength. She should know by now that nothing will cleave me from her side, save death.*

He looked towards the woods, the last of the light fading as night fell, anxious to see her, to have her near him. He knew that once she was with him she could use his emotions to help heal herself, and he was certain that Bryn would help her as well. When he spoke to his brother his voice was at a normal volume. "Allie is with the kelpie, who is bringing her back here now. The Dark court agents have fled."

Zarethyn sheathed his sword, prompting Jess to follow suit. "A pity they escaped him. Wise on their part to flee though. They may well choose not to come back here again, knowing that such a creature abides here."

Jess shook his head slightly. "Can you not now compel her to seek sanctuary at the Outpost?"

"I have said that I would not, and indeed it may serve our purposes better to have her here when she keeps drawing those we seek to herself. We barely needs must hunt them when they act so blatantly." The Guard captain replied.

Jess frowned. "You would use her as bait in a trap but that puts her in great danger."

"Not so great, little brother, "Zarethyn said. "She is well guarded, not only by you but by others who care for her. And if we seek to catch those who we must catch, for the sake of our duty, then we must be willing to accept some degree of risk. In the months we have sought for the agents of the Dark court who are hiding here we have found nothing but shadows and hints."

"I do not want her life put at risk," Jess insisted.

"Nor do I if it can be avoided," his brother agreed. "But she is herself a member of the Guard now and she has a duty as well as we do. We cannot leave these agents free to fester like an infected wound and spread their darkness into the Queen's realm. Or worse to create war between Fairy and America. No single life is greater than that cause."

Jess bowed his head in acquiescence, although his heart rebelled. Zarethyn whistled, the sound high and sharp, calling the rest of the squad back in from their positions reconnoitering in the woods. As they waited for the other three elves to join them Jess saw movement at the far edge of the yard and a moment later the kelpie emerged, in the form of a black horse sleek and shining, with Allie clinging to his back. The last of Jess's anxiety left him at the sight.

The kelpie picked his way carefully across the lawn, head down, heading directly for them. Allie rode like someone unaccustomed to the experience, her face and body tense, clinging to the fairy horse as if she expected to fall off at any moment. Jess's lips twitched in amusement, although he also felt sympathy for his lover who, despite her own elven heritage, was so utterly a product of this modern human world.

He moved forward to meet them, uneasy at being so close to the mercurial and dangerous Lesser Fey but wanting to reassure himself that Allie was truly unhurt. Kelpies were fearsome enemies and difficult to defeat in battle, being both strong and clever, but they were also known for their loyalty. Jess felt that it spoke highly of Allie, for her to have such a friend. This close to the fairy horse there was a faint odor of dampness, as if he were near open water, and he could see the small droplets dripping from the animal's mane and tail, in defiance of the dry conditions he stood in. Jess edged around the sharp hooves and teeth and reached up to help Allie down.

She slid off, landing awkwardly on one foot and wincing as he took most of her weight to keep her from falling. Touching her he had the vaguest impression of her emotions, like an echo, anxiety and fear. *"You are safe my heart"* he thought to her pulling her against his chest even though the armor was a wall between them.

Even as he sensed her relaxing against him the rest of his squad began to filter out of the woods, Mariniessa from the left and Natarien and Brynneth from the right. They each regarded the kelpie with concern, but mirrored their captain and sheathed their blades. He was proud to see the discipline they displayed under the circumstances, which reflected well on him as their commander; even the normally prickly Mariniessa was behaving well.

Jess glanced over at Brynneth and made a subtle motion to call the healer to his side. Keeping a wary eye on the kelpie Bryn complied. Allie glanced around, her balance shifting clumsily, fingers clutching at the seams on the side of his armor. She used her chin to point at a stone jutting up out of the earth a few feet away. "Help me over there and I can sit down."

He hesitated, eyeing the uncomfortable looking rock, but then nodded. Brynneth quickly joined him and with the two elves bracing her on each side she hopped over and sat down heavily. Frowning Brynneth knelt down next to her, his fingers gently probing her ankle, seeking the location of the injury. Jess turned back to the kelpie just as he heard Mariniessa gasp, and he found that standing behind him was not the horse but a dark haired man. He held his own shock in check with great effort; he had never seen a kelpie in this form before, although he was of course aware that they were able to take human form, as well as equine and canine.

The kelpie's black eyes held his. "You will heal her?"

"I will do everything in my power to heal her," Brynneth said, unperturbed as usual. Jess was pleased at his friend's words. Bryn did not need to make such a promise, but Jess knew that he genuinely liked Allie and was willing to do more for her than he would for most others.

"You are the elven healer who helped her after she was injured before, yes?" the kelpie asked, his tone hard to read.

"Yes," Brynneth confirmed, his hands now wrapped around her ankle. Jess could feel the healing energy from where he stood as Bryn channeled it to the injured area. He felt reassured that if he was only channeling energy and not using any spells her ankle could not be too badly injured.

"I pursued the ones who were chasing her, but they fled before I could catch them. If they return here they will not escape me a second time. I find it…greatly concerning that the one who harmed Allie before is seeking her out again here, at her home. Should they return I cannot guarantee my temper, nor that they will still be whole and living when you arrive," the Lesser Fey creature spoke in that same inscrutable tone, his words not quite asking permission to mete out justice nor exactly promising to do so.

Jess inhaled sharply, stunned by the revelation that it was not merely any Dark court elves who had been here but that the same elf who had caused her such grievous harm on two previous occasions had returned seeking her. His brother was nodding, telling the kelpie that the Guard would consider any action he took against the Dark court elves helpful – tacitly giving him permission to bend the Law and take elven lives, something normally strictly forbidden – but Jess barely heard it. "*Allie?*" he thought, knowing she would feel his fear and anger. "*Why did you not tell me?*"

"*Jess, I – I would have. I was going to. I just hadn't had a chance yet,*" she thought back. She looked up at him over Brynneth's head, her face pale, eyes wide. She looked so young and vulnerable in that moment that it tore at his heart.

"Aliaine – Allie – are you certain that the one who chased you here today was the same one who caused your injuries before?" Zarethyn asked. Allie's attention shifted away from Jess, and because he couldn't bear to see her looking so small and helpless he moved over to her, rules and regulations be damned, and took her hand. She leaned against him, taking a deep, steadying breath.

"I never actually saw them, only sensed them. There were two of them. One I don't think I knew, although there was something…but I can't put my finger on it. But the other…yeah, him I recognized. The same one from my store a couple months ago and from Walters' house," her voice was flat, emotionless, and Jess saw Brynneth glance up, concerned. "I'd recognize him anywhere."

"I saw them," the kelpie said. "One fair haired the other cloaked and hooded. Both male, and neither a mage by my judgment."

"And how can you be sure of that?" Mariniessa asked, her voice far more polite than usual, although her words were typically brisk.

The kelpie regarded her for a long moment, making the young mage shift slightly and look away. His nostrils flared as if he were scenting something on the wind. "Because I can smell magic on those who have the ability to use it as you do Fair Lady. Also although I frightened them greatly when I charged at them in the woods they cast no magic at me only metal. And metal harms me very little, as they quickly realized. Had they any magic to use beyond what all elves naturally possess they would doubtless have used it as soon as they realized their blades would not help them."

Zarethyn nodded at the logic of this. "I doubt they will risk returning here again, knowing now that you are here and willing to defend Allie."

"I agree, but should they return I shall be ready for them," the kelpie said and then without a further word he shifted back into his horse form, turned with an agility that defied the size of that shape and galloped back into the woods, leaving the surprised elves in his wake.

****

Salarius was the first to break the silence after the two Dark elves returned to the hotel they were holed up in. As Ferinyth peered out between the blinds that he had pulled tightly closed, Sal sat down in one of the thinly padded chairs, only just catching his breath. He was certain he had never run so fast in his entire life, "We cannot tell my father of this."

Ferinyth took a second away from staring out the window to turn and glare at the younger elf. Sal ignored the fierce look, reaching one hand up to push his damp hair out of his face. "I am serious. If we are lucky word will not reach him that we played our hand so poorly and the girl not only escaped but the Elven Guard was alerted to our presence."

"We do not know…"Ferinyth started, but Sal cut him off, almost mid-word.

"Don't be a fool. She escaped and even if by some miracle she didn't see us or recognize us then the kelpie surely knew us for what we are. He will have told her and she will have told the Guard by now." Sal said, the words spilling out quickly in his agitation.

"So what shall we do, having failed?" Ferinyth said bitterly. "Slit our own throats? Crawl home and beg forgiveness? Turn ourselves over to the Guard and trust their mercy will be greater than your father's?"

Sal flinched, thinking furiously. "No. No, if he doesn't know then we should stay here and keep trying…"

"Keep trying?" Ferinyth scoffed. "We have no chance now. It is clear she cannot be taken at her home, and she is never left alone anywhere else that we have any chance to overcome her. Today, this evening, that was our best chance. Our moment to capture her and return home."

Sal shook his head slowly. "You are too impatient. It's true that if the kelpie is there, and we may as well assume he will be, we have no hope of taking her from her home. And she is rarely alone otherwise. But with patience and enough time our opportunity will present itself."

Ferinyth finally moved away from the window, although he continued to cast worried looks at the door. They had been unbelievably lucky to escape, and he did not entirely trust that they actually had. "And so you propose that we continue as we have been, lurking and skulking and stalking her, wasting our time watching her do nothing of interest? Hoping that at some point we will see a chance to seize her when she is alone and unguarded?"

"More or less," the younger elf agreed. "Is this town and its diverse pleasures so unbearable?"

To his surprise the older elf did not reply with a scathing retort but hesitated. "Perhaps it is not so bad as all that. And if we are agreed never to speak of this to your father, then we can wait until the girl's guard is down again."

Sal nodded, shocked that the obstinate elf was going along with this, but undeniably pleased. He was quite enamored of this Bordertown and all the diversions that it offered. The longer they stayed the better to his mind. "Indeed, and having apparently been chased off she may well believe we have given up."

Ferinyth nodded. "Perhaps. Perhaps. We will fall back and observe again and let her think we have fled. And when next we strike we shall not fail."

****

Allie sat on the uncomfortable rock outcrop, trying not to fidget as Brynneth finished healing her ankle. It was getting cold now that the sun was down and she could smell rain on the air. Since the immediate crisis had passed she felt silly for making such a big deal out of it and rousing the entire Guard squad out of the Outpost. She should have waited until Ciaran had returned and then she would have known that the Dark elves had escaped.

"I'm sorry I got you all out here for nothing," Allie said, shivering.

The Guard captain frowned at her, his head tilting to the side as he regarded her intently. The other elves also gave her puzzled looks. "Hardly for nothing. We now know with certainty that agents of the Dark court remain here. Before we had only rumor. Now we can set about to hunt them down and deal with them properly."

Allie shivered harder her eyes fixed on the broad back of the house. Jess reached up and stroked her hair. He met his brother's eyes, his expression challenging. "I am going to bring Allie in the house. We can continue discussing it there if necessary."

Zarethyn hesitated, then nodded slowly. "Yes, bring her back into her home. Brynneth go with them. Mariniessa, Natarien return with me to the Outpost. I want you both to look for a pattern in the petty crimes that have been plaguing us. I believe now, after what Aliaine told us about the gremlins and after this attack tonight that there is a larger hand guiding these problems. If we can find the pattern behind their actions we may be able to put an end to this plague of difficulties and if we are fortunate to catch those behind them."

The two junior Guard bowed slightly to the captain and turned to head back to the Guard vehicles. Zarethyn hesitated a moment, stepping over to Allie who had stood up with Jess's help. He reached out and grasped her shoulder, "Allie, I am…glad…that you escaped relatively unscathed. Do not forget that you are always welcome to seek shelter in the Outpost if you wish it."

Allie was tucked against Jess's side and she could feel him relax at his brother's words, even as she felt the flow of worry and tension from the Guard captain. It was a bit disorienting. She shook her head slightly. "Thank you for the generous offer, once again captain, but I really want to stay here. As long as it's not putting anyone else in danger…"

103

Zarethyn's hand squeezed her shoulder gently, and he smiled reassuringly. "I think it unlikely that they will try to attack you again here, knowing how well protected you are."

"And if they do," Jess added his tone still challenging, his eyes on his brother, "then we will see that it is the last thing they do."

The rain that had been threatening finally broke, fat drops hitting the ground and bouncing off of the elves armor. Jess pulled Allie back and she went without resisting, Zarethyn's hand slipping off her shoulder. With a last nod to the Elven Guard captain she, Jess, and Brynneth headed quickly for the shelter of the house.

Allie's hand found the light switch on the wall without thought as she walked in the back door and the overhead lights flickered on, illuminating the kitchen. The rain had fallen hard as they had crossed the last section of yard and water now dripped off their clothes and bodies onto the linoleum, puddling around all of them. Allie shivered again, her eyes moving over the familiar kitchen as if she was expecting something different to be there. She felt herself starting to shake, not from the cold or rain, but from a deep internal conflict as her mind struggled against a rising sense of panic which came up against the healing that Brynneth had been giving her to help handle the emotional trauma she'd been through. She didn't want to leave her home, and her stubborn determination to stay there had become almost an obsession which she clung to in defiance of everything. And yet she looked around now and she felt a deep seated fear that she was not safe here anymore, that nothing was safe anymore.

The next thing she knew Jess was shaking her gently, but hard enough to force her to focus on him. His worried face filled her field of vision and she could hear his voice as if he were speaking from very far away. "Allie? Allie, answer me."

Brynneth was there with him, his face also close, his concern for her less immediate than Jess's but also clearly present. She looked slowly from one elf to the other, thinking over and over *if I hadn't sensed them, if I'd stayed in the house, if I'd tripped, if I hadn't gotten up when I fell, if I ran just a little bit slower*...her own voice startled her when she spoke, harsh and low. "I won't let him hurt me again, I won't go through that again. I'll kill myself first."

She felt Jess's horror at her words and she threw a hand up to cover her mouth, tears spilling over, "I'm sorry I don't know why I said that."

Jess pulled her against his body, his armor gone now, his clothing soft as she burrowed her face into his chest to hide her weeping. Wordlessly he surrounded her with his love and worry and she took a deep breath instinctively pulling in his emotions, using them to strengthen herself and recover her own emotional equilibrium. Brynneth reached out and touched the back of her neck, then pulled away. "It's going to be alright Allie. Keep letting Jess's emotions ground you."

Allie shuddered harder, trying momentarily to fight against the instinctive way her body pulled in what he was feeling and transmuted those feelings into energy she could use. It was futile, like holding her breath after a short time she could feel herself straining against the deprivation. She gave in and let herself take what she needed as he rubbed her back and wrapped his feelings around her like a physical weight. She was suddenly aware though that while taking from Jess in that moment was out of her control she was able to fairly easily resist pulling from Brynneth, even though she could also sense his emotions, albeit less strongly.

"Better?" Bryn asked her after several minutes.

She stepped back slightly from Jess, still held within the loose circle of his arms. The truth was having absorbed Jess's radiating emotions she did feel better, less shocky and on the edge of a panic attack and more stable. She hated to admit that though when it made her feel like the basest Dark court creature, using another living thing's energy as food. "A little. I'm sorry I said that. I'm just upset. I thought…I thought that was all behind me."

"It is behind you," Jess said gently.

"But it isn't," Allie said, as Brynneth watched impassively. "Not as long as he's out there, still trying to get me."

"Why do you think he came back for you Allie?" Brynneth asked quietly.

"It must be about the book again," she said slowly. The two elves exchanged a long look that made Allie shake her head. "I can't believe after a couple months he decided to come after me for some sort of personal reason. That doesn't make any sense. But if he – his people – still want what was in the book, then, well that I can understand."

Brynneth's expression turned grim. "If that is so Allie then they will not stop pursuing you until they have what they seek."

It was Jess who shook his head then, his arms tightening trying to pull her back in against his body. "I will not discount that he may have a personal reason for seeking you out. And I will not allow you to be harmed again."

Allie closed her eyes, for a moment feeling overwhelmed by everything that was going on – the shooting, the murders, trying to root out whatever conspiracy might be behind the murders, now the reappearance of the Dark court elves. She wanted to run away and hide, to find somewhere safe. For an instant she was actually tempted to go to the Outpost… *This is too much for me! I'm not a cop or a warrior. I'm not even a fighter. I just want my normal life back...* and then she felt a surge of resolve. She felt something break inside, as if she had reached some internal limit and then surpassed it. *No.*

No more running, she thought with unexpected hardness. *No more fear. What good has it done? I'm afraid of getting hurt but being afraid doesn't keep me safe, it doesn't keep me from getting hurt it just makes me miserable. I can't run from this. I can't hide. I have to turn and face it and start fighting back. Let the bad guys be the ones to hurt this time.* Without consciously intending to she found herself thinking of the contents of her grandmother's grimoire. There were several spells in there she could use to deal with this situation, to end the threat…she remembered the feel of the dark magic flowing through her when she'd cast the spell to punish Corey and shuddered slightly. She'd nearly killed him with her magic, and for what? For scaring her and breaking her windows? *No* she thought trying to push away the seductive idea of giving the Dark court elf a firsthand taste of the magic he wanted from the book.

Jess was frowning at her, his expression worried and she forced herself to relax. "No one can promise that I won't get hurt again. That's life. But I – we – have to do what we can to stop this. To catch the killer and to catch the Dark court elves."

Jess looked at Bryn, his expression searching, "Allie you do not sound like yourself."

"No, I guess I don't," she agreed sagging against him, suddenly exhausted. She felt the weight of the whole day as if it were pressing down on her shoulders. "But I'm just sick of feeling scared all the time and waiting for something bad to happen. I feel like…I feel like I was so afraid of him coming back and trying to…and then suddenly he was there and he was chasing me and it's like waking up from a nightmare and realizing that the nightmare is real. I can either curl up on the ground and give up or I can stop running and start fighting. And I just…I guess I want to start fighting."

"She is using your emotional energy to heal herself, to heal her mind," Brynneth said with his usual calm. Allie turned and looked at him and he continued. "I suspected you were capable of as much Allie, but something always held you back. In all honesty you do a better job healing yourself in this way than I have been doing, although you should be cautious not to let yourself be overcome with a false sense of confidence."

"What do you mean?"

"Only that you are healing yourself but you are not healed. Not yet. It will take some time yet, even with you embracing this ability and not struggling against it. You may find that while you feel courage now and have less anxiety at the abstract idea of facing this enemy, should you actually be captured or face that same pain again all of that fear may return just as before," he replied.

She looked down, her forehead resting on Jess's chest, his hands continuing to caress her back. She understood what Brynneth was saying and the sensible part of her knew he was probably right. But the rest of her was overwhelmed by a rising anger that bubbled up and settled under her skin. She was tired of being a victim. And she wasn't going to let herself get hurt again without fighting back. *And there's always what I know from the grimoire* Allie thought then immediately shoved the thought away, seeing dead birds behind her eyes. *No, no I can't let myself be tempted by that again. Just because I know that dark magic doesn't mean I can let myself use it. Its' too easy to hurt others to get what I want and justify it as being a good thing...although it would serve that heartless bastard right...no, no I can't even let myself think like that....*

Brynneth was watching her closely and she struggled not to let her thoughts show. She knew that the elven healer was very perceptive and after the repeated healing sessions he had given her he knew her very well. She tried to cut off that entire line of thought by shifting her focus to Jess.

108

For the first time she was consciously allowing herself to fully connect to and pull energy from him, without reservation. His love and concern were like a tangible thing, like incense that she could see and taste and smell, and the emotions wrapped around and through her. She imagined that she could see herself, her aura drinking that smoke-like emotional energy in, could feel it being absorbed and transformed into what she needed. Suddenly, inexplicably, she had the almost overwhelming urge to push Jess down and take him right there on the kitchen floor, audience be damned, knowing on some level that then she could truly and completely tap into the emotional energy she craved from him. The unexpected rush of arousal, so intense it was almost painful, on the heels of the rest of the evening's extreme negative emotions left her feeling embarrassed and confused. *Dear Gods* she thought uncomfortably *what is wrong with me? Am I having a nervous breakdown or something?* And yet somehow she felt more calm and stable than she had in a long time, with Jess's energy still curling into her. The more she opened herself to it the more she wanted it.

"Are you alright Allie?" Jess asked her, tensely.

"Yes," she said softly, her voice husky. "Just tired. I think I'd like to go lay down for a while."

Brynneth nodded. "Of course. I will leave you for tonight then. If it can be arranged I will see you tomorrow and be certain that you are well."

"Thank you, Brynneth, that's kind of you," Allie said in that same low voice. Her gaze drifted up to Jess's face, her mind ignoring all of the traumas of the day to wedge itself solidly in the gutter. She was pretty certain it was either part of her accepting her ability to use his emotions, or else a really weird psychological survival mechanism, but at that point she didn't care. Feeling anything besides terror and anxiety was fine by her.

Jess's eyes met hers and she saw understanding flicker across his face. *"Allie?"* he thought tentatively.

She looked away, watching politely as Brynneth saw himself out. Then she thought back to Jess, *"I want you to make me forget that today ever happened."*

He hesitated, as if he were going to argue with her, but then seemed to think twice and instead scooped her up into his arms. *"If this is what you need, my love, then of course. Anything."*

Chapter 4 - Wednesday

He followed the girl slowly, making sure to walk far enough behind her that she wouldn't notice him following. He kept his eyes down, the hood of his sweatshirt pulled up over his head to cover most of his face leaving only a tunnel of clear sight in front of him. His eyes stayed trained on her feet as she walked, her scuffed white sneakers moving with a purpose on the sidewalk. His hand gripped the hilt of the knife so tightly his fingers had started to go numb, and he could feel his blood singing with the desire to hear her screaming.

She was the fourth girl he'd followed today, but each of the other three had escaped into a crowded area, or disappeared into stores and not come back out before he lost his patience. He had a feeling about this one though, a lucky feeling, so he paced behind her hoping she'd head into an alley or better yet into one of the deserted little parks that pocketed downtown.

After another few minutes of walking he got his wish. The sneakers turned onto a dirt path at the edge of a small park. He lingered, not wanting to be obvious, but watched her progress carefully. There was a man sitting in the grass at edge of the park playing guitar and he stopped nearby pretending to listen as the girl walked further in. The musician's long brown hair swung in time to the rhythm of the song he played, something distinctly heavy metal even on the acoustic guitar he was playing. His nimble fingers flew across the guitar's neck as he played, seemingly oblivious to everything around him, his eyes tightly closed.

Jerry moved into the park, senses alert for the girl's passage. He found her easily, sitting under a tree eating a sandwich. She looked relaxed, and he assumed she must come here often to eat her lunch. She was petite, barely five feet tall and thin in a way that made her seem delicate; her pink blouse and jeans hung off her frame. Her skin and hair were the exact same pale brown color, and her nose had an odd look to it, as if it was an afterthought added on rather than truly part of her. He felt an extra thrill as he got a better look at her; he'd never taken a part-Brownie before and the idea of it excited him.

He shifted the knife, getting a better grip on it, then walked out of the trees towards her. Her large brown eyes immediately tracked the movement, fixing on him. She didn't seem alarmed, just curious. He smiled, continuing to walk towards her, watching as her expression went from curious to uncertain.

He had almost reached her when several things happened at once. She started to open her mouth to say something and he lunged forward swinging the knife. Faster than he could believe anyone would react she was jumping to her feet, shoving him away with inhuman strength. By sheer chance as he was pushed back the knife, swinging wildly, embedded itself in her shoulder.

She screamed, falling back, the knife pulling free of her body. He scrambled over to her on his hands and knees, clutching the weapon. He backhanded her with the hilt, hearing bone break under the blow, the metal tearing a bloody gash across her cheek and jaw, and she collapsed to the ground. She lay still, her eyes rolling slightly as she fought not to pass out. Reaching out with both hands, the knife held awkwardly, he yanked at her blouse until the buttons popped and it opened, then he used the blade to cut off the rest of her clothes, suddenly anxious to feel her small body under his. She was stronger than he'd expected and he was afraid of her waking up before he was done with her, but his lust overruled his fear. Nonetheless he hurried, not taking the time to enjoy her the way he usually would have.

112

As he was finishing with her he heard someone shouting behind him. The guy who had been playing guitar as he'd walked into the park was there, rushing forward, guitar in hand, his face angry and horrified. Jerry staggered up, growling at the intrusion, the bloody knife still gripped tightly in his hand. The musician saw the knife at the last moment and skidded to a stop, swinging his guitar like a club. Jerry dodged, falling to one knee, stabbing up blindly towards the other man's body. Once again he was saved by pure luck; the knife seemed to find its target on its own, slicing deeply into the musician's body.

Jerry lost his balance and landed gracelessly on his back, rolling in anticipation of the next attack, but it never came. Looking up he saw the other man writhing on the ground, his guts spilled across the grass from the gaping wound the blade had opened in his abdomen. For an instant Jerry froze, utterly fascinated by the gory sight, but then he remembered what he was doing here. The others would be angry he had killed a human, and he felt a rush of anxiety at the thought. This was not part of his glorious purpose.

Since it was too late to do anything else he advanced on the musician's prone form, deciding he could at least put an end to the man's suffering. That was the humane thing to do and the others would appreciate that he's tried to be merciful. He moved forward, slowly lifting the blade, prepared to slit the man's throat when a wave of magic hit him from the side and knocked him off his feet again. He scrambled back up and saw the mixed blood girl on her hands and knees crawling towards him, blood still flowing from her shoulder wound and head, but obviously about to cast another spell at him. The expression on her face was one of blind fury.

Jerry turned and ran.

****

113

Allie was just finishing ringing out a customer when her cell phone rang. The woman buying the books was one of her oldest regulars who didn't care about any of the drama that had gone on, not even the recent shooting in the parking lot, as long as Allie had her special orders for her to pick up. Allie was disproportionately grateful for at least one person who didn't even mention police or murder investigations, and who only wanted to discuss when the new shipment from earth would clear customs. The cell phone ringing startled Allie who had gotten used to the phone sitting silently in her pocket and never doing very much. She carried it as much because it made Jason feel better as she did to actually use, since she could always contact Jess directly when she needed to.

"Have a nice day Mrs. Davidson," Allie said quickly, fumbling the phone out of her pocket and rushing to get it opened before the call went into the irretrievable black hole of her voicemail. Her customer gave her a disapproving look and sighed, waving over her shoulder as she carried her purchases out the door.

"Hello?" Allie answered the phone tentatively, only then thinking to wonder who would be calling her on it.

"Ms. McCarthy?" detective Riordan's voice sounded strained even over the phone line.

"Detective Riordan?" Allie said.

"Can you get over to the clinic?"

At first she thought she'd misheard him, and then she glanced at the clock. It was a little past one. Riordan's voice on the phone was anxious now. "Ms. McCarthy? Are you there?"

"Ummm. Yeah, I'm here," Allie said, frowning at the worn wooden counter in front of her. "Did you just ask me if I could go to the clinic?"

114

"Yes. We have a situation here, and I could really use your help."

"My help?" Allie repeated, feeling like an idiot. "What's going on?"

"There's been an assault, and a murder," Riordan said, his voice tired. "The elves are here but…they aren't exactly being diplomatic. And the victim isn't cooperating. I was hoping maybe you could help, because we aren't getting anywhere right now."

"Could you hang on a second detective?" Allie asked, feeling her stomach drop. Then, "*Jess?*"

A moment's hesitation where she resisted the urge to project to him and see for herself what he was doing. "*My love? What is wrong?*"

"*Nothing. Riordan just called me and asked if I could come out to the clinic to help you question a victim. What is going on?*" she knew her mental voice sounded perturbed but she didn't care. He should have called her himself.

"*Yes there has been an incident, and it is likely our suspect, but there is no need for you to come out here,*" he thought back, his anxiety plain.

"*Well Riordan thinks there is.*"

"*Do not worry about it my heart. We will take care of it.*" Something in his tone made her frown. He didn't want her to go there and perversely that decided her.

"*I am on my way,*" she thought firmly.

"*No Allie, do not…*"

"*I'm on my way- I'll see you soon,*" she though then put everything she had into blocking him. Refocusing on the phone she took a second to make sure she was composed and her voice would be calm. "Detective?"

"I'm still here."

"I'm leaving now, I'll be there in a few minutes," Allie said, determined to find out why Jess didn't want her there and to see what she could do to help.

"Hey Jason," Allie called to her friend, who was sitting reading a novel in one of the chairs set up on the left hand side of the store. "I have to run out to the clinic to help the police with something. Do you want to run up and visit Bleidd while I'm there?"

Jason shoved a bookmark in his novel and stood up. "Sure. What's going on?"

"I don't know," Allie said, limping up to flip the sign to closed and sending up a prayer that she wouldn't lose too much business. She locked the door and gestured at Jason. "Let's go find out."

****

Allie found most of her squad of Elven Guard and the two police detectives outside one of the small private rooms in the emergency room area of the clinic. Jessilaen, Brynneth, and Mariniessa stood in a small cluster to one side and the two human detectives to the other. To Allie's surprise Sam was also there, although he was walking slowly around the hallway as if he were deep in thought. Everyone turned and stared at her as she approached and she reached down and adjusted the badge clipped to her waist to be sure it was in place. Touching the badge had become like touching a talisman; it gave her confidence in a stressful situation. There was something surreal about the entire thing but at the same time Allie was painfully aware that barely a few months ago she was the victim sitting in the hospital room with the police gathered in the hallway trying to decide how to handle *her*.

Riordan looked relieved as she walked over. "Ms. McCarthy, I'm sorry to have called you out here but we're hoping the victim might be more willing to talk to you."

116

"She won't talk to you?" Allie said. Of all the reasons they could have needed her to come out this one hadn't occurred to her, and she was even more puzzled that Jess hadn't wanted her there. She had just automatically assumed they needed her for her empathy, maybe to help read the victim's emotions to see if something was being left out of the statement.

"No," Brynneth said, his frustration evident. "She will not speak to the Elven Guard at all, nor when we are in the room."

"And all she'll tell us is that we have enough physical evidence that we don't need her statement," Smythe said, sounding as puzzled as Allie felt. "She won't even give us her name. She's in here as a Jane Doe."

"Okay," Allie said slowly. "Why is she here? I mean, what happened? You said there was a murder and an assault?"

Riordan made a face, reaching up and rubbing his temple as if his head hurt. "Right. We got a call about a disturbance at Lincoln Park, it's one of those little pocket parks off River Street..."

"Yeah," Allie interjected, thinking *It's not that far from my store actually.* "I know where it is, I've been there a couple times."

Jess looked concerned, but she tried to ignore him to focus on Riordan who had resumed his story. "Right, well we get out there and find this guy Skip Penney, he's a musician who plays guitar around town, I'm sure you know him, everybody knows him, we find him laid out dead in the grass. I guess he was still hanging on when the first patrol got there and the medics but there was nothing they could do for him. I'll spare you the details, it was pretty gory. And the patrol officer tells us he called because there was also a female victim, mixed Fairy blood, raped and stabbed, and she ID'ed our suspect in the other cases before the ambulance took her. Best guess at the scene was that

Penney showed up and interrupted the assault before Standish could finish the victim off."

Allie nodded slowly, feeling the disgust and anger rolling off of the two human detectives as they remembered what they had seen at the crime scene. She tried to push the feelings away, but it was like trying to hold back water. Without thinking she gravitated towards Jess, wishing she could drop her attempt at a professional appearance and touch him to help ground herself. Looking away from the cluster of human and elven police she noticed Sam peering intently at her, and had the uncomfortable thought that he knew exactly what she was struggling with. Bracing herself she pushed through the feelings with sheer willpower. "Okay. So we know it was the same killer, but this victim survived."

"Right," Smythe said. "But we need to know from the victim what happened. If we're going to catch this guy we need to know the details. It's possible some little thing she saw or something he did will give us the key to finally get a step ahead of him."

"Except she won't tell us anything," Riordan finished.

"Detective Riordan called us to alert us of the additional victims," Jess said, breaking his silence. "And in the hopes that we could compel her to break her silence but she is even less willing to speak to us than she is to speak to them."

"Okay, but ummm. What exactly am I supposed to do to help?"

Riordan sighed, "I'll be blunt. You're the survivor of an assault yourself, or at least an attempted one. You're mixed too, like she is. You're female. We're hoping that she'll be willing to open up to you."

Allie looked down to hide her reaction, her automatic rebellion at the mere idea of opening up in any way to a stranger about what she'd been through. *And*

118

that's probably exactly how she feels too she thought unhappily. "Doesn't the department have an expert for this kind of thing?"

"There's a psychologist with the state police that we call in when we need to," Riordan said reluctantly. "But she feels that we should wait and not pressure this victim to talk if she isn't ready to."

"You disagree?" Allie said, looking not at Riordan but at Brynneth, who frowned.

"We feel that we have no time to waste," Riordan said.

Allie nodded, then thought to Jess *"Last time I checked Mariniessa was female. Can't she go in there and talk to this woman?"*

Under different circumstances she might have laughed at the way his face twitched as he tried not to show a reaction. *"My heart, Mariniessa may be female but a hedgehog has fewer sharp edges. If I send her in there alone she's likely to end up in a fist fight with the victim."*

"True," Allie thought back, repressing an unexpected surge of jealousy as she remembered that Bleidd had found the elven mage enticing enough to have a one night stand with, sharp edges or not. She tried to shove the thought away knowing it was ridiculous, since one night stands were the typical elven approach to sexual relationships. And that she had flat out told him to do it, when he had offered not to for her sake, because she was with Jess and wouldn't adopt the elves' polyamorous attitude. *Ugh I can't keep disliking her because she slept with someone I'm in love with, when I'm the one who is choosing not to be with him for someone else's sake. That's not fair*, Allie thought, but she had to fight not to shoot a glare at the other woman. Allie forced herself to stop that train of thought and refocus on the task at hand.

She did not want to go in to that hospital room and face someone whose situation was so similar to one she had

119

gone through and gone to great pains to forget. She was afraid to ask how badly the woman had been hurt or any other details of the assault. The truth was she didn't want to know. But she did want to help if she could and she knew at some point she had to stop avoiding her own past. She had enough healing and perspective at this point to know that it was unhealthy to keep insisting that nothing had happened.

"Okay," Allie said unhappily. "Okay. I'll try to talk to her, but I wouldn't count on her being any more willing to say anything to me than she is to you."

Riordan visibly relaxed. "Thank you Ms. McCarthy. I know this is out of your purview and that it's asking a lot of you. If I – we – thought there was any other way we'd go with that, but nothing is working."

"Right," Allie said hoping her voice didn't sound as bitter as she was feeling. "So what am I supposed to be asking her?"

"Just try to find out what happened," Smythe said.

Jess was frowning and Allie looked at him, worried by the feelings of indecision she felt from him. "Mariniessa go in with her, but say nothing. I mean absolutely nothing, under any circumstances. Do anything you can to disappear so that the young woman forgets you are there, but you can be a witness to her words."

Allie was sure her face must have shown her shock, after Jess had said, privately anyway, that Mariniessa was the worst person to send in there she couldn't believe that he was doing exactly that. The elven mage looked very serious though, and Allie felt a grim determination from her that she hadn't expected. Maybe this would still work out.

Allie started to step towards the door of the room but Jess stopped her. With an apologetic look he reached up and pushed her hair back behind her ears. Allie bit her lip and fought the urge to put it back. Her ears – neither the delicate, upswept point of elven ears nor the gentle rounded curve of human ones – were a source of embarrassment for her. She usually went to great effort to hide them, but she understood his logic. If this woman was hostile to the elves and mistrusted humans she might feel some kinship with another person of obviously mixed ancestry.

Bracing herself, and with Mariniessa a silent shadow behind her, Allie slipped into the small room. It was much the same as the one she had been in after the Dark court elf had attacked her in her store, not surprising really. She assumed most of the rooms in this section of the clinic were probably mirror images of each other. Nonetheless it made her stomach clench to walk in and see the small figure huddled on the wooden hospital bed, much as she herself must have looked not that long ago. It sent a stab of unexpected sympathy through her, not just for the woman's situation in general but for the woman herself in a very personal way. She felt an immediate kinship with this stranger.

The woman looked very small and young but Allie quickly revised her initial assessment when she realized the woman was part brownie. Brownies tended to be short and petite, but were very strong for their size, and like all Fey could be quite old without looking it. Her brown skin and hair stood out in stark contrast against the shocking white of the hospital pillow and sheet. The left side of her face was covered in a bulky bandage, and another similar larger bandage was visible beneath the hospital gown covering her left shoulder. She wore a nasal cannula, the plastic tube snaking under her nose, the hiss of the oxygen filling the quiet room. The slow beeping of a heart monitor was the only other sound, and after a moment Allie could pick out the wires for the monitor against the pillow, disappearing in a cluster of bright colors into the sleeve of the hospital gown.

Mariniessa faded into the back corner as Allie stepped forward towards the bed. The woman watched her,

121

her expression hostile at first as she took in the badge, but fading to a dull confusion as Allie's jeans and t-shirt destroyed the impression of an Elven Guard. Allie repressed a nervous laugh, knowing that no Elven Guard would be caught dead working in anything as grubby as the worn jeans and faded t-shirt she was currently wearing. *Well if I'd known I was going to get drafted today to play Guard I'd have worn my nice jeans and fancy t-shirt* Allie thought irrelevantly. When the woman spoke her voice was stronger than Allie had expected and she spoke in English. "Who are you?"

"My name's Allie," she said, stumbling over how to properly introduce herself. "Allie McCarthy. I own a bookstore here in town and I, umm, sometimes help the Guard out. I've been helping them try to track down the guy who hurt you today."

Her face gave away nothing, her voice challenging. "So why are you here?"

"Just to talk," Allie said, feeling her way carefully around the painful tangle of the woman's emotions, which were twisted and sharp like jagged metal.

"I don't want to talk," she said flatly.

Allie sighed, not too surprised that the woman didn't offer her own name in exchange for Allie's. It was extremely rude, by Fey standards, but if anyone deserved a little leeway she supposed this woman did. She was also starting to suspect that mixed-blooded or not the woman might not know that much about Fey culture. It was only a hunch but the way she defaulted to English and the way she acted…she was either taking a huge risk by being rude to someone of higher rank or she didn't have a clue about how that all worked. It was a possible explanation for why she feared the Elven Guard so much too, since their reputation tended to be even more extreme among the humans of Ashwood than among the Fey population.

Allie moved slowly over next to the bed sitting down carefully in the chair that had been left there. "I hope you don't mind if I sit down, my ankle's bothering me today. I need to rest it for a bit. And I don't blame you for not wanting to talk. If I were you I wouldn't either."

That caught the woman off guard and Allie could tell she wasn't sure how to respond. *She was probably expecting a typically elven attitude*, Allie thought, *or maybe that I'd order her to start cooperating. Because the elves really can be pricks when it's expedient and they just expect the Lesser Fey to toe the line, even when those Fey are crime victims. Well, I'll sit here in silence if that's what she wants until I think I can get away with leaving, but even with the healing Brynneth gave me and the healing I guess I gave myself with Jess's help my ankle is still sore today and I'm not going to stand the whole time.*

She stared hard at Allie for a full minute, the hands on the bland hospital clock ticking slowly around. Then possibly deciding to try to provoke Allie with rudeness into leaving by throwing etiquette out the window, if she was aware of it, or perhaps just in a lot of pain, the woman asked bluntly. "What's wrong with your ankle?"

"Well, I'm not sure you really want to hear that story," Allie said, not really wanting to tell it, but when the woman's eyes narrowed and she felt the hostility returning, she gave up. There didn't seem to be any way not to get into her own personal pain, and she guessed that was as good a segue as any. Now to give her the version of events that stuck to total truth but edited out the Dark court's quest for her grandmother's spellbook. "Okay. Well. A couple months ago I got hit on by an elf and I told him to go look for a bedmate at the Fey groupie club downtown. He didn't take it well."

The half-brownie's eyes widened and Allie felt her interest focus entirely on what the she was saying. Allie stopped and swallowed hard. The other woman spoke into the background hum of hospital machinery, but now her voice was softer, less hostile. "You're...half elven?"

"Yeah," Allie said simply, not sure what else to add to that.

"What happened?"

Allie felt her mouth stretching into a grim smile against her will as that damn inappropriate laughter tried to bubble up. "He didn't take it well. Said I should be honored that he'd even consider bedding someone like me. Needless to say I didn't share his opinion, but...getting into a physical fight with someone who's a lot stronger than I am wasn't a great idea. It didn't end well for me."

The other woman wasn't bothering to hide her interest now, leaning forward slightly in the bed so that the mattress crinkled underneath her. "He broke your leg?"

Allie swallowed hard again, waiting for the usual upwelling of panic that came when she thought about the things she'd been through. Instead she felt a deep sadness, looking at the tiny woman in the hospital bed and thinking of her going through a similar ordeal. She took a deep breath aware of the woman's eyes trying to meet hers. Instead she looked down at her hands. "It's a long story. We got into a fist fight which I lost, badly. He broke my nose, I ended up with a concussion and a bruised throat and he...he tried to rape me" she forced the last word out with a physical effort, hating the sound of it.

The woman on the bed made a small sympathetic noise but Allie forced herself to keep going, knowing that if she stopped now she'd lose her nerve. She had never spoken of this to anyone afterwards, instead doing her best to act as if none of it had happened. Some small irrational part of her tried to believe that if she just pretended that it hadn't happened she could unmake the experience, bury it underneath her denial. But she had made a lot of progress with Brynneth and recently in letting her own empathy heal the broken places in her mind. And she knew, on some deep level, that the only way to really get this woman to trust her was to be completely honest about the most painful parts of her own story. "But then he…found me again later. After I'd recovered from the first time. He's a very sadistic person by nature. My ankle was broken and he crushed it, stomped on it, which is why I limp now and always will, and he broke my arm, and…and raped me…and stabbed me. I almost died, would have died, both my lungs were punctured…but the Guard arrived and I was healed in time."

She was surprised that once she'd said it, out loud, past all taking it back or denying, she didn't feel the way she'd expected, the way her upbringing in the Dark court had taught her to feel about being a victim. She didn't feel weak or helpless. She felt an odd sense of peace, and that same anger she'd felt the night before when she'd thought about the same elf returning to torment her again. She didn't want to run away anymore – she wanted to hurt him. *Which maybe isn't the most helpful way to feel* Allie thought to herself. *But I'm done with letting him make me suffer in my own head, because he hurt me. I'd rather hate him than hate myself.*

She finally looked up, meeting the woman's eyes and she was shocked to see the tears running down her face. "And did he…was he punished?"

"He wasn't caught," Allie said, watching the other woman frown and wipe her tears away. "But I lived, and if I'm lucky he still will pay for what he did. Eventually."

"Did you...I mean," she said, obviously embarrassed, "I'm glad you're okay now. But did you feel like it was your fault? What happened?"

"Yeah I did. I suppose in some ways I still do. Afterwards I tried to act like it didn't happen at all. But I've…it's been really hard," Allie said with brutal honesty. "Nightmares, anxiety, being afraid to be alone. Part of that is because I do feel like if I'd just done something different, maybe not offended him to begin with, it, none of it would have happened, even though I know that isn't true."

"Yeah," the other woman said softly, her fingers reaching up now to touch the bandage on her face. "I keep thinking if I'd just moved faster, if I'd just realized sooner what he was going to do…"

Allie felt her pulse speeding up, as she quickly debated whether to push or not. Finally she asked, as gently as she could, "What happened?"

The woman licked her lips, her deep brown eyes locked with Allie's as if seeking support. This time Allie didn't look away, but held her gaze. "I was on my lunch break and I walked down to the park to eat. I do that a lot because it's nice there. I had noticed this guy in a hoodie following me, but I didn't pay attention. I mean lots of people walk that way and go to that park. And I went to my favorite spot and was eating and this guy walked up the path and right towards me, you know? It was weird but I just thought, maybe he was a tourist who was going to ask for directions or ask me some lame question about being part Fey – I get that a lot because of how I look – but he wasn't slowing down he was just coming straight at me, kind of fast. And then I realized something wasn't right and I started to get up and then he was swinging this knife, and…and it was in my shoulder. I didn't think anything could hurt that bad."

She stopped, looking down, "I'm sorry, I've never been stabbed before."

"It's okay. It does pretty much suck," Allie said, earning a soft chuckle from the woman.

"Yeah," she agreed looking up again. "The doctors said it broke my collarbone. I didn't know that at the time just that it hurt like crazy. And then he hit me, I think maybe with the other end of the knife. And I don't remember much after that. I mean it's all hazy. I remember enough to know…to know what he did. But it was like it

126

wasn't really happening. And then someone was yelling. I guess that was Skip…"

"You knew him?"

"Skip? Yeah, I'd share my lunch with him sometimes he's – was – a nice guy," she said. "And I rolled over and I saw him, the guy, with a bloody knife and I used the earth energy to throw him, except everything was still kind of spinning, I was really dizzy from getting hit, and I missed. He ran away before I could try again. And then…then I saw Skip…and I found my phone and called 911."

Allie nodded thinking that the killer had some very perverse luck. Brownies had a special talent for manipulating earth energy; if she'd managed to hit where she was aiming she might have knocked him out, and that would have been the end of it. "I think you're very lucky to be alive. And that he's lucky you missed."

The woman nodded slightly. "Do you think he'll be caught?"

"Gods I hope so," Allie said sincerely. "Thank you for telling me that, I know how hard it was to talk about it."

She nodded again. "I suppose it's stupid of me not to talk to the cops. I mean I don't want to talk to the Elven Guard because, since when have they cared about what happens to the Lesser Fey? They just care about the letter of the Law and preserving order, and I don't need anyone in here telling me to do anything…but I know Ashwood's cops are good people."

"So why didn't you tell detective Riordan anything?"

She heaved a heavy sigh. "Because my dad's a cop with the state police and – it's stupid because he's going to find out about this anyway right? – but I didn't want him to know."

"Believe me," Allie said reaching out across the space between them for the first time and taking the other woman's hand. "I completely understand."

****

As they were moving through the door Allie grabbed Mariniessa and whispered quickly, "Jess doesn't know what I just told her; don't repeat it."

She felt the other woman's disbelief and moved past her quickly before she could respond to what Allie had said. Out in the hallway all the police, elven and human, were still gathered. Allie rubbed her temple, unconsciously imitating Riordan. "Her name is Joy Piburn."

"Piburn? Why does that sound familiar?" Smythe asked, frowning.

"Well her father's a state cop," Allie said.

"Shit," Riordan swore with real feeling.

"She told us what happened and gave us a description of Standish," Allie continued. "The cliff notes version is that he seems to have followed her for a little bit on the street – she didn't think anything of it – and then just walked right up to her as soon as she was alone and stabbed her."

"Yes," Mariniessa said unexpectedly, her voice more subdued than Allie had ever heard it before. "It appears that the second man, the musician, arrived during or immediately after the sexual assault and Standish turned his attention from his victim to attack the one who would have aided her. The woman recovered enough while the other man was being mortally wounded to attack Standish herself, magically, and drive him off."

"That was bravely done," Jess said quietly.

Still looking troubled Mariniessa nodded. "Yes. It may give him some pause in choosing or attacking his next victim."

"We can hope," Riordan said, without much hope in his voice.

"Allie," Sam said, speaking for the first time, "would you be willing to go with me out to the crime scene and do whatever it is that you do to see if you can pick up anything we might be able to use to catch him?"

"Oh, ummm, sure," Allie said.

Jess stepped forward, resting a hand protectively on Allie's shoulder. "I am not sure anything can be gained from Allie going to that location. We already know that it was our suspect."

"Obviously," Sam said nonchalantly. "And I appreciate your concern about Allie going to a place so rife with such abhorrent emotions given her clear issues with her own abilities, but trained or not, shielded properly or not, we may be able to use her like a dowsing rod to find the killer's trail."

Allie winced as Jess's emotions swung from concern to outrage. Sam could not possibly have chosen a worse way to phrase things. Even Mariniessa and Brynneth were looking from their commander to the human mage as if they expected Jess to throw a punch. When he spoke though Jess's voice was utterly devoid of any emotion at all – something that should have warned Sam of how badly upset the elf was. "She is not a tool to be used at your convenience. I think it was expecting too much of her as it is to ask her to come here and expose herself to the emotions of the victim. Turning around immediately after that and wanting to drag her out to the scene of the crime is asking too much."

Everyone's eyes shifted back to Sam, waiting for his response. The human mage rolled his head, cracking his neck in a way that made Allie wince. "I think that I asked Allie and she said she'd do it."

Jess's hand tightened on her shoulder and Allie swore to herself, wishing that she hadn't reflexively agreed. "Allie is a kind hearted person who is always willing to help others whenever she can," Jess said in that same flat voice. "But she is also a poor judge of her own limitations. I will not stand by and allow her to be put in a situation where she will be exhausted or harmed in her effort to help you do your job."

"Now, I think we all just need to calm down," Riordan tried to interject, realizing how angry Jess actually was.

Sam, as usual, ignored him, continuing in a light pleasant tone as if they were discussing the weather. "I wasn't aware that you were her keeper, to decide what situations she did or didn't put herself into. Or maybe you don't care if she breaks her word, having said she'd go already."

Allie felt Jess's anger spike and knew that whatever he said next would almost certainly be neither calm nor civil, and probably ruin the new atmosphere of cooperation the police and Elven Guard had. She spoke quickly into the brief pause that hung in the air after Sam's final word.

"Jessilaen is my fiancé," her subconscious supplied the word, which flowed off her lips so naturally she was almost overwhelmed by hysterical laughter. Jess was so distracted by the formal proclamation of their status, he shifted instantly from angry to something else entirely. She didn't dare look at the other two elves, who were radiating shock so strong she could taste it, thick and heavy as cream. She saw Riordan blink and look at her in wide-eyed surprise but she pushed on. "So you'll understand why he has a right to be concerned about my well-being. And I said I would go with you and see if I could find a trail but I never said when."

130

Sam looked at her, his face totally blank. "I...see. Indeed. Well, that does put a rather different spin on things then doesn't it? Especially as I understand that elves only marry for the purpose of procreation, I imagine he would have a vested interest in your safety."

"Sam," Smythe said sharply, "I'm saying this as your friend, but seriously shut the Hell up, or when the commander kicks your ass I'm going to cheer him on."

Sam stepped back slightly, his expression flustered. "What? I was apologizing. I didn't mean any offense to begin with of course but if he's her boyfriend then naturally...*what*? Why is everyone looking at me like that?"

Riordan was rubbing his temples again, this time with both hands. "Kensington, for Christ's sake stop before you get your entire leg wedged in your mouth with your foot."

Sam's mouth shut with an audible click and Allie realized with some trepidation that he really didn't understand what he'd said that was so offensive. He was either so used to being brash that he was mistaking rude for friendly or, like some other mages she knew, he really was just that abysmal with social cues.

"*Don't be too angry with him Jess, he does mean well, in his own way*," she thought at Jessilaen. He relaxed his hand on her shoulder as if he'd only just realized how hard he was holding onto her.

"*He is of no consequence and clearly mentally deficient*," Jess thought back, as if waving away what she'd said. "*It was worth every word he said to hear you declare us betrothed.*"

"*Yes, well, I'm not sure Bryn and Mariniessa will ever get over the shock, but since your family has accepted the contract*," Allie thought back. "*I mean it's just a matter of it being written up and reviewed, so...I was right to say that wasn't I?*"

131

"Of course my love," Jess said, his happiness overflowing into her. *"Once accepted the actual writing and signing is mostly formality. And then we shall be wed."*

Allie felt a rush of panic at that word 'wed', despite the ease with which she'd just thrown around fiancé. It was one thing to accept in an abstract way that she was agreeing to marry him but the cold hard reality of it was overwhelmingly terrifying. Kind of the same way that she'd always talked with Syndra about how fun bungee jumping would be, but actually standing on the bridge counting down to jump was an entirely different experience. *Oh Gods Syndra I wish you were here, and not dead. Or at least show up in a dream where I can talk to you about something besides murders and conspiracies* she thought feeling an unexpected stab of renewed grief for her friend. She realized Riordan was talking and struggled to focus outward.

"…so we'll meet at 10 Friday morning and compare notes," he was saying. "We should have some results on the physical evidence analysis by then. At least preliminary results."

"Yes," Jess agreed. "And we should be finished comparing the possible connections between the three known members participating in the ritual murders."

"And…I mean would Friday be a good day to go out to the crime scene and have me check it out?" Allie said, fumbling slightly as she tried to walk the line between pleasing both groups. Sam rolled his eyes at her, and she sensed his annoyance.

"Friday's fine by me," he said, his voice perfectly civil. His eyes fixed on Jess who said nothing, clearly not willing to advocate her going forward with this plan, but also choosing not to stop her.

"Good," Riordan said, glancing from the mage to the elven commander to be sure that there would be no more disagreement. "Could you go before our meeting? It would be helpful if we could get your input at that point."

Allie looked at Sam, who shrugged. "I'm not a morning person, but with enough coffee I'll manage."

Allie nodded, "I'm okay with that."

"Alright," Smythe said, "I need to notify the next of kin here and we have a lot of evidence to go through from this incident. I think we should all get moving on our separate missions today and see what we can turn up in the next few days."

Everyone nodded and Allie felt a rush of relief. At least there was some kind of plan and everyone was working together, for the moment anyway. She turned to head towards the exit, Jess still by her side, when Sam jogged up. Jess tensed, as did the other two elves walking nearby, but Sam ignored them. "Allie hang on a second."

"What's up?"

"I've been thinking," he said, shooting the elves a suspicious look. "If you're interested. I know someone who can train you so that your empathy would be under control."

"Why do you assume it is not?" Jess asked coldly. Obviously he had taken a strong dislike to Sam and Allie repressed a sigh, knowing that he'd probably dislike the man for the next thousand years. Elves were legendary, literally, for their long memories and ability to hold a grudge, even over things humans found trifling. She felt bad for Sam's unborn great-great grandchildren who would probably never understand why they had such bad luck with elves....

Sam shrugged, "I'm not assuming. I know it isn't. I can see the way she flinches every time someone gets really pissed off or upset and the way she relaxes when people are happy. That just screams unshielded empath. No offense Allie."

133

Allie shrugged, "None taken. I spent most of my life until a few months ago ignoring my empathy, and I could shield just fine, but then I made a mistake. I don't know exactly what I did, but I opened myself up to my ability in a way that short circuited everything. My shielding's been erratic at best since then."

"Hmmm," Sam murmured thoughtfully, as Jess tensed. Allie knew he didn't like her giving away so much personal information to the mage, but it was clear Sam already knew or had guessed a lot of her problem anyway. "Yes, I definitely know someone who can help you."

"And what cost will this help come at?" Jess asked, his voice stiff.

"Now that I can't say. But it'd be up to Allie to decide if it was worth it or not."

Allie nodded slightly. "So who is this person? A friend of yours? A former teacher?"

Sam actually blushed a little, looking uncomfortable. "Well as it happens, neither. It's my great-aunt. She's an accomplished mage in her own right and is particularly knowledgeable when it comes to training people's innate gifts."

****

Allie grabbed Jason and went back to work after leaving the clinic, deciding it was better to re-open the store for a few hours than lose the entire day. It proved to be something of a waste since she didn't have any customers, probably she thought because her hours lately had become so erratic. She did manage to get several internet orders packaged up and mailed though so the afternoon wasn't a total waste.

Jason left to work second shift at the firehouse and Allie tried not to worry too much during the few hours she was alone in the store. It was a relief when the time came to close. Feeling tired and a bit depressed she went and picked Jess up at the Outpost after work. As soon as he was in the car her mood lifted and she turned and smiled at him. He smiled back but she could feel that he was unhappy about something.

"What's wrong?" she asked, tilting her head to one side.

"Nothing is wrong, my love," he replied reaching out to take her hand. "It's only that I worry for you."

"There's no reason to worry," she said.

"Allie," he said gently, "You have been under a great deal of pressure lately. You are only just beginning to overcome the mental trauma you went through a few months ago. You were just shot as was someone you…are fond of. Then the person who harmed you so grievously returns unexpectedly and pursues you. Last night you were obviously in shock and wrestling with the memories brought up by that person. Expecting you to be able to handle the emotions surrounding this victim and crime scene is expecting too much. The police may not care about pushing you too hard, nor even may the other Elven Guard, but I will not – cannot – stand by and watch you pushed to breaking."

"Jess, I understand why you're worried for me, I do. And I know that I haven't been as strong as I should have been…"

"Do not," he cut her off, his voice hard, "say that. You are stronger than most others I know and certainly stronger than you give yourself credit for. If anything your need to appear strong hurts you in the end, because you do not allow for your own weakness."

Allie looked down, frowning. She didn't understand what he meant. He sighed. "My heart, there is nothing

135

wrong with being weak. There is nothing wrong with admitting that something is beyond you or that you need to rest. Or that something is too upsetting for you to deal with."

"But it has to be done," Allie said slowly. "And I have admitted all of this – I told Syndra….oh, ummm. Right. I may not have mentioned that to you. I've been dreaming of Syn. She's stuck here, on the earth plane, and she wants me to help find out why so her spirit can move on."

Jess gave her a long look, but before he could ask her why she hadn't mentioned that sooner she rushed on, "And anyway I have told her I can't do this that it's too scary and I'm not strong enough."

He sighed. "I will spare you my opinion on whether or not confiding in your dead friend in a dream is the same thing as telling a living breathing person while you are awake. And you continue to push yourself harder and harder. Everyone has limits. Even you."

"I know that," she replied, stung.

"Then why not tell the police and their pet mage that you cannot go to the scene of that crime?"

"Why shouldn't I? I've been to others, and this one might help us find Standish…in fact I might be able to track him from there."

"Yes, that has occurred to me, which is why I will accompany you when you go. But do you really think it's wise to go somewhere and open yourself to the emotions of such a scene?"

"I think it's necessary," she said stubbornly defending Sam's idea.

"And what will it stir up in you? How much of your recent progress with this healing will be undone if you are put in touch with the feelings of that woman, the feelings she experienced during her assault?" he insisted, just as stubbornly.

Allie felt something click into place, something she'd tried to deny just as much as she'd tried to deny the event itself. Her hand tightened on his. "You...you know what happened? To me, I mean? All of it?"

He met her eyes, his face full of sorrow, "I knew when we found you that night."

"Oh," she said, feeling stupid. "Of course you did."

"*It changes nothing,*" he thought to her, reaching out to connect to her mind, although she wasn't sure if it was to comfort her or reassure himself. "*I love you no less. I value you no less. You are the most precious thing in my life Allie, and nothing can alter that.*"

"*No,*" she thought slowly, feeling his love around her, filling the air, "*It does change something – it takes a weight off of me. I don't feel like I'm hiding a secret from you anymore.*"

"*I knew you would tell me when you were ready to,*" he thought calmly.

Allie nodded, pulling her hand from his so she could start the car. She really did feel as if a weight had been lifted, although part of her had worried it would change how he felt about her, about wanting to be with her, finding out that he'd known from the beginning made it hard to hold onto that fear. Releasing it was like setting down something heavy she'd been carrying, and she drove home silently, turning the idea over and over.

When she parked in front of the house she noticed that while Shawn's car was still gone both Liz and Jason were home and she relaxed even more. She had barely seen her cousin since the shooting and she had begun to fear that Liz was avoiding her on purpose, either because of Jess moving in or because she wouldn't take Liz's suggestion to leave town for a while.

She scanned the yard reflexively for Ciaran as she walked up to the door with Jess, but there was no sign of the kelpie. Allie had no doubt though that he was nearby, probably laying low trying to lure the Dark court elves back by pretending to be gone. It was reassuring to know that he was out there, wherever he was, protecting her.

It had been a long day, but an oddly satisfying one. She knew that Jess expected her to be an emotional wreck with everything that was going on, but she felt better than she had since the shooting. Talking – finally talking – about what had happened to her several months ago with someone who knew exactly what it was like to go through that same thing had been cathartic. She didn't feel alone anymore, and even better she had finally talked about it with Jess. Yes the Dark court elves were back, and the one who had hurt her was hunting her again but she didn't feel afraid. She felt angry, and oddly relieved. She didn't have to worry about whether she'd see him again, whether he'd hurt her again. He was back and she knew it and the terrible uncertainty was gone.

She was still thinking about this when she walked into the house and Jason called from the living room. "Hey Allie, I've got a surprise for you."

She and Jess exchanged a puzzled look and then walked into the other room. Liz was sitting primly on one of the high backed chairs; Jason stood by the window as if he'd been watching for them to get back. And sitting on the couch, leaning back as comfortably as ever, was Bleidd. For an instant Allie stood, stunned, feeling her own shock reflected by Jess.

"Bleidd!" she cried and ran across the room. She skidded to a stop a few feet away from him, wanting to throw her arms around him, but afraid of hurting him. "You're home! Are you – I mean how are you feeling?"

His expression was as cynical as his words, but the feelings around him let her know he was basking in her excitement. "I'd like to say I successfully escaped but I think they just grew tired of dealing with me."

Her face hurt from smiling and, deciding it would be safe enough if she were careful, she leaned forward and gave him a gentle hug. He of course took advantage of the moment to wrap his good arm around her and pull her as close as possible, almost throwing her off balance. She said, "I'm glad you're home"

He whispered into her hair, low enough that no one else would hear, "I would not be anywhere else with so much excitement going on."

She tensed, pulling back. He let her go with obvious reluctance. She turned to Jason, putting her hands on her hips, "Jason, what did you tell him?"

"Me? What?" Jason said nervously, his eyes darting between Allie and Bleidd and then at Jess. Allie knew he was still very nervous around the Elven Guard, even with Jess living here. Or possibly more so with Jess living here, and she felt a brief stab of guilt. Especially since Liz was making a point of refusing to acknowledge Jess's presence. *Why can't I be happy without the thing that makes me happy making other people unhappy* she thought *Is it some sort of universal law?*

"About what happened yesterday?" she prodded.

"Oh, ummm that," Jason said faintly. "Well, yeah. I told him. I mean I had to tell him Allie he does live here too and…"

"Wait," Liz cut in frowning fiercely, "what happened yesterday?"

Uh oh Allie thought as a thick silence fell over the room. "Ahhh, well…."

"There was an incident here yesterday," Jess said, calmly, "Two people came here and chased Allie, who fled into the woods. Her kelpie friend came to her aid and drove them off."

Allie blessed Jess's discretion, in saying people and not elves. Even so Liz frowned harder, her expression reflecting something uglier than just her judgment.

139

"People? What people? Allie this is getting completely out of control. I can't even feel safe in my own home anymore."

"I'm sorry, Liz," Allie said.

At the same moment Jason spoke up. "It's not her fault Liz."

"I'm not saying it's her fault," Liz said but the guilty look she shot at Allie belied her words. "It's just that she's done enough. She's helped them enough. How does it do them any good now if she gets herself killed?"

Jess reached out and pulled her back against his shoulder. "I will never allow Allie to be killed, not while I live."

To Allie's shock Liz gave Jess a cold look, her emotions a tangle of anger, resentment, and something almost like hatred. Allie frowned at her cousin. She knew, of course, that Liz didn't like elves and that she blamed the Elven Guard for a lot of the trouble that had gone on in the past few months. She also knew that Liz resented Jess moving in to the house, something the cousins had argued bitterly about right after the shooting. But she had honestly believed that her cousin understood how important Jess was to her. What she was feeling from her now though made her question that.

"Well," Allie said, looking away from the only surviving family she had any contact with, someone who was more like a sister than a cousin. "Let's not ruin Bleidd's first day home with this. We should be celebrating."

"Right," Jason quickly agreed. "How about some Dynasty Moon? My treat?"

Both the elves agreed eagerly, not surprising given the high quality of food at Dynasty Moon and the elven love of sensual pleasures including the epicurean ones. Liz hesitated, obviously wanting to disagree but also not wanting to make a scene. Finally she gave in, forcing a smile but Allie knew she was still seething inside.

The rest of the evening passed quietly as Bleidd, Jason, and Jess ate and then settled into a long, meandering conversation about the history of Ashwood. It was exactly the sort of thing that normally would have captivated Allie, since the elves were not talking about second hand stories but sharing their own memories of the town over the years, but she sat quietly watching her cousin. It was finally sinking in that Liz was really unhappy about the way things were going, both the danger Allie was putting herself in and Jess living there and Allie started to worry that she was being selfish by insisting that she had to have her own way. It was Liz's house too, but Allie wasn't giving her cousin much choice but to accept the situations. It made her feel bad, and ruined both Bleidd's coming home, which should have eased the last of her worry about his health after the shooting, and also an evening where he and Jess were in the same room and not sniping at each other. That was truly miraculous, although Allie thought that it probably had a lot to do with Jess feeling so much more secure in their relationship now that they were going to be married.

So she sat on the couch after the food was cleared away, halfheartedly listening to Bleidd and Jess talk about the Sundering, the Great War, and the impact on Ashwood, but really watching her cousin. Liz sat on a chair across the room pretending interest, her mind really a million miles away; Allie recognized that detached look on her face from all the times they'd sat through boring lectures by their grandmother as children.

Allie was really worried that with the way things kept amping up something was going to have to give soon. And the last thing she wanted was for her cousin to get hurt because of her choices.

Chapter 5 – Thursday

Bleidd moved slowly down the hallway towards the kitchen, hating the way his body still ached from his injury. It was leagues better than it had been even the day before, but he was not accustomed to dealing with any physical limitations. His time recovering in the clinic had been absolutely maddening and more than once he had nearly called on Brynneth, to see if the healer could do any more for him. Only the knowledge that he was already in the healer's debt because of the first aid he'd been given immediately after the shooting had stopped him. The Elven Guard would be far too willing to use any such debt to manipulate him to its own ends, something he knew too well having long ago been a Guard member himself.

That train of thought had proved fruitful however as he'd realized he could use the debt to further his own agenda. As soon as Jason told him about the Dark elves attempting to kidnap Allie he knew that, whatever it took, those elves must die or they would be an endless threat to her. He had convinced the doctor to release him from the clinic, fully intending to set about hunting down and destroying this threat. But it quickly became apparent that he was in no physical condition to accomplish anything except finding his own death, for although he could undoubtedly locate them he could not defend himself. The thought of fighting an agent of the Dark court, no doubt skilled in countless Machiavellian methods of combat, was laughable. But, if he went to the Guard, who were certainly already hunting the same quarry, he could say that he wanted to find the Dark court elves for them, to relieve his debt. And once they were found the Elven Guard would become his blade, putting an end to the threat to Allie's safety with limited risk to his own.

And so he walked stiffly down the hall, carefully rehearsing what he would say and trying to ignore his own obvious weakness. He could have gone to the Outpost and petitioned the Guard captain directly, but last night there had been something different about Jessilaen; less hostility and more conviviality. Bleidd knew that Brynneth answered first to Jessilaen, and that the debt owed to the healer had been accrued through his position in the Guard and could therefore be discharged through service to the Guard. It was within Jessilaen's authority to negotiate and accept such a thing and Bleidd was fairly sure the other elf would be receptive to his idea.

He found the Guard commander sitting in the kitchen drinking coffee. Jason had already left for work, and Liz was asleep so it was a safe assumption that the distant sound of the water running upstairs indicated Allie's location. Perfect. Given Allie's love of lengthy showers he should have plenty of time to talk with Jessilaen without her being aware of it. The last thing he needed was for her to get wind of his plan and force him to make a promise that would tie his hands entirely.

He fixed his own cup of coffee, with generous amounts of milk and sugar. With a sigh he joined Jessilaen at the table, sipping the drink despite its temperature. It was worth coming home early just to escape the black sludge the clinic tried to pass off as coffee...

"Commander," Bleidd said politely, after he'd savored his drink for a bit. "I would speak with you if you have the time."

Jessilaen tilted his head, setting his own cup down and giving the former Outcast all his attention. "Certainly."

"It is weighing heavily on me that I owe Brynneth a debt." Bleidd began carefully. "But I am also aware that you are seeking to find the Dark court elves that are hiding in Ashwood. I believe I can be of assistance with this."

"Why are you so willing to aid the Guard in rooting out these agents of the Dark court?" Jess asked.

"I have offered and done as much before," Bleidd pointed out, refusing to let the other elf bait him. "And now I have a debt to pay."

"Yes, but why offer to do so again now?" Jessilaen pressed. "And do not act as if your debt motivates you. We both know that Brynneth did very little for you that day, and what he did do hardly warrants risking yourself hunting such a dangerous enemy."

"Because they are here to harm Allie," he said, struggling to stay calm. He did not want to confess his true reason, but he also knew that Jessilaen of all people should understand well enough that motivation.

"And you are willing to come here and ask me to allow you to help us, officially, because you are so certain you can track them down where we cannot?" Jess pressed.

"Whatever it takes to keep her alive I will do. If I must get down on my knees and kiss your arrogant ass, then so be it," Bleidd said, the words forced out between gritted teeth as his temper slipped. Damn the fool for making this so hard, when it should be simple. "But I will not let her die because I was too stubborn to compromise and work with you."

Jessilaen regarded the former Outcast cautiously. "You must love her a great deal."

"You have no idea," Bleidd said. "I love her far more than you do."

"I doubt that. She is my life now, without her I will die," Jessilaen said, his own voice cold, even as he acknowledged his own weakness. "You must hate me for standing in your way."

"There have been times recently where I did hate you," Bleidd agreed. "When I watched you in my own home with her. Ten years I have known her, ten years of loving her and waiting for her to grow up, and there I sit

144

watching you in what should be my place. Knowing that she loves you too, knowing that she can't choose between us and that you are with her because you acted when I waited. The torture of being in the same house while you enjoy the privilege of bedding her, when it should be me spilling my seed between her thighs. Oh yes, it's easy to hate you for all of that. But I am not so young or foolish, or even blinded by my love for her, that I don't realize my hatred for you is rooted in my own jealousy, because you have something that I want. And in hating you I reduce her to nothing but a prize to be won and that is...unworthy of her."

Jessilaen's paused, for once not answering with a quick retort. Finally, slowly, he nodded. "Yes, it is."

"And so I am willing to work with you," Bleidd said, "because it will negate my debt – however small you believe that debt to be – and because it will protect her life."

Jessilaen nodded again. "Yes. I will accept your assistance in finding the location of the Dark court agents within the bounds of this town, in payment for the healing that Brynneth rendered to you. But let us be clear, you are to find them only. I will grant you no authority to confront them."

Bleidd controlled his face carefully making sure that he looked properly annoyed by that, despite his elation. "Those terms are very restrictive. If I find them and do confront them should I be worrying about repercussions from the Guard?"

"Those are the terms I offer," Jessilaen insisted, exactly as Bleidd had expected him to. "When you find them you will alert me and I will handle dealing with them."

Bleidd took another drink of his coffee, as if debating what the other elf had said. He had to be careful not to answer either too quickly or too slowly. "If those are your best terms then I accept them. Without my help tracking them down you will certainly never find them."

To his surprise the commander agreed. "Yes, you have a much greater chance of success than we do."

Seeing Bleidd's surprise, Jessilaen merely inclined his head in a shrug. "There is no reason to deny what is obviously true. They have been here, likely since they first attacked her, and we have not only been unable to track them down to wherever they are lairing but have been oblivious to their presence these past months. I would have to be a fool not to let you aid us in finding them."

Bleidd's eyes narrowed. "You planned to ask me for help with this, yes?"

"I had been considering it," Jessilaen agreed.

"And yet you let me come to you," Bleidd said, angry despite his real reason for being there. Since he was using the Guard as a means to his own end it should not ultimately matter whether they approached him or he approached them, so long as he found the target and they eliminated the threat to Allie. Yet he found himself disproportionately annoyed.

"I said I was considering asking you, not that I had decided to do so," Jessilaen replied holding his hands up in a calming gesture.

Bleidd realized that he had started to stand up in his anger, and he sat back down carefully, feeling the muscles in his chest and shoulder pull against the motion. "And what made you hesitate, if you agree that I am your best chance to find them?"

Jessilaen didn't answer immediately, drinking slowly from his own coffee. Bleidd began to think that the proud elven commander was not going to answer him at all, but then he did speak, his voice soft and low. "What you will be doing is dangerous. Even if you do not confront them there is risk to you, that they will discover you following them for example. It has become clear to me that

146

you matter very much to Allie and it would grieve her greatly if you should be killed."

"And you do not want her to blame you for my death?" Bleidd asked, intrigued by this sudden turn. A week ago he'd have thought Jessilaen would gladly have handed the blade to the Dark court agent if he thought it would remove him as a rival for Allie's heart.

"I do not want her to suffer more than she already has," Jessilaen said simply. "When you were both wounded all she could think about was saving your life. When she awoke after her own injury was healed the first thing she did was ask if you still lived. I could see then how much she cares for you, and I do not want to see her lose part of herself with your death."

Bleidd sat back, stunned at the other elf's words. After a moment Jessilaen smiled, "And perhaps I am starting to see that you have some redeeming qualities. Certainly you are very loyal and have proven true in many difficult circumstances."

The compliment was wholly unexpected and caught Bleidd off guard. He responded with proper courtesy and offered a compliment in return automatically, "As have you. You have shown yourself remarkably loyal to her far beyond what I had expected."

He saw a flicker of understanding move behind the other elf's eyes, and he was certain that Jessilaen knew now that Bleidd was aware of the secret he kept for Allie. The other elf nodded slightly, his expression softening. "We both love her enough to do what we must to protect her."

Uncomfortable with the sudden surge of respect and even friendship he felt for the Guard commander who had been his rival, Bleidd was compelled to add, "Of course you might only be feeling anything kind towards me because of the way your link with her affects you."

Jessilaen smiled widely at that, giving Bleidd an appraising look, "You underestimate yourself Bleidd. But if it is her influence I do not mind."

Certain he must look as shocked as he felt Bleidd watched as the Guard commander stood and carried his now empty mug to the sink. He found himself thinking, for the first time, *When he isn't being an arrogant ass he's actually quite personable. And it's not hard to see why Allie is attracted to him, he is quite handsome.* That led down a fairly inevitable track, before he stopped himself. Bleidd shook his head, then forcibly reminded himself *And I should not forget that he has her and I do not. Sitting here and fantasizing about him gains me nothing but more frustration. I have a mission now, and better if I accomplish it sooner rather than later.*

****

Sam had arraigned to meet Allie in front of his great-aunt's house the next afternoon, as soon as she'd closed the store and he was off duty. Allie had been nervous all day, and either luckily or not the store had been slow so she had spent a lot of time worrying over this meeting. Part of her wanted very much to find an excuse not to go through with it, but her common sense kept winning out. She could not go on the way she had been for the past few months, with her empathy controlling her and other people's emotions influencing her actions. She needed to be able to help catch this killer and that wasn't going to happen if her own psychic gift was dragging her along like a leaf on the wind.

She parked her car on the street in front of the house at the address Sam had given her, glad she'd arrived first and he couldn't see her reaction. Located in one of the best areas downtown the huge Victorian sat behind a heavy iron fence. The yard was a sprawling expanse of well-manicured grass and topiaries. The long, perfectly kept driveway ended at a huge carriage house that could not ever be called anything as simple as a garage. In fact everything was in such great condition that Allie not only felt overawed by the luxury of it but also oddly as if she'd stepped back a hundred years in time.

As she sat admiring the giant house a long black hearse pulled up and parked behind her. With a growing sense of inevitability Allie stepped out of her car and went to stand on the sidewalk, watching without surprise as Sam emerged from the driver's side of the hearse. He was still dressed all in black and carried his dragon headed cane, a big grin spreading across his face as he watched her reaction to his vehicle.

"You drive a hearse," she said, not sure if she should be amused or horrified.

"It's an excellent vehicle, very dependable," Sam said innocently. "And roomy."

"Right," Allie agreed thinking to herself *and so convenient if you need to move bodies.*

Sam stood regarding her for a moment as if waiting for her to say something else. When she didn't he gestured towards the house, "Well, we might as well get on with this. I'll bring you in and introduce you. After that, well you'll see how she is. Either she'll be willing to teach you or she won't."

Allie nodded wordlessly and followed Sam over to a gate in the fence. He punched in a security code and swung the gate open; Allie walked through eyeing the wrought iron cautiously. Sam must have seen the look she gave the fence. "Does iron bother you that much? I'd have thought being half human it wouldn't."

"Well it's not my favorite thing," Allie answer vaguely as they walked down a decorative mosaic path towards the front door. The house was even more intimidating up close and she bit her lip reminding herself that this was necessary. She suddenly wished that she had given in and brought someone with her, but Sam had been insistent that his great-aunt would not allow anyone else in the house. She didn't know what he'd said to get her invited in but she gathered that the elderly woman was living as a recluse and hated company. She'd had a difficult time convincing Jess to let her go alone, and in the end only the fact that the police mage would be there too had soothed him enough for him to stop insisting on sending one of the other elves from their squad.

They were met at the door by a maid in uniform and Allie struggled against the nervous laughter that always seemed to overtake her when she was in tense situations. The hallway to the house was expensively decorated, making the reason for the security system clear. The maid greeted Sam as "young Mr. Kensington" and nodded politely at Allie before escorting them to a parlor off to the left. This room would have made any antique collector have fits of envy; it was all vintage Victorian era and all pristine. Not to mention luxurious and expensive. Allie caught herself before she could apologize for wearing sneakers on the thick oriental carpeting.

The maid left and she and Sam waited several minutes in silence. A slight noise at the back entrance of the room drew Allie's attention and she turned in that direction. The woman who entered the room walked slowly and carefully, like someone unsure of their balance. She was tall, nearly six feet, and even extreme age hadn't stooped her proud shoulders. Her body was gaunt, the skin stretched tight over the angles of bones and pooling in paper-fine wrinkles everywhere else. Her light blue eyes peered out sharply behind small round wire rimmed glasses, taking in everything with obvious acuity. In defiance of the current trend that dictated even elderly women color their hair in imitation of youth, her hair was completely white, pulled back into a mercilessly tight bun. Her clothing was as expensive as the décor of the room, but the styles were all years out of date, and Allie couldn't help but wonder if she had them specially made to her own taste.

All of Sam's usual impudence had disappeared and he was the image of complete respect. "Good afternoon great-aunt Amelia. This is my friend Allie, who would like to train with you."

"Your friend?" the old woman's voice was strong, and she managed to pack an enormous amount of derision into those two words.

Sam actually flushed under her scrutiny. "I'm sorry great-aunt Amelia if I misspoke. I know Allie through the police department. We are working on a case together."

"Well," the old woman said, seeming mollified, "it's always interesting to meet one of your co-workers."

She turned to Allie, her sharp eyes speculative. "So you are the untrained empath Samuel told me about."

"Yes ma'am."

"Call me Miss Amelia," she said, then glancing at Sam. "You may go Samuel."

Sam opened his mouth as if to argue, then obviously thought better of it. "Yes great-aunt Amelia. Allie I'll meet you outside when you're done here."

Allie nodded numbly, wanting him to stay but afraid to ask. It was obvious Miss Amelia wasn't someone that people argued with.

After Sam left the room the old woman turned back to Allie. "So you have come here seeking training."

"Yes ma'a – er, ah, Miss Amelia," Allie said.

"How old are you? Twenty? And you're helping the police with an investigation even though you have no training?" her words were scathing and Allie could feel the disapproval filling the air around her.

"No Miss Amelia. I'm thirty-seven. And I am helping the police but technically I sort of work for the Elven Guard and the elves don't know how to train empathy."

The woman's attitude changed so quickly it was miraculous, the stern disapproval giving way to a wave of nostalgia and longing. Her face and voice gave away none of this but Allie could sense it all as clearly as if the other woman was yelling it out. "You are part elven?"

"Yes, I am. My mother was an elf," Allie replied cautiously.

Miss Amelia looked closely at her for a long time, her face softening. "I had an elven lover once myself. Back before the worlds were joined and reality Sundered. There were gateways back then connecting the realms that people could pass back and forth between. He liked to come here to be with me, and he taught me many things…"

Her voice trailed off as she lost herself in her own memories of some distant time. Allie stared back, stunned. *Before the Sundering! That would make her…at least, what? A hundred and twenty?* Allie guessed. *How is that possible?*

"He taught me many things," Miss Amelia repeated, sighing. "Certainly enough to help you learn how to help yourself."

Allie nodded, still speechless and her shocked expression finally pulled the older woman back to the present. "I'm sure you are trying to guess my age. You won't be able to, I assure you. I was given the gift of extra years, of time, and nothing is more valuable, but there is always a cost." Miss Amelia stared at Allie, her gaze challenging. "So the question is, what price are you willing to pay little half-elf?"

Allie struggled not to wilt under the scrutiny. "What price are you asking?"

Miss Amelia closed the distance between them and placed one hand on Allie's forehead. Allie could feel the other woman's energy going through her, weighing and measuring something. Miss Amelia dropped her hand with a sigh. "You have no idea what you are, do you?"

"Ummm," Allie mumbled caught off guard. "Apparently not."

The old woman nodded. "You'll find out in your own time. For now I can teach you how to control your empathy. And in payment I want you to visit with me and remind me of the elves."

"Remind you how?" Allie asked carefully.

"Surely you speak Elvish? And you know stories, children's tales, songs?" at Allie's nod she went on, "Then you can come here and entertain me with those."

"You speak Elvish?" Allie asked hesitantly.

"Not much nor well, but I love to hear the sound of it," Miss Amelia said. "It reminds me of better times. Do we have a bargain?"

"I will agree to stay after our lessons for the same length of time that the lesson lasts and speak to you in Elvish, or tell you elven children's stories, or sing to you," Allie agreed.

For the first time Miss Amelia smiled, the expression softening her face. Allie imagined that she must have been quite striking when she was younger. "Spoken like a true elf. Then our bargain is made. The first lesson begins now."

Allie followed the woman obediently to the closest couch where they both sat. Miss Amelia perched on the cushion with her back ramrod straight. "You know how to ground and center, yes?"

"Yes."

"Shield?"

"That seems to be my problem," Allie admitted reluctantly.

153

"Your problem is that you deny your true nature and try to be something you are not," the woman said sharply. "Is it not true that you can gain energy from other people's feelings, especially other people you have bound to yourself?"

"Yes, how did you-? Wait bound to myself? What does that mean?" Allie felt the words tumbling out as she tried to process what the woman was saying.

"I know because I've seen another like you before, a full elf," Miss Amelia replied cryptically. "He didn't fight against what he was though. He embraced it."

"Did he ever hurt anyone?" Allie asked quietly.

The old woman grinned wolfishly. "Not with his gift, only with his fists, a sword, and his words. Using his gift to wound might have been less painful."

Allie looked down, embarrassed, and Miss Amelia shook her head slightly, her expression sobering. "So shielding. You say this is a problem for you?"

"Yes," Allie said, trying to keep her expression calm. "I can't seem to hold my shields. They stay up sometimes and then they collapse others."

"Indeed. And let me guess, when you shield you visualize a wall surrounding yourself, keeping everything out?"

"Of course," Allie said, confused.

"And that is why they fail," the old woman said, shaking her head.

"What do you mean?" Allie said, frowning. "That's how everyone shields."

"Of course it isn't." Miss Amelia said dismissively. "It's how you were taught, and it's the basic method that many witches use but it's hardly how everyone does it. You of all people should know that the elves use color. I'm disappointed that such a basic fact escapes you actually. I was under the impression that you knew more than you obviously do about different magical systems."

Allie blushed, suddenly remembering her mother holding her close when she was a little girl, whispering 'Picture the silver light all around you Laine[1]. Can you see it? It will keep you safe..." She had not thought of that in decades. Only her mother had ever called her Laine, her father had found it too hard to pronounce and had nicknamed her Allie instead...and when she moved in with her grandmother she had been taught other ways to shield and had stopped using the light. "I...am sorry Miss Amelia. I did know that but I had forgotten it."

The old woman looked at her shrewdly. "Forgotten or been told it was the wrong way? Well it doesn't matter, elven shielding won't solve your problem either, it's too dependent on ambient magic. You'll find it unreliable on mortal earth as well as the sections of Ashwood with less magic."

Allie blinked slowly, thinking *how do you know all this?* But the elderly woman was already going on. "So your first lesson is this: as an empathic being it is imperative that you not block yourself off from the emotions you need to sense and draw on, but also that you be able to filter and control what affects you. Putting up a shield that acts as a wall is like trying to cut off your vision or hearing and then function – your own subconscious mind rebels against the idea, and that is why you fail. Your instinct, whether you realize it or not, is to use your ability to protect yourself, to read other people in order to know if you are safe or in danger..."

"But I don't want to read people," Allie protested.

Miss Amelia looked at her as if she had just declared breathing passé. "Why ever not? Dear Gods child next you'll say you don't want to look at people you're talking to since that might give you visual clues about how they feel!"

---

[1] Lawn-yuh

Allie frowned, "Of course not, but anyone can do that."

The old woman sighed. "Of course they can't or at least not equally well. You've been born with an ability that gives you extra insight, its foolishness to the point of insanity not to use it. If you had exceptionally good hearing would you stuff your ears with cotton so that you were on the same level as everyone else?"

"Well, no, of course not…" Allie mumbled, frowning harder.

"Of course not," Miss Amelia echoed. "So why cripple your innate empathic ability just because not everyone else has it?"

Allie shook her head wordlessly and Miss Amelia continued. "So, shielding. You cannot use a wall or solid structure, because your own mind will poke holes in it to reach what you subconsciously seek. You cannot use the colors as the elves do because you will find it too imprecise. Instead you must learn to visualize something like a heavy screen; something that is strong enough to protect and filter out other people's magics and dangerous influences, but will leave tiny openings for the emotional energy to enter."

"How do I do that?" Allie asked, intrigued despite herself.

"My friend once said that for him most magic was heavy like a physical presence, but emotions were light as smoke. Perhaps you will find the same is true for you," Miss Amelia said, shrugging her thin shoulders.

Allie nodded slightly, taking a moment to test this idea. She could sense the energy around her, the magic woven into this house over decades of living by its occupants. Now that she had some frame of reference she could understand what Miss Amelia was saying; the energy did feel heavy like mist or fog in the air, something solid that could be touched and manipulated. She turned her attention to the old woman and felt her emotions, curiosity and a dull excitement, rising off of her like thin tendrils of smoke, something that was barely different in substance than the air around it. Carefully Allie visualized her shields but not as the usual solid wall surrounding her, instead she pictured herself covered by a heavy white mosquito netting like energy. This new shield was finely woven and offered only tiny openings for energy; it took her several minutes of experimentation to find the exact right sizing that kept out the spells of the house but let in that fine smoke of emotions. After she had anchored these new shields she found that she could still sense what the other woman was feeling, although not as an overwhelming distracting presence but rather as a simple awareness of them. At the same time while she was aware of the ambient spells she was insulated from them.

For the first time in the months since she had fully opened herself to her gift and short circuited her abilities – or perhaps she realized more accurately awakened her abilities – she had full, stable shields back. She heaved a sigh of relief, feeling an enormous weight lifting.

Miss Amelia smiled liked a cat with a bowl of cream, "And now, tell me a story."

****

Jerry paced the confines of the spare bedroom that was his home for now, feeling restless. He was staying with another member of the group, Ken, who worked for the town maintenance department and made more money driving the town trucks, and keeping them running, then Jerry had in all his years at the gas station. The house was expensive and in a part of town Jerry had barely ever driven through before. The room looked like it had been

157

decorated by an old woman, full of lace and quilts, and he'd bet money that Ken's mom had picked it all out. There were even framed quilts on the walls.

Sometimes, to break up the mind numbing boredom he'd walk around the room touching everything. The heavy wooden bedframe was smooth as silk. The sheets were softer than any he'd ever felt in his life, softer even than the ones at that nice motel his mom had taken them to hide in after she'd finally left his dad. Even the stitching on the quilts was soft to the touch. He'd lay down on the floor and run his hands over the hardwood to the edge of the heavy throw rug next to the bed, working his fingers through the fibers. Soft, everything was so soft in here. Sometimes it comforted him and he could spend hours just touching everything.

Other times though all the softness reminded him of his girls and that didn't comfort him, it made him remember her, the special girl he'd kept. She should have been his forever, she was perfect...but the Elven Guard had come and taken her away. And then he'd remember that this fine expensive house wasn't his, that he was just staying here because he had to. And that made him angry, because he wanted all these things to be his, and he wanted that girl back, and he wanted his freedom. And then he'd sit and rock and hit the side of his head with his hand until everything faded. Or until he couldn't bare it anymore and he had to sneak out and find a new girl....

That last girl, the brownie, she'd been nice enough but the whole experience wasn't any good. He hadn't been able to really enjoy it, and she'd ruined it at the end by fighting back, by scaring him. He frowned as he walked, remembering the cold fear clenching in his gut as he'd run through the little park after she'd tried to use magic on him. *These Fairy things they don't know their place*, he thought restlessly. *She should never have dared do that. She should have realized how powerful and terrifying I am. She should*

*have been afraid of me, been begging me not to hurt her.
Stupid defiant slut.* The more he thought about it the more
the residual fear was replaced by anger. *Damn that bitch
and damn the Elven Guard. They ruined everything. They
all ruined everything. This is exactly why we have to do the
ritual, why the worlds have to be separated again. So their
corruption is gone and we'll be free...*

He walked, and started to fantasize about the next
girl. He'd be sure the next one was perfect. Soon. Very
soon.

****

After leaving Miss Amelia's house Allie found Sam
and Jess both waiting for her on the sidewalk. The two men
were eyeing each other in tense silence and Allie sighed
slightly, some of her good mood fading.

"Alright guys," she said. "I have functional shields
again. Do we want to go the site now?"

To her annoyance they both reached out with their
respective magics and tested her shields. Sam looked
surprised; Jess looked pleased.

"You're a quick study," Sam said thoughtfully.

"I do my best," Allie said, shrugging. "Now, can we
go check out the location of the last murder?"

Jess still looked hesitant, but Sam smiled eagerly.
"Yes, why wait until tomorrow? I'm looking forward to
seeing how you do what you do."

"Don't get your hopes up," she warned him. "I
don't think you'll be able to duplicate it no matter how
much you study what I do."

"You don't think I'm skilled enough?" Sam scoffed.

"Not at all – I don't doubt you're quite skilled. But
this is an innate gift not a learned skill, so...I just don't

159

think it's something you can imitate," Allie said, automatically trying to soothe the mage's ruffled feathers. Jess sniffed disdainfully, unconcerned by Sam's ego.

"Well, we shall see," Sam replied, regaining his usual nonchalant cheer.

"Are you certain you are ready to do this?" Jess asked quietly in Elvish, earning a frown from Sam.

Allie nodded, then mentally added "*I am sure. These shields are good, and I think now I won't be totally overwhelmed by the emotional traces.*"

She could feel his reluctance, still as strong as if she were unshielded. Clearly their spell-bond meant that she was connected to him on a level too deep to shield out, something she would have to keep in mind. But while she could clearly sense Sam's emotions – excitement, impatience, and a touch of envy – she wasn't feeling them with him, only sensing them as an outside presence. There was no overwhelming pressure, no echo of his feelings within Allie. It was a huge improvement and she felt relief to know that she wouldn't be at the mercy of whatever other people were feeling anymore. Well, except Jess who still seemed to influence her as strongly as ever.

"If you insist on doing this," Jess said, "then let us proceed."

Sam grinned broadly, gesturing at the hearse where it sat in all its macabre glory. "If we want to go together in one car, I'd be happy to drive."

Jess gave him a look that would have withered most other people, "Absolutely not."

Sam, undaunted, turned to Allie. "What about you? You want a ride? We can talk ritual murder on the way over."

Allie's lips twitched into a smile but she managed not to laugh. She didn't want to encourage Sam when she could feel Jess growing angrier with each thing the mage said. "Sam, we'll meet you at the scene, okay?"

"Suit yourself," Sam said, sighing melodramatically. "No one ever seems to appreciate my car. Clearly a lack of good taste."

Swinging his cane Sam walked over to the hearse, whistling cheerfully. Jess continued to glare at him, even as Allie grabbed his hand and tugged him over to his own vehicle. One of the really annoying things about elves which Sam was clearly underestimating was their ability to hold a grudge, particularly against non-elves. Once an elf decided they really didn't like you, changing their mind became impossible, and elves were capable of some truly obnoxious behavior around people they didn't like. Allie could only think of a handful of situations that had gone against this general rule and they usually involved exceptional circumstances. At the rate Sam was antagonizing Jessilaen the Elven Guard commander was going to hate Sam's entire line down to his great-grandchildren, on principle.

"Come on Jess," Allie coaxed. "Why don't we drive to my store and I can drop my car off there, then I'll ride with you to the scene and home after. If you can give me a ride in to work tomorrow that is."

"Of course my love," Jess said, his emotions lightening as his attention finally shifted. "Perhaps when we are home later we can watch another movie. I am becoming quite fond of those movies Jason likes."

"That series of horror movies about the possessed doll?" Allie smiled relaxing into his energy. She normally didn't like horror movies at all, but she had to admit the ones Jason had picked out lately were less about gore and more along the lines of psychological thrillers. They still weren't her favorites, but it was entertaining to listen to Jason, Bleidd, and Jess argue over the details of the plots of the films.

"Yes," Jess said as he opened the door of the Guard vehicle, standing for a moment to finish what he was

161

saying before getting into the car. "I think we are on the third one now and I would like to see if they will find a way to finally end the threat. It is quite a fascinating story."

Allie giggled as she got into her own car and clipped her seatbelt. *Leave it to an elf to discuss a cheap horror movie like it was fine art,* she thought, careful to keep her mind closed to his.

Despite everything that was going on with the marriage contract and her difficulty adjusting to sharing her living space with someone, she was glad that she had Jess with her. She was slowly accepting that she did need him in her life, not only as a romantic partner but as a friend. Over the years she had gotten used to never really letting anyone in, but Jess had challenged her from the beginning, pushing to get her to open up to him and share her own emotions. Now that she was finally doing that it was surprising how much she enjoyed feeling like she could depend on him. Instead of worrying about needing him too much she found herself looking forward to being able to count on him to be there for her. It was still a strange new feeling but one that she liked.

Less than half an hour later her car was sitting in the lot of Between The Worlds and she and Jess were together in the Guard vehicle pulling up to the park were the assaults had happened. Jess parked in an open spot by the curb. Getting out Allie looked but there was no sign of Sam's distinctive hearse anywhere. Catching Jess's eye she shrugged and inclined her head towards the dirt path leading into the park.

Jess frowned slightly but moved ahead of her, leading the way in. Allie followed, nervously reinforcing her new shields to be absolutely sure they would hold once they got to the crime scene. She could feel it coming, like a storm in the air, a taste of ozone to her empathy, sharp and unpleasant. She could have easily led Jess to it, but she was relieved to realize that although she could sense the stain of fear, pain, despair, and death just as easily as before there was no overwhelming tidal wave of emotions pulling her into a trance state. She had no problem keeping herself separate from the feelings while still following them, by choice this time. It was such a relief she almost wanted to laugh. Instead she carefully described the experience to Jess, hoping that he would also be reassured.

"That is good," Jess said. "But let us not relax our guard until we are inspecting the scene itself. That will be the true test."

He glanced back at her, his eyes flicking down to her waist and sighed. "Allie you should wear your badge here, since this is an official investigation."

Allie blushed and fumbled the badge out of her pocket. She had been so worried about how she would react to the emotions at the scene she had completely forgotten about the badge. *Damn* she thought *maybe I should just staple it to my waist.*

To her surprise she heard Jess's amused voice in her mind, responding to what she had intended to be a private thought. *"I'd rather you did not, I quite like your waist as it is. And I imagine stapling anything to your body would be very painful."*

Her lips twitched into an almost-smile even as she worried about how easily she slipped and projected her thoughts to him now. She was going to have to be more careful about that. *"True, true, but I'm always forgetting to wear it when I should."*

"Do not worry my love, I will always be here to remind you," he thought back, pleased at the idea even as he thought it. She may have misgivings about the speed and permanence of their relationship but Jess clearly delighted in both. Walking behind him, certain that he couldn't see her she shook her head, caught between exasperation and amusement.

163

This time she carefully blocked her thoughts from him. *How can he be so certain so quickly about everything with us as a couple? We barely know each other, really and yet he has always been so utterly sure that he loves me and we belong together.* And yet, when she tried to imagine her life without him she couldn't; all that happened was a horrible sinking feeling in her stomach and a rush of anxiety. *Is that how he knows? Is that what love really is? The inability to imagine life without that person in it? Somehow he has become as essential to me as my own life, I just can't even begin to think of life without him in it.*

She pushed the thoughts away as they broke through a small cluster of trees into a clearing and found Sam standing patiently. Even if he hadn't been there waiting though she would have known this was the place. The energy here reminded her of walking into an area where a skunk had sprayed; the lingering emotions were like an acidic stink in the air, burning the back of her throat. Her nose wrinkled, despite the lack of a physical smell, and she unconsciously gravitated towards a place at the edge of the clearing where the grass was trampled down. There was a faint copper-tang smell of blood here.

"That's where the man died," Sam said, confirming what Allie had already guessed.

Turning she saw that both men were watching her closely. Jess's expression was guarded; Sam's was eager. Allie looked back at the ground. "The feelings here are strange. Not like the other locations. I think…Standish was afraid and also…there's something like regret here. I don't think he wanted to kill this guy."

"You think he gutted him by accident?" Sam said, his eyebrows arching up in a perfectly manicured expression of disbelief.

"Yes, that's what it feels like," Allie said frowning. Sam looked thoughtful and peered at her more closely as she moved around the open space. At the far end of the

164

small clearing was another area of emotional disturbance, although outwardly there was little sign to indicate this place was of any importance. But Allie could feel the familiar emotional trace of Standish, thankfully fully outside of her own energy now, its pulse of lust-joy-anger blending with frustration and fear. She tilted her head to the side trying to consciously filter out the victim's feelings and focus only on Standish. It was harder than she'd expected and she struggled with it. Finally, still unsure, she said, "This one was different for him. Maybe because she fought back? I'm not sure, it's hard to separate her anger from his. But he was definitely frustrated and afraid this time which he wasn't before."

"Could be because his normal process wasn't followed through," Sam said slowly. "If he's a real serial killer – not just a ritual murderer – then he'd need to complete his entire personal ritual or he wouldn't get his fix."

"His fix?" Jess said, frowning at the unfamiliar expression.

"It means he wouldn't get the emotional rush out of the experience he needed. It's what motivates him to do what he's doing," Allie explained, grateful to all the books she'd read on the topic of serial killers during the long hours at the store. At the time it had just been a way to pass the boring hours when business was slow, and later she'd justified it by saying it let her recommend books to customers; she'd never expected her reading to be useful in any practical way.

"Ah," Jess said. "So then if he has not gotten his 'fix' he will be seeking it still, yes?"

Sam flinched. "Shit. You know I'd hoped maybe almost getting caught would drive him further into hiding, which might be bad for us in catching him but would at least slow the body count…but I think you're right. I think he'll kill again, and soon."

Allie found herself nodding, her own heart sinking slightly at the prospect. "I think you're right. This all feels...incomplete. The emotions are all tangled but he, Standish, definitely feels...unsatisfied. Frustrated."

"Can you tell where he went from here?" Sam asked, for once no trace of humor in his voice.

She shook her head. "I'm sorry. I can't. There's a weak trace in the direction of the entrance of the park, but it fades as it goes....I think he projects the emotions I can follow the strongest when he's thinking about killing or hurting someone. Here he was just running away, so there's no strong emotion lingering."

Sam sighed. "That would be too easy wouldn't it? Alright well this still tells us he'll strike again, and soon. And if you are right..." Jess growled slightly startling Sam into flinching and giving him a wide eyed look "...erm, well, yes I should say if he hesitated to kill our Good Samaritan, then that could provide us some advantage if we can find him."

"Now we just need to need to find him," Allie said.

"Yes," Sam agreed, still eyeing Jess uncertainly. "Well, I'll fill Jim and Mark in on what you've said. I may try some trace spells as well, although I don't expect to have much luck. Notoriously tricky things. But at this point it can't hurt."

"Alright, then we'll leave you to it," Allie said, sick of the stink of emotional suffering permeating the air. Sam nodded absently and she turned and headed back the way she'd come, Jess a silent shadow with her.

As they left the clearing behind Jess matched her stride and reached out for her hand, twining his fingers with hers. She sighed and let herself pull in his emotions – love, pride, concern – not fighting against the way her body reached for his feelings and used them. Even as she felt his emotions filling her, she felt her own fatigue and stress

166

melting away, until she might as well have just woken up, or drank a large cup of coffee.

His voice was gentle, the Elvish words flowing and beautiful. "If that is an example of what you can learn from this teacher then I retract my concern. That was very well done."

She replied in kind, realizing that she was speaking Elvish so often now that it was becoming second nature instead of a concentrated effort. "Yes, the new shields held beautifully. There was no point when the emotions overwhelmed me, but I could still sense them just as clearly."

"This is a good thing, my heart. It will give you a great advantage in working such cases," he said, his pride and pleasure in her success flowing into her.

She couldn't help but feel her stomach drop at his words though, one hand going to the badge clipped to her waist. Her fingers traced the design stamped in gold, wondering again how she had been foolish enough to get tricked into working for the Elven Guard when all she wanted was her ordinary life as a bookshop owner. But of course the answer was walking next to her holding her hand, oblivious to her unhappiness with the situation.

Chapter 6 – Friday

Bleidd parked his car at the curb in front of the small pawn shop, sparing a derisive glance at the building. Nestled between a dollar store and a laundromat, Gold Street Pawn was an unassuming looking place, lacking all of the flash and allure of most pawn shops. The building was a drab grey with the store name painted in yellow on a flat sign above a large display window to the left of the door. The window was filled with an uninteresting assortment of junk. It was exactly the kind of place that the eye would slide right over, and for that at least Bleidd grudgingly respected the owner, since it was well known by the less law abiding residents of town that Gold Street Pawn was the place to go to buy or sell less-than-legal things, including information.

He paused for a moment, sitting in the car, gathering himself. His body still ached in the aftermath of his injury, and without thinking he reached a hand up to touch the scar pulling across the right side of his chest, feeling it through the thin material of his t-shirt. Already it was amazingly healed in the scant few days since he'd been injured, yet he chafed at the sense of time crawling by. And if he was totally honest he'd have to admit that the knowledge that his fair flesh would always be marred now with a not inconsiderable scar was depressing.

Pushing away thoughts about something he could not change, and reminding himself yet again that he should be grateful to be alive, he slid out of the car. He paused momentarily, using the cover of locking the door to set wards around the vehicle and adding a simple glamour to discourage anyone from entertaining the desire to touch the car. Possibly a bit paranoid, but in this part of town it was always better to be careful.

Crossing the cracked sidewalk he pushed open the door to the pawn shop and felt the slight tingle of active magic. It was far too weak and crudely constructed to have even a minimal effect on him, but he could feel it like smog in the air and he repressed a sneer. If Will was going to go to all the trouble to waste magic on spells to confuse and distract customers he would have thought he'd at least have invested enough money to hire a decent witch or mage to do the job. He shrugged off the annoying sensation and walked past the racks of cheap used items, each a piece of someone's desperation, towards the back counter.

He was in luck, the owner was working today. Will leaned against the counter reading a pornographic magazine and smoking a cigar. The heavy blue smoke dispersed in the air and made the already dim lights at the back of the store appear hazy. Bleidd had known the original owner, Will's father, having the occasional need to make use of the shop for one reason or another and so he knew that despite appearances Will was only in his mid-forties. He could easily have passed for a man in his sixties, despite the obvious dye job that made his hair look like an oil slick. His face was a roadmap of deep lines, his eyes so bloodshot the whites looked pink to the elf's sensitive vision. Will always wore jeans and a t-shirt sporting a motorcycle, even though he didn't ride, and was always smoking and reading the same sort of magazine whenever anyone came in. Bleidd had long suspected the man intentionally cultivated an image he thought would throw people off to give himself an advantage in any haggling, a suspicion that was somewhat confirmed when Will glanced up, realized who it was, closed the magazine and snuffed the cigar. "Oh, it's you. Selling or buying today?"

"That depends," Bleidd said levelly, refusing to flinch at the stench of cigar heavy in the air. He didn't know how the man could bear it. "On whether or not you have what I'm looking for."

"Right, same old same old then," Will said shrugging like it didn't matter to him. Of course given Bleidd's willingness to pay cash without trying to argue the price down for the information he needed, something Will could count on whenever he came in 'looking', the elf knew it mattered very much to the human.

"I'm wondering if you've acquired any merchandise recently from unusual sources that you may not have been as scrupulous about checking ID for," Bleidd said, choosing his words with care.

Will pursed his lips. "Well now that's a broad question. Always getting things coming and going from unusual sources and maybe I don't remember to check IDs the way I should all the time."

Bleidd nodded trying to walk a fine line between staying vague enough that if the Dark elves questioned Will themselves about anyone hunting them he wouldn't be able to point a finger at Bleidd, and not being so vague that even the quick witted pawn shop owner couldn't decode what he was saying. "This would be larger amounts."

"Ah," Will said snapping his fingers. "Now that you mention it I did get a weird guy, an elf and you know they don't sell in here very much, in a few weeks ago. Had a book that was pretty pricey. Might have seen something like it on a police fax a little later, but well...I'd already paid the guy."

For some reason that sounded familiar to Bleidd. Frowning he said. "Can I see the book?"

Will shrugged again but reached down for his keys. That peaked Bleidd's interest; it must be an expensive book if the normally paranoid pawn shop owner had it in one of the few locked displays. A moment later the human returned carrying a very battered copy of an elvish treatise on water magic. Not the sort of thing he expected a human pawn shop to be peddling, but there was something naggingly familiar about the book. After a moment he realized what it was – the book had been stolen from Allie's store. He felt an surge of triumph at having unexpectedly found her property when the Guard had failed both to find it and capture the thief, but that was quickly followed by an equally unexpected wave of remorse. He knew that Jessilaen and the other Guards had very quickly been distracted by more serious things, including threats to Allie's life.

Will was watching his face eagerly. And Bleidd quickly decided to use this to his advantage not only in pleasing Allie but to cover his real reason for being here. "How much are you asking, and what can you tell me about the elf who sold you this?"

"$700 firm," Will said without blinking an eye at the outrageously high amount. "And he was a strange one like I said. Twitchy for an elf. Short hair, maybe shoulder length. Don't think he was planning to stay in town for very long."

Bleidd pulled out his money and counted out seven crisp hundred dollar bills passing them into Will's hands without a word. He knew already there would be no talk of taxing the purchase. Will didn't bother to even pretend to put the money in the register, instead stuffing it directly into his pocket. "So why do you care so much?"

"It was stolen from my friend," Bleidd said, knowing in this case absolute honesty was best. Will likely already knew where the book was stolen from and when. It wouldn't hurt to let him know that Bleidd considered that particular store of personal interest; it might encourage him to immediately alert the former Outcast elf if anything else belonging to Allie ever showed up in his place.

"Must be a good friend," Will said cautiously.

That Bleidd ignored, letting his silence speak for him. Then, "Anything else from this strange elf?"

"No," Will said, as expected. It would look odd though if he didn't ask.

"You are certain?"

"Like I said I don't get many elves in here selling, and when I do it's not usually expensive stuff," Will said, then added offhandedly, "There is another elf that's been selling in here regularly lately, decent stuff. I feel like I'm financing his mistress if you know what I mean. But he's got no connection to the other one."

"How can you be sure?" Bleidd pressed, trying not to show his interest. This sounded promising, since he knew that if the Dark court had agents here they must be financing themselves somehow and they obviously couldn't go to the bank and do a regular currency exchange without raising suspicions. That was his entire reason for coming to the pawn shop to begin with. If he were them he would pawn stolen goods to get the money he needed, and so it was logical to start at the store that was most well-known for handling stolen items without questions.

"Oh, I'm sure," Will said. "The guy with the book was dark haired and like I said he was looking to rabbit. I could practically smell it on him – he was probably out of town before sundown that night, one direction or another. This other guy he's blond and like any other elf – long hair, big attitude. And he's been in a couple times, same routine each time. He's hanging around, I'd bet my cigars on it."

Bleidd nodded slightly, thinking *And there we have you my not-so-clever Dark court agent. Now to find out where you might be...* "That does sound unrelated. You understand though that I have a personal reason for wanting to find anyone who wants to steal from my friend."

"Ha," Will laughed without humor. "I'm betting this is the sort of friend you spend horizontal time with. Trying to earn some points by playing white knight and catching the bad guy?"

Oh if only I had a chance to be horizontal with her I would surely take it Bleidd thought repressing a smile *but alas so far things have not fallen out in my favor.* To Will

172

he simply said "More or less yes. So I'd like to be certain that the person is truly gone..." *hopefully spitted on the end of an Elven Guard's sword dying slowly* "...I'm sure you understand."

"The crazy things we do to get laid," Will said smirking. "I hope she – or he, whatever floats your boat, I don't judge – is worth it. But like I said I'd bet that elf was outta here as soon as he could find a way out after he sold that book. This other guy's not going anywhere, not the way he keeps coming in. The way he goes through money the girls over at The Gentleman's Club have probably built a shrine for him."

Of course Bleidd thought *Where else would a Dark court elf go in this town to kill time but the strip clubs? That was where I picked up their trail last time as well...let's see if it proves more fruitful this time.* He stepped back from the counter holding the book carefully on his bad side. It still ached slightly to use that arm and he wouldn't risk being attacked and having to take the time to drop anything to free his good hand. If all kept going well it should be almost normal within another day, but the last lingering feeling of vulnerability irritated him. "I'm sure you are right that the one who stole this book is long gone. I am glad that I found it at least. That will please my friend well enough."

Will laughed, relighting his cigar, "I hope you get thanked repeatedly until things start to chafe."

He waved slightly and walked out, thinking *Oh, if only...*

****

"Hey Jason you ready for lunch?" Allie asked her friend, looking up from the box of new books she was checking in.

"Are you kidding?" Jason asked. "Am I ever not ready to eat?"

Allie laughed and shook her head. "Good point. I really don't know how you do it, if I ate the way you do I'd explode."

He shrugged, tossing his head to get a stray lock of hair out of his eyes, "I have a fast metabolism."

Allie looked her friend over from his scuffed work boots to the fire department t-shirt she'd been teasing him earlier about wearing on his day off. At 5' 9" Jason was solid muscle and tended to give the impression of being bigger than he actually was. His eyes were so dark they looked like they matched his black hair, although Allie knew they were really dark brown. His father was Japanese and Allie suspected that Jason looked a lot like him, since he didn't look anything like the picture of his mother she'd seen. She could relate to that; she looked far more like her mother than her brown haired, green eyed father, which meant she also didn't look much like her grandmother or cousin. Jason always radiated an air of quiet confidence that gave the impression he could handle anything that came up, something that made sense given his job, but had always intrigued Allie given how high-strung Jason could actually be.

"What?" Jason asked, shifting uncomfortable and clutching the book had been holding up to his chest like a shield to ward off her scrutiny. "Why are you looking at me like that?"

"Just thinking that your fast metabolism has good results," Allie said, smirking. "I'm sure Tony appreciates that great body even if you do eat him out of house and home."

Jason blushed at her words. "You've been hanging out with elves too much, that polyamory stuff is rubbing off on you. And don't get any ideas, I'm so totally not into girls."

Allie laughed again louder, "No worries, you are probably the world's most expensive date anyway."

"Truer words were never spoken," Jason said grinning. "But like you said, I am worth it."

"Okay are you trying to talk me out of ogling you Mr. Ego or into it?"

Jason laughed with her. "Well it's hard to deny my own awesomeness."

They both started giggling then and every time they'd start to wind down they'd glance at each other and crack up all over again. Before long Allie couldn't even remember what was so funny, and she was bent over the counter wiping tears from her eyes. The laughter released the last of the subtle tension that had lingered between them since Allie had discovered the secret Jason was hiding about his heritage. She took a deep breath, staring resolutely at the countertop, and thought *Oh that was good. I needed that. We needed that. I guess maybe laughter really does cure everything.*

"Okay, okay," Jason said, his voice still thick with amusement. "Lunch. Must get lunch."

"Yes," Allie agreed, struggling to sound serious. "I don't really want the sandwiches we brought, to be honest. I was thinking maybe we could order a pizza or something?"

"Sounds fine to me," Jason said. "Didn't they feed you at that meeting this morning?"

"At the police station?"

"Unless you've been to more than one meeting today," he teased making Allie blush.

"They had bagels and coffee but I wasn't that hungry," she said. "Listening to detective Riordan discuss, in detail, the evidence from the crime scene didn't exactly help my appetite."

Jason laughed. "No I guess it wouldn't, but I bet you a slice of pizza that all the cops – human and Fairy – ate like it was nothing."

Allie rolled her eyes. "They did. Not me. I must have a much lower tolerance for gross than a real cop."

"Any progress with all of that?" Jason asked more seriously.

"Hard to say. The victim's doing well, which is good, but she couldn't tell us too much, really, that we didn't already know. I didn't get anything breakthrough worthy at the scene either, except that he probably isn't going to wait too long to try again."

"Hmmmm. That is frustrating," Jason agreed. "So no emotional trail to follow?"

"Not this time," she said, making an exasperated noise. "And no real physical evidence that tells us anything we didn't already know."

Just then the bells over the front door jingled and they both turned reflexively towards the front.

"Bleidd!" Allie said, torn between being glad to see him and worried about him being out so soon after his release form the hospital. She and Jason both hurried around the counter to meet their friend in the open space between the book shelves on the right and loose assortment of seating on the left.

Jason stopped a few feet away but Allie went up to Bleidd and gave him an enthusiastic hug. She could sense his tension and worry blended with happiness as his arm came up around her shoulders. She also felt the hard corner of what could only be a book jabbing her in the ribs. "What's that?"

Bleidd stepped back slightly, his arm sliding reluctantly off her shoulder. "I have brought you a present."

"A present?" Allie glanced back at Jason who shrugged. "You didn't need to do that."

Smiling he handed her the book. It was an old copy of Terevelien's treatise on water magic and weather working. For a second she looked at it, puzzled, and then her eyes flew up to his in shock. "How did you...? Where?"

He laughed lightly, looking pleased with himself. "I found it in a pawnshop downtown. Since the Guard hadn't had any luck getting it back for you I took it upon myself to liberate it and return it to its home."

"Bleidd," she threw her arms around him again in a tight hug, "You didn't need to do that. How much do I owe you?"

"I wanted to do it, and you owe me nothing," he said, enjoying the feeling of satisfaction that came with her gratitude.

"But, it had to have been..."

"Allie," he said, reaching up to stroke her hair, making her blush. "I was happy to find it and get it back for you. It is a gift. Don't question it."

She leaned into his hand for the barest moment and then stepped back. "Well, if you insist. Thank you so much. Oh, hey we were just about to get lunch, would you like some?"

She turned to Jason who was giving the two of them a strange look. He nodded, "Yeah, hang out for a bit and eat with us."

Bleidd hesitated but then nodded. "Alright. I can spare some time."

As they headed back towards the counter she could feel his eyes on her back, like an itch between her shoulder blades. "What is it?"

"Hmmm?" Bleidd said, distracted. "Oh, nothing. Your shields are different."

Allie felt herself beaming, reveling in the joy of having functional shields again. "By which you mean I have shields again and they are actually decent."

"Well," he said, a smile in his voice, "if you want to put it that way. It's been so many weeks since you had strong shields, I must admit I'm relieved to see them back. It's a different method than you used before, yes?"

"Yes," Allie agreed, reaching under the counter to pull out the small stack of take-out menus she kept there for the occasions when she decided to splurge and order food. She dropped the pile of menus on the counter and then set the book down next to them. "The mage who works with the police department offered to hook me up with his great-aunt for some training and I decided to take him up on it. Don't give me that look Bleidd, I'm not naive enough to jump into something like that without thinking it through."

"And the cost?" he asked, his tone as ambivalent as his feelings.

"For the same amount of time that she teaches me each day I stay and tell her stories or sing," Allie said feeling a bit self-conscious. Her voice was a low alto and she wasn't a terrible singer but this was definitely the first time anyone had asked her to sing for them. "She doesn't speak Elvish, but she likes to hear it spoken, so I go back and forth between the two languages."

"Hmmmm," he made another thoughtful noise. "She is very old, this woman?"

"Yes."

"Does she live in the great house with the iron fence around it?"

Allie looked at him, wide eyed. "You know her?"

"I did years ago, when I first came to Ashwood, but I have not seen her in many years. In truth I assumed she would have died by now," he said thoughtfully. "She was a very skilled mage when I knew her; some called her a sorceress because of her knowledge of Elven magics. She could be an ideal teacher for you."

Allie bit her lip, unaccountably disturbed that Bleidd knew Miss Amelia. Then she had the truly unsettling thought that maybe he had been the elven lover she'd spoken of, until she reminded herself that he couldn't have been. From what the old woman had said that affair had happened long before Bleidd was Outcast, and so before he'd come to Ashwood. Jason watched both of them, his eyes darting between their faces as he pretended to read the menu for the closest pizza restaurant.

Bleidd was also watching Allie's face and she felt his emotions through her new shields shifting from nostalgic to amused. "Do not be jealous Allie. We were never lovers, she and I – she was already very old when I knew her and uninterested in male attention. As far as I knew anyway."

Allie blushed furiously, but couldn't deny that she was relieved. She decided to try to make a joke of it. "Well it's reassuring to know there's at least one woman in town you haven't slept with."

Bleidd grinned widely, giving Allie a pointed look, before retorting. "More than one."

Jason snorted loudly. Allie was sure her face was probably crimson. She cleared her throat loudly. "Right, well. She taught me a way to shield that protects me fully but doesn't block me from sensing emotions."

"Ummm, isn't part of the point of shielding to block those emotions out?" Jason asked.

"You know I thought so too, but she said that's why my old shields were so erratic, because subconsciously I kept trying to read things through them and knocking my shields down myself," Allie said shrugging.

"Huh. That actually kind of makes sense," Jason said as Bleidd nodded.

"Yeah and it works really well," Allie agreed. "My shields are strong now, and I can feel the emotions but they don't hit me the way they used to. Now it's like sensing something outside myself instead of feeling it with the person."

"That is surely an asset," Bleidd said smiling at her eagerness. Through the new shields she could sense his genuine happiness for her and that brought a smile to her own lips. "It should give you an enormous advantage in dealing with others."

"Yeah," Jason agreed. "It'll turn a weakness into a strength. Hey does this mean that now you won't need to touch someone else to ground yourself when things get really overwhelming?"

Allie looked down, embarrassed. He was, of course, referring to the fact that during the investigation so far whenever she ran across the emotional trail of the killer it sent her into a sort of semi-trance state that forced her to follow the emotions back to their source. The most recent time it had happened she'd been with Jason and he'd had to forcibly restrain her to keep her from walking up to the killer's door, and then on Jess's advice via cell phone had ended up cheek to cheek with her to get her to snap out of it. It was not one of her best moments and she was keenly aware that if not for Jason she'd probably have gotten herself killed. She tried to keep her voice nonchalant when she answered. "Well, I guess there's no way to know for sure until I'm in that situation, but that's the hope. I mean in theory yes. These shields should keep any outside emotion from controlling me, but still let me sense them. I was able to visit a crime scene yesterday without a problem at least."

"Then let us all hope the reality follows the theory," Bleidd said more seriously.

She shrugged, then decided to change the subject. "So what are we getting? I'm hungry enough that anything

180

is fine by me. Anything but anchovies or mushrooms anyway."

"What do you have against mushrooms?" Jason groaned. "They're delicious."

"They're fungus." Allie shot back. Bleidd looked from one to the other with the same disbelief that Jason had been giving himself and Allie earlier, which made Allie giggle. For the second time that day she found that once she started she couldn't stop and soon Jason joined her. Bleidd's look turned from disbelief to displeasure as he tried to decide if they were laughing at him.

"You two are worse than children," he said finally.

"I thought in your opinion we were children?" Jason said between snorting laughs. Allie giggled harder.

"Your ages aren't usually indicative of your maturity, but I'm starting to wonder," Bleidd sniffed.

"So tell me, how did you get on with that nurse when we weren't around? Stay nice and passive?" Jason asked. Allie's mind immediately jumped back to the nurse's comments after finding her kissing him in the hospital bed and she lost it entirely. She ended up kneeling on the floor laughing so hard she couldn't catch her breath. Jason was barely more coherent than she was. At first Bleidd stood and glowered, annoyed at being the butt of anyone's joke, but his decades living among humans had given him a much better sense of humor than most elves. Eventually he gave in and cracked a smile.

"I don't think that one would know what to do with me if she had me," Bleidd said, trying to turn the joke around in his own favor.

Allie had recovered slightly, but that almost sent her back onto the floor. She managed to gasp out, "Oh don't underestimate her. You have to watch out for those quite ones."

Jason kept laughing but Bleidd sobered a bit, his eyes fixed on her. She sensed his longing, and the sadness that went with it and that wiped away the last of her own humor. Straightening up and clearing her throat loudly she said, "Well, okay. I have to get this book back into inventory. You guys order whatever you want."

"Allie," Bleidd said softly, reaching out and grabbing her wrist, while Jason struggled to compose himself, for once oblivious to what was going on with his roommates.

"I'm sorry," she said meaning it, even though she wasn't entirely sure what she was sorry for. There was so much at this point that she could apologize for, she decided he could pick what to apply it to. "But I really do appreciate you finding this book. Maybe it's a sign that things are finally turning around."

He opened his mouth to say something and she could almost see him change his mind. He hesitated, then said, "Yes, perhaps things are turning in our favor now with all the things that have been going on."

She slipped out of his grasp and headed back into the shelves, leaving the two men to discuss pizza toppings. As she looked for the section she kept her small collection of elven books in she turned his words over and over in her head. *What did he mean by that? Did he just mean looking for the killer? Or was he implying things with him and me?* She thought chewing her lip. *Because that hasn't changed, if anything there's even less chance now because I'm not just with Jess I've agreed to marry him.* She felt a predictable surge of panic at the thought of marriage.

Finding the spot where Terevelien's treatise went on the shelf she shoved it back between its previous shelf-mates with more force than necessary. *But if he is implying that, why? It's not like he's worn me down at all in my choice to go with human monogamy over elven polyamory. I mean sure I admitted I love him too, but he's known that. And I did kiss him, but that was just to pay back a debt. Even if I did enjoy it…*

At that thought her mind wandered off, remembering the feel of his mouth on hers, his hand holding her head, his body pressed hard and ready against hers as they lay together in the hospital bed. She leaned back against the bookshelf, trembling, fantasizing about what might have happened if the nurse hadn't come in….She only stopped when she realized how aroused she was getting and the embarrassment of knowing the subject of her fantasy was only a few dozen feet away ruined it. Knowing that he would be thrilled if he knew what she was thinking only made it worse. *Gods damn it! I feel like I did when we'd just met, before he made it clear he wasn't interested.* Back then Bleidd had been the almost obsessive focus of her sexual fantasies, as she'd lusted after him before she'd gotten to know him well enough to call it love. She covered her mouth with her hand to smother her groaning. *Damn it, damn it, damn it. I do want to sleep with him. But I can't. Even if I was willing to, Jess has made it really clear he doesn't want me with anyone else, but especially Bleidd. Gods! This is such a mess.*

Thinking of Jess made her feel a surge of guilt, but then offered the perfect distraction, as she realized she should let him know the book had been recovered. Needing to hear the sound of his voice, even if it was just in her head, and to feel like she was still a loyal girlfriend despite her traitorous thoughts of someone else she reached out carefully to his mind. *"Jess? Are you busy?"*

"Allie? No, I am not busy. Sitting in a quiet place enjoying my lunch," he replied, his words colored by his pleasure at hearing from her.

She relaxed. *"I have news. Do you remember the book that was stolen from my store?"*

"Yes," he replied. *"Brynneth and I opened that case but we have made little headway with it."*

"I appreciate your effort," she thought back, not wanting his feelings to be hurt when she told him the book

183

had been found. And by who. *"Bleidd brought it back to the store today. He said he found it in a local pawnshop. He knew it was stolen from here so he bought it himself and returned it."*

"*Did he?*" Jess asked. His emotions were not what she had expected; there was no jealousy or annoyance at the mention of Bleidd's name. Instead he seemed genuinely interested, his feelings curious. *"That was kind of him."*

She had the sudden suspicion, purely intuitive, that something strange was going on. It was unlike Jess to pass up an opportunity to make a snarky remark about the other elf. She realized, once she thought about it that he had actually been reasonably nice about Bleidd since the shooting, he'd even been fine with her kissing him. She almost questioned him about it, but then shook her head slightly deciding it was better not to poke the bear. She was certainly sick and tired of playing referee between the two of them; if they could be civil to each other that was fine by her. Friendship was probably asking for a miracle. *"Yes, it was. He was trying to help. And I am just as glad to have the book back. I wanted to let you know though in case you need to talk to him about finding it, you know for the case."*

For some strange reason this pleased Jess. She could feel his happiness through their link and it puzzled her. *"Yes my heart I will likely need to speak to him further about the details."*

"*Well,*" she thought back slowly, "*You can probably find time at home later.*"

"*I will do so,*" he thought back and then she felt him turning his thoughts back outward.

Allie pushed off the shelf and headed back out to see if the pizza had been ordered, feeling off balance. *That was weird* she thought. *If I didn't know better I'd almost think Jess was eager to talk to Bleidd. But unless I just woke up in the Twilight Zone that's impossible. If I didn't know better I might worry that Jess was having the same*

184

thoughts about Bleidd that I am. Certainly not impossible, given the elves lack of sexual preference, but since they kind of hate each other...or at least strongly dislike each other...oh! Unless he's picking up on my feelings and I'm influencing him... That was a strange thought too. A tiny part of her tried to fantasize about the three of them together but she couldn't quite get her very sexually inexperienced mind to go there. Instead she ended up imagining her boyfriend leaving her for her crush. That made her smile as she was walking out from the book shelves. *And somehow I think that would serve me right if this really is the result of me influencing Jess somehow...*

"Okay guys, what'd you order?" she struggled to keep her tone light as she watched her two friends leaning against the counter waiting for her. *And that's all Bleidd and I will ever be* she told herself firmly. *Friends.*

****

He walked down the street with his hood pulled low, surreptitiously glancing around as he walked. The sun was high and he felt a thrill at being out in town in broad daylight. Everyone wanted him to hide. Everyone wanted him to wait around and do nothing until they needed him again. Screw everyone. He was sick of it all.

The more he thought about the last girl the less satisfied he was with her. The only silver lining there was the paper said her dad was a cop and that idea made him really happy. He hoped that her dad had been told about what he'd done to her in detail. His own dad would've told him it was his own fault, if he were any kind of victim, just like he'd always said it was Jerry's fault when his dad beat him. But he liked to imagine that last girl's cop-dad being all broken up and crying over his poor baby girl. Served the

185

bastard right for breeding with something not-human. That train of thought though just brought him back to his frustration that he hadn't killed her. It would've been so much better to be able to imagine her dad crying over her dead maimed body…

He shook himself slightly, pushing the thoughts away. He needed to stay sharp and find the next one. He *needed* another girl, and he needed this one to be perfect. He'd snuck out as soon as he could, as soon as Ken left for work, and he'd been wandering the street aimlessly since then. He'd seen a couple potential girls but they weren't quite right. He wanted perfect this time and wasn't going to settle.

Finally he saw her, younger than the others, maybe thirteen or fourteen. Young enough not to fight back or know any magic. Her hair was red, just like his favorite girl that the Elven Guard had taken away. She sparkled with that glow of other-ness that drew and repulsed him. He shifted course to follow her, starting to get excited as he thought of how perfect she'd be.

She was walking with an older woman; after a moment of careful eavesdropping on their conversation he decided it was her mother. His lip curled in a sneer as he thought about the human woman betraying her entire species by screwing some Fairy thing. She was worse than they were because they had no choice about their nature but she chose to spread her legs for something Fey. It made him furious to think of all the hard work he and the group were doing to save the human world when people like her were throwing it away. He gripped the hilt of the knife tightly and waited for his chance. He'd show that blood-traitor what happened to people who betrayed the human race. And then he'd enjoy her daughter, and it would be perfect….

"Is there any pizza left?" Allie asked, drinking the last dregs of tea from her cup.

"Sorry," Jason said looking sheepish. "I just ate the last piece."

"It's okay, I've probably had enough anyway," she said, knowing it was true. It had been really good pizza though and she would have forced another piece down if there had been one, full or not. Allie was leaning against the sales floor side of the sales counter; Jason sat on the stool behind the counter. Sitting in the closest chair in the seating area Bleidd sighed and Allie sensed his contentment. It made her happy, and for a moment she simply relaxed at the general friendly atmosphere.

In the next instant though she felt goose bumps raising on her arms and her head swung to the right as she tried to sort out what was going on. She could feel something, something off, but understanding emotions coming through her new shields was a bit of a learning process.

Seeing her frown and shiver Bleidd sat up straighter. "Allie what is it?"

"I don't know," she said, perturbed. "I feel something weird. I'm not sure what it is. Strong emotions, really close I think. I've never felt anything like this…"

She took a few slow steps forward, and Jason ran around the counter and grabbed her. "Hey!"

He looked apologetic. "Sorry Allie but I don't want you zoning out and walking into traffic."

"Thanks," she said, hoping she didn't sound too sarcastic. "But I'm fine. The new shields make a big difference. I think I – ummm, we – need to see what's going on."

The two men exchanged an uneasy glance. Bleidd shook his head, reaching up to rub his chest absentmindedly. "If there's anything bad happening we should alert the police."

"Right," Allie said, as the emotions she was sensing sharpened into what she was almost certain was pain. "What am I supposed to tell them? I have a vague sensation with my wacky empathy that someone somewhere might be in trouble?"

His lips flattened into a disapproving line. Jason let her go though and reluctantly agreed. "We can at least go see if it is anything. Then call the police."

Bleidd closed his eyes for a moment, as if gathering his strength, making Allie worry that he was still in pain. Then he stood up. "Alright let us go."

"Bleidd maybe you should stay here…"

He quelled her with a look. "You two clearly need adult supervision."

"Well, alright," she said, still worried for him but unable to ignore what she was sensing. She grabbed her keys and then they all headed for the door.

Out on the sidewalk, with the store locked behind her, Allie took a moment to get re-oriented. As soon as she found the emotions again she started moving towards them, walking quickly down the sidewalk away from downtown. At the end of the block she turned towards the residential area. There was a section of empty lots slowly being overtaken by trees and brush between the downtown commercial district and the lower income residential area. Allie slowed, her sneakers scuffing on the cracked concrete; the two men slowed with her. Their tension was distracting her, making it hard to focus on the thread of disturbed feelings. She hesitated, passively waiting for the emotions to come to her more strongly because she had no idea what else to do. After a moment she felt them again,

188

more to her right, but different now. She moved off the sidewalk, into one of the empty lots.

"Allie that's far enough," Bleidd said stiffly.

"But Bleidd, what if someone's hurt?"

"What if we're walking into an ambush?" he shot back, his eyes scanning the densely packed trees and brush.

"What? Who would…" she started, but her protest was interrupted as a man staggered out of the bushes a dozen feet away.

The man stopped in obvious surprise at seeing anyone on this quiet side road. He stared at them, his hands covered in blood. A bloody knife was held in one hand, almost as if he'd forgotten he was holding it.

"Holy shit," Jason swore, his voice low. Next to her she heard Bleidd swear in Elvish, the musical tones of the language softening the strength of the words he used. Allie's eyes met those of Jeremiah Standish for the second time in their lives, and she saw recognition spark in his. The pulse of rage-joy-excitement that always radiated from him reached her at this close range, but it was bearable through her shields. As he stared at her his feelings shifted more solidly into rage and Allie stepped back instinctively.

The knife shifted in his bloody hand, now gripped tightly and ready for use. Allie felt a surge of panic as she realized that this close she might not be able to outrun him, and if she turned she'd be giving him her back which even she knew was a bad idea.

"You fucking bitch!" he snarled, "You ruin everything. Everything! This is a grand plan and the group needs me to complete it. To fix the worlds! I can't let you stop me!"

His voice rose on each word until he was shrieking, spit flying from his mouth. And then he ran at her, crossing the distance between them in leaps. She froze, seeing only the bloody knife coming at her. Bleidd's arms were around her even as Standish charged, pulling her back and trying to move her behind him – a futile effort since it would only mean he would be killed first.

The sound of the gun firing next to her was shockingly loud. Allie screamed and covered her ears, dropping to her knees and dragging Bleidd with her. Standish fell, his own momentum carrying him forward so that he landed on his face a few feet from where Allie knelt, having already crossed most of the distance between them. Everything happened in the space of a few seconds.

Allie huddled in Bleidd's arms staring at the body on the ground. She knew he was dead, if only because the pulse of his twisted emotions was gone. There was nothing but silence now. From Bleidd she felt a mix of fear and satisfaction. From Jason…

She turned her head slowly towards Jason who had been standing a little bit behind her and Bleidd, closer to the sidewalk. He still held the gun up, gripped in both hands, aimed at the body as if he were ready to shoot again if Standish so much as twitched. Allie knew of course that Jason carried the gun almost all the time. He had a permit to carry concealed and he wore it in a waist holster clipped to his belt in the back most of the time. She was so used it being there that she didn't even think about it most of the time. But knowing he had it and knowing he'd just used it were two different things.

Bleidd hugged her closer for a moment and then released her, getting to his feet with some effort. He walked stiffly over to Standish's body and checked it, glancing back at Jason and shaking his head slightly. Then he looked in the direction the bloody killer had come from. He turned back to the other two, his face grim. "Stay here."

He moved into the woods, looking Allie assumed for the source of the blood on the knife.

"*Jess,*" she thought miserably, not knowing what else to do, but sure he was going to be furious about the situation.

"What is it my heart? You sound upset," he thought back, his own mental voice distracted. She was interrupting something, she knew it. For an instant she had the completely irrational urge to tell him to forget about it, but her eyes drifted back to the body on the ground, blood pooling around his head in a way that made her swallow hard.

"Jess," she thought again, *"You need to get out to the side street by my store, ummm, Crestmore Ave. A lot, empty lot there. I was…I had sensed some strange emotions I wasn't sure what was going on but I thought someone might be in trouble so we – Jason, Bleidd and I – were trying to see what was going on."*

"Allie," he cut in his voice reproachful. *"That is not wise. You could walk into any kind of danger blindly that way."*

"Yeah, well," she thought back, wincing. *"That's pretty much what happened actually."*

His voice and emotions changed immediately from worried and distracted to afraid. *"Are you hurt? Are the others injured? What has happened?"*

"Umm, well…we… were walking following the emotions I was sensing…" she began, aware that she was stalling, but not wanting to tell him how much trouble she'd gotten into.

"For the love of the Gods Aliaine just tell me!" he thought back.

"We found Standish, covered in blood in a wooded lot about two blocks from my store. He charged at us with a knife and Jason shot him," Allie blurted out.

She had to stuff her fist in her mouth to stop the nervous laughter that wanted to spill out as she felt his utter shock at her words. She would not let herself sit there and laugh next to Standish's still warm corpse. She felt all the stress and tension suddenly catching up to her, remembering the knife coming at her. Then she started to

191

cry. Jason was there, on one knee, his hand on her shoulder. "It's okay Allie."

"It's not okay, I almost got us all killed," she mumbled through her tears.

"No you didn't. A gun is always going to win over a knife," Jason replied, his feelings both sad and grim.

"Allie? You are not hurt?" Jess asked again.

"No I'm not hurt. Neither are Bleidd or Jason. But Standish is dead. Bleidd went to see if...if he could find the victim," she thought, knowing that there had to be a victim back there. *Oh my Gods* she thought to herself, *that's what I was feeling before. I was sensing him assaulting and killing someone.* It was too much for her and she staggered up and away from the scene, managing to reach the pavement before she threw up.

****

Jess pulled the Guard vehicle up to the curb near where he could see Allie sitting on the ground and Jason standing. The second car pulled up behind him. The entire squad was with him, as well as the Guard captain and he had no doubt that the human police would not be far behind. Getting out of the car his nose wrinkled at the smell of vomit and blood that filled the air.

"Allie," he thought to his lover, *"I am here but I must see the body first."*

"Go," she thought back, sounding exhausted. He knew that she had been under a lot of strain in the past week, and that the emotional trauma was having an effect. She was certainly holding up better than many had expected her to, given her lack of training and experience, but he worried about how far and hard she pushed herself.

He walked over to the man's body lying on the grass. Clad in a dark grey hooded sweatshirt and jeans, the

192

clothing was non-descript enough that he had probably
been blending in easily. Jess crouched down, aware of the
other elves standing around him observing, and lifted the
man's head. The cause of death was obvious: a single
gunshot through the right temple. Knowing the police
would not like them moving anything before the detectives
arrived he hesitated, but then shrugged it off. It wasn't as if
there was any question about who had killed him or that it
was self-defense. He rolled the body over carefully and was
surprised to find the killer's own knife embedded in the
body's chest, the man's hand still clenched tightly around
the hilt.

"He must have fallen on the blade after being shot,"
Zarethyn mused.

"Better then he deserved," Mariniessa said quietly.
Several others nodded. As they stood around the body there
a slight sound from the wooded area and they all reached
reflexively for their swords. Jess relaxed as he saw Bleidd
walking towards them.

"You found the body of his victim?" he asked the
former Outcast in Elvish.

"Bodies," Bleidd corrected. "Two of them. A
human woman, probably in her early forty's and a girl,
mixed ancestry, very young."

"How young?" Zarethyn asked.

Bleidd inclined his head in a shrug. "I cannot be
certain, but she looks no more than fourteen."

The Guard captain nodded, his expression giving
away some of his anger. "If you would show Mariniessa
and Brynneth?"

Bleidd hesitated, his eyes going to Allie, then
nodded. "Of course. Follow me."

The three disappeared back into the brush. Jess felt
an unexpected sympathy for the other elf since he would
also rather be comforting Allie than focusing on work. It
was an odd sensation but he ignored it to focus on the job at

hand. "Natarien check the perimeter, be certain we are missing nothing essential."

The young Guard nodded slightly before jogging off. Jess turned to his brother. "Another killer dead."

"Yes, and again Allie is at the heart of it," Zarethyn replied.

"You think this is significant?"

"I believe that synchronicity moves strongly in all of this and that Allie is tied somehow to the underlying pattern," he said thoughtfully.

"Her grandmother was the undoing of the original coven," Jess pointed out.

"Yes," the captain agreed. "But she also participated in several of the ritual murders."

"What is the significance of that?"

"I'm not sure," Zarethyn admitted. They both paused at the sound of police sirens in the distance. "Go and question Allie and her friend. Despite the new emphasis on cooperation I do not trust that the police will not arrive and try to take over entirely."

Jess nodded and headed over towards where Allie was still sitting on the ground, looking pale and stunned. Her friend Jason was obviously nervous, shifting from foot to foot and watching the Guard the way an injured baby bird watches a snake. *Odd*, Jess thought, *Surely Jason knows we all realize it was self-defense. I would hardly be angry with him for saving Allie's life!*

He approached them both slowly, not wanting to agitate Jason, even as the sound of sirens grew louder. Allie looked up when he was a few feet away and then launched herself at him, wrapping her arms around him and pressing her face into his chest. He stroked her hair and murmured comforting words until she relaxed a little bit, but her first words caught him off guard. "You aren't angry at me?"

"Angry?" he repeated, baffled. "Wherefore?"

"Huh?" Jason said, then bit his lip and looked like he wished he hadn't said anything.

Allie sniffled slightly and Jess realized she'd been crying recently. "Wherefore means why. And because I followed some random emotions into a deserted area without calling the police or you first and confronted a killer and almost got myself and my friends killed…"

"Allie!" he interrupted. "You took a risk yes, but no harm was done and thanks to your action – not alone but accompanied by two people more than capable of defending you - the killer had been stopped."

She took a deep breath. "Yeah, I guess you're right I just feel like I keep walking into these things."

"Well you do have a unique talent for finding dangerous things no one else can find," he agreed. "But good always comes from it in the end."

She swallowed hard and nodded slightly, pulling away from him. "I suppose we need to give our official statements?"

"Yes, please," he said, listening carefully and writing everything they both said down as they relayed in fits and starts the series of events that had led to Standish's body cooling on the ground. He was particularly disturbed by the last words they both told him the killer had said, and he had the sinking feeling that Standish's death would not be the end of anything.

****

The meeting was breaking up, people clustering together to chat. An air of desperation hung over the group, despite the leader's best efforts to inspire them after Jerry's loss. The woman knew deep down that it was too many setbacks in too short a time.

She kept thinking about Jerry; she found it impossible to reconcile the friendly smiling man who had always been socializing with the other group members with the terrible things she knew he had done. It just didn't seem possible that someone who had been so nice here could have been so brutal out there...

The group's leader appeared at her side, reaching out and grabbing the woman's arm. "You promised you'd stop her."

The woman flinched, trying not to look guilty. The truth was she'd been avoiding the entire situation, unsure what to do. "I know...I will. We have time..."

"We won't have time if she keeps pointing the police right at us." the leader hissed, her eyes shooting around the room to be sure no one was noticing the tense exchange.

"She wouldn't have helped catch him if he'd stopped sneaking out and..."

The leader waved a hand dismissively, her manicured nails glinting in the electric lights. "That's not the point."

"But..."

"It's not the point," the leader said, her normally charismatic voice brisk and dismissive. "The police had nothing, but she found him. You're supposed to be dealing with her, keeping her away from what we're doing. Not only is she not staying away she's even more involved than ever."

The woman frowned, frustrated. "I'm working on it, but it's not that easy. I can't be too obvious or she'll get suspicious."

"I'm starting to think you don't really care about keeping her safe."

"Of course I do! I've told you how much that matters to me..." the woman's voice started to rise, and then glancing around she remembered where she was and that she needed to stay quiet. "You know how important it is. But it won't do any of us any good if I get caught now will it?"

The leader nodded, looking thoughtful. "Alright, well if you haven't been able to think of anything..."

"I just need more time!"

"We don't have time, the next ritual is almost here, and now we have to find another replacement. Don't worry though, I have an idea," the leader said, pulling a tiny plastic bag out of her jacket pocket. The bag was the sort that drugs were often sold in, but what it contained was like no drug the woman had ever seen: a dull grey metallic powder. She blanched and looked up at the leader, shaking her head slightly. The leader's voice was reassuring, persuasive. "Don't worry. You just need a tiny little bit. Barely any at all."

The woman reached out and took the tiny bag slipping it quickly into her own pocket. She nodded, biting her lip. "Okay. Okay. We'll do it your way."

"You'll see," the leader said, relaxed and smiling. "This is a good plan. It'll work perfectly. Just a tiny bit will be enough to knock her out of things and no one will know it's not just the flu. By the time she's on her feet again the next ritual will be over, and then we'll have an entire month to get everything straightened out."

Chapter 7 - Saturday

Allie clutched the edge of the toilet, gasping, consumed by the sensation of lava filling her stomach and intestines. She gagged again but there was nothing left anywhere in her system to come up. The pain was so intense that she could barely think around it; it was becoming her entire world.

At some point she realized Liz was there with her, stroking her hair out of her face. She could hear her cousin speaking but the words were like water, flowing over and around her. "I'm so sorry Allie. It wasn't supposed to be like this. It wasn't supposed to be like this at all. It was just supposed to make you a little bit sick…"

Finally the words actually registered and Allie turned her head slightly towards her cousin's voice, unable to get her eyes to focus. When she spoke her voice was a barely recognizable croak. "You…you did…this?"

Liz's hand stroked her back. "It wasn't supposed to be like this. I only used a little bit of iron. It was just supposed to make you a little bit sick. Just enough to stop helping them"

Allie felt her entire world collapsing. The pain came in waves now, never getting better but spiking into a blinding agony that drove away rational thought. She managed to force out one word. "Why?"

As if from very far away she heard Liz say, "You were helping them too much and they were getting too close. It was ruining everything. I was supposed to keep you distracted but nothing was working."

Allie felt everything shifting and then the floor was cold against her cheek. Somewhere above her Liz was crying. She could hear Jess's voice too, in her mind, but she couldn't follow what he was saying or form a reply. She didn't care anymore about anything but the pain. Then

Liz's voice was there again, in her ear, "Hang on Allie, I'm calling an ambulance."

Her body convulsed, eyes rolling up, and the entire world became the sensation of molten knives tearing her apart from the inside out.

****

Brynneth took a deep breath, stepping back slightly from the hospital bed. Sweat dripped from his face and he grabbed the bedframe, clearly exhausted. Zarethyn looked alarmed; Jess didn't look away from Allie's still form on the bed. Her face was ashen and she lay so completely still it was hard to be sure she was breathing.

"I am sorry Jess," Brynneth said, meaning it.

"You can do nothing?" Jess asked, already knowing the answer.

"I tried everything that could possibly be done. If she were fully elven she would be dead already, but her human heritage is slowing the iron poisoning somewhat. But...there is nothing that I can do to reverse the damage." Brynneth said.

"How long?" Zarethyn asked, his voice flat, his eyes on his brother.

"Hours," Brynneth said. "Perhaps less."

The Guard captain nodded, his expression grim. He inclined his head slightly towards the door and he and the elven healer quietly stepped out, leaving Jessilaen alone with Allie.

He sat by the edge of the bed clutching her hand, watching for every slight sign that she still breathed. He reached up, smoothing her hair back from her face, her skin cold beneath his fingers. *"I cannot lose you Allie,"* he thought to her silent mind. *"There must be a way to heal this. I know you can use emotions to heal yourself. Use mine, now. Let my feelings give you strength..."*

She remained still and silent and he felt a furious desperation growing in his chest. He could not let her die. But he was no mage or healer, nor did he have any particular gift. Again and again his mind returned to the idea of her speeding her own healing when she drew on his emotions, yet he also knew that she took the most energy from the more positive feelings, especially love and happiness. Certainly what he was feeling now was not anything she would normally allow herself to pull from…and yet he had also seen that when she was exhausted she would pull from him reflexively, even when she didn't want to do so consciously. He was certain that her gift could help her now, at least pull her back enough to save her from death, and just being close to her she should draw on him even if she were unconscious.

He bit his lip, certain that there was a way to save her if only he could figure it out. Skin to skin contact made it easier for her to connect to him. He clutched her limp hand in his own, but that was not enough. He tried to remember every time he had been aware of her using his emotions to strengthen herself, looking for any hint of a way to trigger the reflex in her. *When we are close and touching* he thought rubbing his eyes with his free hand. *When we lie together.....*That thought stopped him. *When we lie together she connects to me completely* he thought more slowly. *The combination of the close contact and the heightened emotions…that might do it. She connects without thinking about it then, as if it were a reflex…as if were second nature.* He frowned as the full realization struck. *Or as if it were her nature, to use the emotions of desire and arousal.* Jess had not served over two hundred years in the Elven Guard not to understand what that meant. He looked at her still form in the bed and shook his head slightly. It didn't matter what her true nature was, if he could use that nature to save her now.

It was a mad idea and for a moment he hesitated. It might not work at all and if anyone walked in….but what choice did he have? She would die if he did nothing and crazy or not this was the only thing he could think of that might help. Nothing else had any effect. But if he tried this, if he could get her to connect to him on that deep level and take his emotional energy reflexively…He nodded, suddenly determined. He would try, and if it failed then he was certain that he would die with her or soon after, and he would at least know that he had tried everything to save her.

Physically joined with her he could feel her there with him, her mind somewhere dark reaching out to him. He reached back with everything he had, giving her all of his emotions. When he could feel the emotions subsiding again he pulled away from her, his eyes seeking any sign that what he had done had accomplished anything. He had given her everything, had felt her through their connection drinking in each emotion until he could not feel more than he already was. His heart had been full to a point that was nearly unbearable and he let her feel all of it with him.

He felt a surge of excitement to see that although she was still pale her face was no longer grey-tinged and her eyes moved restlessly beneath the lids. Sliding from the bed he grasped her hand again and his heart lifted to feel her fingers tightening on his.

And yet…it wasn't enough. She was certainly better, but even he could see that she was still dying. His desperation surged anew and he gritted his teeth in frustration. If she could connect on the same level with someone else, perhaps drawing on another person's emotions as well would be enough, but he knew that neither Brynneth nor his brother were close enough for Allie to willingly draw from, even on an unconscious level.

201

Her friend Jason might work, and Jess was sure he would be willing, but he was not entirely certain that the necessary connection could be established between them, not if he were right about her nature and sexual attraction was a necessary factor.

And that left only one possible person. Jessilaen hesitated for a moment feeling a mix of jealousy and denial. He frantically cast around for any other option, but could only come back over and over to the same conclusion. He looked at her lying on the bed, her form appearing somehow smaller as if some vital substance had been lost. What he had done was enough to revive her slightly and her hands opened and closed on the sheet that covered her. She looked like she was in pain now, no longer deeply unconscious but aware again of what her body was going through. Seeing that decided him. He leaned forward and whispered against her ear, hoping she would understand him, "Be strong my love, I will not let you die."

Now that he was resolved to do it he stood quickly and crossed the room in a few long strides, throwing the door open. The other elves in his squad had been in the middle of a discussion; they fell silent as he burst out into the hallway. He ignored them, his eyes fixing on Bleidd who was standing apart from the others, a look of naked anguish plain on his face. He was by the other elf's side before anyone realized where he was going and he could see the sudden alarm on his brother's face, as he grabbed Bleidd by his good shoulder and forced him towards the hospital room. The other elf went with him as much from the shock of the unexpected situation as any willingness.

He pushed the former Outcast into the room ahead of him before the heavy door had swung shut from his exit. Turning to his companions he locked eyes with his brother, "No one enters."

Zarethyn opened his mouth to say something – whether it would be agreement or not Jess was unsure – but he was already turning away and he never heard it. He slid back into the hospital room and as the door shut he pushed a chair in front of it. A flimsy barrier it was and nothing that would hold back any significant attempt to force entry, but it should give him enough warning if anyone were trying to come in.

Allie lay as he had left her, her head now rolling side to side from the pain, her eyes fluttering. Bleidd had moved to stand next to her, clutching one of her hands much as Jess himself had earlier. The dark-haired elf wept without shame, but when he spoke his voice was choked with rage not sorrow, "Whoever did this, I will find them, and I will kill them."

"I believe we can save her," Jess said, his own voice thick.

"It cannot be done," Bleidd whispered. "Your own healer said she has very little time left."

"She can help herself with her gift."

"What do you mean?" Bleidd asked sharply, turning to lock eyes with Jess.

"I had suspected it before, but I was certain after she was shot." Jess said carefully. "Brynneth healed the injury as best he could but you know full well yourself how slow and painful it is to recover from an iron wound. It should have been so for her yet within a few days she was fully healed."

"How?" Bleidd asked, leaning forward. Jess knew then that he would help, would do anything, and he felt his own hope surging.

"She uses the emotions of others, of people she is connected to - especially love and sex - to empower herself and I believe to help speed her own healing," Jess said, still choosing his words carefully.

Bleidd frowned slightly, "Do you understand what that means?"

"Yes," Jess said simply. "I also know that it means you can save her now if you let her connect fully to you and draw on your emotions."

"Why do you not do this if it will help her?" Bleidd asked his voice low.

"I have already given her everything I have to give," Jess replied, watching the other elf's eyes go wide at the implications. "It has helped, but not enough."

"Why me?"

"Because you love her," Jess said. "And she loves you. She will connect to you even if she isn't fully conscious and take what she needs."

"What must I do?"

Jess struggled to keep his face expressionless. "Lie with her and let yourself feel everything, every emotion fully. Let her connect to you."

"Lie with her?" Bleidd's was incredulous. "Are you mad? Here? Like this? Even if I was willing to I don't know that I could."

"Yes," Jess said. "I am not absolutely certain but I believe it's necessary to make the connection as strong as possible. And if she accepts you, your emotions, then she will help you. She will amplify what you feel, any desire you have, until everything else falls away."

"And that's what you just..." Bleidd trailed off. "You have lost your mind."

"You told me once that you would do anything to protect her life. Will you stand there now and let her die?" Jess challenged him directly and saw a flare of the same determination in the other elf's eyes that he himself felt. And he knew that he would do what needed to be done.

He just hoped it was enough.

Allie floated in darkness. Brynneth had been there with her in the black and she knew he had used as his skill to try to help her. His healing magic had looked like green fire against the darkness but soon enough it had faded and she was left alone. It was quiet here and peaceful. She did not mind so much being in the dark. There was no pain here, no fear, only an endless dark.

Then Jess had come, his emotions filling her, drawing her back to herself, back towards life. His feelings were like fire too in the darkness but they burned red and gold, warm and full of love and need. The darkness was driven back before the sheer force of his emotions and she could feel herself feeding on his feelings, drinking the energy in, as reflexively as a flower seeking light. For a short time she felt nothing but what he felt and she struggled to live, to emerge from the shadows, as his will to survive consumed her as well.

She surfaced from the dark place into a grey limbo of pain. She could not wake fully but she also could not return to the peace of the place she had been before. Her body burned from the inside and she wished for Jess's beautiful red-gold fire to come and chase it away again.

And then there was someone in the grey place, but it wasn't Jess. Allie pushed this person away at first, afraid and hurting, but then she thought – or imagined – she could hear Bleidd's voice somewhere far away. She reached for the sound frantically, searching for him with her empathy, and then he was there with her, his own fire illuminating the shadows with a light that was also red and gold but somehow not the same as Jess's. For a little while she pondered that, the difference that the same colors could have. She could feel him reaching out to her, holding his feelings out like an offering, and she knew that it was her choice, to accept what he was offering or to reject him. If she rejected him that beautiful fire would be extinguished and the desire that she felt from him, tentative and uncertain as it was now, would be destroyed. She also knew, on an instinctual level that she could choose to take what he was giving her, to accept the emotions and amplify them, make them into the same glorious conflagration that Jess had felt. She tried to take them, suddenly frantic to be filled again with the desire to live that Jess had given her. But she could not pull enough in from him. She could feel that it was there, but she couldn't quite get to all of it. And she wanted all of it, in the same way she had gotten it from Jess.

Her own physical pain and fear overwhelmed her, but it also reminded her of something, of another time when she had been desperate to reach someone, when her survival had depended on it. Without thinking she reached out, back to that place, her mind blurring the boundaries between that situation and this one, between Jess and Bleidd. The energetic battery still hung in the air in the rough shed where she had been held prisoner, where she had created it, shimmering. She tapped back into it, feeling the power filling her. It hurt terribly, like straining a torn muscle, to direct the magic, and the added pain goaded her to reach out for Bleidd, overwhelmed by her need for him. The power arched between them, colored by the red and gold of his love and a deep dark crimson which Allie slowly realized was her own energy, sluggish and tainted by the poison that was killing her.

The realization gave her the strength to push through the pain and complete the connection with him. She felt herself breaching an unseen barrier, surging through into his essence, which flowed back through the connection and filled her. His emotions were like an ocean, immense and surging, and she was overwhelmed with a greedy desire to take it all in. She was in his mind then and his heart, and somehow Jess was there too like an echo, and both of their feelings opened to her. She absorbed Bleidd's emotions as fast as they flooded into her, her own reactions and feelings amplifying his, the energy revitalizing her. She nurtured that little flame into something stronger and more powerful, enjoying the way it filled her, encouraging it until it reached its full potential, the red and gold flames mesmerizing in their beauty. Finally, after what seemed like an endless time in that grey place, reveling in his feelings, she snapped back into full consciousness, back into the waking world entirely.

"Mine," she hissed, her voice strange in her own ears, that greedy feeling still resonating in her. And then she woke fully out of the odd trance, realizing that his face was inches from her own and her hand was clutching his hair so hard it had to be hurting him. She forced her fingers to unclench with an effort. Then the disorientation hit in full force as she tried and failed to understand where she was and what was going on.

Bleidd was looking at her with an indescribable expression, fear and joy chasing themselves around his heart. She could feel what he felt too clearly and somewhere in her mind alarm bells went off, even unshielded he should not be coming through that strongly, and she could feel her new shields still in place. An instant later she realized that she was in a strange bed, and Bleidd was there with her, his body still pressed against hers, leaving her no doubt even through her confusion that they had had sex. A shadow of memory tried to surface, of his feelings filling her, of red and gold fire, and she remembered feeling that she needed to make a choice, between rejecting his desire or accepting it. She had accepted and magnified what he'd felt, fanned it into something much stronger, and she had no doubt that what had happened in her mind, with the fire, was directly related to what had happened physically. And despite not knowing why this had happened she did not regret her choice....the hand that had been clutching his hair stroked his head gently, as she tried to sort out what could possibly have happened to result in this scenario. Jess was standing off to one side, his face also unreadable, his emotions a tangle of worry, love, and fear. Her body still hurt in a terrible way, but the pain was not so all consuming. She took a deep breath, and it seemed to her that both men released theirs.

"*What is going on?*" she thought, unable to frame a more coherent question.

To her utter shock it was Bleidd's voice that answered in her mind. "*Forgive me Allie...*"

"*Wait- what?*" she thought cutting him off. She stared at her friend in complete shock.

"*What did you do my heart?*" Jess thought to her – no Allie realized as Bleidd's head swiveled around to look at the other elf, his expression stunned – to them.

"*I...I don't know. I don't...I was...there was darkness and shadows and I felt him with me, his feelings, but I couldn't get enough of them, I mean I couldn't connect enough,*" Allie thought at both of them, still not understanding what was going on. "*And I was reaching and I needed more...*"

"*It's alright, it will be alright,*" Jess thought back soothingly, seeing her agitation.

"*Yes,*" Bleidd added tentatively, his shock still plain. "*Yes, it will be okay Allie. What matters is that you will live.*"

"*I'll...*" Allie thought, trying to grasp the thought. She forced herself to speak aloud then, unable to handle the implications of the three way mental conversation. "I'll live? Was I...I was dying?"

The two elves exchanged an indecipherable look, and she had the oddest feeling that they were now speaking to each other silently. Bleidd tried to pull away from her

208

but she grabbed his neck, holding him where he was. She might not know what had happened, exactly, or why but she did know that she was freezing and he was very warm, so as far as she was concerned he could stay where he was for a minute. Certainly Jess seemed to be okay with it, as strange as that was. *It figures,* Allie thought repressing a frown *I seem to have finally managed to get over one small aspect of this monogamy obsession I have and I don't remember anything about it.*

"Yes my love," Jess said gently, stepping over to the bed and reaching out to stroke her face. She tried not to let herself think about how weird that seemed, considering Bleidd was still in the bed with her, because she knew for the elves who had no concept of committed relationships outside of contracted marriages this situation really wasn't that strange. Her human upbringing though was pitching fits in the back of her mind. The worry on Jess's face distracted her. "You were dying. You were poisoned with iron and not even Brynneth could save you. But I knew that you can help speed your own healing by drawing energy from the emotions of people you are closely connected to. I did what I could for you but it wasn't enough so I got Bleidd to help as well."

And this whole situation just got that much weirder Allie thought trying to process the idea of Jess sleeping with her first while she was unconscious and then talking Bleidd into doing the same thing. *Not that I mind Jess doing whatever he had to if it saved my life. And Bleidd...its not like I haven't fantasized about sleeping with him or wanted to, it was only feeling like I'd be betraying Jess that kept holding me back. Being conscious would have been better, but it was his energy that pulled me back.* She remembered both of them finding her in the darkness, giving her the will to live she needed, the energy to pull herself back.

"Allie," Bleidd said, using her momentary distraction to extricate himself from her. "What happened? You were fine when we left this morning."

Jess added, "It must have been something you ate or drank. Try to think of what might have caused this."

"I don't know…" Allie said slowly trying to sort through memories muddled by agonizing pain. And then, far worse than the physical pain, the flash of memory came. She closed her eyes as if she could shut the realization out that way, but she could hear Liz's voice playing in her head *'I'm sorry'*.

Bleidd tried to step away from the hospital bed, afraid he was the cause of her distress, but Jess held him in place. "Allie what is it?"

She shook her head hard. In her mind she was reliving that morning. Walking Jess to the door, because he had to leave early to get to the Outpost. Bleidd was already gone, as was Jason. Shawn was finally back from his visit to his mother, but he was still sleeping. She walked into the kitchen and found Liz making breakfast. Tension hung heavy between them making Allie wince. She started to walk over to get coffee and Liz was handing her a mug. "Here Allie I fixed it for you. I know how you like your coffee in the morning, lots of milk." Liz's emotions were all over the place, hopeful and nervous and worried but Allie had just thought it was because they'd been fighting so much lately. About her helping the Guard and about Jess living there. She'd taken the coffee and drank it. All of it. Smiling and thanking her cousin…

"Oh Gods," she moaned out loud, covering her face with her hands.

"I should go," Bleidd said, and she felt her heart spasm in her chest.

"No!" she sobbed, the tears spilling over. And then despite her own aversion to dealing with what she'd done she reached out to both of them, because she knew they loved her and they had gone to extraordinary lengths to save her. *"Please, don't go. Stay. Both of you. I need...I need you here. Don't leave me. I can't...I can't believe this..."*

"Allie what is it?" Jess asked again, his fear washing over her. She didn't care, his feelings were better to deal with than her own. She didn't know it was possible for a heart to actually break until that moment. Liz was more than just her cousin, she was like a sister to her. She had protected Allie from the moment Allie had moved in with their grandmother. The two didn't always agree, and Allie knew that Liz didn't particularly like elves, but she had always been able to count on the anchor of her relationship with her cousin. It was one of the constants in her life, like the store and the house.

"Allie," Bleidd thought tentatively, his mental voice unsure. *"Please tell us what is wrong. If you are angry with me..."*

"Angry with you? What? Why?" she thought back, miserable and confused. *"No of course I'm not angry at you. You just saved my life. Both of you did. You should be angry at me for...this."*

"Oh Allie," he thought back, his feelings too mixed even for her to read.

"Then what is it? What happened to put you here?" Jess pressed.

She pressed the palms of her hands hard into her eyes, wanting to shut the whole world out. She couldn't believe that her cousin had done this to her. The pain, even now, was terrible. But if she told them she had no doubt they would kill Liz, not because it was the Law – she actually had no idea what the Law said about this sort of thing – but because they loved her. As her friend for more than a decade she knew Bleidd well enough to know that he would seek revenge for her and it would not be pleasant. Jess, well she did not know him for as long or in all honesty as well, but she suspected he would also want to see the person behind this dead. How could she do that to Liz? Even if Liz had been able to do this to her.

"If you don't remember Allie, it's alright," Bleidd said into the silence. *"We will get to the bottom of it. Between the Guard and myself we can trace back your steps today and sort out what must have caused it. And who."*

It was so tempting to lie, even by omission, and let them believe that she couldn't remember. But Bleidd was right they would figure it out quickly enough. Really who else could it be? And then the end result would be the same…

"Please," she whispered aloud, her voice ragged. "Please, promise me you won't hurt her until I can talk to her. I have to understand why she did this."

"Her?" Jess said, puzzled.

Bleidd however knew immediately who she meant, drawing up to his full height, shaking in rage. "Liz? *Liz* did this to you?"

"Please," Allie said again, moving despite the pain to grab his hand. It made her lightheaded, and she would have fallen out of the bed, railing or no railing, if they both hadn't moved to catch her.

Two sets of hands eased her back down onto the pillow. Her whole body hurt, in a way that reminded her of having the flu. She didn't think she had the strength to sit up; even moving to grab Bleidd's hand left her weak and shaking. There was still a terrible burning from her throat down, but it was more bearable now. Since she should be dead it seemed petty not to be grateful, even for the pain. She felt a wave of exhaustion, and she fought against it. "Please, promise me, both of you."

The two elves exchanged a long look, and Allie could hear in her mind, the debate between them.

"We should find her quickly, before she flees and kill her," Jess thought.

"Yes," Bleidd agreed, *"We should but Allie wants to speak with her. Certainly Liz owes her that at least?"*

"Any delay risks her escape," Jess thought back. *"Or further harm to Allie. I think it's too great a risk, especially with the killer dead."*

"Hmmm. This may have been retribution you mean? Then Jason's life may be in danger as well."

"That is so, although I meant that with their killer dead the conspiracy may melt back into the shadows," Jess thought.

"We must capture Liz then. There is no other reason for her to have done this, except that she is part of the conspiracy." Bleidd thought.

"There is synchronicity to this," Jess thought gravely. *"Their grandmother was part of the original coven who first helped them and then stopped them. Now her two granddaughters each follow one of those paths, one helping, one seeking to stop them."*

"Perhaps so," Bleidd agreed. *"You may find that bringing Liz here to confront Allie may compel her to speak about what she is doing far more effectively than anything else you can do."*

Jess nodded, then said out loud to Allie, as if she hadn't heard that entire exchange, "I will promise to bring your cousin here to speak with you."

Because you think she'll confess Allie thought bitterly. "Unharmed."

Jess shook his head. "I cannot promise that Allie. Please understand. There is no way to be certain that in finding her and compelling her to come here she will not resist or attempt to harm myself or others. To promise not to hurt her would give her an enormous advantage that could get someone else killed."

Allie sighed, feeling defeated because he was right but without that promise she knew that there was no guarantee that Liz would not be terribly hurt. And she still couldn't bring herself to want that.

"Just please, try not to hurt her," she whispered, crying again and too tired to care.

Both elves were frowning and she could sense their anger, which was not aimed at her, and their confusion, which was. Bleidd spoke slowly, standing next to the bed, but leaning away as if he wished he could step back. "Why are you so concerned for her safety? She tried to kill you – she very nearly succeeded. You should be furious. Tell me that you want her head and I will bring it to you."

She shook her head, the motion making her dizzy. "No. She said she was sorry. She said it wasn't, that it wasn't supposed to be like this. I don't think…I can't believe she was trying to kill me. Make me really sick maybe, but not kill me."

Identical looks of disbelief met her words, and she knew, with a sinking feeling that they both thought she was being very naïve. *Damn it, why do they have to start getting along and agreeing with each other now?* she thought.

Jess reached over and stroked her hair out of her face, then leaned over and kissed her forehead gently, the barest brush of lips against skin. "Do not worry about this now my love. You are still very sick. You must rest and try to recover. I will go and send Brynneth back in and see if he can do any more for you now. And I will tell the others what happened, and we will set about finding your cousin."

Allie closed her eyes again, utterly miserable between the physical pain and the knowledge that Liz had done this and that now she would become the quarry of the Guard. She wanted to point out to him that as a human resident of town Liz should fall under the jurisdiction of the human police, but she was sure he already knew that, and more importantly if they called in Riordan she would not

214

get to see her cousin. Liz would be found and arrested and taken away. Allie had to be able to see her and know why she had done this, even if it meant trusting that the Guard would not kill her.

Jess started to leave and to her dismay Bleidd followed. She felt a rush of panic at the idea of being left alone in the clinic, and more at the thought of Bleidd going out to find Liz on his own. She struggled to sit up and failed to do more than push herself up a few inches and fall back, setting off a painful protest from her body. It was enough to stop both of them, even before she reached out with her mind, *"No don't go! Don't leave me here by myself!"*

"Allie I must go," Jess said, his voice soft but firm. Bleidd opened his mouth and then closed it again, looking between the other two.

"I know but Bleidd can stay," she thought back desperately, then directly to Bleidd, *"Stay with me. Don't leave."*

"Allie," he thought back, his mental speech more confident but his feelings still raw and uncertain. *"I have spent far too much time here recently and I can tell you the staff will not let me stay. I am amazed we have gone this long without interruption from a nurse or doctor. They will make me leave anyway, and I must let Jason know what has happened."*

"Make him stay Jess," she begged, wishing for once that she could use her empathy, or their bond – if that is what she had just forged between herself and Bleidd – to make him do what she willed. It was finally starting to really register that she had in fact almost died and although she was unbelievably tired she was afraid to go to sleep, afraid she wouldn't wake up again. If Brynneth came back in whatever healing he could offer would surely knock her out and the idea of being back in that terrible darkness, now that she understood better what it was, terrified her.

She could sense Bleidd's resolve crumbling beneath her obvious desperation, even as Jess, his own emotions a chaos of hard to read things thought back, "*I cannot compel him in anything,*" then to Bleidd, "*But if you will stay I will ensure that the clinic allows it. I can tell them that she was poisoned and I want someone with her at all times until the person responsible is apprehended.*"

Bleidd looked at his erstwhile rival, obviously confused by this sudden willingness to encourage him to get closer to Allie, when he had so far tried to separate them. The Guard commander could assign anyone to watch her if he were truly concerned about her safety, and Bleidd was not even a member of the Guard, so he had to be doing this purely to please Allie. Just when she was certain he was going to refuse, Bleidd nodded and stepped back towards the bed. "*Alright. I will stay as long as I am able to. And I will certainly protect her life against any threats.*"

Allie relaxed back into the pillows, feeling the hard knot of fear ease. She would not be alone, and if he had saved her from the darkness once he could do it again. "Thank you," she whispered, then to Jess, "Thank you, too. And please be careful. Please, I can't believe, even if I know it's true that Liz has done this. But she has and that means I have no one, no family left that I have any connection to. You two, and Jason, you're all I have. I don't think I can bear to lose any of you right now."

"I will return to you as soon as possible, and I will strive to let no harm come to myself," Jess said, smiling slightly. "Until then I will let Jason know what has happened, and ask that he come here as well, for his own safety, and Bleidd has said he will stay with you, so you need not fear for him."

"Jess? Don't tell Jason that it was Liz please," Allie said reaching out and clutching Bleidd's hand like a life line.

"If you wish it, I will not tell him yet," Jess agreed, inclining his head in a shrug.

She nodded, the barest motion of her head, fighting to keep her eyes open. Bleidd's hand was warm against hers as she heard Jess walking slowly towards the door. *Maybe this is all a bad dream* she thought feeling the anguish rising up again even as exhaustion pulled her down towards sleep. Bleidd leaned forward his hand gentle against her cheek, "It's okay Allie. Everything's going to be okay. I don't know how, or when, but it will be."

"Stay with me," she mumbled, losing her battle with sleep. "Don't leave me in the darkness."

"Never Allie," he said, and she could sense his own anguish now merging with hers. "Never. I am right here. If you truly wish it I will stay for as long as you like."

"Forever," she murmured recklessly, unable to force her eyes open anymore. She knew no elf would ever agree to that, it was too close to a promise and it was impossible; to promise it would mean eventually to be foresworn and elves took their honor too seriously for that.

"Forever is a long time," he whispered gently.

"I know," she thought to him, too tired now to speak, right on the edge of sleep.

"Go to sleep Allie," he thought back. *"I am not leaving I will be here when you wake up."*

"I'm afraid to sleep," she said, more honest in this liminal state between sleep and waking than she might usually be.

"Wherefore?" Jess's voice drifted into the conversation.

"If I go to sleep I'm afraid I won't wake up. I don't want to die," she thought back simply.

Their joined grief buoyed her up slightly back closer to waking. Jess said, *"Oh no my love you shall not. You shall live. Sleep and be safe."*

She could feel Bleidd's hesitation, and then suddenly, the words quick as if he was afraid himself, "*If you want me to promise you forever Allie then I will promise it. For as long as you want it. But do not fear to sleep. We, Jessilaen and I, are with you. I will watch over you while you rest and no harm will come to you. I swear that I will put my own life before yours, but do not fear to sleep. You are safe.*"

She felt Jess's shock at Bleidd's words, then, "*Yes Allie, we are with you. Forever, if that is what you wish. Sleep peacefully. You are safe.*"

Her last thought as she lost the battle with her own exhaustion, was that she must already be dreaming, because that could not have just happened....

****

Jess walked out of the room, leaving Allie and Bleidd alone. His own heart was a sea of conflicting emotions as he tried to process everything that had happened so quickly. He was overjoyed that Allie would live, although it was clear that she was still very ill. He was also both relieved and pleased that his greatest fear – that given the chance she would choose another and reject him – had proven groundless. It was a shocking and unexpected turn though that she had bonded to the other elf in the same way that she was bonded to him, and while he could not regret the actions necessary to save her life it did make him jealous to have to share that unique aspect of their relationship. And yet...and yet, he had come to respect the former Outcast and he knew that Bleidd loved Allie as much as he himself did, something he had long refused to believe given the elven predilection for rejecting strong emotions and avoiding close emotional ties outside of blood-kin.

He pushed the thoughts away as he emerged back into the hallway where the rest of the Elven Guard where waiting. Their faces made it plain that they expected him to announce bad news. He looked to Brynneth, relieved that in the intervening time the healer seemed to have recovered somewhat. "Bryn, would you go check her again. I believe you will be able to help her now."

The healer's head went to one side, his curiosity evident, but instead of asking any question he moved quickly past his friend and into the room. Jess had no doubt that he was eager to see for himself what was going on. His brother however frowned. "She was dying Jessilaen. What could have changed that Brynneth can help her now?"

"She was dying but she is not now," Jess said simply, earning a gasp of disbelief from Mariniessa.

"What have you done?" Zarethyn asked, his voice low and worried.

"What I had to do to save her," Jess replied calmly, thinking *even if saving her means sharing her. At least she will live*. Seeing the concern on his brother's face he added. "I didn't break any Laws, nor cause any harm to anyone, nor do anything against anyone's will."

They all looked baffled now. He didn't care. Let them wonder – if it mattered that much to his brother he would tell him later, privately. It was nothing that could be duplicated for anyone else anyway, and they had more important issues at hand. "She told me who poisoned her, but she has asked that the person be brought here before any justice is dealt, and I have promised as much."

Now his brother looked really shocked, although whether it was because Allie knew who had caused her such grievous harm or because he had been willing to give such a promise Jess wasn't sure. Either way he forged on, with Mariniessa and Natarien watching the exchange in silence. "The person is human and so beyond our legal reach, but she may have vital information about the conspiracy and the ritual murders. I believe if we allow Allie to confront her directly we may learn something essential."

Now Zarethyn was nodding, his eyes narrowed thoughtfully. "Yes, I had assumed the culprit would likely prove human and that puts us in a bad position. The punishment for trying to kill any member of the Elven Guard, even one with a nominal position such as Allie's, should be death. Yet we lack the authority to mete out such a punishment on a human resident of town. Knowing what I do about the human legal system I fear their justice will not be something we will recognize."

"Have you alerted the human police yet?" Jess asked, trying to decide how best to proceed. Zarethyn had not yet asked him to name the suspect, knowing he would do so in time on his own, but once named, they would need to move quickly to try to find and capture her. He feared that the task might prove more difficult if the human police were already involved.

"Not as of yet," the Guard captain said, his head tilting to the side. "Allie is half-blooded and within our jurisdiction. Up to this point although it seemed logical to assume that this attack on her was related to our investigation there was no proof of anything."

Jess nodded. "Her cousin, Liz McCarthy – I believe her full name is Elizabeth McCarthy – is the one we need to find."

Natarien shook his head sadly. "Her own cousin? That is a grievous thing."

"Indeed," Jess agreed. "Although Allie believes that she did not intend to kill her but only to sicken her enough to ensure Allie could no longer help us."

The looks of disgust on the faces of the elves in the hallway made their opinions of that idea clear.

"So we must find her and bring her here," Mariniessa said thoughtfully. "If Aliaine is wrong and her cousin was seeking her death it may be that she will try again. We may not need to seek her if she comes here on her own."

"Yes," Zarethyn agreed. "That is a possibility we must consider as well. It would be unwise to leave her here alone. We will take shifts staying with her."

"Bleidd is staying with her as well, at her request," Jess said, ignoring the searching look his brother gave him. It was too complicated to try to explain at the moment why he not only wasn't upset about it but had encouraged it. "I have told both of them that we will ensure the staff allow him to stay."

"Easily done under the circumstances," Zarethyn agreed. "But given his own recent grave injury I will still leave one other Guard here to ensure her safety. Have we any indication that her cousin is a mage or witch?"

Jess shook his head. "None that I am aware of, even having stayed in the same home with her. But the original coven consisted of practitioners, it is quite likely if she is herself a member of the new coven she has some talent and training."

"Synchronicity," Zarethyn murmured, frowning. "We must assume then that she has some magical ability, perhaps well hidden. If that is so, then only Mariniessa and I should risk pursuing her."

Jess began to protest but the Guard captain held up his hand to forestall it. "I understand your feelings in this matter, truly, but she is an unknown factor. It may be that she has a great deal more skill than any of us realize and if she were to attack either you or Natarien magically she might escape or do you great harm. No we shall pursue her and you two shall return to Allie's home and seek out any clues that can be found. Examine her cousin's room and possessions. Look for signs to whether she has fled, or remains. We will find out where she works and begin tracking her there."

"She works in the theater, O'Neill's Theater, downtown," Jess supplied. "But I doubt greatly she is there now. It was she who called the ambulance that brought Allie here. I had thought it odd that she left when we arrived, but it can be hard to understand why humans do the things they do sometimes. Of course now it is obvious why she fled."

Zarethyn nodded. "Then we will begin by questioning the staff who talked with her when Allie arrived..."

They were interrupted by the arrival of a harried looking doctor accompanied by a determined nurse. The doctor was an older woman, her grey hair pulled back in a severe way that made her face seem very round. The nurse was younger, her brown hair short and held back by a headband, a clipboard in her hands. The doctor looked unhappily from one elf to another before addressing Zarethyn. "Captain, I'm sorry if I'm interrupting, but with all due respect, we really must check on the patient now. It's normal protocol to check critically ill patients no less than every fifteen minutes while they are in the emergency room, and it's been almost two hours since we've seen Ms. McCarthy. Please understand..."

"I understand doctor Bierry. Our healer is in with her at the moment. As long as you do not disturb him there is no reason for you not to enter as well."

The young nurse was regarding them all suspiciously, but the doctor looked relieved. "I hope your healer can help her, sir. Honestly there's nothing we can do for iron poisoning. I'm sure you know that. Just make the patient comfortable."

"I appreciate your efforts on Aliaine's behalf," Zarethyn said gravely. "Whatever those efforts may be. I must tell you that I know you have strict rules about visitors, however we believe that Aliaine was intentionally poisoned and her life may be in danger until we apprehend the person responsible. I am ensuring that someone will be with her at all times, around the clock."

The doctor frowned. "Of course, of course. I'll notify all the staff. I assume you want to restrict any visitors to her room? Here and if - when we move her to a room upstairs?"

So they think she is dying as well Jess thought, not terribly surprised. Iron poisoning was always fatal to elves, and he did not think it had ever yet been seen in a half-elf. It was clear that his brother had done as he'd asked and kept everyone from entering the room while he and Bleidd were in there, and he felt a surge of gratitude for that.

"Yes," Zarethyn said simply. "I will provide you with a list of my Guards who will take shifts here and of the other approved people who may be here as well."

"Doctor," Jess said suddenly breaking his silence. "May I ask if you saw Aliaine's cousin when she first arrived?"

"Brown hair? Arrived in the ambulance with her?" the doctor asked.

"Yes, and I believe so."

"Yes I did. I was the physician who handled Ms. McCarthy when she was first brought in. I remember the woman who was with her," the doctor said, obviously puzzled.

"Did you tell her of the seriousness of Aliaine's condition?" Jess asked, and he saw his brother's eyes light up. The Guard captain turned to give the doctor his full attention.

"Ah, yes, yes I did," the doctor said, glancing towards the door of the room. "I told her that her cousin was critically ill but there was really nothing we could do for her except try to minimize the pain."

"Did you tell her that Allie was dying?" Jess said bluntly.

The doctor's eyes widened, but after a moment she nodded. "Yes. I felt it was best to be honest with her about her cousin's condition and not give her any false hope. People tend to think that coming in here will fix anything but that just isn't the case sometimes. I didn't want there to be any…any unrealistic expectations. And I thought if she wanted to say goodbye or call anyone else to do the same she needed to be aware to do that."

"Thank you doctor," Jess said, and then in Elvish to Zarethyn. "So Liz arrived her without her own vehicle and left thinking that she had killed her only family. Perhaps it may prove fruitful to track her from here?"

Zarethyn nodded but before he could speak Brynneth was emerging from Allie's room. The elven healer looked stunned. He started to speak and then saw the two humans and stopped. The doctor looked relieved to see him. "You're the healer? Did you have any luck stabilizing her?"

Bryn gave Jess a long look out of the corner of his eye, but answered the doctor calmly. "She is stable now and I believe she will recover. She is still, of course, gravely ill, but her life is out of immediate danger. In time – perhaps a few days with additional healing – she should fully recover."

The doctor and nurse both looked as stunned as Brynneth had when he'd first walked out of the room. "Well that's…amazing. You must be truly skilled. If you don't mind I'm just going to go in and examine her myself."

Brynneth shrugged one shoulder noncommittally at the doctor; the nurse was already heading into the room. "She is sleeping now, but you will see from her vital signs that she is significantly improved."

224

As soon as the two humans were gone Brynneth turned sharply to Jess. "What have you done?"

Jess repressed a sigh. This was getting tedious. As his friend, a rare and cherished thing among elves, Bryn had a right to speak bluntly to him but he had no intention of responding in kind in front of everyone. He ignored the question and answered with a question of his own, "How is she doing?"

Brynneth gave him a long look, but let his avoidance go for the moment. "She is still very ill and in pain, but she will live. I cannot predict the rate of her recovery."

Jess nodded eager to push on to other topics before anyone else could interject a question he didn't want to answer. No doubt Bryn would corner him later and get the details he wanted. "Allie's cousin is the one who poisoned her. We must find her with all speed. Bleidd is to stay here, at Allie's request, but you will stay as well to guard her."

"Is anyone else permitted to enter?" Brynneth asked, seemingly unperturbed by the revelation of the perpetrator's identity.

"Only her roommate Jason," Jess said. He knew that Bryn would remember the human well enough; he still spoke of him sometimes. Apparently their single night together had left an impression, and Brynneth had asked about Jason's wellbeing at the scene of Standish's shooting.

Brynneth looked thoughtful. "I will stay and be sure no one else enters as a visitor, but what of the staff? If this is a wider conspiracy can we be certain they are all trustworthy?"

Zarethyn frowned. "At this juncture we cannot be certain of anything. We do not know the numbers of this new coven, nor any living members, save Liz McCarthy and that is as much assumption as certainty."

"Could Aliaine be moved?" Mariniessa asked. Jess had not expected any concern from her over Allie's safety or health, but then again it could be simple pragmatism.

Brynneth hesitated for a long moment and then shook his head. "I could not swear that it would be safe to do so, no. I have never seen anyone survive iron poisoning before and it's difficult to know what the course of her recovery will be. Perhaps tomorrow if she is stronger and in less pain."

"Then we have no choice but to guard her here," Zarethyn said.

"Could we not alert the human police and get their aid in this?" Natarien said quietly. Jess turned to the young elf who he had almost forgotten was there.

"If they find Liz before we do they will have her in their own system and we will likely never get to speak to her, nor will we be able to bring her to see Allie," Jess said.

"And you think that essential?" Mariniessa asked.

"I think that Allie will be able to get her cousin to talk more effectively than any of us will," Jess said simply.

"Yes," Zarethyn agreed. "But if we don't inform detective Riordan it could be problematic later as well. We will call him and tell him what has transpired but not that we know who is behind it. Jess, Natarien go now and examine Aliaine's home; as soon as the police are notified they will surely do the same and I want us to inspect it first. Mariniessa and I will go seek Liz as soon as I speak to the police. Brynneth stay here until Jessilaen returns."

Each of the Elven Guard bowed slightly to their captain and set about fulfilling his orders. As Jess walked down the hallway towards the entrance he felt a grim resolve filling his heart. One way or another he would see that this new coven was rooted out and the threat they represented was ended once and for all.

Whatever it took.

Chapter 8 - Sunday

Saturday afternoon had passed in a blur of feverish delirium and pain punctuated by intervals of lucidity. She had vague memories of Jason holding her hand and talking to her, although the words had just been a blur of sound, and of Brynneth's cool touch easing some of the worst of the suffering. It was pretty clear to her that she was still dangerously ill, even though she did feel better as the day wore on.

Despite dozing on and off most of the afternoon Saturday when night fell she was seized with a terrible certainty that if she went to sleep she'd never wake up again. Nothing either man said could convince her otherwise and she'd been increasingly agitated until they'd both agreed to stay with her. Allie had fallen asleep late Saturday night sandwiched, at her own insistence, between Bleidd and Jessilaen. It was irrational and she could see more psychological healing in her future, if Brynneth was willing to work with her on it, but she was afraid to sleep. Only when she was safely tucked between them on the not-meant-for-three-people hospital bed had she felt safe enough to sleep, knowing that one or the other of them could help her if she needed it.

As she slept she dreamed and found herself sitting back in her own kitchen at home. She felt a surge of unhappiness as she looked around, thinking of her cousin in that very room fixing her the drink that would nearly kill her. *How could you do it Liz?* Allie asked herself, fighting back tears. *How? We are all the family we have. I could never do anything to hurt you....*

Her melancholy thoughts were interrupted by her friend Syndra drifting in from the hallway. Somehow Allie wasn't surprised to see her friend, although she had hoped that maybe Syndra's spirit had passed on by now. Syndra seemed confused though, almost dazed, distracting Allie from her own worries. "Hey Syn, what's up?"

"You tell me Al," Syndra said, moving slowly over to sit at the table. Everything about her was hesitant as if she wasn't quite sure what she was supposed to be doing.

"What's wrong?"

"Once again, you tell me." Syn said, her fingers tracing patterns on the table.

"I don't understand," Allie said softly.

"You called me here, so you tell me why. Damned if I know. Figuratively I mean, pretty sure I'm not actually damned."

"Huh?" Allie said cleverly. "I called you here?"

Syndra looked frustrated, as if she was being very dense. "Wow, I always forget how slow you are when you're dreaming. Yeah, Al, you called me here. Not that I mind, but I'm not sure why."

"Well, don't look at me," Allie said, totally baffled. "I didn't do it on purpose. I don't even know how I did it. If I knew how to call you I'd talk to you more often."

Syndra sighed, "Well, I'm not complaining. I like it here where I can really feel things again."

Allie looked away, out the window into the endless night that seemed to be the norm in this place. "So you know we found the killer?"

"And Jason shot him, yeah," Syndra agreed. "I also know you and Bleidd were shot last week. Couple things there by the way, since we're on the subject, you really have to stop trying so hard to get yourself killed because I was only kidding about you keeping me company here. And what the Hell are you doing screwing things up with Bleidd?"

"Screwing things up?" Allie frowned. "It's not like I wanted him to get shot…"

"I'm not talking about that," Syndra cut in. "I mean screwing around with his heart Al. I didn't think you were the type to do that. So what the fuck are you thinking?"

"I'm not..." Allie started, only to be interrupted again.

"You are. Okay I get that the whole him sleeping with you thing wasn't exactly your fault – don't give me that look. I was here waiting for you, to meet you when you crossed over, except you didn't, so I saw what happened. And I'm glad you aren't dead, props to Jessilaen for that, but you know how much he, how Bleidd, feels about you and you totally friend zoned him but you're also pulling this damsel in distress don't leave me crap. That's not fucking fair Al."

"I know it isn't," Allie mumbled, regretting all the times she'd wished to be able to talk to Syndra like this. She knew her friend was right but she really didn't want to hear this right now. Or ever. "I know it isn't fair, but I...I need him Syndra. I don't mean I just need him as a friend or even as more than that, I mean I *need* him. Like I need Jess. I can't even get my head around the idea of him – them – not being there."

"Is this some weird elf thing I don't understand? Or do you just need major therapy?" Syndra said, drinking from a coffee cup that was now on the table in front of her. Allie wondered if Syn could manifest stuff like the drink intentionally or if it only happened when she wasn't thinking and forgot the cup wasn't supposed to be there.

"I don't know, maybe it's a weird empath thing. Maybe it's a weird me thing. Maybe my best friend died a few months ago and I was shot a week ago and almost died horribly today and found out my own cousin was the one who tried to kill me and I can't deal with any of this," Allie said, her voice rising on each word until she was close to yelling. "Maybe I can't stand the idea of losing one of the few people I really care about that I have left."

229

Syndra watched her calmly, sipping her coffee. When it was clear Allie was done she put the cup down. "Feel any better?"

"Not really."

Syn laughed. "Yeah, life's a bitch that way. But all I'm hearing is 'me, me, me'. What about him? Are you going to leave the other guy for him?"

"I can't do that Syn."

"Well where does that leave him then?"

Allie groaned and dropped her head to the table. "What if I can't leave Bleidd either?"

"Well that's great, it's Sophie's choice for shallow people."

"Hey!"

"What? You don't like the truth? You want exclusivity in your relationship right? You don't want the person you are with to be with anyone else, right? So that means, Miss Raging Hypocrite, that you can't string them both along. Pick one and stick with that choice. And if you don't like that then change your expectations and let them have multiple partners too," Syndra said.

Allie closed her eyes and shook her head. She couldn't put into words that it wasn't that easy. Not anymore, not since she had a spellbond with Bleidd too now. Even if she was willing to walk away from him entirely unless she could get herself out of his head she'd be aware – intimately aware – of every single time he was with someone else. Which was going to happen anyway now, she realized. Once she thought about it she had no illusions that Bleidd, like Jess, would choose celibacy if she wasn't an option. She knew too well from their decade of friendship how strong a drive sex was for him. She groaned, as the realization hit that like it or not she'd be an eavesdropping witness to his future assignations, which were likely to be frequent and enthusiastic. Even if she did choose a more elven approach and sleep with both of them that wouldn't change Bleidd's lifestyle. *Damn* she thought *I could not possibly have screwed this up more.*

"You know what? I don't want to talk about this anymore," Allie said, lifting her head.

Syndra gave her a long look, her coffee somehow having changed into a beer while Allie's head was down. She drank slowly, watching her friend. "Okay. Be in fucking denial. Don't say I didn't try to help. So back to business. The second killer is dead courtesy of Jason. And your cousin tried to kill you."

"Nicely recapped," Allie said, making a face.

Syndra stuck her tongue out, then took another drink. "So are these two things related?"

"Well it's an awfully big coincidence if they aren't," Allie said grimly.

Syndra stopped, putting the beer down. Her eyes narrowed. "So...that would mean...that Liz – fucking *Liz* – is part of the group behind the killings?"

There was something in her tone that made Allie tense. "Didn't you already know that?"

"I'm dead I'm not fucking omniscient," Syndra snapped. "Or I'd just tell you all the answers and boom, done. But I'm right, aren't I? You and the elf brigade think Liz is part of this new ritual group, don't you?"

"Looks like there's a good chance."

"So *fucking Liz* is part of the reason I was killed?"

"Ummm," Allie was caught off guard by the sudden rage coming from Syndra. "It looks like she's at least part of the same group. I mean I can't believe she'd be part of a plan to have you killed..."

"She fucking tried to kill you!" Syndra yelled, making Allie flinch. "Why the fuck should she think twice about me? Holy fucking shit! No wonder I'm fucking stuck in Ashwood purgatory!"

"Ahhh, Syndra," Allie started, not sure what to say to calm her friend down.

231

Syndra ignored her, standing up and radiating righteous wrath. "Now I understand why I'm stuck here. Why I can't fucking move on. Not just because I need to help catch the killer, or because I need to stop this conspiracy but because I need to see justice come to the person I fucking trusted who sent me to a fucking altar to get raped, tortured, and murdered! That motherfucking bitch!"

Allie was sitting wide eyed, pinned in place by the intensity of Syndra's anger. It was like sitting out exposed under the full summer sun; she felt like she was baking. Finally she managed a weak, "Ah, Syn…"

"I trusted her! Oh I'm not sitting on the sidelines for this one. I'm going to find her myself," Syndra said, still furious. "And we'll see if this ghost can jack up her day in a way that matters."

Syndra started to fade out, making Allie shake her head and rub her eyes. But it was no good, as she watched her friend grew translucent and then was gone leaving Allie sitting alone in the kitchen. Allie stood, turning around the empty space and calling her friend's name over and over….

She woke to Jess's hands on her shoulders, shaking her gently. He was calling her name, his voice worried, but at first she was too disoriented to respond. She could still feel Syndra's anger like a burning coal and the emotional sensation merged with the very similar feeling of the residual iron poisoning in her gut, creating an overwhelming sense of being on fire. Jess's hands felt like ice against her skin.

"What's wrong?" That was Bleidd she realized after a moment, his voice coming from somewhere towards the door. An instant later he appeared next to the bed, his worried face mirroring Jess's on her other side.

"I don't know," Jess said anxiously. "She was sleeping but then started to struggle as if she were fighting something. She was calling out her friend's name, the one who was killed, and I can't wake her…"

"I'm awake," Allie mumbled, still feeling disoriented.

Bleidd reached out, his hand cold against her cheek. "It's another fever. Is Brynneth still here?"

"No he's gone to find his own rest. He exhausted himself yesterday," Jess answered unhappily. "Damn! I thought we were past this."

"Guys," Allie said, struggling to sit even as they pushed her back down. "Really I'm awake. I was having a, ummmm, well not a nightmare exactly. I was talking to Syndra."

Bleidd looked grim, "Is she hallucinating again?"

"Hallucinating? I am not – wait when was I hallucinating?" Allie said, even more confused.

Jess relaxed slightly. "Allie do you know where you are?"

"What? Of course. I'm in the clinic," she replied.

"And do you know why you're here?" Bleidd asked, still tense, his hand brushing her hair off her face.

She made a face. "What's with the twenty questions? I'm here because someone I trust – trusted – slipped iron into my damn coffee."

Bleidd and Jess exchanged an amused glance and she could feel their fear and worry dissolving into a sort of exhausted concern. Bleidd kept stroking her cheek, the coolness of his hand unexpectedly pleasant. Jess met her eyes, "You are running a fever Allie, so we wanted to check how rational you were. Yesterday you had several bouts of high fever where you were…not."

Allie's eyes went wide. "Define 'not'?"

"You were hallucinating. The details don't matter but it is a good thing that Bleidd or I were always here with you because at times only speaking to your mind would calm you and Brynneth advised against any sort of sedation," Jess said.

"I thought…I think I remember Jason being here?" Allie said uncertainly.

"Yes," Bleidd said. "He was here visiting for a little bit. I think it frightened him to see you so ill."

"Oh Gods he doesn't know who did this does he?"

"No, my heart," Jess reassured her. "No one has told him yet. He thinks we are investigating and didn't ask too many questions."

Allie closed her eyes and took a deep breath. "Have you found Liz yet?"

Jess shook his head. "No. She has not returned to your home, nor has she gone to work. Zarethyn and Mariniessa are attempting to track her, but she is proving elusive."

"Why the two mages? Why not you or Natarien?" she asked after a moment.

He smiled, "It is good to see your mind is sharp. It was decided that there was a risk that she might be a mage or witch if she truly is associated with this new ritual group."

"Liz?" Allie said, blanching. "No. She was never interested in any magic."

"Allie," Jess said so gently that she knew bad news was coming.

"No," she repeated shaking her head. "I can't believe that I've lived with her all this time – that Bleidd lived with her – and we never knew she practiced any kind of magic."

Bleidd sighed. "I did not want to believe it either, but truly how would we know if she never actively cast anything around us and was careful not to act like she knew anything?"

"But she never had any shields…" Allie said weakly.

"Perhaps she trusted her safety to something else, like a talisman, knowing that shields would give her away," Jess said. "But I assure you, she does practice. When Natarien and I examined her room we found the clear evidence of her art, well hidden as it was."

Allie lay there, stunned. It was almost more of a shock to hear that her cousin was a witch than it had been to find out Liz had poisoned her.

Allie tried to sit up again, annoyed at trying to hold a conversation while flat on her back. It was embarrassing to realize that something which should have been easy was such a struggle but a moment later Bleidd lowered the side rail and slide in next to her, pulling her up until she was sitting leaning against him. As his arms wrapped around her, supporting her, she relaxed back into him, but not without a twinge of guilt. She couldn't get Syndra's words about him out of her mind. At least she felt nothing negative from either elf about Bleidd's closeness – there was no jealousy from Jess and no challenge from Bleidd. They were both perfectly relaxed.

"I saw Syndra, in my dream," she said, and then added when she realized she hadn't told Bleidd about that. "She comes to me sometimes when I'm sleeping and talks to me, mostly about the murders."

"Her spirit is trapped here?" Bleidd said, his voice flat and emotionless, at odds with the deep sadness he felt at the thought.

"Well, yes. It seems that way. At the ritual site, although she can go other places sometimes too. She said she was here to get me when I died, except that I didn't."

Jess inhaled sharply at that. Bleidd's arms tightened around her. Allie sighed. "Its okay guys, really. I didn't die, so it's not a big deal…"

"Allie," Bleidd said, as Jess stared at her, speechless, "I'm starting to believe you have no sense of proportion whatsoever."

"What do you mean?" Allie said, irritated. "I understand I almost died, but I didn't – you, both of you, saved me. It's not like she was saying she was here to take my soul or anything. I find it comforting that she would have been there for me, if you know…I'd gone."

"Last night you wouldn't sleep without both of us staying with you and now this morning you're acting like nothing of import happened," Jess said. "Can you not see how baffling that is?"

"*I don't want to talk about this,*" Allie thought to them both, knowing she sounded like a pouting child and not caring.

"*Allie,*" Bleidd thought back, his words clumsy as he struggled with this form of communication. "*You don't have to be strong all the time. It's okay to be frightened, and to admit that a situation is overwhelming.*"

"*I…*" Allie started, then stopped, gathering her thoughts. She wanted to deny what he was saying, to insist that she was strong. But she couldn't even sit up without help. It made her feel like she had after the Dark court elves had attacked her in her store in March, back when all of this had first started, and she hated the feeling. "*Okay. Okay, maybe you're right. Maybe I feel…weak, and helpless and frightened right now. And stupid for trusting someone…for loving someone…who tried to kill me. Maybe I'm really, really scared that I almost died and that makes me feel ashamed because Syndra did die, and you, Bleidd, you almost died too, and I should just be able to keep fighting like you do…*"

"*You judge yourself too harshly,*" Jess thought, his emotions heavy and sad.

She sighed. "*Listen. I mean really listen. Maybe I should just fall apart right now and be upset and cry and all of that, but I can't. I can't. You asked me to be honest about how I feel and that's how I feel. If I sit here and really think about that it's just too overwhelming. I have to*

236

keep fighting. I can't just give up now because this is too hard. And so what if I did? It won't change anything. If I say that I'm scared and I can't do this it won't change that we have to find Liz, that we have to root out this group before they complete the ritual cycle and rip a hole in reality, or whatever. It won't change that the Dark court is still after me."

"That is true Allie," Bleidd thought. *"But we are here to help you and it is concerning to see you rush headlong into danger as if you have no concern for your own life. When you speak of almost dying yesterday – yesterday! – as if it were nothing it frightens me. You take such risks already with yourself, it is…unnerving…to think that you have no fear for your own life at all."*

She could feel their concern like a joint force pressing against her, wrapping around her. It stopped her arguments before she could make them because she knew that what they were saying was born of a genuine worry for her. She didn't know how to explain that she had grown up surrounded by death and learned early that life gave you two choices: you got up and kept going, or you laid down and gave up. She could not see any other possibility and she wasn't ready to give up, which meant that her only choice was to get up and push forward.

"Alright, give me some time to process all that," she thought slowly. *"Back to Syndra, I told her that Liz was probably part of the ritual group and she didn't take it well. She thinks that she's earth-bound because her death was partially due to Liz in some way."*

"How so?" Jess asked.

It was Bleidd who answered, before Allie could even form a thought. *"Because she trusted Liz and even if Liz was not directly involved with Syndra's murder if she had told us what she knew about what was going on it could have been prevented. She certainly knew Walters was behind the killings."*

Jess tensed, his anger washing over Allie, sharp and bitter. "*If this is so then she could also have aided us in finding Allie when Walters kidnapped her.*"

"No," Allie said firmly switching back to verbal communication to give herself some space from their emotions. Their feelings may have fed her but she was unused to trying to deal with two sources at once. Handling twice the intensity and depth of emotion made her head swim, especially when they were both upset. "No, I can't believe she knew where I was. She was really shocked that it was Walters who had kidnapped me and genuinely upset that I was hurt."

Bleidd took a deep breath and nodded. "Yes, we must be careful not to jump to conclusions. We know she is part of this conspiracy but we do not know how deep it runs or what exactly Liz's involvement is."

Jess frowned but was forced to agree. "Perhaps you are correct. Nonetheless Syndra believes Liz bares enough responsibility for her death to hold her spirit here."

"Yeah, she does," Allie said. "And she said she was going to look for Liz herself and try to see if there was anything she could do against her."

"Hmmmm," Jess said thoughtfully. "Interesting. That is good to know. Ghosts have limited influence on the earthplane, but even a small action, well timed, could be critical."

"If Syndra finds Liz do you think she'll tell you where your cousin is hiding?" Bleidd asked.

"I don't know. Maybe."

They were interrupted by a knock at the door. Bleidd tensed, his body rigid behind Allie, his arms tightening around her. Jess moved quickly around the bed, his hand reaching towards his empty belt only to have his sheathed sword appear just as his fingers touched the hilt. Allie had to admit that was an impressive bit of magic, and she felt a twinge of jealousy. *Not that I'd know what to do*

238

with a sword if I had one, but I wish this elven ancestry could let me do things like that; it'd be nice to be able to call a weapon or shift my clothes, Allie thought wistfully. *Like right now I'd kill to be able to change this stupid hospital gown for jeans and a t-shirt...*

Jess opened the door slowly, hand still grasping the sword hilt. She guessed who it was as soon as she saw Jess relax, even before Jason stepped into the room. To her surprise a step behind him was Shawn. They both looked nervous. Jason saw Allie sitting up, more or less in Bleidd's lap and he smiled, some of the tension going out of his face. Shawn, of course, was smiling widely at everything although Allie could sense his uncertainty.

"Hi Jason, hi Shawn," Allie said, trying to sit up further. Bleidd pulled her fully onto his lap then and she prayed she wasn't blushing, then fought back a nervous laugh. She was in the hospital after almost dying and she was embarrassed about her roommates seeing her sitting on someone's lap? Even Allie couldn't deny that it was a ridiculous thing to be worried about at the moment. *Oh Gods* she thought as the realization dawned on her that at some point she'd have to explain the new relationship situation to her other roommates. *How the Hel am I going to explain this? After I spent all that time convincing Shawn that I wasn't into polyamory and wasn't dating Bleidd...now I have to tell him, well something. Something that doesn't sound stupid. If that's possible...*

Shawn kept smiling widely, "Hey Allie. Wow, you look really good. I mean not good, but better than I thought you would. I mean..."

"It's okay Shawn," Allie said, feeling sympathy towards her newest roommate. He finally relaxed a little bit his smile changing from exaggerated to more normal.

Jason's eyes were fixed on her position in Bleidd's arms. "Hey Allie. Feeling any better?"

"Yeah, much better today," she answered honestly. "I remember you coming yesterday though. Thanks for visiting."

Jason looked surprised. "You remember that? I didn't think you would. You were pretty out of it."

"Yeah, well," Allie said, certain she was blushing this time. "I couldn't tell you what you said to me while you were here, but I do know you were here."

Jason's lips quirked up in a lopsided smile. "No worries. I was just babbling on about how if you went and died on me I'd find some cut rate witch to trap your soul in a pickle jar for eternity."

Allie giggled, even as the other three men in the room gave the two of them odd looks. "That's low Takada. I at least rate a pretty decorative bottle."

Jason chuckled, "Hey if you'd died you would have deserved pickle jar fate."

"Wow, remind me not to die around you."

"See now we understand each other," Jason said, not entirely joking. Jess was giving him a quizzical look, but she could feel Bleidd's amusement at the exchange. Jason walked over to the edge of the bed, his eyes still on Bleidd's arms around Allie instead of Allie's face. "But seriously, I'm glad to see you sitting up and talking. I've buried enough friends this year."

She had been ready with another joke, but his words stopped her, making her reach out for him. Silently she grabbed his wrist and pulled him into an awkward hug, releasing him before Bleidd could complain. "Don't count me out yet. Apparently I'm tougher than I look."

Jason smirked, "Yeah, to be honest you don't look tough at all. But after everything you've been through I guess you might be the toughest person I know."

Allie snorted, "Hardly, but thanks for the thought. If it wasn't for the healing Brynneth gave me in March and

240

when I got shot, and Jess and Bleidd this time I'd be dead a few times over by now."

Jason shook his head slightly as if he wanted to argue, but before he could Shawn said. "Oh, hey we brought you flowers. Seems like the thing to do. I mean I assume. I've never actually visited anyone in the hospital, er, clinic before."

"Thanks," Allie said meaning it. She normally didn't like cut flowers, knowing that they were doomed to die just so she could look at them in a vase for a few days ruined the idea for her, but it was a nice thought. She really hadn't expected Shawn to visit at all.

Jess continued to stand by the door, obviously on guard while Jason and Shawn went into the small bathroom to try to get the flowers set up in the little vase they'd brought. Allie relaxed back against Bleidd, watching. Then as it occurred to her he wasn't long out of the hospital himself she thought to him *"I'm not bothering your shoulder, am I?"*

She felt his surprise, then his arms shifted slightly, holding her closer in an embrace rather than just holding her to keep her balanced. She felt an odd surge of longing and melancholy from him that puzzled her, then his voice was in her mind, *"My shoulder is much better Allie. I barely notice any stiffness in it and the arm moves well now. Don't worry that you are hurting me."*

"Oh good," she thought back as Jason and Shawn emerged carrying the vase together as if it were much larger than it actually was. Her lips curved into a smile as they carefully discussed exactly where to put it in the small room. *"Because I'm really comfortable and it's nice to be sitting up, but I don't want to hurt you."*

He whispered in her ear, his voice barely a breath against her skin, "I've waited a long time to get you in this position, and I'm thoroughly enjoying it."

241

She turned her head slightly, keeping her eyes on the two men fussing over flower arraigning, and whispered back. "What position?"

"Half naked on my lap," he said, and despite his amused tone she could feel the sharpness of his emotions increasing.

"Bleidd…" she started to say, but the phone ringing on the small table next to her startled her into almost falling out of his arms. He held her in place and she reached out instinctively and picked up the phone after the second ring. "Hello?"

"Allie?" Liz's voice sounded tinny and far away but Allie recognized it immediately. She held the phone, speechless, as her brain tried to process this unexpected turn. Liz spoke again, uncertain, "Allie? Is that you? Are you there?"

"Ummmm. Yeah. Yeah. It's me, I'm here," Allie said reflexively. Jess's head swung towards her, the tone of her voice giving away her shock.

His voice in her head was tense, *"What is it?"*

At almost the same moment Bleidd asked *"Who is it?"* their mental voices overlapping oddly making her eyes twitch.

"Hang on a second," she mumbled into the phone, then to the chorus in her head, *"It's Liz."*. Then before they could react, she spoke to Jason and Shawn, knowing Liz could hear her too, "Hey guys? Do you think you could run down to the cafeteria and grab me something to drink? Maybe some milk? I'm super thirsty."

Jason looked from her to the phone, obviously not fooled, but nodded, "Sure. We'll be right back. Come on Shawn, let's go make a snack run."

"I thought she wanted a drink?"

"Yeah, a drink for her, snacks for us," Jason said, already moving past Jess out the door. Shawn jogged behind him, hurrying to catch up.

As the door swung closed Allie focused back on the phone clutched in her hand. "Are you still there?"

"Yeah," Liz said, her voice still distorted. "I'm here."

Jess moved swiftly over to her side, his steps silent. Bleidd leaned forward resting his chin on her shoulder, almost against the phone, turning so that he could hear too. As good as elven hearing was she knew both men would be able to hear Liz as clearly as she could. She wasn't sure how she felt about that but there was nothing to do to change it, except to let Liz know the conversation wasn't private and she was afraid Liz would hang up if she thought anyone was listening in.

The silence stretched out until Allie started to wonder if Liz had gotten nervous and hung up, but then she finally spoke again. "Are you alone?"

Allie's heart sank even before Jess shook his head slightly. *"Do not tell her we are listening."* He said, his emotions equal parts fury and anxiety.

"Jason and Shawn were here visiting," Allie said, hating herself for misleading her cousin. "I asked them to go get me a drink. They're gone now – we should have a few minutes before they come back."

"Allie…" Liz said, her voice thick. "I am so sorry. I know…maybe you don't believe that…maybe you think I was trying to hurt you, but I really wasn't. It was just supposed to make you sick. Just enough that you'd stop helping them."

"I know Liz," Allie said, resolutely ignoring the waves of rage coming off of the two elves. "I know you'd never do anything on purpose to hurt me."

Liz started to cry, her sobbing crackling across the phone line. "It was just supposed to make you sick. I guess that doesn't make me a good person either, that I'd do that to you, but after you were shot I was afraid if I didn't do it they'd really hurt you."

243

"Liz…are you…" Allie started to ask, and then switched to a different topic. "I mean, did you know I was going to get shot before it happened?"

"Not shot no," Liz said, sniffling. "No, I wouldn't have allowed it. She promised, after you were hurt so bad before that you wouldn't get hurt again. But – it's just so frustrating, you have no idea. You are such a stubborn person Allie. The more I did to try to drive you off the more you insisted on being involved. And you just kept handing them leads. They never would have found Walters without you and then after that they never would have known we were still working on the ritual if you hadn't started helping the Guard look for Jerry."

"So you were doing what exactly? To drive me off?" Allie asked with a sinking feeling.

There was a moment of silence, then, "I deleted part of your computer program so that the cameras wouldn't record and…I left the animals."

"You did that?" Allie said, appalled. "You killed those animals?"

"They were just animals," Liz said, her voice closer to it's normal businesslike tone. "It was supposed to scare you. And when it didn't, not enough anyway, I cut your tires…"

"Liz!"

"Just to scare you!" Liz said defensively. "And let me tell you that was a lot harder to do than you'd think. And how was I supposed to know that the knife Rick gave me for protection was a God damned murder weapon? But you just kept helping them, more and more. So she decided to… I wasn't doing enough and she had Amy go to take that shot. It was just supposed to be a warning shot."

"Well, it wasn't," Allie said, her voice bitter in her own ears. The two elves listened in absolute silence to the exchange between the cousins, but she could feel Bleidd's fingers moving on her wrist where her hand clasped one of

244

his around her waist. The touch was reassuring and she drew a long, shaky breath.

"That wasn't my fault. I don't know why she shot you when she wasn't supposed to, and the damned Guard didn't need to kill her. I'm not saying what she did was right, but no one died because of her," Liz said. Allie closed her eyes and saw again Bleidd's still bloody body on the ground, felt the dark magic twisting around her as she used the spell from the Grimoire to save him. Saw the dead birds.

"Liz, how could you do it though? You know I can't...you know what iron does to me," Allie whispered, her own pain and grief suddenly overwhelming.

"I'm sorry Allie. I already said I was sorry, but I'll keep saying it if that's what you need to hear," Liz said, and Allie's heart broke a little more at her cousin's defensive attitude, as if she really believed that Allie was the one being unreasonable. "It was only a tiny amount. Just a little bit of powdered iron in your coffee. It should have made you sick, but not...not like it did. And that's why I called the ambulance. I didn't want you to die."

Allie pulled her hand free of Bleidd's and covered her mouth, trying to smother her own sobbing. It was one thing to know that Liz had done it but to hear her talk about it as if it were all some big mistake and not a cold blooded, premeditated act was something else. She shuddered, feeling a keening cry rising in her throat and Jess, his face a cold mask, reached for the phone. She jerked away, forcing down the tears. "Liz," she said, her voice thick, "I just don't understand why you're doing this. All of this. You're part of a group that's killing people."

"Allie....I know this is hard for you, especially now because they've got you brainwashed into thinking that their ways are better than human ways, but it's wrong the way the world is. It's not supposed to be this way," Liz said. She sounded soft and persuasive, even over the bad phone line. Genuine. Allie shuddered again, and she felt Bleidd's arms tighten around her in a reassuring hug.

"But this is how the world is," Allie said. "This is our reality."

"But don't you see it doesn't have to be," Liz said eagerly. "Grandmother knew that, that's why she helped the original coven. She lost her nerve, but she kept the book because it was our legacy. It told the story Allie, of what the original group stood for, and of their magic."

"You've read it," Allie said, genuinely shocked. She didn't think anyone but herself had read the book before she'd burned it.

"I did," Liz said. "A long time ago, before grandmother died. But then I couldn't find it again and I don't have your crazy memory for things. If I'd known she'd kept it in the house – but I thought she'd taken it out to the store or maybe somewhere else..."

"Why didn't you tell me you were a witch?" Allie said dully, feeling as if her entire world was collapsing.

"I wanted to," Liz said. "But...it was too dangerous for anyone to know. They monitor witches and mages, you know, and I had to be under the radar."

"Who monitors them?" Allie asked, confused.

"The Fairy beings," Liz said softly, her voice intense. "They keep track of human mages and witches and what we can do, to make sure we don't get too strong."

Jess was frowning and she could feel her confusion reflected back by both the elves. Jess shook his head slowly. Allie tried to sound reasonable, "Liz, I don't think that's true..."

"Oh it is, it is true," Liz insisted. "They want to destroy us Allie. That's why what we're doing is so important. If we don't stop them by separating the worlds again, by setting everything right, they'll slowly enslave us all and destroy our way of life. They'll make us just like them, debauched, perverse, and amoral. And humans will be a slave race...I know you don't believe me but it's true. We have to do whatever we can, whatever the cost, to fix the worlds. I know I can make you understand, if you'll just listen to me."

"I'm listening," Allie said, knowing her voice sounded skeptical. "But killing innocent people?"

"They weren't innocent," Liz said confidently. "They were part of the problem. Their Fey blood corrupted them, but dying for the cause saved them, don't you see?"

Allie gaped at the phone, unable to think of a single response. What Liz was saying was insane, no matter how logical she made it sound, and worse despite the way Liz seemed to exempt Allie from this bizarre world view she knew that what Liz was saying should apply to her as well. And that hurt, deeply. That her own cousin, her flesh and blood, could feel no remorse at being involved in the torture and death of young girls just like Allie, because one of their parents came from the wrong world...Allie closed her eyes again, the last shred of hope she had for her cousin dissolving.

"Where are you Liz?"

Silence. Then, "Are you going to be okay?"

You're asking that now? Allie thought dully. *Not the first thing out of your mouth, but as a distraction, 'oh by the way are you still dying or is that better now?'* She felt raw anger joining the burning after effects of the iron poisoning in her gut. "Thanks to Jessilaen and Bleidd, and Brynneth for healing me, I'll live."

Liz cleared her throat loudly. "Well, that's good, but what will you owe them for it?"

"Owe them? It isn't like that," Allie said, feeling her anger growing. Her cousin didn't even seem that grateful, just worried about what Allie might have to do to pay back the elves who had helped her.

"Don't be naïve," Liz said briskly. "Nothing's ever free with them. What will you have to pay them?"

Allie's eyes met Jess's. She didn't need her empathy to know how furious he was. His voice in her head was icy, causing a physical shiver as his emotions rippled through her. *"Nothing. You owe us nothing. As a member of the Guard you are entitled to healing, and as well Brynneth agreed to heal you."*

Bleidd's voice was calmer but just as adamant. *"You owe me nothing Allie. If anything I owe you."*

She had no time to contemplate what he meant as she had to push both their voices aside in order to keep the flow of the conversation with Liz. "I don't owe them anything Liz. Really. I'm sure."

"You're so young Allie. You don't seem it and I know you're my age but you really are," Liz said, sounding tired. "You don't understand how the world – worlds – work. But I do. And you need to trust me that I'm doing what's best for us. For you."

"Liz…"

"No Allie, just listen," Liz said, her voice suddenly intense. "Someday you'll understand. I'm doing this to make the world right again, for both of us. I know you don't believe me right now, because *he's* got you convinced, he's seduced you, made you think that their ways are better. But once everything is fixed you'll understand why I did this."

Allie swallowed hard, wondering if she'd ever really known her cousin at all. "Liz, you're talking about half my heritage."

"No," Liz said. "You're heritage is my heritage. You read the book. Grandmother's book. You know what she and the original group believed and did. That's your heritage. Not this, this elven nonsense."

"Where are you Liz?" Allie asked again.

"I love you Allie," Liz said. "Stay safe."

And then the line went dead.

****

Ferinyth walked down the sidewalk of the dull human Bordertown, keeping his head down. Salarius had told him about the girl being rushed to the hospital and after spending a night in near panic at the idea of her death – and his ultimate failure – he had decided to take the great risk of going to see for himself.

Luckily what passed for a medical facility here was small and understaffed with negligible security. When he reached the clinic he slipped in a side door, moving easily through a deserted hallway. He grabbed the first person he found, a human male in drab matching linens who smelled of antiseptic, and wrapped the man's mind in glamour. He grinned savagely as he watched the human's eyes dilate, his breath speeding eagerly. *As if I would ever have any real interest in this boring creature*, Ferinyth thought knowing that his magic would ensure the man would do anything he asked. "There is a girl here, a half-elven girl. She was brought in by ambulance. I must know where she is."

The human pressed up against him, thoroughly caught in the thrall of the elf's glamour. "I...I don't know. I'm not sure who you're looking for." The man grimaced, his face writhing between confusion and lust. "I shouldn't tell you anything. I'm not allowed to...and I don't understand why I'm...what's going on? I don't..."

Ferinyth enjoyed the man's fear and confusion. It was tempting to let him feel it, but he didn't have the time to waste. He strengthened his magic, coiling the energy around the man's will like a snake getting ready to constrict its prey. The human's eyes went blank, emptying of everything but the desire to please the elf who was enchanting him. "I know she's here. There is probably at least one Elven Guard with her. You must tell me where she is."

The man nodded slowly. "Elven Guard. Yes. On the third floor. Room 313. I don't know…who is there. But no one can go in without clearance. And there is a Guard at the door. Everyone's been talking about it."

Ferinyth felt a thrill of triumph. "And what sorts of patients are normally kept on the third floor?"

The man gasped slightly, blinking sluggishly. "The third floor…recovery."

So the girl still lived. That was excellent. All the better for him if she was injured or ill, she'd put up less resistance. Of course there was still the problem of getting to her through the thrice-damned Guard, but Ferinyth would find a way. Perhaps Salarius could finally be of some real use. The human man tensed slightly as the elf's distraction allowed the magic to slip a little bit. Ferinyth watched the revulsion slide across his face as he tried to understand what was going on and why he was acting against his own inclinations. The Dark elf smiled again, relaxing and reveling in the knowledge that he could make this human do whatever he wanted, no matter how much the man didn't want to. The Bright court were all fools to worry about kindness towards these human cattle who could be controlled with simple glamour.

He knew where the girl was and that she was injured but lived. He had time to find the best way to move against her, so all was not yet lost. Perhaps Salarius was right in that he rushed too much instead of waiting for the best moment. This time he would be certain to move only when the time was ideal.

Hoping that whatever the circumstances were the girl was suffering, he wrapped his magic even more tightly around the man's mind.

Chapter 9 – Monday

Ciaran was waiting on the front lawn, sitting in the grass in his dog form, when Allie arrived home Monday morning. She still felt tired and ill but it was so much better compared to the day before that she didn't want to complain. She had continued to draw on both Jess and Bleidd to help heal herself and there was no denying how much it helped; even Brynneth had told her that she could do more for herself now than he could do for her, not that he didn't also try.

She climbed out of the car with effort, but refused to let anyone help her. That earned an annoyed look from Jess and a long suffering one from Bleidd, both of which she ignored. She had learned over the past two days that the biggest downside to having both of them spellbonded to her was that she was outnumbered in most arguments and they almost always agreed on subjects relating to her independence or self-sufficiency. It was beyond annoying.

"Hi Ciaran," Allie greeted her friend, doing her best to ignore the residual burning in her gut that was aggravated by the movement out of the car. "Do you have a minute?"

The kelpie cocked his head to the side, "Certainly."

"Come on in for a bit then, I'd like to talk to everyone at once."

She could feel the curiosity her comment aroused, but they'd all just have to wait. She didn't want to have to repeat herself. Ciaran shifted to his human form, his dark eyes reminding her of the water of his pond. "If you wish. I wanted to tell you and the Elven Guard that twice there have been disturbances in the woods. Once when the ambulance was here, and I am sorry but I was distracted and by the time I turned to see what was going on whoever was testing the borders had fled. The second time was last night, when everyone was gone. The house was empty so I was resting and again by the time I arrived here whatever was pressing against the wards had left."

"I am glad you are here to watch the boundaries," Jess said gravely. "Especially during such troubled times."

Ciaran inclined his head in a shrug, but she could feel his surprise and pleasure at the praise. Before they could move two more cars pulled up: a Guard vehicle and an unmarked police car. Ciaran tensed and a moment later his form shifted again, back to the large dark dog. Allie feared he'd bolt as the Guard and police got out but he held his ground. Allie nodded at the two detectives, police mage, and the Guard mages, realizing she should probably say something formal and polite and just too tired to care. Instead she led the way into the house, Ciaran close at her side.

Jason and Shawn were both waiting in the living room, each projecting anxiety. Allie managed to get to the couch and sat down, wishing she didn't have to deal with any of this. Ciaran lurked by the door; the police of both species found seats on the assorted chairs and couches around the room. Jess and Bleidd sat down next to Allie on the couch, one on either side, while her roommates stood by the fireplace. Allie was grateful for her new shields as the emotions of the people crowded into the room pressed against her. "I asked if everyone could meet here today because it seemed easier to get this all over with at once."

"How are you feeling?" Smythe asked.

Allie hadn't expected the personal question. Without thinking she reached out and grabbed a hand on each side, letting herself draw on both of the elves she was increasingly starting to think of as hers, which was dangerous territory. "Better. Slowly better, but better."

"I'm glad," Riordan said quietly. "I hope once this is over with you can be...safe."

"Yeah," Allie said sincerely. "Me too."

252

She glanced over at Zarethyn and Mariniessa; the elven captain nodded slightly. They had made no progress finding Liz and it was clear they needed the extra resources the police department could provide. And since Allie had already spoken to Liz she had released Jess from his promise to bring her cousin to her, agreeing that all that mattered now was finding her. Taking a deep breath she cut to the chase. "So, the thing is, the person who did it, who poisoned me, was my cousin."

Shawn looked truly shocked, and turned to Jason, who was standing there dumbfounded. The human police looked grim. Sam, predictably, was undaunted. "So your family is much like mine. Although mine would have gone with a bit of arsenic or belladonna in the tea rather than iron in the coffee."

Jess hissed in anger but Allie couldn't hold back a laugh, surprising everyone. "I wish it had been arsenic or belladonna, that probably wouldn't have done very much. Maybe a stomach ache. But the important thing is that Liz is who we need to find and she's part of the conspiracy group, the new coven."

"You're sure?" Jason asked, his voice weak. He'd always liked Liz.

"Yeah, I'm sorry Jason," she said. Bleidd squeezed her hand, his fingers tangling with hers, even as she could feel Jess's rage burning on the other side. Bleidd believed, like Allie did, that Liz hadn't intended to really hurt her but Jess had reached his limit with the things the group had been doing with Liz's help to harass and hurt her. There was neither forgiveness nor understanding in his heart for her cousin. Allie worried that he was building like a volcano and that when he finally truly lost his temper he would not be satisfied until someone died. She could feel his rage simmering beneath the surface even when he seemed distracted by other things and she worried about the bloody turn his thoughts had taken. She was afraid that this

253

was exactly why the elves discouraged strong emotions, because his anger had become a force on its own that wanted death and blood as much as he wanted her safe. She shook her head, trying to push the thoughts away. "She called me in the hospital, to apologize, sort of. More to try to explain why she'd done it so I wouldn't be mad at her."

"So why'd she do it?" Riordan said, frowning.

"She, and I guess the whole group, believe that Fairy is corrupting earth, that there's some plot by the Fey to take over and enslave humanity," Allie said, trying to keep her face neutral. "They think the only way to stop it is by separating the worlds with this ritual."

"You said the ritual wouldn't work," Riordan reminded her.

"I know, and it won't. The magical theory just isn't sound. You can't force two types of energy into separating by weakening the layer between them."

Sam was nodding now. "No that would – should – have the opposite effect. It should pull things closer."

"Or create an instability into a third reality," Zarethyn suggested, making Sam wince.

"As if we don't have enough to deal with, with two worlds. I can't imagine the chaos of three overlapping."

"Exactly," Allie said. "But they're fanatical about it. Liz hid that she was a witch for decades because she believed that all human magic users were monitored and controlled by the elves. That's how strongly they believe what they believe. I don't think anything will convince them that this ritual won't work."

"Even if they complete it and it fails?" Smythe asked.

"Honestly I think if they manage to get the next three done, when the worlds don't separate they'll convince themselves it's because the elves found a way to ruin it, or because multiple people were involved in the ritual casting…I don't know, but they'll explain the failure away."

"Allie," Jason said, breaking his silence suddenly. "Why…why you and Liz? I mean why does it all seem to hinge on you two?"

"Synchronicity," Zarethyn answered calmly, his eyes shifting to Riordan who looked down, making Allie wonder what exactly they'd been arguing about when the task force had first re-formed.

"But what does that really mean?" Jason asked, still looking upset.

"From the beginning," Zarethyn said carefully, "many things have centered on Aliaine, her store, her home, and her cousin, although we did not see all they layers and connections. Synchronicity is a force that moves in all things, that holds reality together by joining things on a metaphysical level. Allie's grandmother first helped, then thwarted the original coven – so too one grandchild aids the new coven and the other seeks to stop them. I believe that just as Allie has found herself in pivotal places, able to influence the outcomes of our investigation, so too her cousin has been in equally pivotal places able to help the new coven. It preserves a certain balance."

"You mean that's why Allie found the book, and was kidnapped, and was drawn to the second killer, and all that?" Jason asked.

"Her fate is interwoven with the coven's, yes, whether she or we knew it or not."

"What does that mean in practical terms for us now?" Riordan asked.

"Allie has always been the key to solving this. We must allow synchronicity to work in our favor to find the last few pieces of this puzzle," Zarethyn said.

"What does that mean?" Smythe asked, clearly frustrated at whet seemed to be a series of non-answers to him.

The elven captain sighed. "It means that we must continue to give Allie her head and follow where she leads, trusting her to bring us where we need to be."

The police frowned but the elves were all nodding. Allie felt her poor, battered stomach fluttering nervously. She did not like the idea that everything rested on her randomly bumbling her way to the right solution, but she also couldn't argue that it was a method that had gotten them where they were today. She hadn't believed in synchronicity before, not really, but she had to admit now that so much of what happened that should have been unrelated was actually part of this bigger plot that it was hard to deny a larger force moving in it all. *I just hope Liz and I survive this* Allie thought *I've almost died three times now. I should have died this last time, and I don't think it was synchronicity that I didn't. I think I should be dead right now and I'm not...* Allie cleared her throat. "Ummm, about that. I agree about the synchronicity. There's no other reason for me to be so in the middle of all of this. But I don't think that's going to take us any further."

Zarethyn tilted his head to the side, gazing at her intently. "Why should it not?"

"Because...and I'm not sure I can explain this exactly...but because I think I was supposed to die a couple days ago. I think when I was poisoned that should have been it. The - I don't know whatever you want to call it with this case – karma? Fate? Connection? Whatever it was through my grandmother that created the synchronicity with all of this, I think part of that was that I was meant to die when I was poisoned. Because she really wasn't trying to kill me, but that's what would have happened."

"But you lived." Riordan said, frowning as he tried to wrap his head around elven metaphysics. The elves were all contemplating her words in silence.

"Right, but only because of an, ummm, exceptional intervention. Something that shouldn't have been possible and relied on things completely unrelated to this case," Allie said, thinking as she spoke. "I've almost died three times because of this. That third time should have been it. But I lived. I just feel like from this point out my synchronicity with this situation has run its course. Because I shouldn't even be here anymore."

"What does that mean though?" Smythe repeated, irritated, his frown matching his partner's.

"It means that you can't count on me to come through with some lucky connection or to just randomly be in the exact right place at the right time," Allie said, letting go of the hands she was holding to rub her eyes. "It also means, if Liz and I have some kind of inverse or mirror synchronicity going with this that her life is in great danger right now."

"You think she'll be killed?" Jess asked, his voice flat. She could feel his eagerness though and it made her flinch behind the cover of her hands.

"I think that maybe we were both meant to die at the end of all of this," Allie said, lowering her hands and looking around the room. "I didn't so maybe she won't either. I don't know."

"Well, elven synchronicity or not I can see her life being in danger just from the situation," Riordan said. "This group is going through members pretty quickly and until we know for sure who killed the woman who shot you we shouldn't assume they aren't willing to get rid of their own loose ends."

Smythe nodded in support. "And this close to finishing they'll be desperate not to get caught. If they think she's talking to anyone outside the group they could decide she's dangerous to them."

"Then it is imperative we find her quickly," Mariniessa said, speaking for the first time.

"Yes, and in that Allie you can still aid us," Zarethyn said. "You know her well. What do you think she is most likely to do?"

"I don't know how well I really know her if I never suspected she was part of all of this," Allie protested weakly. "But if she's not here or at work…I guess I'd talk with her boyfriend, Fred. He works in town hall."

"Are we sure she is still in Ashwood?" Smythe asked.

"Not positive, no," Allie said. "But the way she was talking on the phone made it sound like she was still trying to help complete the ritual. I'm pretty sure she's still here."

Riordan nodded pulling his notebook out of his pocket. "What's her full name?"

"Elizabeth Anne McCarthy."

He wrote quickly. "I'll get an APB out and notify the bridge not to let her pass through to mortal earth."

"So you have the same last name?" Smythe said. "You're fathers were brothers?"

"Ummm, no," Allie said. "My father was her mother's brother."

Riordan stopped writing and glanced up. "Then why do you have the same last name?"

"What is this about?" Zarethyn asked before she could answer.

Allie sighed. Elves didn't use last names and, of course, being matrilineal, clan names passed through women's lines. To the elves Allie and her cousin having the same last name as their grandmother had a certain logic to it. "McCarthy wasn't her original last name but my grandmother changed it when she adopted Liz and her brother after their parents died."

Riordan looked at her sharply. "What's her original last name?"

Allie had to stop and think about that for a minute. "Tavish. Her father's name was Miles Tavish. So that must have been her original last name."

Riordan wrote that down. "Okay. She might be using that name now, if she thinks we're looking for her."

"She certainly knows we seek her detective," Jess said.

Riordan shrugged. "Any chance she may have contacted her brother?"

"I don't know," Allie said. "If you'd asked me a few days ago I would have said no. They haven't spoken in decades. My cousin, my other cousin, ran away as a teenager and has been estranged from the family since then. I've never spoken to or met him myself. But at this point I'm not sure I can say anything about Liz with certainty."

"Alright," Smythe said looking at the elves. "Then if it's okay with everyone let's do this. It seems that this new coven has more than one tie to the old. I think we need to track down all the descendants of the original members and vet them. We can also check out Ms. McCarthy – Liz McCarthy's – boyfriend and see if she's hiding with him or if he knows where she is."

Zarethyn nodded. "Be very careful detectives. We must assume that these people are all mages or witches, and as such they should be considered quite dangerous."

"Yes," Sam said suddenly. "I should probably go with you when you question people. Just to be safe. If this group feels its back is against a wall at this point there's no telling what they may do."

"Will they try to kill Ms. McCarthy – Allie – again, do you think?" Smythe asked. Ciaran looked at the human with narrowed eyes, and Allie realized that this was the first time in the entire conversation that the kelpie had been truly interested in what was being said.

"It's impossible to predict," Zarethyn said. "I agree with her that her part in this may finally have run its course, but whether or not the group believes that is a different matter. To be certain we will leave a Guard with her."

"There was an incident at the hospital this morning," Riordan said, frowning as if he were thinking hard. "I hadn't thought about it until now, but if these people are all witches…"

"What happened?" Bleidd said, his voice tense.

"A nurse killed himself," Smythe said. "Jumped off the roof."

"Seemed straightforward," Riordan added. "It's tragic but these things do happen sometimes. But now I'm wondering."

"How would that connect to me?" Allie asked unhappily.

"I'm not sure, but it happened while you were there. And everyone swore the guy had no reason to jump and no indications he was depressed. Makes me wonder now if someone made him do it, with magic."

"But why?" Allie said again.

"Maybe trying to get to you, or even just get information about you," Riordan said, thoughtfully.

Allie inhaled sharply, even as the elves all looked at her. *"Jess? Could it have been the Dark court elves?"*

"It could. They are capable of such. If they used glamour on the man, the only way to hide the evidence of it would be to kill him," Jess thought back unhappily.

"It makes sense," Bleidd thought, his voice grim. *"If they still hunt her and knew she had been taken to the clinic they may have sought to find out if she could be taken from there."*

Allie felt something pass between the two elves then, something she didn't understand. Bleidd nodded, the barest downward movement of his head and Jess returned the gesture. *Oh crap* Allie thought to herself, carefully blocking her thoughts from the other two *I am so outnumbered here. Whatever they are up to they don't want me to know about it.* The temptation to read their thoughts was tremendous but she managed to resist. Forcing herself to focus all her attention on the conversation between Zarethyn and Riordan, who were arguing details of strategy.

"Alright," Riordan said. "Let's get moving then. We'll get all the old records to you for your people to go through to track down the descendants. We'll find Liz McCarthy's boyfriend and talk to him while you see if there's anything here you can use to track her magically."

Allie swallowed, hearing that last. The elves were not playing around if they meant to use spell-tracking to try to find Liz. Clearly Allie had underestimated how much of a threat they felt Liz and the dark coven actually were. The rest of the group were nodding and breaking up, except for Jason and Shawn who looked a bit shell-shocked. Bleidd stood up, his hand caressing her arm as he rose, and then walked over to talk to Ciaran before the kelpie could slip out. Jess stood as well, intending to head over to where the other Guard were standing and Allie struggled to her feet with him.

"Sit and rest my love," he said, gesturing for her to return to her position on the couch. "I must speak with Zarethyn briefly but I will be back."

"I know, I just…are they really going to…" Allie swallowed hard, feeling anger at her cousin and worry for her safety in equal measure. "Are they so worried about what Liz might do, or this group, that they're really going to use the major tracking spells to find her?"

He looked at her in genuine surprise, his expression almost comical. "Allie, you are a member of the Elven Guard. She tried to kill you, and in a manner that is considered the most painful way any elf can die. For the sake of the justice you deserve we will do whatever must be done to find her."

261

"Oh," Allie said, stunned. It was hard for her to wrap her head around the idea that the Guard was going to such extreme lengths for her sake. Magical tracking spells were a high level magic that required an adept mage, an item from the person being tracked which contained their essence – usually something of deep personal significance – and a huge amount of magical energy. They were rarely used because the success rate was only about fifty percent and the effort needed was so high.

She stood there, still trying to process that as Jess walked over to his brother.

"I'm sorry Allie," Jason said quietly, coming up next to her in the chaos of everyone else leaving.

She looked at him, sensing his sympathy hanging between them heavy with his own grief about the situation, and nodded stiffly. "Thanks Jase."

"I just can't believe it. I mean if you'd said anyone else I could maybe see it, but Liz? That just seems impossible. She acts more like your mom than a cousin. I just can't get my head around the idea of her hurting you at all never mind trying to kill you."

"Yeah, well," Allie mumbled, looking away. Her eyes roamed to where Jess was talking to the police and then over to Bleidd who was still with Ciaran. He'd been acting odd since she'd woken in the hospital; staying with her as she'd asked but clearly pulling away as much as possible. Every now and then a bit of the old Bleidd would shine through with some innuendo or teasing, but much of the time he seemed to be trying to treat her with a politeness that made her feel as if she'd offended him somehow. Syndra had accused Allie of playing with his heart but she felt like it was hers that was being played with now, which made her feel guilty since she still couldn't offer him anything but friendship. Even if she wanted to. Even if she kept thinking that there was no reason not to anymore. In the hospital Jess had subtly encouraged her to spend time alone with Bleidd, even when Jess was there, finding excuses to step out for periods of time, but nothing had happened between them. It left Allie feeling unsure and vulnerable, afraid of his rejection, and equally afraid to simply ask Jess what his thoughts were on the situation so she had distracted herself with trying to keep helping the police and the Guard. Jason was still waiting for her to say something so she made herself add, "I didn't want to believe it either but she called me at the clinic and admitted it. I don't think she was trying to kill me though. I really don't, and Bleidd doesn't either. I think, I mean I'm sure, that she just wanted me to get sick."

She glanced back at Jason, and realized he was watching her watching Bleidd. She pulled her eyes away from the elf and focused on Jason. He nodded. "I'd believe that before I'd believe she was trying to kill you. I mean Liz can be a bit overbearing, and she can be blunt, and she really doesn't like elves, but she was always nice to me. She made me feel welcome here and we had fun when we hung out. And we talked a lot, enough that I know she really does love you. I can't imagine her poisoning you, unless it was just to make you sick."

Allie relaxed slightly, relieved that Jason wasn't flatly condemning Liz. "Yeah, I really think that's what happened. I think she just underestimated how strongly it would affect me."

"I can understand that," he said wincing. "No offense Allie, but you really do look pretty human. It's easy to forget sometimes that you aren't, even though I know you aren't. And it seems like iron does hit you as hard as the full elves."

"Yeah, I guess," Allie said, embarrassed. She intentionally tried to pass as human most of the time, but it was awkward to hear Jason saying she did it so well even he forgot she wasn't. Maybe that was how Liz convinced herself that Allie was exempt from the coven's

263

worldview....Allie's eyes tracked to Bleidd again, distracted. *I wish I knew how to handle this*, she thought. *What should I do? Act on what I want because it seems okay with Jess now? Talk to Jess first? What if Bleidd isn't interested anymore?* That thought was as embarrassing as Jason's comment; she didn't want to admit her desire to Jess and risk then having to tell him she'd been rejected...

"I hope it doesn't bother you, me saying that," Jason said.

"No," Allie said, shaking her head. "I understand what you mean."

"Okay, spill it," Jason said, peering at her closely.

"Spill what?"

"What is going on with you and Bleidd?" he asked, and she could feel his worry, his emotions held out by her shields but still with the unusual intensity that only Jason had.

"Ummm," Allie mumbled, her eyes automatically going back to Bleidd, then flinching away when she realized she was staring. "Well...it's kind of complicated..."

"Allie!" Jason cut in, grabbing her wrist and squeezing lightly. "I'm not blind. Something weird is going on. I can see it. I know he's totally freaked that you almost died, but it's more than that."

"Yeah, see it's just..." she faltered, then pulled him across the room into the corner, trying to get some privacy. "I was dying Jason. Really dying. Brynneth couldn't help me."

She felt his shock like a wave of cold air, making the hair on her arms go up. His grip tightened on her arm. She forced herself to continue. "And Jess thought there was a chance I could heal myself, or at least enough to save me from dying and let Brynneth help me, if I could just use his emotions. So he tried but it wasn't enough."

"I would have helped too," Jason said, his voice subdued.

"I know you would have but, ummmm," she could feel herself blushing now and looked down to try to hide it, aware that the room was still full of people, including Shawn who was now talking to detective Smythe and looking like he might pass out. "Ummm. Unless you've developed an interest in girls in the last few days I don't know about you couldn't have helped."

"Oh," Jason said frowning. Then, as her words really sunk in, "Oh!"

"Right. So he, ummm…and that did help but not enough and he asked Bleidd to…"

"Holy shit," Jason whispered, his eyes cutting over to where Bleidd was standing.

"Right," Allie said again, feeling like she was explaining this badly. "And he did – help I mean. And it saved my life. He saved my life. But I, ummm, the thing is, I was pretty out of it and I could sense him, his emotions but I couldn't connect enough, so I, ahhh, well, I ended up creating the same kind of spellbond with him that I have with Jess."

Jason's mouth fell open and he stood and gaped at her. She shifted nervously from one foot to the other, the silence starting to freak her out. Finally she burst out with, "You think I'm a terrible person don't you?"

"What?" Jason said. "No. No, of course not. That's just, wow Allie that's a lot to take in. Are you…I mean, are you okay about it? About what happened?"

"What do you mean?"

"Ummm. Does it bother you that you were out of it and they…"

"Oh! No," she said, shaking her head. "It wasn't like that, exactly. I mean I was out of it, yeah, but I knew who it was, who was there with me. And I didn't know exactly what was going on, ahhhh, you know physically,

265

but I wanted the emotions. I was, ahhh, encouraging that part. As much as I could on the mental end of things. That's participation, sort of. I'm more worried that I influenced their emotions to get what I needed. And they saved my life. And I would have been…I mean if I was totally conscious I would have encouraged it too…"

"Okay, okay," he cut in. "You're babbling. I get it. I think it's a little weird, and if it was me, it would bother me, but it's your life and your body, and if you're okay with it, I'm okay with it."

"I'm okay with it," Allie said firmly. She wished she could explain the way the red and gold fire had been in the darkness, the way that their emotions and will to live had filled her. The way that she had drunk it in greedily until there was nothing more to take…and her own certainty that she could have refused, could have stopped either one of them by killing their desire in that blackness, putting out the beautiful flames, if she had wanted to.

"So are you and Bleidd and Jessilaen all, I mean…how's this going to work now?" Jason asked, obviously uncomfortable.

She flinched, looking down again. "I don't know. I think I've really screwed everything up, but there's too much going on right now to deal with it, you know?"

"Well. Ummm. Wow. Is this bond thing something you can fix? I mean undo?"

"Honestly I don't know," she said, biting her lip. "I think so. I mean in theory I should be able to unbind him. I think."

Jason's expression softened as he reached out to lift Allie's chin so that she had to look at him. "Is that what he wants?"

"What do you mean?"

"Allie!" Jason's dark eyes searched her face as if he were looking for something important.

"What?" she mumbled uncomfortably.

"He loves you. He's been trying to get into your pants for months now. Maybe he won't want you to undo this," Jason said as if that should have been obvious.

She made a face. "Yeah well he might be re-thinking that."

"And what does that mean?"

"That sometimes getting what you want makes you realize you don't really want it," she said, embarrassed at the tears that threatened to spill over.

"Hey, don't cry," Jason said, alarmed. Then, realization dawning in his eyes. "You really love him don't you?"

"Ugh," she groaned, trying to pull away from her friend. "Yes. I really do. And I really love Jess too. And I'm really contracted to marry Jess. And Bleidd really did save my life. And I really tied myself psychically to both of them. And it's all just a huge mess now and damned if I have any idea how to fix any of it. Really fix it. Because it seems like anything I do is just going to mean breaking someone's heart."

"Including yours," Jason said.

"I think I'm pretty screwed at this point," Allie said sincerely, earning a small wry smile from Jason.

Allie jumped as a hand landed on her shoulder; she watched Jason's eyes go wide. Then Bleidd's voice was in her ear, "How so Allie?"

She swallowed hard, feeling his worry through their connection. Only that, and after a moment she decided he hadn't overheard much of the conversation. Probably only the last few comments. Jason was projecting panic and she knew in a minute he'd open his mouth and start babbling and the Gods only knew what he'd say once he got started. "I just meant that…this entire situation is so complicated. I can't think of any easy way for it to be resolved."

Jason looked even more shocked and she prayed he'd keep his mouth shut while sending up a simultaneous prayer that Bleidd would assume she was talking about anything else but her love life. To her relief he said "Yes, I know you feel responsible for much of the situation, even though you should not. I also know you are still hoping that Liz will be captured alive. I hope though that you are prepared for it to end badly Allie."

She looked away, out the window at the heavy grey clouds. "Do you think it might rain later?"

Jason rolled his eyes. Then, as much to himself as either of them he said, "Ummm. Why don't I walk Shawn out before he falls over?"

Bleidd let his hand fall from her shoulder, his emotions now hesitant and uncertain. "Allie, no one wants her to die…"

"Sure they do," she said. "Syndra does. Jess does."

He sighed. "Alright. But the police and the majority of the Guard intend to capture her alive. And Jessilaen may wish her dead but he would not actively seek to harm her. He knows how much that would upset you."

Allie inclined her head in an elven shrug at the same time she lifted her shoulders in a human one. "I'm really tired. This meeting took a lot more out of me than I thought it would."

Bleidd looked for Jess who was still talking with the other Guard, then took her arm gently guiding her out of the room. "Let's get you to bed then. You should be resting."

"Will you stay with me?" Allie asked, afraid to look at him, her voice shy.

She could feel the surge of desire and longing that went through him and then was overwhelmed by an iron-clad determination. "I can't. I have to go out. But I'm sure Jessilaen is planning to stay with you and I asked Ciaran to keep a closer eye on the house. You'll be safe."

She nodded, swallowing more tears. *Of course he wants to go out* she thought bitterly *He's been stuck by my side for days, only leaving to go to work. He's probably thoroughly sick of me. Wanting to get in my bed and actually dealing with me being so damn needy are two different things.* She pulled her arm out of his loose grip and began limping down the hallway. "It's okay. I understand. You go do what you wa- need to do. I can manage to get upstairs by myself."

"Allie," he said, his voice equal parts tired and annoyed. They had reached the bottom of the staircase and she started to step up only to find herself swept up in his arms. She let out a small undignified sound in protest and she could feel his laughter vibrating through his chest. She clutched him tightly, burying her head against his shoulder, as he began moving quickly up the stairs towards her room. "You are so ridiculous sometimes."

"I'd argue," she muttered into his t-shirt, "but I don't feel like getting dropped right now."

"How about now?" he asked a moment later, his voice teasing, and then he really did drop her.

Her heart spasmed as she fell, in the instant before she hit the mattress of her own bed. She couldn't restrain a giggle. "Oh, that was evil."

He looked down at her, his amusement changing into something else entirely. She sobered as the storm of his feelings flowed through her.

"Stay here," he said, his voice husky. "Get some rest."

"Bleidd…" she whispered, not sure what she wanted to say to him.

He hesitated, then with the uncanny speed of the Fey he bent down and kissed her, pressing his mouth against hers. Eyes closed she reached up and tangled her fingers in his hair. His tongue moved between her lips and she opened her mouth for him even as his hand found her breast. She moaned against his mouth, her free hand sliding down his body, brushing lightly across his hip…and then he was gone.

She opened her eyes and caught a glimpse of him disappearing out the door. One fist pounded into the mattress as she was overcome by desire and frustration. "Damn!"

****

"How could you let them know it was you?" the group's leader's voice shook with rage. Liz had never seen her friend so angry and despite feeling that she was the one who should be angry she held her hands up in a peaceful gesture.

"They already knew. They knew as soon as they realized it was iron poisoning," Liz said.

"How would they have known that?"

"How couldn't they have?" Liz shot back, some of her own anger showing through. "When it was obvious it was poison it was pretty clear it had to have been me. No one else was there when she got sick and iron is too fast acting for her to have drunk it earlier."

"Why did you call the ambulance?" the leader fretted, pulling aside the heavy curtains to pear out the window. Liz knew that was a waste of time. No one was out there; the police and Guard had already checked here but they didn't know about this secret room, a small annexed space that had long ago been sealed off from the main building. That was what made it such an ideal meeting place.

"Of course I called an ambulance! You should have seen her, it was horrible," Liz shuddered at the memory. "She was dying. I couldn't sit there and watch her die."

"No, of course not," the leader muttered insincerely. "But it shouldn't have affected her so strongly. It should have just made her a little sick."

"Yeah, well it didn't," Liz said. "It was killing her. I knew it and the doctors said the same thing."

"Then how did she survive?"

"She said the elves healed her," Liz said reluctantly. It galled to admit the elves had done anything helpful.

"I'm sure they did," the leader sneered, her voice full of innuendo. "And I bet Allie paid for it."

"Hey," Liz said, shifting uncomfortably at the implications.

"I think we need to face the reality that she's been subverted," the leader said, and Liz could see her convincing herself with each word. "She's been seduced into their beds and corrupted by their ways. Who knows what magic they've done on her and with her?"

"She's a good person," Liz insisted stubbornly. "And she's my cousin. We grew up together."

"I know that," the leader said, her voice still hard. "We grew up together too didn't we? But some people choose darkness and they can't be saved."

Liz shifted again, the old wood creaking under her feet, not liking this line of thought. "But we need her. To tell us everything that was in the book."

"Yes, the book that you let her burn," the leader said, her voice acidic.

Liz inhaled sharply. "We've been over this. What was I supposed to do? And it's all still there in her head. She has a very good memory for details she reads."

"Yes, and do you think she's going to help us by telling us everything we want to know?"

Liz looked away, knowing that Allie would never help them do anything that might hurt anybody. She was too soft for that, which is why Liz had never even tried to get her into the group. "She may eventually. When she sees that we're right."

"You know she won't unless we…persuade her."

"Persuade her? How? By hurting her?" Liz blanched, suddenly seeing Allie the night they'd brought her home from Walters', pale and smelling of blood, bruised, unable to walk. She shook her head violently, her eyes still fixed on the wood grain of the wall. "No. You can't."

"I think you're losing sight of the real goal here," the leader said carefully. "No single person matters more than success. We all have to do what we have to do to make this work."

Liz heard the floorboards creak as the other woman walked across the room towards her. She sighed. "I need to get out of town. Let me take Allie with me. I can make her go with me, trust me, I can. And she'll be out of your way until this is over."

"I'm sorry Liz, but I have to do what's best for the coven. I've done my best to cover for you every time you've failed but I can't let it go this time," the other woman's voice didn't sound sorry. She sounded determined and that raised the hairs on the back of Liz's neck.

"What are you talking about?" she asked as she turned towards the group's leader, her friend. She looked down in dull shock at the blade in her chest, the manicured pink nails of the hand gripping the hilt. A small grunt escaped her lips but no other sound came out.

"I'm sorry Liz. Really I am," the leader said calmly as Liz went to her knees and then collapsed onto the floor. "You're my best friend but I can't let that get in the way of doing the right thing. Now that they know you're involved they'll find you, no matter how we try to hide you. She'll find you for them, the same way she's found everyone else. And they'll get you to tell them everything, name names, point out the rest of us. Everything we're worked for will be destroyed. I can't let that happen. I'll tell everyone else you're in hiding so they won't be upset over another death in the group. And Fred can take over for Jerry handling the sacrifices. His loyalty to you held him back before but I think he'll be quite capable of doing what's needed. Now that you'll be…away. And when we get Allie don't worry, I'll watch out for her but she'll tell us what we need to know. One way or another."

Liz looked up at her friend, her lips moving in a silent question. The other woman shook her head. "Oh honey don't act like you wouldn't have done the same thing in my place. All that really matters is fixing the worlds. Whatever it takes."

****

Bleidd moved carefully through the club, ignoring the pulsing lights and blaring music. This was not a place he would have come willingly, one of the lowest of the strip clubs to be found in town and the kind of place that catered to many less than legal activities. But it was just the sort of place he was more likely to find his quarry. His eyes scanned the crowd, mostly men, both humans and Fey, who were absorbed in watching the girls dance.

It was hard to focus knowing that Allie was finally home from the clinic. He had spent the last two days by her side, despite his own worry that she did not truly want him there. Certainly she seemed eager for him to stay but she was also still in shock over her cousin's betrayal and gravely ill. If he closed his eyes it was all too easy to remember the last several nights spent sleeping in the narrow hospital bed with her, and sometimes with her and Jessilaen as well, Allie clinging to him, or both of them, like a child afraid of monsters under the bed. The iron

273

poisoning may not have killed her but she had been extremely ill, unable to eat, spiking high fevers....he had stayed because he had given his word that he would and when she was delirious from the fevers and calling his name, or confessing things to him he would never have imagined from her, about how much she needed him, he was glad that he had stayed. It was still difficult though to hear her say many of the same things to Jessilaen and to know that ultimately, even if he had gotten what he wanted in a way, the Guard commander was still the one she was choosing to be with. He would forever be the friend, perhaps closer now than any friend was meant to be but still just a friend, looking in at someone else getting what he truly wanted.

There were times, in his bitterness, he wanted to leave her there, or to go to the bar and use the balm of alcohol as he had for so many years to forget this new pain. But somehow he could not do it, not when she needed him so desperately. Even now when he had forced himself back on the trail of the Dark court agents, knowing that the threat they represented must be eliminated, part of him wanted nothing more than to go back and stay by her side. The memory of her lips pressed against his was more than a small distraction, and the knowledge that she had wanted him in her bed was a torment. He had almost lost his resolve, feeling her hand slide along his body, but somehow he had found the willpower to leave. She was too emotionally raw after the betrayals of the last few days and he could not let her do something in a moment of physical need that she would regret.

She'd been clear for months that she preferred monogamy and equally clear that she had chosen Jessilaen, something he had not truly understood until he saw them together in the hospital. She really loved Jessilaen, and he loved her. Up until this point Bleidd had truly believed that Jessilaen did not – could not – love Allie as much as he did, and that the other elf was just fixated on enjoying the experiences associated with her. But seeing the lengths he had gone to to save her, even his willingness to give up his exclusive claim on her if it meant she would live, had forced Bleidd to reassesses his opinion. Bleidd had left the hospital with them knowing that if he forced her to choose between them he would destroy Allie's love for him. The past two months he had thought if only he could get her to see that he loved her more, that he was the truer, she would choose him willingly, but now he understood that Jessilaen was not the shallow affair he had assumed. She was willing enough now, in her pain and weakness, to cleave to him, but he knew how often people as young and inexperienced as Allie mistook physical love for emotional support. How could she not come to hate him if he took advantage of her current weakness to get into her bed when he was certain that was not what she really wanted? And yet he could not stop thinking about her.

If this was the effect she had on Jessilaen he could understand much better the apparent madness that drove the other elf…

As he slid around one of the tables in the back he found a girl blocking his way.

She was one of the dancers, clad only in a g-string. Her long blond hair reminded him of Allie and he felt a stab of grief and desire. The girl's eyes had the unfocused look of someone who is not sober, but her words were steady, "Hey handsome. You looking for a private party?"

Of course Bleidd thought, weighing the girl's offer. *Most of these girls make their real money illegally. I've never understood the human insistence on outlawing what should be a perfectly respectable profession, or for that matter why anyone should have to pay for sex at all, but humans are such an odd people.* The girl, who was more than a foot shorter than he was, reached up and put her hand on his chest, taking his silence for interest. She licked her lips leaning into him. "I'll give you a good price and I can be really, really friendly."

Bleidd tilted his head to the side, *There's no harm in a slight delay* he thought *I could enjoy some sport with her and then get back to my hunt. I haven't been with anyone since Allie.* That thought made him wince slightly although thinking of Allie was always a pleasant thing. He started to step forward towards the girl and only then realized that his body was not cooperating with him, despite the fact that a bare few hours ago he had been more than ready to lie with Allie. He should have been more than ready now to enjoy what the girl was offering but although the mental interest was there the physical arousal was not. Such a thing had never happened to him before and he didn't know what to do about it. He gently moved the girl's hands away and stepped back, murmuring, "Perhaps another time."

She looked disappointed but moved on. He stood there for a moment frowning. *Perhaps it was just this one time* he thought uncertainly. *Or perhaps....perhaps this is part of the cost of being bonded to Allie. That would explain a great deal about Jessilaen as well.* That thought was a difficult one. He did not regret saving her life, nor even being tied to her mind, although he greatly feared that she would not waver from her preference for Jessilaen alone. However the idea of not being physically able to bed anyone else but her when she was in a monogamous relationship with another person was hard to come to terms with.

He shook himself slightly, directing his attention back outwards. He needed to focus on finding the Dark court elves hiding within the town. He could worry about his sex life, or lack of one, later. He was getting close now, he could feel it, and the sooner they eliminated this threat the better.

276

He moved up to the bar and waited for the bartender's attention. A few minutes later a harried looking older woman came over, "What'll it be?"

"Orange juice, straight," he replied, keeping his eyes on the crowd.

"Virgin juice?" the woman asked, clearly amused. She was short, barely five feet, and thin. He might have thought her a retired dancer but she was far too homely to have ever earned money stripping, even here.

He allowed his lips to curve into a small smile as he slipped her a hundred. "Indeed."

The woman's grey eyes went wide. "I can't change this, not this early."

"I don't need change back," he replied easily. "But I am curious about something."

"Right," the woman agreed, then to his surprise switched to low Elvish. "And I can keep the change if'n I satisfy yer curiosity, then?"

Bleidd switched languages easily, looking more intently at the woman. "You can keep the money either way. But if you happen to know anything about dancers disappearing or being hurt, or about strange elves causing trouble in here, that would certainly satisfy my curiosity."

She grunted, sliding a large glass of orange juice his way. "I wouldn'ta thought the cops 'ud care about strippers."

"I'm neither a police officer nor an Elven Guard," Bleidd said calmly. After another moment of study he decided the woman was a goblin. Probably outcast from her clan if she was working here.

"Aren't ye then?" the woman said suspiciously.

"No. I was Outcast many years ago," *and no need to tell you I was redeemed* he thought. "And I have a friend in this town who has mixed ancestry that is in danger from these elves."

The woman peered intently at him, her whole demeanor thawing. "Mayhap I heard o' ye. And yer trying to help yer friend?"

"One of these elves hurt her badly several months ago. They tried to hurt her again last week. I intend to find them and see how they enjoy the experience themselves," he said savagely.

The goblin woman grinned approvingly. "Well enough then. Yeah I know 'em. Come in here every couple days and start trouble. Drink too much, mess wit the girls. Use glamour on and mess with their heads. Hurt 'em sometimes real bad."

"And the owner puts up with this?" Bleidd said coldly.

"The owner'd sell his mother's liver for a bit o' cash," the bartender sneered.

Bleidd took a long drink of the juice. "When do you expect them back?"

"Tomorrow," the goblin said, her eyes glinting viciously.

He nodded. "Keep the money."

He stood up, pushing the remains of the drink away and walked out through the crowd. Outside a cold rain was falling, and he shivered feeling a slight twinge in his injured shoulder. *Tomorrow* he thought *Tomorrow they will come here, and they will not leave again. At least not in one piece....*

****

"Wait here," Allie said to Jason as she struggled out of the passenger seat of his truck.

"Ummm, Allie, this is a bad idea," Jason said weakly.

She ignored him. "Wait here. I'll be right back."

She marched through the rain up to the gate in front of Miss Amelia's house leaving Jason sitting unhappily parked by the sidewalk. She knew it wasn't fair to him to make him drive her here, but she wasn't allowed to drive, in case she passed out, and she was so furious she would have walked if she had to. Bleidd was still out, Jess was at the Outpost, and she needed to see the old mage. After what she'd unintentionally witnessed that afternoon she had to know more about what she'd done to the two elves who were spellbound to her, and this was the only place to find any answers. And Allie had no intention of leaving without answers.

She limped heavily across the lawn, her body aching with the effort. At the door she held the doorbell down until the maid answered, then pushed past the startled woman. The maid tried to stop her, but Allie was on a mission. She dodged around the heavyset woman and into the parlor where Miss Amelia was sitting with a cup of tea.

"I need to talk to you," Allie said, over the maid's loud protests.

"It's alright Lucy," Miss Amelia said, totally unperturbed by Allie's behavior. "Let her in."

Allie ignored the fuming maid who bowed out of the room with obvious ill grace, her eyes meeting Miss Amelia's. "You said I had bound them to me, what did you mean?"

"Them? I was under the impression you had only one person bound to you," Miss Amelia said, stirring sugar into her tea.

"Not anymore. Now there is another," Allie said, flustered and then found herself explaining. "I was dying and he – Jess – tried to help me but his emotions weren't enough so he brought someone else, someone he knew I loved, and I…I didn't mean to, it wasn't on purpose, I was semi-conscious and I needed his feelings and I couldn't get to them so I…I guess I did what you said, I bound him to me. I don't even really know how. I thought it was a spell, I mean I know there was a spell involved too, but there was something else…"

"You bound him – them I suppose – because you need what they give you once they are bound to you. Casual relationships aren't enough of a connection for you to draw what you truly need from them," the older woman said, adding honey to her cup.

"I don't want them to be bound to me!" Allie said, her voice rising with each word.

"Why not?" Miss Amelia asked, calmly sipping her tea.

"Because it's not fair!" Allie shouted.

The old woman raised an eyebrow. "How so? You give them something special, something they couldn't get otherwise, a purity and intensity of feeling that very few people ever experience. And they give you the emotions you need for your own energy."

"I don't want to feed on anyone," Allie said, fighting tears.

"There's no need for childish hysterics," Miss Amelia said, still perfectly calm. "You are what you are Allie. You do them no harm. I imagine they are more than willing to give you what you need."

"That's not the point," Allie said, struggling to control herself. "They do it because I make them want to do it. That's not the same thing. I feel like some kind of freaking drug, the way I influence them to do what I need."

"The fact remains that you need them. You can draw on anyone's emotions and gain some…value from them. But unless your mixed blood makes you entirely different from the one I knew, you need to have this bond with someone to truly get the energy you need, in the way that you need, to stay strong, to heal, to empower yourself."

"And if I don't?" Allie said rebelliously.

One white eyebrow arched gracefully up. "Then you'll weaken and pull energy from emotions, feed on to use the crude term you prefer, anyone around you. Like living on watered milk instead of cream. And the emotions will influence you because you will be forced to take whatever you can get."

"I wasn't like this before."

"Of course you were. You always have been," Miss Amelia said dismissively. "Although you certainly have your own unique approach to everything and the way you manifest things is not what a full elf might. But what you are hasn't changed. You never saw it because you had never bound anyone to yourself before. Now you know what that level of energy is like. Quite frankly I don't know why you'd want to go back, to be weak and at the whim of other people's feelings again."

"Because I don't want to see people I care about changed into something they shouldn't be." Allie gritted out, annoyed by the other woman's cavalier disregard for that aspect of things.

"Does it harm them so much?"

"It makes them different. Not like other elves. They don't want anyone but me, for one thing, which goes entirely against their culture. They feel possessiveness, jealousy, things that shouldn't be an issue in their culture, and now I realize they can't be with anyone else but me…and my preferences influence them. How am I supposed to feel about that?"

"Relieved?" Miss Amelia suggested, sipping her tea. "Don't give me that look young woman. There's nothing you can do about what they feel because of their binding to you. I'd guess it's a defense mechanism, to ensure that those you bond to stay with you and keep giving you what you need. And if you agonize so over the morality of it, then comfort yourself with the knowledge that you genuinely care for them and they for you. As you've explained it you did not bind them – either of them – until you knew they already loved you. If it were otherwise, if you had taken unwilling people and bound them, forced them into this situation, then perhaps you could feel guilty and call yourself evil."

"Aren't I evil?" Allie said bitterly.

"Nonsense," the old woman waved her away. "You have a right to get what you need, as much as any living being does. You harm no one and the fact that you have not one but two men who are willing to join with you and give you their emotions as you need them seems to me to be a strong reference to your character. Stop fighting against accepting what you are. It cannot be changed. Accept it and learn to use it."

"And what am I?" she asked softly.

Miss Amelia gave her a long look. "I think you already know the answer to that question."

Allie shook her head. "That's not possible. How would I not have known that?"

"You can call your gift a type of human empathy or you can call it what the elves call it. What difference does it make?" the old woman said.

Allie looked down; her hands were shaking so she clenched them into fists to make them stop. She wanted to keep arguing, but she had heard enough stories growing up about the Bahvanshee, the elves who were able to feed on other people's emotions and sexual energy, to recognize what Miss Amelia was talking about, and to see it in herself. *How could I not have realized this?* she thought, angry at herself. *It was all there, from the moment I bonded with Jess, even before with his strange obsessive attraction to me. I just refused to see it.* Most elves, even in the Dark court, feared those born Bahvanshee because they had the power to force others to their will, to manipulate their emotions, and to drain the life force from anything. Luckily it was an extremely rare thing – Allie suspected true elven empaths were more common than the aberrant Bahvanshee. *Leave it to me*, she thought suddenly tired, *to be the first half-elven one. No wonder I'm so attuned to death that I can track down bodies and murderers.*

"You are what you are. Accept it," Miss Amelia said callously.

"I don't want to feel like I'm manipulating people," Allie insisted.

"We can manipulate people with our words and actions Allie. All of us can do this. Perhaps you do influence those who are bound to you through that bond, but that doubtless goes both ways. They affect you too. It is after all a symbiotic relationship," the old woman stopped drinking and looked off into the distance, as if she were seeing something far away or remembering something she'd almost forgotten. Suddenly everything clicked into place.

"He was your lover," Allie said softly. "The other one like me that you knew. He was the elven lover you mentioned before."

The old woman nodded slowly. "Yes. He died during the Great War after the Sundering. I would have died with him, if I could have but I had…other things holding me here. And then the greatest irony of all, to find out that being bound to him had extended my own life far past his. Some days it seems like a gift, other days it's so bitter its unbearable. But there is some small comfort for me in knowing that I am here now to help you find your way. It almost makes me feel like I have some purpose beyond refusing to die just to annoy my greedy family and keeping my staff employed."

Allie took a deep breath. "Can I find my way Miss Amelia?"

"Oh Allie," the old mage said, setting her teacup down carefully on its matching china plate. "Of course you can. If you want so desperately to be a good person, then stop judging yourself so harshly and do good in the world. It's your choice – it's always your choice – whether you are good or evil."

Allie opened her mouth to argue more and then closed it again. Miss Amelia was right about several things. Allie had no control over what she was, whether she called herself an empath or Bahvanshee. She could however learn to control her impulses and to choose what she did with her abilities. She nodded stiffly. "Thank you."

Miss Amelia waved dismissively. "Go home Allie. It's late and I'm tired."

Allie nodded again, embarrassed now at the way she'd barged in on the elderly woman. She started to walk out when Miss Amelia's voice stopped her. "I'll see you promptly at 7 p.m. Wednesday for our next lesson."

Allie smiled. "Yes Miss Amelia. Have a nice night."

She walked back out into the rainy darkness trying to decide how to tell Bleidd and Jess what she'd just learned. Maybe they had already guessed, but she couldn't assume. If they chose to stay with her, either of them, they had a right to know what they were choosing.

And she was tired of ignoring problems and pretending things were fine when they weren't.

It was time to start confronting problems head on.

Chapter 10 – Tuesday

"She's dead."

"What?" Allie asked, turning slowly towards Syndra who was pacing around the living room. Her friend was wearing her police uniform, including the jacket, looking exactly as she always had when she'd headed out for work when she was still alive. She paced around the room frowning at the wood paneling and chewing her lip now, her blond ponytail bouncing as she walked.

"I said she's dead, how hard is that to follow?" Syndra snapped.

Allie sat down hard on the closest chair, a plush Victorian style seat that managed to be uncomfortable in spite of its welcoming appearance. Despite everything that Liz had done to her, despite everything she'd said on the phone, Allie was overcome by grief. "What? How?"

Syndra sighed, smacking the wall with her hand, and then wincing as if she'd forgotten that it would hurt. "I found her where she was hiding. Clever, clever little bitch. And I figured I'd wait and see if I could do anything...I don't know maybe shove her at the top of the stairs or something. Turns out I was wasting my time. Her own friend killed her. Stabbed her. Not in the back by the way. In the front. Right in the chest."

Syndra made a stabbing gesture and Allie winced. "What is it with this group and knives?"

Syndra snorted. "Well fuck they shot you so clearly they aren't that picky."

"Gee, thanks for that Syn," Allie said.

"Obviously they go with whatever works. Probably knives because they're quiet," Syndra said, shrugging.

"Okay, so why are you still here then?" Allie snapped, suddenly angry at the cavalier way her friend had told her of her cousin's death. She wanted to grieve for Liz, but she was also angry at her too, and that left her feeling conflicted.

"Fuck if I know," Syndra said, smacking the wall again. "Maybe...maybe...fuck! Whatever. I don't care."

Allie relented when she saw how upset Syndra was. "Well, I've been thinking about it..."

"That's dangerous."

"...and I think maybe you're tied there until the residual energy from the spell is released," Allie said.

"What do you mean?" Syndra spun and crossed the room towards where Allie was sitting, looking eager.

"Well, the spell uses the pain of the girls who died to create an energetic battery, right? And that echo-energy remains active, as if the torture and death is still happening all the time, or out of time, at the ritual site. That's what's powering everything there, all the weirdness, the weakening of reality at the site. But I was thinking, maybe part of that, because it also involves tying in the death energy, maybe tying in the death energy actually ties in the souls too, trapping them here."

"Well that's completely fucking horrifying," Syndra said softly. "Wait I wasn't killed in the real ritual though. Just an imitation."

"But it was a real ritual at the site, it just wasn't part of the bigger cycle."

"So you think it counted enough to trap my soul anyway?"

"I think so yeah," Allie said slowly. "Which means until the elven adept gets here and takes it down you're probably stuck."

"Well isn't that just fan-fucking-tastic!"Syndra groaned, then flopped down herself on the couch.

"So Liz is really dead?" Allie asked after a few minutes of silence.

"Yeah, really really," Syndra said. "She and this blond Stepford wife looking chick were arguing about Liz blowing her cover. I guess the other woman decided Liz was a liability. Walked up to her and stabbed her in the chest, then dragged her body into a crawl space."

"Wait…where was this?" Allie asked, realizing she needed to tell the police where they could find Liz.

"At the theater."

"It can't be Syn," Allie said shaking her head. "Everyone searched there."

"It's a back room. It was blocked off years ago and the only way in is behind what looks like a wall," Syndra said.

"Like a secret room?"

"Yeah, I guess," Syn shrugged. "They were talking about the group meeting there."

"The new coven? When?" Allie asked eagerly.

"Tonight. Oh I get it you're going to tell the task force so they can ambush everybody. I like it. Yeah, they said today, this afternoon at 5. At the theater in the secret room."

Allie nodded, trying to hold onto all of this in the shifting dreamscape. "Okay, tell me exactly where…"

She came up out of the dream like a fish jumping out of water. She startled Jess awake as she sat up, gasping, and he quickly moved to support her, although she found that she was feeling better already than she had been when she'd gone to sleep. It was amazing how quickly she was healing now that she wasn't fighting against her own nature but instead allowing herself to fully pull from Jess…and Bleidd, even if he was avoiding her like a plague victim.

"Allie, what is it?" Jess asked, concern coloring his words.

"I dreamed of Syndra again," Allie said, and then, realizing they were alone in the room. "Where's Bleidd?"

"Sleeping in his own room," Jess answered.

Allie felt a surge of annoyance followed by embarrassment. Of course he was in his own room. *This isn't the hospital anymore and he had no reason to assume I wanted him with me at home.* She shifted unhappily in the bed, Jess's arms warm around her body, thinking *and I have no reason to assume he wants to be here with me now either. Even if he did kiss me earlier. He also took off. And when I got back from running off to yell at an old woman no one was home. I have no idea when he got back or where he's been or what he's been doing...except that I know he hasn't been sleeping with anyone else because thanks to me he can't. If I were him I'd be pretty pissed about that. Maybe the last thing he wants is to be around me right now...*

"Allie?" Jess asked, his voice soft.

She pushed away her recriminations about the situation with Bleidd for the moment and tried to focus on the issue at hand. "Liz is dead. Syndra was following her and saw her being killed."

"Truly?" Jess asked, eyes wide. She could feel his relief and happiness at the news and she tried to ignore that as well.

"Yes. Stabbed, Syndra said," Allie said. "At the theater. There's a secret backroom blocked off from everything else and that's where Liz was hiding."

"I am sorry for your loss, my heart," Jess said. "I know her death grieves you."

"It does, but I can't deal with that right now. What matters is that Syndra overhead them planning a meeting of the dark coven today, this afternoon, at the same place."

Jess sat up quickly. "Indeed? And you know the time and exact location?"

"Yes, I do," Allie said, then as she thought more about what Liz had said on the phone and something Syndra had said about the woman who had stabbed her.

288

"And I think…I think I know who someone else in the group is."

"How?" Jess asked.

"Things that Liz and Syndra both were saying, if you add them together…I think someone else in the group, maybe even someone up in their hierarchy is Liz's friend Candice," Allie said. "I'm not sure if knowing that helps you any."

"It may. Although likely setting an ambush at the theater will be more effective than tracking down individuals," Jess said thoughtfully. "Let me contact Zarethyn and inform him of these developments and we will decide how best to proceed."

"Okay," Allie agreed. She hesitated as he slid out of the bed and dressed, knowing that she needed to tell him about what she had learned about herself, but afraid of how he might react. "Jess?"

"Yes my love?" his voice was distracted and she lost her nerve.

"Never mind. It can wait," she said, feeling like a coward.

He leaned over and kissed her forehead. "I will be back later. I do not think you should open your store today – stay home and rest one more day instead."

She found herself nodding in mute agreement, and he smiled as he turned to leave. Glancing at the clock she realized it was still early, just past 6 a.m. and sighing she decided to try to get some more sleep. She'd worry about everything later. "Jess?"

"Yes?"

"If you see Bleidd," she said slowly, "could you just make sure he's okay?"

Jess tilted his head, curious. "Certainly. Are you worried about him?"

"I'm worried he's upset…about something," she mumbled. "If you see him just, if you could just talk to him. Try to make him feel better?"

"If it pleases you," Jess agreed. "I have grown fond of him as well and I will see if I can cheer him up."

There was something in the way he said that last that made Allie pause. If she didn't know better she'd have thought it had a sexual overtone to it. She smiled slightly at Jess and cuddled back into the blankets. *No* she thought to herself. *I'm imagining things. I just realized they can't sleep with anyone but me, so why would I think Jess and Bleidd would hook up?* Not that it was at all odd from an elven perspective, given the lack of sexual preference among elves, and Allie had to admit a small prurient part of herself enjoyed the idea. But she might as well imagine Jason suddenly developing an interest in her….She rolled over and went back to sleep, still thinking of her two love interests being interested in each other.

****

Jessilaen moved silently down the stairs of the house, keenly aware of the absence of Allie's cousin. He had always felt a vague sense of hostility while he had been staying here, but that was gone now, as if the house itself had relaxed. As much as he knew it hurt Allie to have lost her blood-kin he was pleased that the woman was dead, and his hands were clean of her blood. Allie would get over the loss in time with the support of people who truly valued her and cared about her and she would come to see how treacherous her cousin had truly been.

As he moved down the first floor hallway the door to Bleidd's room opened and the former Outcast stepped out. Jess stopped, waiting to see what the other elf would do.

"Is everything alright?" Bleidd asked, his voice low.

"Should it not be?" Jess asked.

"Don't play word games with me commander," the other elf said sharply. He looked as if he had not slept well, or at all. "Is she okay? I felt something, I thought perhaps she had a nightmare…"

His voice trailed off and he looked uncertain; Jess was sympathetic, even if he did not understand why the other elf was avoiding the woman they all knew he loved. "She is fine. She dreamed of Syndra again, if indeed it was a dream at all. Her friend told her that her cousin had been killed and that the new coven was set to meet at the theater later today."

Bleidd's eyes reflexively looked up towards Allie's room, his expression unreadable. "She must be very upset by this news."

Jess reached out carefully to the other elf's mind, making sure he blocked Allie out so that she could rest. *"Why do you not go to her? I must inform the Outpost of what I've learned and arrange an ambush of the coven, but she would welcome your company."*

Bleidd twitched at the words, although Jessilaen was unsure if it was the manner of speech or the message itself that caused the reaction. His response was slow as he tried to imitate what Jess had done to speak to him. He tried to change the subject *"Speaking of ambushes, I have found where the Dark court agent will be tonight."*

"That is excellent news. If luck is with us we will see the one who harmed her so grievously dead before another day has dawned."

Bleidd looked at the Guard commander in shock and was rewarded with a wolfish smile. *"If I find him I will surely kill him for what he did to her. I appreciate that you* have kept your word and not done so yourself, as I do not doubt you feel the same."

Bleidd nodded stiffly. "*I would be more than happy to see that one dead, yes.*"

Jess paused and then, "*Why do you not go to her now?*"

"*I do not assume she would be so pleased to find me in her bed when she clearly prefers you.*"

That is certainly a change in attitude Jess thought to himself, puzzled. Then to Bleidd, "*She asked for you after she woke. She was very insistent in the hospital that you stay with her. And you did give her your word that you would stay until she did not want you to stay any longer.*"

Bleidd looked away, the muscles in his jaw working. "*And this does not bother you commander?*"

Jess tilted his head, genuinely puzzled by this behavior. "*Call me Jess, as she does. And why should it bother me? It's not as if she loves or desires me any less. Nor as if she is spreading her legs for everyone she meets. You are an exception, but an understandable one.*"

Now Bleidd looked as confused as Jess felt. "*She is contracted to marry you and even if she were not, she prefers only one lover, as have you since you have been with her. It seems that being bonded to her means she is the only one either of us can be with, and since she has chosen you I need to accept the situation for what it is.*"

Jess leaned forward placing his hands on Bleidd's shoulders. "*Do not be so certain that she does not want both of us, and is not willing to take a more elven approach to this. She is young, as you yourself have said, and her upbringing was very human. Monogamy is normal to her, but she is also elven and that is part of her heritage too. Compromise is always a possibility. And as to the marriage contract, such situations have been arraigned before.*"

Bleidd frowned, unsure where this sudden turn had come from. "*Why the change...Jess? Not so long ago you seemed perfectly willing to harm anyone who got too close to her. Now suddenly the territoriality is gone and you are willing to share? I find that hard to credit."*

"If it were anyone else I would still not allow it, nor would she want it. But she loves you. That is not the same as lust. The more I understand her the more I see that love is a force that drives her and that she needs both of us in her life. To lose either would be a true loss, especially now that she has created this bond between us. Between all of us." Jess thought to him, knowing that it was true. Bleidd frowned but his expression was more thoughtful than angry. Jess hesitated for a moment, debating the amount of time he could spare before he must report what he had learned. The obvious unhappiness and hint of vulnerability around the other elf decided him. *"And Bleidd? She is not the only person we can feel desire for."*

He leaned forward and kissed the other elf, gently at first and then when he felt Bleidd's responsiveness with more force. Bleidd's hands wrapped around his waist, pulling their bodies close, and then tugging him gently back towards his room. Jess followed without any further urging.

✳✳✳✳✳✳✳✳✳✳✳✳✳✳✳✳✳✳✳✳✳✳✳✳

Allie woke for the second time that day to sunlight on her face. She squinted and rolled over, then realized if the sun was up high enough to be in her face it had to be after 9. Yawning she threw back the covers and rolled out of bed, glad that she was feeling better today, if not entirely well yet. Already the ordeal of the poisoning was starting to fade into an unpleasant memory, with many of the details lost to pain or fevers. She was surprised though by how much better she was feeling, almost as good as she would have felt if she'd taken strong energy from Jess. Or, she supposed Bleidd. But there'd been none of that going on, unless she counted a very intense dream she'd had before waking up about Jess and Bleidd sleeping together. She hadn't thought her imagination was that good, honestly, but she'd enjoyed the dream. If only they could get along that well in real life.

She dressed as quickly as she could, still mindful of the dull ache that permeated her body and then headed downstairs to see who else was home. If she remembered correctly Jason was on first shift today and should be at work, but she doubted Jess had gone very far. It was increasingly difficult to resist the temptation to read Bleidd's mind to find out where he was and why he seemed to be avoiding her, but she managed not to give in by focusing on the hope that he might be in the kitchen.

Following the smell of coffee she found Shawn washing dishes and Jess sitting at the table.

"Morning Shawn,"

"Good morning Allie," Shawn replied. She watched him for a minute, waiting to see if he'd say anything else, but he seemed nervous. Understandable with everything going on, so Allie left him alone. She knew he was probably worried about the state of their living arrangements, since the house was in Liz's name and Liz was currently – as far as he knew – fleeing the police and wanted for attempted murder. It didn't seem right to tell him now that Liz was dead and that the house would go to Allie, so she said nothing. He would find out soon enough anyway.

She sat down at the table, contemplating breakfast before deciding to wait for lunch. "Hi Jess,"

He gave her an odd look. "Good morning my love. How are you feeling?"

"Oh, well, still kind of achy but better," she said, then reluctantly, "Is Bleidd around?"

Jess glanced at Shawn and switched to speaking Elvish. "He is sleeping."

"Oh. Good," she mumbled back in the same language, frowning at the table.

"Is something wrong?"

"What?" she said, distracted and trying to decide if she should wait to talk to them together or just tell him what she'd learned from Miss Amelia now. "No, nothing."

"Allie," Jess said, in what she was starting to think of as his stop-being-stupid voice, "something is obviously bothering you. If you are worried about Bleidd you can tell me, I will not be upset by your concern."

"Well he does seem to be avoiding me," she said. "And I guess I do feel bad about, the ummm, situation."

"It may take him time to adjust to the mental bonding but you should not feel bad about that. You might find if you talked to him that he does not mind it so much. And I doubt he is avoiding you, but just as you feel bad about what you feel you have done to him he may worry that you do not want him in the way he wants you."

"It's not what I think I might have done it's what I know I have done."

"I don't understand," he said, tilting his head to the side in confusion.

"I...ummm. I kind of accidently was in his head a bit yesterday and there was this woman he wanted to sleep with but he couldn't. I mean literally couldn't," she said feeling her cheeks coloring. "And - well how can I not feel bad about that? If he can't be with anyone else but me, that's my fault. I did that."

"Ahhh," Jess said slowly. "You need to talk to him Allie. With elves it is almost reflex to take any opportunity to indulge in a pleasurable activity, especially sex. You may find that he was more interested in the activity than the person."

"I'm not – I mean it's not that I'm jealous. Really. I mean maybe a little bit, but not really. I know he sleeps with other people, he always has as long as I've known him. But now he can't. And I just…is he angry about that? Is that why he's avoiding me?"

"Allie," Jess sighed, shaking his head slightly. "Talk to him. And…he can be with someone besides you, just not random strangers."

"He can…" she had a sudden flash of insight, a bit of what she'd thought was a dream from earlier flash through her mind and she could feel herself blushing harder. "Oh. Oh. Right. You…and…right. I thought I was dreaming that."

"You dreamt it?"

"Obviously not a dream," she said, mortified that she'd eavesdropped on something so personal, however unintentional it had been. *And now I know why I feel even better this morning* she thought *apparently I can pull from both of them when they are feeling something intense like that even when it's not with me.* "Probably the emotions drew me, even in my sleep, through the bond…"

Jess was watching her closely. "Does it upset you? To know that I bedded him?"

"No," she said quickly. "I mean, I don't know. I never thought there was any possibility of that happening. You two never seemed to like each other much – and please don't tell me how with elves you don't have to like the other person. That won't make me feel any better. Or that you just did it out of reflex because the opportunity was there."

He smiled, reaching out to take her hand, "My love, I have come to admire him and I think I see, at least in some small measure, what it is you love in him. And he is an attractive person. But I did it because he needed the comfort of it and for whatever reason he will not seek you out right now."

296

"Maybe he is angry at me," she said despondently, still trying to process that the two people she loved had slept together. She wasn't angry at either of them, but she did feel frustrated. She couldn't get Bleidd to stay in the same room with her and yet he was jumping into bed with Jess. And she had started to take for granted that Jess didn't want to be with anyone else but her, and she was surprised by how insecure she suddenly felt at the idea of him going back to a more elven approach, even though she knew he could not be with anyone else except her. And apparently Bleidd. Part of her even thought she should be grateful that in bonding all three of them together she had unintentionally given them the option of each other, that all of their sexual satisfaction didn't rest solely with her. But she couldn't quite shake the fear that having that option they would decide they didn't need her...

"Are you angry?" he pressed as her silence drew out.

"No," she said meeting his eyes. "I guess maybe a little worried. I think I know how you were feeling for all those months now, worrying that I'd choose someone else."

"Oh, my heart, no," he said, rubbing his thumb across her hands. "I would never forsake you."

They both looked up as Shawn walked to the end of the table, standing awkwardly looking at them. "Umm, sorry to interrupt. If it's okay with you guys I'm just going to run out and pick up some groceries. Do you want anything?"

"Thanks, Shawn, I think we're all set, unless you want to grab some cat food," Allie said, forcing a smile. Shawn nodded stiffly, then headed for the back door.

"Jess," she said, deciding that she needed to tell him what she'd learned before she lost her nerve. "There is something I need to tell you, but I'm afraid you'll...think badly of me."

He frowned, but nodded slightly, so she pressed on. "Yesterday, while you were at the Outpost and Bleidd was out I had Jason drive me out to talk with the mage who is training me to use my abilities."

"Allie!" Jess said, his anger filling the air around her.

"I know it was a stupid thing to do to go out without anybody but Jason, but it was after I'd seen what happened with Bleidd and I was upset. I feel like I'm ruining his life, and yours…"

"Allie," he started, his feelings now sad and worried, but she pushed on ignoring the interruption.

"I wanted to know about this…binding you to me thing. Because she'd mentioned that when I was there learning how to shield but I hadn't paid much attention then. So I asked her about it and she said I do it, bind you to me, because I need your energy, your emotions, and in exchange I let you – make you – feel things more vividly, more intensely," she swallowed hard. "And I wanted to know if I could *not* do it and she said no, if I try to draw on people I'm not bonded to it's not enough anymore, now that I've had the deeper energy, and people's emotions will influence me. And it didn't sound like empathy exactly and she was talking like she knew what I was. So I asked…"

"Allie," he said more forcefully. "I already know what you are."

"What?" she said unsure if they were talking about the same thing. "You know that I'm…"

She hesitated to say the word so he said it for her. "Bahvanshee, yes."

She looked at him speechless, so he went on. "Bleidd knows too."

"How? How do you know? I didn't know," she sputtered.

"I suspected, but when Tharien said you were an empath and described the abilities of empaths, some of

298

which you do have I was unsure," he said gently. "But when I realized you can heal yourself with the energy you draw and more that you pull the most energy from sexual encounters, then I was certain. Only a Bahvanshee can do that."

Allie thought to herself, *of course I can't just be part elf I have to be a freaky type of elf that feeds on emotions.* And then the irony struck her and she almost laughed, *oh if only my mother had realized this she would have kept me. The Bahvanshee are so rare she must not have understood what I was, but they are almost always Dark court because people are so afraid of what they can do.* She looked at Jess, who was looking calmly back at her and said, "But you…I mean…doesn't it bother you? Aren't you afraid?"

"Afraid? Of you?" he scoffed. "My heart I have no doubt that you truly love me. You have showed me, allowed me to feel it with you. Most of your kind have such an ill reputation because they callously use people, forcing the emotions they need at great harm to the person they are taking energy from. You would never do such."

"How can you be so sure?"

He laughed, "Because if it was in your nature to manipulate people to your own ends you would already have forced Bleidd to conform to your desires."

"Maybe I am like that," she said. "Maybe the only reason you love me at all is because I've made you feel that way. Maybe I made you decide to be with me."

"Do I have no freewill Allie?" Jess asked, frustrated.

"What? Of course you do," she said knowing it was true. Even if she had used her ability to make him desire her, love her, she could not alter his free will, only create a compulsion. That was what kept the Bahvanshee in check; they could create emotions and arousal in others, and if Miss Amelia was right and Allie was any indication bind people to themselves to feed more directly, but they could not remove the person's personality and willpower. There were many stories of those who had been overcome and destroyed by their own victims.

"Then why can you not credit that I chose this?" he said, meeting her eyes and refusing to look away. "From the moment I first met you, the moment I saw you in your store, I knew there was something special about you."

"I don't believe in love at first sight," she mumbled.

"Then do not call it love. But it was something, and it motivated me to pursue you, against all the advice of my family and friends. I wanted to be with you. I chose that. You make me feel alive in a way that I have never felt before. And I will not give that up. Not now and not ever, no matter what your true nature is. I have told you a thousand times you do me no harm in drawing on my emotions. Stop making yourself miserable trying to deny what you need."

"But it changes you…"

He threw his hands up, "Then I am changed. Do you love me the less for that?"

"Don't be ridiculous," she snapped.

"Don't be so stubborn," he shot back.

"But…look at you and Bleidd. A week ago you two couldn't stand each other, now – now that you are both bonded to me, bound to me – now you are lovers and almost friends."

"I do not see how that is a bad thing, my heart, but rest assured that is not because you somehow manipulated us into liking each other. I feared that you might choose him and reject me and I can see now that this is not so, that you can love us both. And I saw that he was willing to do anything to save your life, not to just say that he would but to actually act. You live because of him. How can I not respect that? "

She frowned trying to feel her way around the logic. Despite his words she was certain that part of the change in his attitude towards his rival was because of her own actions in joining the three of them together. "But doesn't it seem at all odd to you that you went from being jealous of the idea of me with anyone else, especially him, to suddenly being willing to, to share me with him?"

"I think that he proved to me that his love for you is truly equal to my own, and that you have shown me that accepting his love won't take anything away from what you feel for me," he said more gently.

She groaned and put her head in her hands. "But I've ruined his life."

"I don't understand."

"He saved me and I bound him to me, and now he can't be with anyone but me, but I'm not with him I'm with you. That just seems cruel," she said, trying to explain.

Jess nodded slowly. "Yes, that is cruel my love. So why are you rejecting him now? Does he displease you so?"

"What?" she said. "No, not at all I'm....I mean it's just that I'm with you. And you don't, you haven't been willing to…I'm so confused."

"Allie," he said, taking her hands in his own and trying to get her to look at him. "I love you, and I know now that you love me and will not forsake me for another, even another that you also love. I…am reconsidering my feelings for Bleidd. There is much worth respecting in him and he is not an unattractive person himself. I do feel drawn to him now, where I did not before, and perhaps that is because of your influence, but it does not upset me. If you wish to share your time with him, or even if you would like us, all three, to be together, courting each other, I am not opposed to it if he is willing as well."

"Three way courting? Would that work?" she said, trying to wrap her head around the surreal conversation. It seemed impossible that things should be able to work out this way, and yet she could not leave things with Bleidd as they were, nor could she choose him over Jess. Unless she wanted to find some way to undo the bonds she had made, if it was even possible, the only workable solution did seem to be to find a balance between the three of them.

"It will work as courting always works, with each of us exploring whether the emotions prove true and valuable. I cannot say, nor can anyone, if or how things will ultimately work out between us. All of us. But I am willing to try," he said, and she could feel with him his eagerness at the potential new experience and she could also feel his love.

"Alright," she said slowly. "Alright. I guess I am as willing to try as you are. I can't deny that it's been really stressful feeling caught between two people I care about. I'll talk to Bleidd and see what he says."

He sighed. "Good. But for today please try to rest."

"Why? What's going on that you want me to stay out of?"

He laughed lightly. "Perceptive. We plan to move on the coven when they meet today, and perhaps address another issue as well. I have asked the kelpie to stay and guard you, but I would feel better if I were not worried that you might show up in the middle of things."

She smiled as well. "Okay, I'll behave. Just...please try not to get killed. I can't lose you...or Bleidd."

He nodded, his expression serious. "I will do my best to see that we both return home to you."

****

Jess moved forward through the underbrush that choked the lot next to the theater, with the other elves form his squad fanning out around him. He knew that on the opposite side Zarethyn was leading a second squad, mirroring this one as they closed in. The human police had also surrounded the building and their SWAT team, a unit of the state police called in to assist, dotted the surrounding roofline, rifles trained on the building. After much debate the decision had been made to send the elves in first, as they had a higher resistance to magic and a better chance of withstanding any spells the human coven might use. The human police had sent their mage, and as well two others also called in from the state police, but those three would be greatly outnumbered even if it proved to be a small coven. And since the group's abilities were an unknown factor this seemed the wisest course.

Nonetheless as the elves moved forward, careful to avoid the side of the building with the hidden room's single window, Jess worried about the danger. The best plan they could come up with was to ambush the group as it left the building after its meeting, but he knew that there were dozens of ways that this could end badly. He knew he could not fail to return to Allie, and also that he could not allow thoughts of that to distract him.

The meeting had begun an hour ago and everyone had been in position, carefully hidden outside the range of any wards, waiting since then. Finally a scant few minutes ago the police had signaled that there was movement in the building and everyone had begun closing in. Jess could feel the tension thick in the air.

Allie voice in his head startled him enough that he jerked to a stop, making the others stop as well, blades held ready. "*Jess!*"

"*Allie, unless this is an emergency, not now,*" he thought back afraid that his own thoughts of her had drawn her attention at the worst possible time.

"*No listen, quickly,*" she thought back and he suddenly had an image in his mind of a human woman, middle aged, blond, tall and stately. The unexpected visual input made him shake his head. *"This is Candice, Liz's best friend. She must be the leader. I'm sure of it. I mentioned her earlier, if you see her, stop her. She's the leader."*

"Cut off the head of the serpent and the body fails?" he thought back, impressed. She didn't answer and he pressed on, knowing his momentary pause had worried the others. But knowing who the leader was he would be certain to find the woman.

They spread out at the edge of the lot around the back door, a handful of cars the only thing breaking up the wide asphalt expanse between them and the building. Jess was confident that his squad could cover the space before the humans could fully react, but it was crucial that they wait until the last possible moment to charge, else anyone succeed in fleeing back to the building.

As he watched the door opened and people began to trickle out. He cursed silently to see them meandering out alone and in small groups, spread apart. He counted nine: four men and five women. The last one to emerge, just as the first couple was reaching one of the parked cars, was the blond woman that Allie had warned him about. He was seized with the certainty that if she was leaving she was the last and he signaled his squad to move.

"Elven Guard! Lay down your weapons and do not resist!" Jess yelled as he ran across the open space towards his target. The rest of the elves in his group spread out as well, and on the other side of the parking lot the four elves from the other squad along with Zarethyn charged as well, making the numbers even. He was dimly aware of the police also identifying themselves and then chaos.

The nearest man, an older human with short grey-ish brown hair and a heavyset frame spun towards them. He felt the spell the man was casting a moment before it was cast and dropped and rolled, the magic passing next to him. He could not identify the spell but it made his side tingle and burn slightly. He rolled back to his feet, prepared to call out a warning to Natarien who was closest to him, but it was too late. Magic was not the only weapon these humans were wielding and as Jess gained his feet again he saw the gun in the man's hand and watched as it kicked up. He moved as fast as he could, closing the distance between them, and swung his sword down hard even as the man started to turn towards him. At the same moment that his blade took the gunman's hand off at the wrist a shot rang out from one of the rooftop snipers and a round wound bloomed in the witch's neck. He dropped to the ground, writhing, unable to speak.

Jess spared a glance back and saw the younger Elven Guard down on the ground and swore, but he had no time to stop. The coven clearly had no intention of surrendering peacefully. He could only hope that Natarien would receive aid from the police following behind and that his injuries were not too serious.

He remembered Allie's warning about the leader and he set his sights on the woman who had crouched down several dozen feet from the building. She watched the mayhem unfolding with an eager expression that surprised him. *She wants to by a martyr* he realized. *She wants them all to be martyrs, if they cannot complete their ceremony.* This was very bad indeed, and Jess redoubled his efforts to reach her, dodging around a younger woman who tried to block his path. He did not kill her, but as he moved around her, avoiding the spell she was clumsily trying to cast, he struck her on the temple with the hilt of his sword knocking her out.

A few feet from the woman she finally noticed him charging at her and hastily flung a spell in his direction. He rolled to the side to let it pass, the movement saving him from a bullet winging out of the chaos behind him. It grazed his armor, sparking and smoking but not penetrating the metal. He had no time to spare to be grateful for that bit of luck though; regaining his feet he crossed the final distance between them and wrapped his arms around the woman, pinning her hands so that she could not shape any major spells.

"No!" she screamed, writhing like a wild thing in his grip. "No! Kill me you bastard! I won't be taken alive!"

"You already have been," Jess said coldly, pushing the woman to the ground. He sheathed his sword and reached quickly for his handcuffs, specially designed to hold mages helpless. The woman would be dangerous until she was properly bound.

As if to prove the need for his caution she began to chant, the words dark and heavy. "Invoco mortem et dolorem…"

He wrapped the silver cuffs around her wrists and her words cut off abruptly with a gasp as the spell within the handcuffs blocked her access to all magic. She groaned like a dying thing, redoubling her efforts to free herself, but to no avail.

He crouched with his knee wedged in her back, pinning her to the concrete sidewalk in front of the building and looked up to take stock of the scene. The two closest coven members, seeing their leader arrested had surrendered and were kneeling with their hands up, their faces shocked and despondent. The woman he had struck earlier still lay prone on the ground. At the far edge of the lot his brother and another member of the guard were dueling a human witch, magic flaring and sparking through the air. As Jess watched one of the state police mages moved towards the group to help. Another coven member was down in the middle of the lot with Mariniessa standing over him, her eyes also sweeping the area. Jess could not tell if that human lived or not, but all he cared about was that he had been subdued. The man whose hand he had severed was being attended to by the police, and Jess had no doubt that an ambulance was already en route. The

306

couple who had first emerged from the building were on the ground next to their car, held by Elven Guard from the other squad. After a moment Jess found Brynneth kneeling next to Natarien's still form. His eye's met those of the elven healer's across the parking lot and Brynneth slowly shook his head.

Jess swore again, with feeling, and he felt the barest shift in his mind. Without thinking, as he held the woman down waiting for the police to move in to his position, he reached out to the two people whose attention he had drawn. *"The raid is over. We have captured the coven."*

"You were successful in taking them alive?" Bleidd thought back, surprised and pleased.

"Yes, but not without cost to ourselves," Jess replied, not trying to hide his grief.

"Who?" Allie asked quietly.

"Natarien," he said and he could feel her grief blending with his own. He had forgotten that she liked the young elf who was in many ways like an age-equal for her.

"I honor your grief," Bleidd said formally, and Jess was glad for the kindness.

"You weren't hurt?" Allie asked, suddenly anxious.

"No, my heart, I was not injured." Jess thought back. He could feel the relief – from both of them – and he relaxed slightly.

The coven would be arrested by the human police and processed through their legal system. As Jess understood it they faced a long list of charges including the murders of all of the victims so far. Natarien's death would be laid at their feet as well, as would Allie's poisoning. Even though he did not trust the human law to provide justice he was confident that there was enough here to hold these people for a long time. One threat had been taken care of.

He had one more to deal with before he could rest easily.

****

Bleidd moved through the twilight, ignoring the flashing lights on the marquee of the strip club. He moved around the side of the building, into an alley that stank of things best not thought about.

"I thought commander," he said to the elf he could not see but was certain was there, "that you were going to pass the information I gave you along to the rest of the Elven Guard. I expected to find a whole squad here, or more, not you alone."

"I don't need a squad to finish this," Jess said calmly, stepping out of the shelter of a dumpster. The Guard commander was not in uniform. Instead he wore black jeans and a black t-shirt, by far the most modern outfit Bleidd had ever seen the other elf in. Dressed so similarly the two elves looked like reflections of each other, one fair haired, one dark haired.

"You think you can capture this agent alone?" Bleidd asked, one eyebrow arching gracefully up.

"No. I have no intention of capturing him," Jess answered honestly.

Bleidd looked at the other elf in open mouthed shock. "You mean to kill him?"

"I mean to do what I must to protect Allie," Jess said, still calm. "If we try to capture him he may escape again. If we do succeed in capturing him he may yet escape from our custody."

"And what of the information he may provide you about the intent of the Dark court here?"

"She and the kelpie both said there were two agents. One can be captured and brought back. But the other must die," Jess said.

Bleidd looked at the other elf for a long time as the last light faded into darkness. "You want vengeance, not justice."

"I want vengeance," Jess agreed. "I am not here tonight as a member of the Elven Guard. I am here as her lover to avenge the suffering he caused her. And then…I will tell the others of the information you provided and where the other agent may be found."

"You realize of course that the second agent may flee after you do this," Bleidd said, his own voice uncertain.

"You and I both know that he will never leave her alone. He will always be a threat to her, as long as he lives. You were in the Guard once, surely you realize that if he is captured and questioning him proves unproductive they may seek to use her to get him to talk. I cannot stand by and see her broken again to gain the obvious information that the Dark court seeks a foothold here, or is fomenting war between our Holding and the humans."

"You underestimate her strength," Bleidd said, even though he knew Jess was right. The only way to be certain she was safe from this particular threat was to remove it. "And you realize that even if you kill this one person there will be others from the Dark court who seek her for her knowledge of the book?"

"They will seek her for what she knows, and they will be dealt with," Jess said resolutely. "But he seeks her for his own pleasure and I will die myself before I allow him to touch her again."

Bleidd was silent again, wanting to ask and not wanting to confirm what he had suspected. Finally, "He outraged her then?"

"I would expect a more modern expression from you my friend," Jess said softly, earning a startled look from Bleidd. "But yes, she was raped while she was held prisoner. And tortured. And nearly killed. Be glad that though you were there that night you did not have to see the way he left her, dying on that floor. I see it still when I close my eyes sometimes, and I know with absolute certainty that he cannot be allowed to live."

Bleidd took a long, deep breath trying to rein in his own anger. "I would, of course, be quite eager to assist you except that I gave you my word I would not."

"If you would aid me then follow the other agent so that we will know where he has denned up," Jess said. "But I do not ask you to be part of this. If I am found out I will lose my place in the Guard, but likely little else. If you were caught killing another elf, even a Dark court one, in cold blood you might forfeit your life and that is too great a risk."

"You don't consider this too great a risk? You would lose your honor," Bleidd said shaking his head and drifting closer to Jess. "I have very little honor to lose."

"Unless suspicion falls on me and I am questioned directly I do not believe I will be found out," Jess said, once again surprising Bleidd. He had not realized that the Guardsman had come to trust him so much, but then again they were bound not only by the magic Allie had woven between them but also by the secrets they already kept for her. There was a logic to everything Jess was saying, and Bleidd could not deny that he would sleep easier knowing this particular Dark court elf was dead.

"Alright," Bleidd said slowly. "I will stand watch while you do what you must."

Jess looked as if this was unexpected, then smiled, reaching out to give the other elf a friendly slap on the shoulder. "Then let us end this, here tonight."

The two elves took up positions near the edge of the alley where they could watch the entrance unobserved. Jess assured Bleidd that their quarry had entered earlier, almost as soon as the club opened. It was only a matter of time and luck.

Just after 7:30 that evening the two Dark court elves stumbled out. One had a girl with him, her steps so clumsy he was all but carrying her. He was cloaked and hooded, but Bleidd knew he was not the one they sought. When he spoke his voice was young. "Come on Ferinyth let's go back to the hotel."

"You go if you want, just don't let that stupid slut make a mess or take all your money," the second elf said, his voice as unsteady as the girl's walk. "I'm going to the Star."

"I don't think..." the younger elf began, the girl hanging all over him giggling.

"No you don't," the one called Ferinyth snapped. "No one's asking your opinion little boy. Go back to the hotel if you want to, but I am not done tonight. The night is young and we are so close to succeeding I can taste it."

The first elf hesitated. "I am going. Just don't do anything foolish."

"Go fuck yourself," Ferinyth snarled.

The other elf snorted and started walking away. "Why bother when that's what she's for?"

Bleidd felt a savage grin stretching his face and didn't bother to hide it. This could not have fallen out better for them. As the younger elf began to walk away Ferinyth turned in their direction and began walking along the sidewalk on a course that would take him directly in front of them. Jess nodded slightly at Bleidd, but he shook his head in response.

"*Follow the younger one,*" Jess thought to him.

"*No need,*" Bleidd thought back. "*I recognize that girl. I can find her here later and ask her where he took her; even if he tries to use glamour to cloud her mind I can uncover it. And you need backup.*"

"*You gave your word not to risk yourself,*" Jess said as the Dark court elf drew closer.

"And I shall not, but I am a mage after all. I can use magic where you cannot and guard your back without ever drawing a blade."

A small smile curved Jess's lips and he nodded, slightly *"So be it then."*

And then he was moving, lunging forward and dragging the Dark elf back into the alley. He flung the elf to the ground a dozen feet back and Bleidd watched in satisfaction as he landed with a painful grunt. The Dark court elf rolled slowly to his hands and knees.

Bleidd leaned against the side of the building, watching as Jess ghosted forward, his feet barely touching the ground.

"Get up," the Guardsman growled at the other elf.

"Why so you can arrest me?" Ferinyth laughed. "Go ahead and try."

"I am not here to arrest you amadan," Jess said, rage filling his voice. That seemed to get through to the other elf, who looked up now with a puzzled expression.

"You're the Elven Guard. You caught me," he laughed again, getting slowly to his feet. "So arrest me. I will escape and you will not catch me again."

"Am I wearing a uniform?" Jess asked, his voice deadly.

The other elf's superior expression faltered, his eyes darting from Jess's black clad form to Bleidd's. "What is this?"

"You gave me a choice once, to fight you or to save her. I chose to save her. Now we fight," Jess said dancing from foot to foot. There was a lethal intensity to the Guardsman that made even Bleidd catch his breath. Beautiful and dangerous, he dared the other elf to combat.

Ferinyth's eyes narrowed. "Yes, I remember you. You are the mixed-blood girl's lover. I hope you found her a better lay after I broke her in for you."

312

Bleidd pushed off the wall, tensing, but Jess laughed. "You are nothing to her but a bad dream that will soon be forgotten."

"Not when she is mine again," the Dark elf snarled. "Then I will teach her her true place."

That did crack Jess's calm and Bleidd imagined he could feel the elf's anger even as his body leaned forward. Bleidd spoke quickly before Jess could make a mistake. "You will be dead before the hour is out. And since you have done nothing but fail to capture her since you lost her months ago I would not be so quick to brag of succeeding now."

The Dark elf threw him a venomous look, but Bleidd was relieved to see Jess relaxing slightly as he regained his composure. Ferinyth shook his head slightly. "I will not die tonight. I will not fight you and you are too honorable to kill an unarmed elf who is offering no resistance."

Jess exerted the tiny of bit of magic necessary to call his sword to his hand. The blade glittered in the fluorescent lights of the alley. "Fight me."

"No," Ferinyth said confidently, holding his hands out from his sides in a sign of surrender. Faster than Bleidd had expected Jess lunged forward, stabbing his blade into the unarmed elf's thigh. The Dark court elf staggered back, his hands covering the wound reflexively. "Son of a whore! You break your own laws!"

"Draw your blade and fight me, or I will cut you apart one piece at a time," Jess said his voice icy. "I imagine it will take you a long time to bleed to death from such wounds."

The other elf's face twisted in fury and raising his bloody hands he conjured his own sword. The leg wound would slow him and Bleidd doubted he could prevail against Jess, but nonetheless he prepared a spell to shatter

313

the Dark elf's sword, holding the magic ready in case he needed it.

The two combatants met in the center of the alley, swords clashing. Bleidd had expected the fight to end quickly but it did not. Jess lunged and parried, meeting the other blade with obvious skill but never delivering a death blow. Every minute or so Jess would break through his opponent's guard and score a minor hit, but never anything truly debilitating. It finally occurred to Bleidd, as he watched the Dark court elf sweating and bleeding from a dozen small wounds, that Jess was toying with him. He smiled and leaned back against the wall again.

At last, when it was clear that Ferinyth was nearing exhaustion, Jess parried one last time, knocking the other elf's blade aside and lunging forward to impale his shoulder. Gasping Ferinyth went to his knees, his sword clattering to the concrete. He glared up at the Guardsman, his face still defiant despite everything. Jess kicked his wounded shoulder, knocking him to the ground and wringing a cry of pain from him.

"And now that you've defeated me, will you drag me back to your Outpost, humiliated, and claim you laid me low in fair combat?" he gasped.

"No," Jess said, barely breathing hard. "Now I'm going to show you what it feels like to die the way you left Allie to die."

****

Allie was sitting out on the steps of the house when they finally returned, Ciaran sitting with her to keep her company. She watched Bleidd and Jess walk across the lawn, feeling a mixture of relief and suspicion. Jess looked like death, dressed all in black, and she didn't think she liked it. Bleidd of course often wore black, his black hair along with the clothes making him look dramatic and artistic. On Jess though, with his pale blond hair, he just looked washed out. There was something different between them as they walked together now, something more than she could explain with the knowledge that they were lovers now. Something had happened tonight, she was sure of it.

Ciaran stood, his form shifting from human to hound, his nose in the air sniffing. He inhaled deeply then gave Allie an inscrutable look before turning and loping off into the woods without a word. *Well that was odd* Allie thought, standing carefully. "Hey guys, I was getting worried."

"No worries my love," Jess said, his happiness vibrating through the link between them. "We are both safe and home, as I said we would be."

Bleidd gave him an odd sideways look at that. Then, "You should be resting Allie not sitting out in the dark. Its getting cold."

"I don't mind," she said trying to decide if the way he was looking at her was concerned or annoyed. His feelings were a tangle of too many things for her to sort out, in stark contrast to Jess's pure happiness. "Jason and Shawn are inside. We thought maybe we could have a little party. I guess its kind of weird since they found Liz's body at the theater and all but we wanted to do something to celebrate the end of these murders. The real end."

"Yes," Jess said solemnly. "The dark coven has been captured and even now have turned on each other. I am loathe to trust the human justice system but in this case I believe the human system is motivated to see true justice done."

"Right. I can deal with all the details of handling Liz's estate and everything later," Allie said, rubbing her eyes. "Probably tomorrow since I need to get the legal stuff with the house settled. But tonight it's such a relief to know the group has finally really been caught. All of them. That we wanted to enjoy the moment a little bit. Now if we could just catch the Dark court elves as easily…"

Jess and Bleidd exchanged a long look. "What? What'd I say? Wait, what's happened?"

Jess nodded slightly to Bleidd, but the other elf seemed hesitant. Finally Jess spoke. "Allie we - Bleidd – found out where the Dark court agents were going to enjoy themselves while they were staying here. He told me and I went there tonight."

"You went alone – out of uniform?" she asked slowly.

"Jess," Bleidd said, his voice carrying a warning. Allie was just as surprised to hear him use a nickname with Jess as she was to hear him apparently cautioning Jess not to speak.

"It's alright," Jess said. "There should be no secrets between us. We know her true nature and the things she has done for us, for you to heal you. She has a right to know this."

Bleidd nodded, meeting Allie's eyes like someone who expects condemnation. "I followed Jess to the…place I knew the Dark court elves would be tonight expecting to find him with the other Guard. Instead I found him alone. We, together, watched the two agents separate. I plan to go back later and trace the one who left to his hotel room."

"And the other?" she asked, feeling a building tension.

"Was the one who hurt you," Bleidd said.

"I pulled him into the alley, fought him, and killed him," Jess said simply. The words hit her with unexpected force.

"He's dead?"

"Yes," they both said together.

She looked from one to the other, guessing that there was more to this story than they were saying. She tried to grasp the fact that the Dark court elf who had almost killed her was dead. Slowly she felt a weight lifting off her shoulders, even knowing that his death didn't mean she was free of the Dark court's pursuit. "Good. But, umm, how are you going to explain that? Officially I mean?"

"I have already notified Zarethyn," Jess said placidly. "I told him we, Bleidd and I, were out on the trail if the Dark court agents and that when we found them there was a confrontation. I said I had no choice but to kill the elf who died, and that we are certain we can find the other."

She looked at Bleidd who nodded, his face unreadable. It was not a lie, but was a version of the truth that left out many essential details, and she was surprised that he would willingly mislead his brother. She had little doubt that Zarethyn had believed Jess without question.

Then again it was his choice to tell or not tell the other Guard the truth. He had protected her not long ago by concealing her use of dark magic in the same way, so who was she to judge him now? Looking from one to the other she said, "Well then let's go in and celebrate."

Bleidd blinked, his emotions pleased but also unsure. Jess laughed and draped his arm across her shoulders. She reached back and took Bleidd's hand pulling him along as they all walked up the steps into the house. For the first time in months she felt a sense of hope for the future, even though she had no idea how so many things were going to work out. The ritual site still needed to be cleaned up and the energy released; until that happened Syndra would be earthbound. She was still contracted to marry one person but psychically bonded to two, and she still only had minimal control of her abilities. There was Liz's death to deal with, and her betrayal to come to terms with. But her life wasn't being threatened by the ritual group anymore, and they couldn't complete the ritual cycle. The worlds – both of them – were safe from whatever the ritual cycle would have done. And thanks to Jess and

Bleidd the elf who had hurt her so badly was dead. Maybe she should be worried about the details of that but right in the moment she couldn't find the energy to care.

She walked into the house, greeted by the smell of roast chicken and cooking vegetables, the two people she loved close at her side. Jason and Shawn were in the kitchen, their voices echoing cheerfully down the hall. Her home felt different without her cousin, but it still felt like a home, and she was determined to move forward and find a way to make everything work out. She'd manage to keep the house, she'd get the store back on track, and she'd find a way to convince Bleidd to give Jess's suggestion a try.

After everything she'd been through, she was determined to find happiness, even if she had to make it for herself.

Epilogue

Allie knocked tentatively on Bleidd's door, unsure of her welcome. After dinner was over he had immediately holed up in his room, and she struggled with the feeling that he was avoiding her. It made her nervous and she kept wanting to leave him alone, afraid that the last thing he wanted was for her to disturb him. She had asked Jess to come with her for this but he had insisted that she needed to talk to Bleidd by herself this time, and so she found herself standing alone outside his door, while Jess, Jason, and Shawn hung out in the den celebrating the successful capture of the coven.

"*Allie?*" the thought was loud in her mind, clumsy, but she was impressed by how quickly he was getting the hang of using their bond to speak to her. It had taken Jess much longer.

"*Yes,*" she thought back. "*Can I come in?*"

"*Of course,*" he thought, and she felt some relief that there was no trace of anger in him.

She slipped into the room, not entirely surprised to see that the light was off. He had always preferred to avoid electric lights when he could. Even with her ability to see well in low light conditions she found herself straining in the dim interior. He was lying on his bed staring up at the ceiling and she went and tentatively sat down on the edge of the bed.

She spoke out loud, staring at the bookshelf against the far wall to avoid looking at him, still unsure of her reception. "How are you feeling?"

"My shoulder is almost entirely healed," he said. His weight shifted on the bed and glancing from the corner of her eye she saw him lifting and rotating his right arm.

"Good," she said.

"And you? How are you feeling?"

319

"I don't know how to begin answering that," she said honestly. "Physically, I guess still tired. Mentally...I have no idea. I feel like my whole life has gone through a blender."

"I'm sorry Allie," he said softly. "I can't even imagine how difficult this must be for you."

"If anyone should be saying that it's me," she said.

He sat up and she could feel his uncertainty, his worry, swirling around her. "Why do you say that?"

"I never meant to tie you to me Bleidd, to take your freedom," she replied sadly, looking down. "I don't like to think that in saving my life you lost part of your own."

"I knew there was risk when I did it..."

"Risk that what, though? That I'd drain all your energy maybe, despite what Jess said?" she asked.

"Possibly. Also the risk that you'd hate me."

"For saving my life? That's a hard thing to hate someone for doing."

"You know what I mean Allie," he said, his voice serious.

"Well, I would prefer being able to remember it, yeah. But that couldn't have been a great experience for you either," she said sighing. "But again, not dead, so....and you know I do love you."

"Even now you can say that?"

"Of course," she said surprised.

"Even though I...did what I did despite knowing how you felt about being loyal to one person?"

"You're being too hard on yourself. Jess was the one who asked you to do what you could to save me," she said. "How can I feel like I betrayed him – or we did, or whatever – when he was right there encouraging it?"

He was silent, but she could feel his thoughts shifting. It was hard not to let it draw her attention enough to listen to what he was thinking, especially when she was this close to him. Now that she was not fighting her own

320

nature anymore, as Miss Amelia would say, she could feel her need for him, for his energy, and it made it difficult not to simply act on what she wanted.

"Bleidd," she said into the silence, "I never meant to change you, and that's what I'm sorry for."

"You didn't," he said, puzzled.

"We both know I did," she said. "I know you...I know about the woman the other day."

"Ahhh," he said slowly. "Indeed. Then you know that nothing happened with her."

"I know that you wanted something to happen and nothing could happen, because of me," she said. "You were right about Jess, that he is the way he is, so focused on me in defiance of elvish culture, because of me, because of this connection we have."

"Allie I didn't give a shit about that woman, or sleeping with her, I wanted to be with you," he said honestly, "But I know, I understand that you aren't comfortable with the idea. So I was just trying to do something to get you out of my mind."

"Except because of me you couldn't," she pressed. "I don't know, I mean we haven't talked about this so I don't know if you want to keep this connection or if you want me to try to find a way to break it, but I want to tell you..."

"If Jessilaen can get used to this then so can I," he cut in. "I still love you Allie, that hasn't changed. I was only trying to make you happy, to give you the space to be with him."

"No," she said finally turning to look at him. "that doesn't make me happy though. I need you both Bliedd. Because I love you both and for me, because of what I am, that makes me...dependent on you. I thought that I'd ruined what was between us, that you were angry with me for this, being in your head thing."

"Well, I'm not certain I like Jessilaen being linked to me in any way," Bleidd said smiling slightly. "Although I suppose he has a few redeeming qualities. And I could get used to him; he's quite…pleasant when he isn't talking."

"Bleidd!" she said, smiling despite herself at the innuendo.

"…and not acting like an arrogant prig," he added. "But honestly I had been jealous of what you had with him. I don't mind feeling like I have a piece of that now too."

"Even if it changes you?"

"Life changes us every day we live it Allie," he said reaching up uncertainly to touch her cheek. "Sometimes in good ways sometimes in bad. But what else do I have in this world that matters except you?"

"Okay," she said, leaning forward, "Because what I wanted to tell you is that I don't know if I can undo this but if you want me to I will. I'll try anyway. And I'll release you from what you promised, if that's what you want. But I've talked to Jess and I've thought a lot about it and you know I'm not an elf Bleidd and I'm not a human either. I'm like this town, I'm stuck somewhere in-between. I don't think I can be monogamous without feeling regret about hurting someone I love, not now not after everything that's happened, and that means Jess and that also means you. But I know I can't – I just don't have it in me to take the elven approach and sleep with everyone I meet that interests me either. Not when intimacy for me is so intense and means connecting to the person's feelings and pulling those feelings in. I'm not sure it would be safe to do that either, since there could be consequences….And it's okay with Jess if it's okay with you for us to all be together, the three of us I mean, if you want to. To all court each other and see where that takes us. I already know you and he are more compatible than I'd thought, and I'm glad for that. Even if you don't want to be with me, if you want to be with him, that's okay. But I'd rather we all be together, even though that's way outside my experience so you'll have to bear with me and deal with me being stupid and naive and oh my gods am I babbling right now? But the thing is I want us to give this a try, all of us together. If you want to."

"Allie…."he looked up at her momentarily speechless, but his feelings encouraged her to keep talking.

"You should know though I have a jealous streak and I'm really possessive, and apparently I engender those qualities in people I'm bonded to, and if you think this is a good idea it might only be because I want you to agree to it…"

He silenced her by pulling her head down to his and kissing her. His feelings swirled around her, and she absorbed them eagerly. The residual pain and aches from the recent events faded as she fed off of his feelings, finally not worried about hurting him.

She pulled back a little bit, "If you're sure?"

"Absolutely," he said. "Although you are still contracted to marry someone else you realize."

"Yeah there is that," Allie agreed. "Maybe I'll just go truly traditional and elven and marry you both."

He smiled. "Polyandry went out of fashion about a millennia ago."

"So? Since when have I cared about being in fashion?" she said flippantly, trying not to get overwhelmed with worrying about how this was all really going to work. If it could work.

"Never," he said trying to pull her down with him onto the bed. "And I'd rather share you with him than not have you at all, even if it means accepting all the unique things that you are."

She smiled and let herself be pulled. "If you change your mind, tell me and I'll understand. But for now – I think this can work. All three of us together."

"I am willing to try, and knowing you, you will find a way to make it work. It occurs to me though that we seem to be together on a bed. Anything you can think of that we might do to pass the time while we're here?" he said, laughing, the sound lighter than she remembered his laughter being before, and kissed her again.

She kissed him back wrapping her arms around his body as his emotions filled her, both of them surrounded by joy.

There were still many things to worry about, and wounds to heal, but for now Allie was content.